Before Redemption

Before Redemption

Teresa McClain-Watson

www.urbanchristianonline.net

Urban Books, LLC
78 East Industry Court
Deer Park, NY 11729

ISBN 13: 978-1-60162-800-8
ISBN 10: 1-60162-800-5

First Mass Market Printing September 2011
First Trade Paperback Printing May 2009
Printed in the United States of America

10 9 8 7 6 5 4 3 2 1

Distributed by Kensington Publishing Corp.
Submit Wholesale Orders to:
Kensington Publishing Corp.
C/O Penguin Group (USA) Inc.
Attention: Order Processing
405 Murray Hill Parkway
East Rutherford, NJ 07073-2316
Phone: 1-800-526-0275
Fax: 1-800-227-9604

ACKNOWLEDGMENTS

I give thanks unto God Almighty, the only true and living God, and unto His Son, my Lord and Savior, Jesus Christ. Without Christ in my life, I am nothing. Without Him, my writings would be as hollow brass. It is He who has sustained me throughout my Christian journey and has granted me the gift of writing. I do not hesitate to praise, glorify, and magnify His holy name.

Additionally, I wish to thank my friends and colleagues who have inspired me throughout the years: Annie Ruth Brookins, Dr. Sonia Williams, Marilyn Enos-Upthegrove, Minnie McClain-Hogan, Shameika McClain, and my first publisher and editor, Steven Murray.

I also wish to thank Joylynn Jossel for her superb editing and inspiring suggestions. She is among those rarest of editors who understand the writer's creed.

And last but never least, I wish to thank my husband and best friend, John. A good man is hard to find, and I thank God for bringing one into my life.

PROLOGUE

1991

"I said Grandmaster Flash," the young man said to a distracted Nikki Lucas as she handed him the wrong cassette she had in her large box of bootlegs. She was too busy staring at the black Ford Bronco that had just pulled up in front of the Bluebird nightclub to even realize her error. Too busy waiting in serious anticipation for the door of that truck to edge open and Walter Dean "Dino" Cochran, the club's owner, to step out.

"Nikki," the young man said with some exasperation.

Nikki finally eased her large eyes away from the truck to realize that she still had a customer. "What?" She was exasperated too. The young man didn't know it, but he was cutting into her *gawking at Dino* time, a habit she knew she had to break, but was too far gone to know how.

"I said, Grandmaster Flash," the young man repeated. "Not no Lou Rawls! You gave me Lou Rawls."

Nikki was so unfocused that it still took her a few seconds to fully register what the young man was talking about. When it registered, she could do nothing but shake her head. "Sorry 'bout that, Joe-Joe." She handed him the correct cassette.

"What's your problem anyway?" he asked her with a frown on his face. "Acting all crazy just because Dino showed up."

"Ah, bump you!" Nikki snapped, determined that her secret crush on Dino Cochran, and thus her weakness, never, ever be exposed. They weren't exactly in Auburn Hills, after all. They were on a busy street corner in the heart of inner-city Detroit, just a few yards away from the famed Bluebird nightclub, and weakness was a trait nobody on those streets could afford to display. Especially not somebody as young as Nikki. Although she knew Dino had run off all of the other hustlers who tried to boost their merchandise so close to his business, and that he had yet to bother her, she still didn't take any chances. She'd been on her own ever since she was thirteen, when she didn't know Dino even existed. She couldn't depend on anybody to take care of her then, and now, five years later, she knew she still couldn't. "Just give me my money," she told the young man. "That's all you got to do, Mister Don't-Know-Squat!"

"How much?"

"What you mean how much, Joe-Joe? You been buying from me for months now."

"How much?"

"Five. The same price it was yesterday and the day before that. And the same price it's gonna be tomorrow."

"Dang, Nikki. Why you always charging so much? Everybody else sells this junk for two at the most."

"Then go to everybody else and give me back my tape."

"They ain't got what I be wantin' and you know that."

"And that's why they only charge two bucks, stupid! They don't have the kind of merchandise I move, boy, and you know what I'm talking about. Now pay up, Joe-Joe, or give it back."

Joe-Joe frowned. He didn't like it one bit, but slapped a five in her tiny hand anyway. He knew the rules. He knew that Dino Cochran had already laid down the law and everybody on the streets obeyed. They could hustle anybody they wanted. They could con anybody they pleased. But when it came to Nikki Lucas, when it came to this snake oil saleswoman, the word was clear: hands off. Period. And it was the law of the land because it came straight from Dino himself, and Joe-Joe knew enough to know that nobody crossed Dino Cochran.

"Thanks, Joe-Joe," Nikki said cheerfully when she received the cash. "Enjoy!"

"Robbin' us blind, Nikki!" he said bitterly as he walked away in the opposite direction of the Bluebird.

Nikki looked at him and placed her hand on her hip. "I ain't robbin' nobody. I don't have no gun to nobody's head, making them buy nothing from me." Then she smiled, knowing that Joe-Joe was one of her most loyal customers and the last thing she needed to do was anger him. "But for real, Joe-Joe; if you like the Grandmaster, you'll love Public Enemy and N.W.A. Those brothers be spinning some serious music. I'm getting it together right now. Come by next week and I'll give you the hook up!"

Before Nikki could finish speaking or even stash the cash Joe-Joe had given her into the pocket of her baggy jeans, a rail-thin young man in high-top tennis shoes bumped her violently and knocked her to the ground. In one swift swoop, the young man grabbed as many of her tapes as he could and took off running. Nikki hesitated at first. She had no idea what had just happened, but when she saw the thief running with her tapes, she jumped to her feet.

But before she could fully react, two men she knew as Wonk and Sugarman shot past her in pursuit of the bandit. Their big bodies were sailing between cars and flying across the street. She attempted to give chase too, but an arm as strong as steel grabbed her from behind and stopped her in her tracks.

"Let me go!" she yelled, her small hands attempting to dislodge the thick arm that now encircled her. Her feet were suddenly airborne and kicking as her small body rammed against the steel arm's massive frame. She looked at her captor as she fought with all she had to be freed from his grasp. Even when she realized it was Dino, the man she dreamed about every single night, her anger was too complete to be repressed. "He stole my tapes, Dino. What you doing!" she yelled.

Dino refused to loosen his grip. "You aren't running after that punk, Nikki." His voice was as calm as hers was hysterical.

"But he stole my tapes!" She was wiggling and kicking even more erratically to free herself from his hold.

Dino pulled her against him with such a force that her entire body tightened and her struggle for freedom couldn't help but cease. He leaned into her ear. "I said don't sweat it. My boys are taking care of him."

Nikki looked first at the strong arm that held her by its catch, and then she looked over her shoulder into the eyes of the owner of that arm. They were gorgeous, oak brown eyes with drooping lids; and they looked out at her with a hardened, all-knowing stare that always unnerved her. His lashes were so black and thick that they leaned over the top tip of those eyes as if to shield the world from the hypnotic appeal within them. Nikki had dreamed of this day for months, from the first moment she'd seen Dino.

That day, she was astounded by those same droopy eyes and that massive, muscular frame he carried around with the kind of swagger that made folks certain that he was not one to trifle with. He had walked up to her, his trademark long dreads bouncing against his strong back, and asked why some kid like her was hanging out on such a dangerous street corner. When she told him to mind his own business, he smiled such a bright-white, lazy smile that it weakened her knees. From that day to this, she was putty in his hands . . . in his big, beautiful hands.

"He stole my tapes, Dino," she said again; only this time with far less fight, her heart pounding, and her eyes unable to blink at the sight of him.

Dino stared back at her, in that concerned, assessing look he always gave her. It was a look that often made Nikki feel vulnerable, as if he was seeing something in her that wasn't quite right. Then he set her back on her feet. "You need to stop worrying," he said as he tucked in his polo shirt, his dreads shining like thick ropes against the late evening sun. "He'll get his."

Nikki looked beyond Dino and saw, for the first time, that his other main man, Max, was on the scene too. She once thought that Max was Dino's bodyguard because he was around him so much. But she came to find out that he, like Wonk and Sugarman, was just another one of his "boys." Max also knew she had a thing for Dino, and she suddenly felt exposed and angry because of it.

"Why you didn't let me get him, Dino?" she asked. "Why you gonna let him knock me down and steal my stuff and neither one of y'all try to stop him?"

"He was fast," Dino said, his remark gaining a laugh from Max.

Nikki looked at them hard. "Oh, and like you're not? What, Dino? You're too old for the chase now? Some punk crackhead can outrun you now?"

Dino should have been offended, but he wasn't. Instead, he smiled that lazy smile of his and dismissed her little comment. But Max didn't dismiss anything. He moved in front of Dino as if he needed protection from little Nikki, his bald, muscle head straining with anger.

"Who you think you talking to?" he asked her. "That's Dino Cochran, in case your lil' skinny behind forgot who you dealing with. He'll eat you alive and spit you out."

"That's enough, Max." Dino grabbed Max by the sleeve as if he weren't almost as big as he, and pulled him back. "I can handle this, understand? Get on back to the club. I'll be there."

Max stared at Nikki a moment longer, his wide nostrils flaring, but then he did as his boss commanded and headed back toward the Bluebird.

Nikki couldn't believe she'd spoken so harshly to Dino. Not to this man that just moments before, she would have given her right arm to get close to. But she couldn't help it. When she got angry she got feisty. And that thief had just ruined her good humor. She moved over to her remaining tapes to see which ones hadn't been lifted.

Dino stared at her a moment longer, as if still conflicted about something, and then moved over by her. "You okay?" he asked.

"No, I'm not okay. I don't like people stealing my stuff. He just took my tapes. These my tapes!"

Dino smiled. "Are they?"

Nikki looked at him. "What you mean? Of course they are!"

"Those tapes are bootlegs, Nikki; come on. You made copies off of one and now you're selling them as if there's nothing in this wide world wrong with that."

"What's wrong with it? Yeah, I copy them. So what?"

"It's an illegal activity, that's what. It's a violation of intellectual property laws."

Nikki looked puzzled. She'd always heard that Dino wasn't some street punk, but was a smart, college-educated brother with an MBA. But sometimes she wondered if he flaunted it. "Intellectual what?"

He smiled and broke it down. "What you're doing is wrong."

"Man, please. Every time you come around me, you always singing that same song. You don't be singing it to nobody else. Just me. Like I'm the only somebody doing this stuff. Like I'm the only hustler on these streets. I'm handling my business, all right? I'm not doing nothing wrong."

"Boosting other people's records is illegal whether you want to believe it or not. What'll happen if you get arrested?"

Dino looked so concerned over what Nikki regarded as nothing, that it made her smile. "Arrested, Dino? For selling tapes?"

"That's right. What'll happen then?"

"I'm not gonna get arrested, okay?"

"But what if you do?"

"Then I'll go to jail and call you. And you'll bail me out."

Dino laughed. "I will?"

"Of course you will."

"And why's that?"

"Because you love me so much." Nikki had a grand smile on her face, knowing good and well that Dino Cochran would probably say, *"Nikki, who?"* if she called him asking for that kind of help.

But by Dino's facial expression, her tongue-in-cheek remark hadn't been funny to him at all. His smile was gone and he stared at Nikki, at this pint-sized, eighteen-year-old in her oversized jersey and jeans, with that trademark backward turned baseball cap on her small head. He removed that cap, something he never failed to do whenever he saw her, and watched with interest as a smooth swath of jet black, naturally wavy hair cascaded past her narrow shoulders. With that beautiful hair and those amazing dark green eyes against her smooth brown skin, even at eighteen, she was a stunner.

"So you think I love you?" he asked, staring into her eyes.

Nikki definitely didn't like the sound of that. It sounded too serious, too *thoughtful.* "I was just playin', Dino. Dang. Don't be making no federal case out of a little joke."

Dino kept staring at her, studying her, and it increased the jittering of Nikki's already raw nerves. And when he wouldn't stop his gazing, she became feisty again. "What?" she asked in a sharp tone.

Dino exhaled. "Just stay out of trouble, all right?"

Nikki grabbed her cap from him and placed it back on her head. "I always stay out of trouble. You, on the other hand—"

"Me?"

"Yeah, you. Ah, come on, Dino. This ain't no Mister Rogers neighborhood. I know what's going down. No brother be owning all of these strip clubs you own and have all of the kind of money you float unless something's undercover."

Dino smiled and then he laughed. He grabbed Nikki's cap and slung it off of her head again. "You're one of a kind, Nikki Lucas."

Nikki grabbed her cap from Dino and placed it back on her head. "And don't you forget it, either." She now had a slight smile of her own.

Dino looked at her longer, his eyes perusing down her small body and back up to her face. His smile dropped into that concerned, anguished look again. Then he began walking back toward his club. "Later," he said as he left.

Less than an hour later, Dino was relaxing in his club with Max. Wonk and Sugarman came in and sat down straddle-style beside them.

"Found him?" Dino asked Sugarman.

"Yeah, we found the little thief. Took a while, but we found him. Had Nikki's tapes still on his butt. He now regrets that particular move, I assure you."

"I wouldn't have even bothered," Max said. "Not for no Nikki Lucas. Got too much mouth on her."

"Yeah, but Dino laid down the law," Sugarman reminded him. "Everybody knows Nikki's off limits. That crackhead knew it too. He violates Dino's law, he pays the consequences—period. Otherwise, what good is Dino's word anymore?"

"But that Nikki Lucas," Max said. "I can't stand that girl!"

"Your boy's here," Wonk told Dino as he looked toward the entrance.

The preacher everybody called Billy Graham, the one always on some street corner sermonizing to less than interested hustlers and bums around the hood, began handing out flyers and talking with some of the patrons. He was the only one who was ever brave enough to approach Dino about getting right with God. Other preachers felt Dino was a lost cause, too far gone for redemption. But Billy Graham, with his thick afro and weather-worn, oversized Bible, didn't hesitate to tell Dino he was a sinner who was going to bust hell wide open if he didn't give his life to Christ. Although Dino wasn't trying to hear that kind of talk, he respected the preacher for telling it to him anyway. And he made it clear to the bouncers at the door that Billy Graham was allowed into the Bluebird whenever he wished, though his message was hardly good for business.

"Hey, Dino," Billy said as he approached their table.

"What's up?" Dino replied.

"Heaven's up." Billy smile as he passed out flyers.

When he tried to hand one to Max, he knocked the preacher's hand away. "You better get out of my face. That's what you better do."

Dino looked at the flyer. It was a cartoon caricature of people burning and falling, with the caption, WHAT IN THE HELL DO YOU WANT, written across the top.

"Hell is down," Billy said. "And y'all going down, too, if y'all don't get right with God. Time is runnin' out."

"We let you pass out your little booklets, Billy; all right?" Max said. "Now get out of here."

Billy Graham looked at Max, and sadness swept over his big, bulging eyes. Then, without responding, he left.

"Why you put up with him, Dino?" Max wanted to know. "These people don't be coming to no club to be hearing that doomsday stuff he be preaching."

"Billy's all right." Dino tossed the flyer on the table.

"Word on the street is that you're thinking about purchasing that strip mall in Dearborn, Dino," Wonk said.

"It's a bad idea," Max stated.

"Everything's a bad idea to you," Sugarman said. "Dino wouldn't own jack if it was left up to you."

Max remained firm. "I still say it's a bad idea! Jake Hampton's got his eyes on that property too, and y'all know it."

"Bump Jake Hampton!" Sugarman said. "Best man wins in this game, boy."

"I'm just saying we don't wanna start mixing it up with Hamp. That's all I'm saying. He and his boys are killers. Stone cold killers. They the kind of brothers that'll pop a cap in your behind and laugh while they watch you dying. Dino don't need that kind of aggravation."

"I'm just checking it out, Max." Dino's response was calm. But as soon as he voiced it, the sound of screeching tires echoed from outside the club, followed by the popping of rapid gunfire.

Dino, and everybody else inside, dashed under the tables, scurrying for their lives. They knew a drive-by when they heard one. Although the Bluebird didn't appear to be the target of this particular one, the shots kept coming, one behind the other. *Pop, pop, pop.* It was as if whoever was the target didn't stand a chance if they had been caught in the open. It was then, thinking about that wide open world outside, that Dino's heart dropped.

"Nikki!" he said in a horrified gasp, quickly pulling out his gun and hurrying from under the table.

"Man, forget her!" Max yelled, grabbing at Dino. But Dino had already taken off.

"What's he doing?" Sugarman yelled. "Is he crazy?"

"Yeah, he's crazy," Max replied. "Crazy about that jive girl!"

"But he's gonna get himself killed!"

"You think I don't know that?" Max asked bitterly just before hurrying into the line of fire.

The shooting was over by the time Dino made it outside and the once busy streets now looked nearly deserted. Two young men lay shot in those streets, both of whom Dino knew were hardcore drug dealers. People were running to aid them and screaming for somebody to dial 911. The getaway car, a Chevy, was speeding off, swerving around the corner with its windows rolling up.

Dino frantically looked down the sidewalk toward Nikki's usual hangout. She wasn't there. He put his gun away and ran in that direction. His years as a college track star and his days in the gym allowed him to move faster than he'd run in years, but there was still no sign of Nikki. Her bootleg tapes were in their usual place, sitting neatly in the cardboard box she carried them around in; but she was nowhere to be found. His only prayer was that she had taken off at the first sign of danger and was out of harm's way by the time the bullets began to sail. She was a survivor, after all. A kid in a grownup world. She knew how to take care of herself. But when Dino looked around the corner, around a narrow alleyway, and saw the body of a young lady lying in a fetal position, his heart rammed against his chest.

It was Nikki, curled up and immobile. For a moment, he was immobile too. All he could do was stare at this lifeless figure and pray for movement; for any sign of life. When his brief paralysis ended, Dino ran, his dreads banging hard against his back. He moved so fast that he nearly slid up to her. He didn't realize she was alive until he was upon her, falling on his knees, and could see that she was shaking.

"Nikki?" Dino's voice was so low it seemed as if he was afraid the sound could hurt her.

"Dino?" She was almost hoarse with fear.

"Yes, it's me." Dino touched her gently on her narrow back. "Are you all right?"

Nikki didn't move immediately, but when she did, she managed to sit up. Dino moved closer to her, looking grief stricken over the sight of this kid who had no business being anywhere near this kind of nonsense. Where were her parents? Who was looking out for her?

"Are you hurt?" His eyes scanned her slender body.

She looked at him, her thin, bottom lip trembling. That cocky look she was known for was now a mask of agony, and all she could do was nod her head. Dino exhaled. He wanted to grab her into his arms and protect her from days like this. But his movement was stifled, not only by the sudden arrival of Max in the alley, but by fear itself.

Dino drove his Bronco into the parking lot of the Paradise Inn, just as Nikki had instructed him. He looked at the small, dingy motel that stood poorly lit on a side street behind a Chinese restaurant, then he looked at Nikki. She was holding up well considering what she'd just been through. But for some reason, he was upset that this was where she had told him to take her.

"You live here?" he asked in disbelief.

Nikki looked at him. "Yeah, so?" The fight in her was coming back easily. "What's it to you?"

"Nikki, this is one of those hourly rate motels."

Nikki laughed. "For real?"

"And you live here?"

"Yes, I live here. Dang. Where you think I was gonna live? I make my living peddling tapes on a street corner. I can't exactly afford no Ritz Carlton." She sighed and added, "It might not be up to your standards, but it's all I can afford. All right?"

Nikki grabbed her box of tapes, opened the passenger door, and stepped out. Dino climbed out and walked with her across the parking lot toward her little room. He couldn't help but think she was a young beauty as he stared at her honey smooth brown skin, her high, graceful cheeks, and her amazing dark green eyes. And despite all she'd seen tonight, despite all she'd probably seen in her short, hustling life, she still had a sparkle in those eyes.

"Who takes care of you, Nikki?" he asked as they walked.

She smiled. "Who takes care of me? What kind of question is that? I take care of myself."

"You do?"

"Yes!" The defensiveness in her voice was strong. She'd always known her life wasn't normal, that people didn't usually start out on their own at thirteen; but what could she do? When she was thirteen, she didn't exactly have the power to make people love her, or to make her parents act right.

"Where're your folks?" Dino inquired.

She shrugged. "Don't know, don't care. They split when I was thirteen."

"Split? They broke up?"

"Split. Skipped town. Punked out on parenting. Whatever you wanna call it. They weren't married and both were on drugs. After my daddy left, my mama decided to skip town too. And she didn't invite me along. Said I'd just slow her down. So she left me with this old man up the block. Some pervert. I stayed there all of about two minutes, long enough for me to figure out that he wasn't exactly the fatherly type. Know what I'm saying? So I hit the road and never looked back."

"And you've been on your own ever since?"

"That's right. Had an aunt in town who wasn't too crazy about me, but she moved to Florida."

Dino pushed out a painful exhale. "Some family."

"I'll never be like my mama was." Nikki's words were so heartfelt that Dino looked at her. "Having a child and then just forgetting about her. What kind of parent is that? When I have a baby, I'm gonna be married and successful; and I'm gonna give my child everything she could ever want. I'll never be a statistic like my mama was."

"What about your education, Nikki?"

"What about it? I got my GED."

Dino couldn't conceal his surprise. "I'm impressed."

"I mean, it ain't no MBA, like what you got."

Dino looked at her. "How would you know about that?"

"I hear things. I hear you ain't your average gangster."

"I'm not a gangster at all."

Nikki chuckled. "Yeah, right."

"I'm not," Dino said, smirking. He removed the key from her hand and unlocked the door to room 17.

When the door pushed open, Nikki looked at him. "Wanna come in?" she asked with a combination of mischief and fear in her eyes.

Dino was torn between doing the right thing by turning her down flat, and accepting her invitation. But he looked at Nikki—at this young woman he couldn't seem to lose interest in, and doing the right thing seemed impossible. "After you," he said.

Three hours later, when it was well after midnight, the door to room 17 opened and Nikki and Dino emerged. Nikki, who had entered wearing jeans, came out in shorts. Dino's polo shirt, which was once tucked in, was now hanging out. But for Nikki, it was beyond a simple physical difference. It was much more emotional. She felt like an entirely different person coming out of her room than she felt going in. She felt happy and scared, lonely and joined, as all kinds of disparate emotions raced through her.

She looked at Dino, at this big, beautiful man walking beside her, and her young heart could barely stand it. Had it really happened? Had she just given herself completely to this man she knew she'd love for the rest of her life? She wanted to take his hand and then jump into his arms again, just to release some of those giddy, unfamiliar feelings. But his demeanor stopped her. She might have found paradise in his arms, but from the stricken look he had on his face, she doubted if he'd found the same.

Dino felt differently too, not emotionally charged like Nikki, but as if the weight of the world was on his shoulders. He must have been out of his mind to let things get so out of hand. But he thought she was experienced. He thought a tough kid like Nikki had been around the block at least a time or two. What street hustler hadn't? And even when he realized his error, even when any fool could have seen that Nikki was about as experienced as a two-year-old, he continued anyway, without even thinking about protection; too selfish and lost in being with her to even consider giving her a chance to change her mind.

Dino opened the door to his truck and sat down, facing outward. He looked at Nikki, and felt repulsed by his own behavior. He took her small hand. "It's not your fault," he said.

She looked at him and knew exactly what he was doing. "It's not yours either."

"Don't believe that, Nikki. Understand me? Everything that happened tonight was wrong, and it was all on me."

Nikki put a hand on her hip. "All on you? How is it all on you? Dino, I'm a grown woman—"

"Barely."

"I'm a grown woman, okay? I knew what time it was. You ain't got to act like you seduced me into doing something I didn't wanna do, or manipulated me, or none of that. Because it's not true. I knew exactly what I was doing."

Yeah, right. Dino's guilt was so searing he felt feverish. "I just don't want you feeling bad about this, Nikki; beating yourself up about it."

Why would she beat herself up about being with the man she loved? What is he talking about? "Don't sweat it, Dino," she said.

But he wasn't finished. "I also don't want you to read more into this than what's there." He immediately saw the responding despair in Nikki's eyes.

Nikki's heart felt faint, but she managed to smile. "You don't have to worry about that happening either."

"You sure about that?"

"Positive, Dino. Dang," she said with her usual frown. "You act like I'm gonna just suddenly fall in love with you because of one night. You got life bent if you think I'm that naïve. Please. You ain't that hot."

Dino smiled; then he laughed. "That's my girl." He pinched her cheek and then placed his feet inside his truck, cranking up the engine. "Need anything?" he asked her.

"Like what?"

"Like anything."

"Yeah," Nikki said after a thoughtful pause. "I need you to let me sell my tapes inside the Blue-bird." Dino immediately began shaking his head. "Why not, Dino? You let all those other girls in there and some of them are younger than me, so don't even go there about my age."

"The Bluebird is no place for a lady, Nikki. Now, do you need anything else?"

She needed many things, not least of which was him, but he'd never know it. "No."

Dino smiled weakly, looked at her one more time with that pitiful look that she was beginning to dislike, and then he drove away.

Days passed before Nikki saw Dino again. And when she did, he got out of his Bronco and hurried into the Bluebird without looking her way, as if he was avoiding her on purpose. He used to always come by and at least speak to her. Now he suddenly had no time. At first she was devastated. She went home and cried every night. Although he'd warned her about reading anything into their night together, Nikki still believed that things would somehow change between them; that he really didn't mean what he'd said. The way he kept avoiding her, however, should have told her differently.

This was especially true a couple months later, when she was too sick to even get out on the street corner and hustle her tapes. She began throwing up and couldn't stop, spending hours in her bathroom. As soon as she felt better, as soon as she could control her regurgitations, she hurried over to the pharmacy and purchased a pregnancy test. When the result was confirmed, when her greatest fear was realized, she slid down on her bathroom floor and cried like a baby. She was pregnant, unmarried, and alone. A statistic. Just like she said she'd never be.

And the father of that baby had to know. That made it almost unbearable. He had already all but told her that their night together was nothing more to him than a booty call. She already knew that she was going to be in this alone, that he really didn't want to have anything more to do with her. That morning brought on a realization so desperate, so horrifically painful, that Nikki lurched forward and started vomitting again.

She still felt lousy; but two days later, she was back on the corner selling her tapes. Dino's Bronco drove up to his club and she knew she had to tell him. Although Nikki was aware that it was going to be unwelcomed news, she also knew he had a right to know. That was why she left her tapes and approached him.

Max was sitting in the driver's seat and Dino was just getting out of the backseat. When he saw her heading his way, he looked almost petrified, like he knew her condition before she could say a word. Nikki was just going to let it rip; tell him that he was the father and let the chips fall where they may. If he denied it, if he suddenly claimed that he didn't know what she was talking about, that he could be one of many possible daddies, she wasn't going to battle with him. She'd look like a fool fighting somebody who could treat her that way.

Dino looked stricken as she approached him, as if he was going to be sick himself. Even Max, when he got out of the Bronco, looked weird, like she was invading some sacred turf. But then Dino held out his hand and assisted a woman out of the Bronco that was so tall and so beautiful that even Nikki couldn't believe her eyes. She was a deep toned, dark-skinned woman who appeared to be in her early thirties like Dino, with a skull-low afro and a big, bright smile. When Nikki scaled the fullness of the woman's body, she quickly discovered that she was not only a statuesque beauty, but also a very pregnant one; as far along as seven or eight months. Nikki nearly died where she stood.

She looked at Dino and tears stained her lids. He was going to be the father of her child. A fact she never dreamed she'd be ashamed of, but now she was. She'd slept with him, not because she was some scandalous woman with loose morals who slept with just anybody, but because she believed that he, unlike any man she'd ever known, was different.

How could she have been so dumb? Why she hadn't guessed it before amazed her. A successful, gorgeous man like Dino Cochran wasn't free as a bird. What in the world could she have been thinking?

"Hello, Nikki," he said as a nervous smile creased his face. "What's up?"

Nikki couldn't say a word. Even if she wanted to, she couldn't.

But when Dino said, "I want you to meet my wife," in a calm, conversational way, those last two words jolted her back to reality.

"Your wife?" Nikki couldn't believe it. Maybe his girlfriend . . . or even one of many girlfriends. But she never would have dreamed for a second that the woman standing beside Dino (or any woman, for that matter) would be his *wife*. He didn't even wear a wedding ring.

"Yes, my wife," Dino said, this time, less smoothly. He could see that Nikki wasn't just surprised anymore, but shattered. "Didn't Max tell you I was married?" Then he turned to his wife. "Sophia, honey, this is Nikki. Max's old lady."

"Hi," Sophia said, her smile even grander as she extended a small hand.

Nikki shook it, but kept her eyes on Dino. She didn't know what to do. Having been alone since the age of thirteen, she'd never depended on any other human being for anything. But then Nikki met Dino. Gave him her heart and then her body. She thought that would mean something special; that her free gift to him would somehow elevate her in his eyes. Nikki would never admit it aloud, or dare let on to him that she felt that way, but that was indeed how she felt. And even after he told her not to expect anything from him, she still trusted him to treat her right. Nobody in this life had ever respected her. Not her parents, not any human being alive. She had counted on Dino. He was her last hope.

Now, even he had let her down. But she didn't make a scene. Why should she? He never campaigned to be her hero. Dino was being Dino. A player who never pretended to be anything else. Why should he be blamed for her foolish hopes?

Gathering her wits, Nikki kept it together and spoke to Sophia, even attempted to smile when Mrs. Cochran commented on her *stunning* eyes. She even allowed Max to place his arm around her waist and talk up their supposed relationship and how lucky he was to find somebody like her. She didn't say a word as Dino and his very beautiful, very pregnant wife said their goodbyes and made their way across the sidewalk and into the club. Dino looked back at Nikki, regret searing his sad eyes underneath his drooped lids, as he followed his wife inside. When they were gone, Max immediately removed his arm from Nikki as if she were a contaminant.

He pointed at her. "Don't even try it," he warned her. "The man is happily married to a real woman, as you can see. And you better not think about messing that up."

Nikki looked at Max, and looked at the bouncers outside the club. A club she'd been itching to join since she first saw its owner. A club no one could now pay her to step a foot into. Nikki turned and walked away. She wanted to cry.

She wanted to scream at a life that had been too harsh too long, but she didn't make a sound. Instead of returning to her corner, she kept on walking, ignoring the calls of Amanda and other hustlers who just knew Nikki Lucas wasn't leaving her merchandise unsupervised. But she was. She was leaving and she wasn't looking back.

"You look like death warmed over, man," Max said to Dino three days later as they drove along the streets of Detroit. They were going to check out a piece of property Dino was thinking about purchasing, and Max couldn't get over how distracted Dino seemed. Max was driving the Bronco, forcing him to keep his eyes on the road ahead. Dino was sitting on the passenger side with a fixed frown on his face. It was late evening, around six o'clock, and the traffic was thick. "What's the story?" Max asked.

"No story." Dino avoided his friend's inquiring eyes.

"Come on, Dino. You look bad, man. For real. What's happened?" As soon as Max finished the question, he realized the answer. "Oh. That scene with Nikki the other night." Dino exhaled and squirmed in his seat.

"That's it, isn't it?" Max asked.

Dino hesitated. "I can't find her." Anguish filled his voice.

"You can't find her? Why would you want to? That chick got too much lip for a kid."

"She hasn't been on the streets in three days, so I went by her motel room. The manager showed me where she'd cleared out. Didn't say where she was going or nothing. Just left."

"Can I ask you a question?"

Dino knew what was coming. "No."

"Man, why you so stuck on that girl? I mean, she's pretty enough. Got a nice lil' bod, nice lil' figure; but so do a hundred other girls on the block. What's so special about that one?"

Dino leaned his head back, his drooping lids nearly covering his eyes. "I don't know."

"But she is special to you?"

"She's a kid, Max; come on. A kid who has no business out here all by her lonesome like this."

"A kid who's got you worried sick about her, when you got a beautiful sister like Sophia waiting for you at home. She can't touch Sophia in the looks department, the class department . . . in no department, Dino. And don't you forget that."

Dino felt a stab of guilt. "You should have seen her face when I told her Sophia was my wife. I thought she was going to pass out."

Max shook his head. "You should have never slept with her, man."

Dino looked at Max. "Who says I slept with her?"

"You should have never slept with her."

Dino sighed. "I know that."

"Not some female like Nikki," Max continued. "She probably thinks you love her now, and have betrayed her trust, and all of that bullcrap. You were already too wrapped up in her before you went down that road with her. Now you got a problem for real." Again, Max shook his large, bald head. "With a woman like Sophia, I can't believe you're all caught up in some Nikki Lucas mess. Man, you crazy."

Dino didn't respond. He couldn't because he knew Max wouldn't understand. His feelings for Nikki weren't something he could just explain away. It wasn't as simple as that. He loved Sophia. She was his wife, the mother of his unborn child; he loved her dearly. But with Nikki it was different. Somehow he felt connected where there should be no connection; bound to her when there was no reason for their bond. But it was there. Strong, willful, and unbreakable.

Dino shook off his mounting concern. She'd turn up in a few days, no doubt. Maybe after what he'd done to her, she just decided to put a little more real estate between them.

The car phone began ringing and Dino looked out of the window, definitely not interested in being bothered right now. His silent gesture was a signal that he wanted Max to take care of it.

Grabbing the phone, Max said, "Max. Speak." He held it with one hand and listened intently, then he looked at Dino. "We're on our way," he said and slammed down the phone.

Dino peered at him. "What?"

"Trouble at the Bluebird," Max said as he made a sharp U-turn and headed back. "Some fools are over there shooting up the place. Wonk says it's Jake Hampton's people; that Hamp's trying to rope you in."

Jake Hampton was Dino's main competition, a strongman who wanted to muscle his way into Dino's terrain. That was why Dino sighed as his Bronco flew through the streets of Detroit. He prayed that Hamp wasn't trying to draw him into some turf battle, some power struggle, but he felt in his gut that that was exactly what was going down.

Dino surveyed the wreckage with a feeling of disbelief. The place looked as if a bulldozer had run through it. There was shattered glass everywhere; knocked over tables, broken chairs. All of the liquor was either poured out, swimming on the bar counter, or still in perfectly fine bottles rolling around aimlessly from wall to wall. Dino placed his hands in the front pockets of his African shirt and exhaled. Other than a bouncer who took a bullet in the arm, nobody was hurt. He was grateful that their normal night crowd had not yet arrived. But he was angry too. Hamp meant business. This was no send-a-message scare tactic. He meant to rile Dino.

The cops questioned Dino, but then moved on to those who had actually been there, like the strippers and waitresses. Max and Sugarman came and flanked their boss, who still stood in the middle of his club.

Max kicked a rolling bottle of wine away from his feet. "We can hit back tonight." His voice was out of earshot of the police. "Just say the word."

"No," Dino said. "That's what he wants."

"Well, what you plan to do, Dino?" Sugarman probed. "We can't let Hamp and his boys get away with this."

"I know that. You think I'm stupid? But I also know we can't go running over there half-cocked." Dino hesitated.

"We don't hit tonight, but early in the morning. Exactly when they aren't expecting it. But we don't hit hard."

Max disagreed. "Bad idea, Dino. Hamp and his boys are killers. You can't play around with them."

"We'll do it my way, Max. I don't want a blood bath. Just a little message to Hamp to let him know that the answer is no. That's all."

"Hit hard or not at all," Max insisted.

"You heard me," Dino said. "We'll do it tomorrow morning."

"And you won't be there," Max said. When Dino gave him a hard look, he added, "Don't look at me like that. You can't be there, Dino. You'll be the first one the pigs come sniffling for after they find out there's been a retaliatory hit. You know that. You've got to let us handle it."

Dino turned his eyes to his ruined club. The final words he said before walking away were, "Then handle it."

And Max did. Hitting Jake Hampton and his boys at their hangout during an early morning blast. Nobody was killed, but the message was sent. Hamp had hit Dino because he wanted a piece of Dino's very lucrative, and substantially legitimate, business action. Dino had hit back because he wanted Hamp to understand that he didn't care what he wanted. He wasn't getting it from him.

The battle had become inflamed, and Dino knew he had to take precautions. He hired more bodyguards and installed more cameras, turning his various businesses into veritable prisons.

Neither he nor Sophia went anywhere without protection, usually one or two bodyguards. And at night, there was always somebody posted outside the door of their house. These were strange days for Dino. Anxious days. And he knew it was just a matter of time before Hamp got bored with his resistance and decided to take the game to another level.

That time came less than a week after the nightclub shooting. Dino and Max were at the strip mall near Dearborn, with Wonk and Sugarman serving as bodyguards as they did a walk through of the abandoned buildings one more time. Dino was still a little wary about investing in such a huge endeavor, especially in light of his less than safe current situation. And Max was trying with all he had to further dissuade him. Max felt that it was too risky all around, and Hamp had already made it clear that he wanted this territory too.

"Don't borrow trouble," he said to Dino as they stepped out of the flimsy door and into the fresh late afternoon air.

And that was when the shooting started. The first bullet caught Max clean in the chest, taking him down to his knees as soon as it struck. Dino grabbed Max and dropped too, while Wonk and Sugarman began returning fire on the unseen assassin.

"Get him inside!" Dino yelled to Wonk as he pulled out his gun and moved behind a post.

Wonk dragged Max back inside the empty mall as Dino and Sugarman returned shot for shot. Soon the blasts across the bough stopped coming and they could see, through the weeds across the highway, a figure running. Both Wonk and Dino ran after the man, who appeared to be as muscular as they were. But he was in a truck and driving away before they were even close enough to get a license plate number. Dino leaned forward, virtually out of breath, amazed at how close a call that really was. Then he thought about Max.

He ran back into the mall and up against the wall where Max lay. He wasn't moving, he wasn't responding, and Wonk had already phoned for an ambulance. Dino fell on his knees and touched his friend. He couldn't believe it. *"Don't borrow trouble,"* Max had said. But he had said it too late.

Max died within hours of the shooting, and Dino's thirst for revenge began to dominate his every thought. He thought he was legit now. He thought that all of those days of old, when he was shooting it up and acting a fool with the best of the gang bangers, were long behind him. Now they were back in spades. Back in the name of a chump like Jake Hampton, who took Dino's kindness for weakness. And he wanted to kill him for it.

Dino fought hard against his feelings. He'd never killed a man in his life, even during his darkest street days. But Max was dead. Shot down like a dog in the street by a brother who wanted to take what he hadn't built; possess what he never owned. And it was eating Dino alive. He felt as if it was all his fault. Max had wanted him to either hit Hamp hard or just forget about it. But Dino thought he could stall the man. He thought he could play nice and wing it. He was wrong. Max's death only proved just how wrong he was.

Even Billy Graham, the street corner preacher who used to always have a word from the Lord to tell Dino, stopped telling him anything. It was as if he, like all of the other evangelists in the hood, wasn't wasting his breath either. And if that weren't enough, word started spreading that Dino Cochran was in a funk, that he wasn't half the man he used to be, that brothers were invading his territory left and right and he wasn't stopping them. He was in trouble. He either had to take Hamp out, or give him what he wanted.

But the real enemy turned out not to be Jake Hampton, or any other punk with a pistol. It was Dino himself. It happened a week after Max's death. He and Sophia had just left a childbirth class and Dino was driving while talking on his cell phone. He was so engrossed in his conversation, so animated over another shakedown attempt, that he didn't see the stop sign until after he ran it. He tried to slam on the brakes, but it was too late. His Bronco skidded through the intersection right into the path of a semi, ramming so hard that the sound of crashing metal was deafening to his ears. The Bronco folded like an accordion, but thanks to their fastened seatbelts, Dino and his wife were saved from what should have been a sure ejection.

Dino blacked out momentarily, but woke up clearheaded enough to understand that he was a very blessed man. His chest was nearly wedged into the steering wheel, and although his breathing was labored, he knew he was going to be all right. He almost released a sigh of relief until he remembered that he had not been alone in the vehicle. His wife and their unborn child were with him. Terror suddenly paralyzed Dino as he slowly and nervously turned toward the passenger seat. Sophia was still there, but her presence brought no relief. Her eyes were wide open, and she was still beautiful to look upon; but Dino knew right away.

He tried desperately to reach out to his wife, but his arms were too short. He was wedged between his disassembled seat and the steering wheel, and could not readjust. All he could do was cry out. All he could do was plead to God Almighty to not let it be, and he cried this prayer over and over and over again. But no matter how much he cried, no matter how much he prayed, it was so. Reality was upon him like that thief in the night.

And it was painfully obvious, even to the truck driver who had jumped out of his truck and run up to the Bronco, his thick body virtually unscathed except for the terror in his eyes. And with those eyes he saw that the beautiful woman in the passenger seat, who was staring into oblivion, was in major trouble.

Dino, however, knew that it was far worse than that.

He dropped his head in agony and sobbed for his wife, his dreads flopping down around him like coiled snakes, concealing the full devastation that masked his unmarked face. He looked at her again and tried to reach for her once more, but he knew the truth. He knew with a certainty that was eating him alive, that his wife did not survive the impact of the crash, nor, to his everlasting shame, the impact of being married to a man like him.

ONE

Sixteen years later

The Big Turn diner sat in the heart of downtown Monroe, Florida, tightly sandwiched between Mary Beth's hair salon and Jeffrey Wainwright's tool and dye shop. It had been a staple of the small town for more than forty years when Alfred B. Macomb decided to take his skills as a rib joint owner in Chicago, and relocate to a less stressful, far more orderly life in the south. He settled on Monroe. Alfred B. once told the wife he met once he arrived in town that he'd chosen Monroe because it was small and homely; a place in great need of some northern style. He believed that Monroe would welcome him and his business savvy with open arms.

The townspeople opened their arms all right, but not very far. Although Alfred B.'s dream had been to launch an impressive restaurant of the first order, with valet parking and imported wines, he ended up settling on a diner smaller than his Chicago rib joint. It was a diner not famous for anything imported. Instead, it was known for its double-stack cheeseburgers and curly-cued fries. And the dream of valet parking materialized into street-side parking that he shared with Mary Beth's salon and Jeff Wainwright's tool and dye.

Then, four years ago, after thirty-six years of barely being able to maintain the diner, everything changed. Alfred B. stepped out of the Providence Bank and dropped dead on the concrete. Right after being warned by a loan officer that he risked certain financial disaster if he didn't learn to appreciate that regular beef sold hamburgers just as abundantly as Angus beef.

At the time of his death, Nikki Lucas was a thirty-yearold single mother who had relocated to Florida some twelve years earlier, rising up the ranks from waitress to the diner's manager. She was particularly crushed when she heard the news.

But his body was barely cold in the ground before his son, Alfred Jr., began seeking out buyers for what he considered was no lifelong labor of love, but a money pit. Although Nikki was no fan of Alfred Jr.'s, and was outraged by his characterization of his father's diner, she was not so

thrown that she couldn't realize that a golden
opportunity was staring her in the face. Who but
she could carry on in Alfred B.'s stead? Who but
she could take care of his diner the way he would
have wanted? After all, she loved Big Turn and
the people who worked there. Owning it would
only reinvigorate her natural entrepreneurial
spirit, a spirit that she thought had long since
died the night she left Detroit. On the spot, maybe even on a whim, she decided to buy it herself,
and nurture it herself.

Nikki hurried to the bank to take out the necessary loan, but she was rejected. And not just
by the local banks, but by every bank in the sur-
rounding small towns and in metropolitan Jacksonville as well. A diner manager with no track
record in owning her own business, with little
credit, with little or no collateral, was a risk no
conventional moneylender was willing to take.

Nikki, however, refused to give up. She all but
begged Alfred Jr. to give her a little more time,
and he had no choice but to do so. Especially
since there were no other takers waiting in the
wings. That gave Nikki the time she needed to
keep on searching. After it became clear that
the conventional moneylenders weren't going
to help her out, she decided to go the unconven-
tional route and take out a loan with a finance

company. And although she signed her name to a loan with an interest rate so inflated that it still made her blood curdle, she had no regrets at the time. She was willing to do whatever it took back then to make her dream come true.

But now, four years later, as she stood behind the diner's counter ringing up a take-out, she wondered if it was worth it after all.

"Of course it was worth it," Tammy "Tam" Ellis, her manager, said as she lifted the hatch and came behind the counter. "You did something the rest of us didn't have the nerve to even think about doing, Nikki. You grabbed hold of your dream. You took a business that hadn't turned a profit in years and at least started breaking even.

"Three ninety-eight, Melvin," Nikki said to her customer and then looked at Tam. Tam was a thirty-six-year-old woman with slanted eyes and long, weaved hair. She had a feistiness about her that kept her young, daring, and admirable in Nikki's eyes. "I guess you're right, Tam," she said as she accepted a ten dollar bill from Melvin.

"Ain't no guess in it," Tam said with her trademark bluntness. "I know I'm right. Alfred B. was good peeps, don't get me wrong. But he was an uppity brother who thought Big Turn was some fancy-dancy place in Chicago somewhere when any fool could see it wasn't. And he spent all that money acting like it was. But you got that business sense, Nikki. You know how to keep it real. And you kept all of us employed when that knot-head, Alfred Jr., would have had us out on our rears before we knew what hit us. So yeah, it was worth it, girl. Don't you ever think it wasn't."

Nikki handed Melvin his change and smiled at him. "You come back now, you hear?" she said, causing him to smile at her exaggerated country twang.

"Yes, ma'am." He grabbed his greasy bag which held the burger and fries and hurried toward the exit.

Nikki, looking flustered, leaned against the counter and folded her small arms. "I hear what you're saying, Tam; and I appreciate having this little place, you know I do." She frowned. "I'm just tired, I guess."

"Aren't we all?" Sebastian Dobbs said as he came and plopped down on one of the counter stools. At forty-one, he was Nikki's oldest employee, a man she hired to be her assistant manager, although such a job wasn't really needed in a diner so small. Sebastian, a handsome, narrow-faced man with a thick mustache and a wonderful smile, had been a star on Broadway; or so he claimed. He had only come back to his hometown of Monroe because his mother had fallen ill.

Of course, everybody knew that Sebastian flopped in New York and came back home, not because of any illness his mother may or may not have suffered, but because he had nowhere else to go. He presented himself to Nikki as this great star who was willing to settle for a job "well beneath him" for his mother's sake. Nikki, no stranger to rejection and hard living herself, saw the pain deep within Sebastian's big, round eyes and didn't have the heart to reject him. She hired him on the spot. He was nosey, talked way too much, and only lifted a finger when he was forced to, but nobody brightened up a day like Sebastian. Nobody could make Nikki laugh or see things in a different light the way he could. And for that gift alone, Tam and Nikki's other employees, who thought their boss was way too serious for a woman still in her prime, were eternally grateful to Sebastian.

"I know you aren't calling yourself tired," Tam said.

Always the drama king, Sebastian quickly lifted his hand. "Desist immediately, Miss Ellis," he demanded. "You saw that lunch crowd up in here. They had me running like I was put here on earth for the sole purpose of servicing them! First, they wanted their hamburgers rare, not well done, mind you, but rare. And when I said, 'Excuse me, but have you not heard of E. coli, that little pesky bacteria that could kill you? Hello?' they wanna get all hot with me. Then one little snot-nosed kid, mistaking my proper speech and manners as some sort of effeminate behavior, I suppose, had the nerve to ask me if I'd been tested for AIDS; and they all laughed at that sick little joke as if it was actually clever on snot-nose's part. Well, I tell you, I nearly came up off of my religion then."

"No you didn't, Seb," Nikki said with a smile.

"God be praised, I didn't. But I almost did. So don't you dare stand up there and tell me I'm not tired, Miss Ellis. I'm fagged!"

Tam laughed. "You said it; not me."

"Fagged means exhausted, Tam," Nikki quickly explained. "An old British term."

"Whatever," Tam replied.

"Whatever indeed." Nikki walked from behind the counter to the bright blue colored tables and banquettes in her establishment. It was a small eatery, but exceptionally clean. The white walls were covered with lively, colorful paintings by local artists who rarely sold anything, but always seemed to find a sympathetic supporter in Nikki. It was after lunch but before dinner, which meant the slowest time of the day. Her current customers consisted of two truckers eating and talking at a table in the center of the diner.

Two of Nikki's other employees were also in the diner: Mookie, her twenty-four-year-old, mildly retarded busboy, and Fern, her youngest and most unreliable employee at twenty-two. Fern was a pretty girl with no other ambition than to meet and marry a pretty boy. She and Mookie sat in one of the booths laughing and talking, enjoying the down time. Nikki had only hired Fern because Mookie, who had a crush out of this world on the young lady, begged her to. Since Mookie was Nikki's best worker and would undoubtedly take up Fern's slack anyway, Nikki caved and gave Fern a chance. She decided that Mookie needed and deserved at least one good friend still young enough to be on his level, and Fern did, at least, talk to him and treat him well. And occasionally, she even did a little work.

Nikki spoke to the two truckers, and then went over to the bulletin board. It was a place where anybody could post want ads, business cards, rewards for lost animals, or nearly anything they wanted. Nikki pulled an index card from the back pocket of her jeans and pinned it to the board. She looked at it for a moment, as if it was a painful post, and then walked away, past the counter and down the hall to her office in the back.

Fern, who'd seen Nikki, nudged Mookie.

"What?" Mookie asked.

"Boss just put something on the board."

"So?"

"So," Fern stated as she stood from her seat, "let's see what it is."

Mookie didn't have to be asked twice. He was a slave to his young friend and followed her, without hesitation, over to the bulletin board.

"What it say?" Mookie asked, his big, coal-black eyes squinting at the board in front of him. He suffered, among many other things, from dyslexia, although he could read better than people thought. But because the words were transposed, because it took him far longer to make sense out of the spellings, Mookie didn't dare try to read at all in public.

"She's looking for a boarder," Fern said.

"A boarder?"

"Yeah. Can you believe it? She's trying to rent out a room in her house."

"Why would she do that, Fern?"

"Why you think? She needs the green." Then Fern looked over at Tam and Sebastian. "Y'all seen this?"

"Seen what?" Tam asked, leaning over the counter.

"Boss is renting out one of the rooms in her house."

"Charming," Sebastian said. "Reminds me of a musical I was in once about this landlord—"

Tam held up a hand. "Spare us, please." She looked at Fern. "Maybe she just has extra space she's trying to fill, Fern. It doesn't have to be a negative reason, you know."

"Yeah, right. I may not be as educated as Seb and Boss—"

"Nikki is not educated," Sebastian quickly pointed out. "She's self-taught. There's a difference."

Fern continued. "The only reason people be inviting strangers up in their houses is because they need the cash flow. Period. It ain't got nothing to do with no extra space or whatever you wanna call it. Now, I've got enough sense to know that."

"Go see if our customers need anything," Tam replied. "Got enough sense to *do* that?"

Fern rolled her eyes, but with Mookie on her tail, she did as Tam had ordered. As soon as she did, Henry, the cook, rolled his wheelchair from out of the kitchen that was located behind the counter.

Tam smiled. "Thought you'd be out back smoking on your break."

"Trying to quit," Henry said and Tam nodded. Henry was an ex-Marine who was shot down, not in any Iraqi desert or on some mountain in Afghanistan, but on the streets of Monroe after a fistfight with a drunk. By far, he was the most reserved of Nikki's employees. "What y'all yappin' about?"

"Nikki's renting out a room," Sebastian said.

"A room?" Henry sat upright in his chair in an effort to relieve his occasional aching back. He was a tall man in his late thirties who still appeared, despite the obvious, too strapping and strong to be wheelchair-bound. "In her house?"

Sabastian nodded. "That's where one's rooms are generally located."

"Ain't no biggie," Tam said. "She knows what she's doing."

"Nobody said she didn't," Sebastian reminded her. "It's just not what you would expect from a woman like Nikki, who generally guards her privacy zealously and has never come across as the *mi casa, su casa* type."

"Anyway," Tam said as she folded her arms, feeling oddly traitorous for talking behind her best friend's back, "the big man is coming today."

"What big man?" Nikki asked as she returned from the back with a stack of papers in her arms. She wore half moon reading glasses that made her look less youthful than she normally did when she wore her jeans, jersey and her hair pulled in a ponytail. She placed the papers on the counter top.

"The bishop's coming today," Sebastian said.

"The bishop?" Henry asked.

"THE bishop. Our pastor resigned; remember?"

"Yeah, I heard about that," Nikki said with a smile. "He was embezzling church funds to pay hush money to his mistress, right?"

Sebastian hesitated, knowing Nikki's penchant for seeing the bad in the good. "Something like that, yes," he finally said.

Nikki shook her head. "Church folks. They are such hypocrites. That's why people don't know what to believe anymore."

"It ain't even like that, Nick, and you know it," Tam said defensively. "Yeah, Pastor Crane wasn't right, but that don't mean all us church folks are like that."

"I didn't put you in that category."

"Well, I go to church. That makes me *church folks* too."

"Me three," Sebastian said, smiling.

"This bishop is coming to take Pastor Crane's place?" Henry asked.

Tam nodded. "Temporarily, yeah. At least until we can find a new pastor. And from what I hear, they didn't send just any old bishop, either. He's the head man, the HNIC of the entire New Life Progressive national organization."

"Ooh, how exciting!" Nikki response was clearly snide.

Tam looked at her. "It's not funny, Nikki."

"Am I laughing?"

"Okay. Keep on picking. Just keep on. But one of these old days, Nikki Lucas, you're gonna fall on your knees to God."

Although Nikki doubted that very seriously, she left Tam and all of her church talk alone just the same.

A jet black Mercedes S550 drove into the parking lot of the New Life Progressive Baptist Church of Monroe, Florida, and stopped in the choice space reserved for the pastor. Dino Cochran, his large eyes weary from his two-day journey, turned off his engine and looked at the modern complex of granite and brick. From the massive sanctuary, joined on by the huge dining hall, to the youth center and basketball courts near the back, it was a sprawling thing of beauty. But Dino wasn't there to appreciate its splendor. The outer shape of the church wasn't the problem. Inwardly, those beautiful buildings represented a church in decay. So much so that in all of his years in the ministry, he'd never heard of such outrageous abuses and moral turpitude than when he received the report about this place. From adultery to embezzlement to extortion, the pastor of this church had gone over the cliff, undoubtedly, taking many of the parishioners right along with him.

Dino had been assigned to clean up the mess. His charge was to right these horrific wrongs, as if he had nothing but time on his hands. In fact, he had so little time that he often sent one of his deputies to handle these kinds of crises; but with the systemic problems plaguing this house of worship, Dino felt that a deputy wouldn't do.

Inside the church, Reverend Cecil Wallace saw the fancy black Mercedes drive into the parking lot and stop in the space reserved for the pastor, but he still didn't put two and two together. Some show-off parking in the first available spot was what he first thought. He turned from the window in his second floor office and headed back to his desk to continue working on Sunday's sermon. As assistant pastor of New Life, he alone had been steering the ship in the weeks since Pastor Crane's resignation. Reverend Wallace was hoping, in fact campaigning, to be named Crane's successor, but it seemed unlikely now. Not only had the national board refused to make him acting pastor, but they insisted that he continue his role as assistant pastor. Fifty-five years old and still somebody's assistant.

He sat down from his five-ten, stout frame and picked up the papers in front of him. His sermons were about as dull as he was; and he knew it. But inspiration just wasn't something he could summon at will. As the back-up man for nearly a decade, Reverend Wallace wasn't accustomed to preaching a weekly sermon. And the congregation was still so divided over Pastor Crane's forced resignation that nothing he preached seemed to interest them anyway. He was just the man for the moment, with no real backing from the national board since many of them, his sources informed him, weren't all that certain that he wasn't as corrupt as Milo Crane.

The door to his office slid open and Roosevelt Atwater, the always colorfully-dressed chairman of the deacon board, peeped in. "He's here, Cecil."

Confused, Reverend Wallace stared at his deacon. "Who's here?"

"Bishop Cochran."

Wallace looked down at his calendar in a sudden sense of panic. The bishop was a full week early. How could he possibly be here now? "He's not due here yet," he said anxiously, searching for the correct date.

"He's due on the twenty-fifth," Roosevelt reminded him. "Today's the twenty-fifth."

When Wallace noted the date, he jumped from his seat and rushed back to the window. The person in the black Mercedes was still sitting inside of the car, which gave the reverend some relief; but he didn't delay. He hurried to his desk and grabbed his suit coat off of the back of the chair.

"What's wrong with you?" Roosevelt asked.

Wallace nervously hurried for the exit. "I forgot. I thought the man was coming next week. I plumb forgot!"

"Lord knows, Cecil. How can you forget something like this?"

Wallace could only shake his head. He had no idea, no earthly idea how he could have been so angry about the decision to bring in the head man that he couldn't keep track of the day of his arrival.

Dino continued to sit in his Mercedes and stare. Not at the two nervous leaders hurrying his way, but at the church itself. It was the largest in the predominately African American town, one that had on its rolls virtually all of Monroe's most influential citizens. It saddened him to know that a church of this magnitude was not a shining light. Dino leaned his head back and wondered about this magnificent temple and the failed leadership that now defined it. He couldn't believe what he was hearing when news came about the problems

that were going on. The details were still highly
upsetting. Not just because of the obvious implica-
tions, but because the drama and controversy went
against everything that Dino believed in.

In all of Dino's life, he'd never done anything
half-cocked. When he was a gangster, he was the
best. When he was a businessman, he was the
best. When he became a minister of the gospel,
he preached and lived that gospel to the best of
his ability. He did all he knew how to do to be
pleasing in the eyes of God Almighty. That was
why the idea that New Life's former pastor could
have done what he'd finally confessed to doing,
made Dino so angry. It was an anger that caused
him to dress down Milo Crane with such a fiery
tongue that he later had to apologize. An anger
he knew he had to get under control before he
stepped out of his car.

Dino's hesitation was enough to race the hearts
of Reverend Wallace and Deacon Atwater as they
waited for the car door to open. They'd heard all
sorts of wild rumors about Walter Dean Cochran.
They'd heard how he was an iron-fisted man who
didn't tolerate anybody's moral lapses. They'd
heard how he believed that those in positions of
leadership in the church had to be above reproach
in every facet of their lives. No exceptions. A stan-

dard that both leaders feared was impossible to uphold. And that was why they stood there, each well aware of his own shortcomings, with a nervousness neither could shake.

And when the car door opened and a pair of expensive wingtip shoes hit the graveled drive, the anxiety intensified. Cochran was a tall, remarkably good-looking man with a strong, straight back, a skull-low, soft-trimmed afro, and a hard, icy look in those light brown, drooping eyes that was so intense that it chilled both leaders.

"Good afternoon, Bishop!" Wallace said nervously as his prepared speech completely failed him. "Welcome to Florida."

Dino buttoned his dark gray Armani suit coat and shook Wallace's extended hand. It was sweaty. "How are you?"

"Blessed and highly favored," Wallace replied with a nervous smile. "I'm honored beyond words to have someone of your stature grace our presence."

"You must be Reverend Wallace."

"Cecil Wallace; that's right, Bishop. We met at the national congress a few years back when it was held in Miami, but I haven't had the pleasure of seeing you since then. Usually, our pastor alone is our representative at all of the national events, so I was fortunate to get to meet you that particular year; especially since I'd heard so much about you and how your tenure as head of the national church has been nothing short of incredible."

"Is that right?" Dino said, amused by the long-windedness of the assistant pastor.

"Nothing short of incredible. That's what everybody's saying. Even Pastor Crane was always very pleased with your leadership style and how you turned the New Life organization into one of the most financially sound and spiritually uplifting family of churches in the entire country. He said listening to you at some of those conventions made him want to come back to our humble church and be the best pastor he could be."

"He said that?"

"Oh, yes, sir. He sure did."

"And when did he say it? Before or after he embezzled church funds? Before or after he paid hush money to his mistress? Before or after he took a mistress to begin with?"

Wallace laughed nervously, unsure if Dino was joking or serious. With Cochran, he couldn't immediately tell because although his voice exuded a kind of lightheartedness, his eyes didn't show that same ease. "I can't answer those questions, Bishop," he decided to say, hoping to quickly distance himself from any talk of Pastor Crane's problems.

"So you can't," Dino said, resigning to the fact that probably nobody in the church could. He looked past Cecil Wallace at the man in the loud, tangerine-colored suit with a knee-length coat and orange alligator shoes.

Roosevelt Atwater swallowed hard when those eyes of Dino's turned to him.

"Good afternoon," Dino said.

"Oh, I'm sorry, Bishop," Wallace said. "Let me introduce you to the chairman of our deacon board. This is Roosevelt Atwater."

"Bishop, it's a pleasure," Roosevelt said with an extended hand that Dino shook. "Wish we were meeting under better circumstances, however."

"Yes," Dino replied, cautiously studying Atwater. The slicked-back hair, the alligator shoes, the orange zoot suit that looked ridiculous on a man his age, gave Dino some pause. It had been nearly sixteen years since his street-running, bad boy days back in Detroit, but he still knew a player when he saw one.

"When we heard you were coming," Roosevelt continued, "we were very pleased. It's not every day that a church gets a man of your caliber to advise it."

"Be not deceived, Deacon," Dino quickly pointed out, "I'm not here to *advise* anyone."

Roosevelt wanted to say, *"No, you're not here to work with us or help us, you're here to criticize us, judge us, and make us straighten up or ship out as if only you can save us now."* Instead, with a smile as chilly as Dino's, Roosevelt replied, "Understood."

"How long have you been saved, Deacon; if you don't mind my asking?"

Roosevelt glanced at Wallace, wondering the reasoning for the bishop's question. But then he smiled at Dino, his gold front teeth gleaming. "Right around four months now, sir."

"Four months?"

"That's right."

Dino nodded. "And you've been a member of New Life for what? About that same time?"

Roosevelt hesitated, unsure where Cochran was going with his interrogation. "About that; yes, sir."

"And in four months time you've already managed to become the chairman of the deacon board?"

Reverend Wallace caught Roosevelt's nervous eye and stepped in to rescue him. With a proud smile, he said, "Deacon Atwater used to be the executive vice president of Providence Bank, Bishop."

Dino frowned. "What the devil does that have to do with anything?"

Wallace was thrown by Dino's response. "Well, he's . . . I mean . . . he's—"

"Well-connected?" Dino offered.

Wallace smiled, relieved that Cochran at least appeared to understand what he was trying to say. "Right," he said. "Well-connected."

"One of the town's chosen few?"

"There ya' go. That's what I'm talking about."

"One of the elite that we appoint rather than appointing an experienced man of God filled with God's Holy Spirit and capable of handling the position?"

Wallace's smile left. "Now hold on there, Bishop," he said. "What I'm saying is that Deacon Atwater here is a man of distinction; that's all I'm saying. He was the executive vice president—"

"Of a bank. Yes, you told me. But that has nothing to do with being chairman of the deacon board. This man has been saved for only four months and you people make him chairman of the board of deacons? No wonder this church is a mess."

Wallace's heart dropped. He didn't know what to say in response, so he didn't say anything. Instead, he looked to Roosevelt, wondering what manner of man they had on their hands.

It was Roosevelt who smiled this time. "Let's go inside, Bishop, so we can introduce you to the full staff and some of the auxiliary heads."

Dino looked down at Atwater's orange suit again, and then nodded. "Good idea."

The two leaders looked warily at each other as they escorted Dino into the sanctuary. Dean Cochran was no pushover. They didn't expect him to be, but they also never expected *this*. They never expected that his reputation of not tolerating problematic leadership would trickle down to where they now felt threatened; to where they now feared that their high positions at New Life could very well become a casualty of that great intolerance too.

TWO

Nikki drove her Volkswagen Beetle into the driveway of her small, three-bedroom home on Firestone Road and took a moment to compose herself before going inside. It had been another long day as the sparse afternoon turned into a dinner crowd that didn't thin out until just before closing time. She even stayed open an extra hour, until nine P.M., to clean up afterward. Now she was almost too tired to move.

Nikki looked at herself in the rearview mirror. Her hair was long and wavy, but she wore it in an unruly, loose-fitting ponytail most of the time. Her clothes still primarily consisted of the baggy jeans and jerseys from her youth, with a pair of bargain basement tennis shoes to round out the package. Although she looked like some stressed out, overworked hardcore to herself, the men of Monroe wouldn't agree. On an almost daily basis, they tried to hit on her, commenting often on her petite body, her gorgeous dark green eyes, her beautiful, albeit, untamed hair. But Nikki wasn't buying it. To her, they were just men in a small town that offered thin pickings; so anybody would do. They saw her as a single, available female who should be glad to get their attention. But they didn't know Nikki. Being alone never bothered her. She'd been on her own since she was thirteen. The idea that she would probably be that way for the rest of her life didn't exactly frighten her.

She finally garnered the strength to get out of her car and walk across the grass to her front porch. Her neighborhood was older and quiet, where all of the houses were small, frame-style structures with awning windows and arched entrance ways; and with small wrought iron fences separating the small backyard from the front. The day Nikki closed on that house was one of the proudest days of her life. She remembered putting Jamal on her hip and walking nearly twelve blocks (she couldn't afford a car then), from the title company to her home. For seven years, she'd been working every hour she could at Big Turn, saving all the money she could until she was finally able to afford the small house. If nobody else understood what an accomplishment it was, she did. Just sixteen years before, she was new in town, heartbroken, homeless, and pregnant; searching for an aunt that could barely stand her when they lived in Detroit.

But that aunt was all she had. When she wouldn't even let Nikki in her front door, forcing Nikki to eventually end up in a homeless shelter, it was the final insult. Nikki swore that she'd never crawl again, or depend on anybody else again; and she kept that promise. But it had been a struggle; one she wouldn't wish on her worst enemy. But what could she do? The turns in her life hadn't exactly been by her design.

"Jamal," she called out as soon as she unlocked her front door and stepped into her living room. Talk about a struggle. Her life on the streets had been easy compared to raising her son.

She dropped her purse and keys on the round table by the door, and headed down the narrow hallway toward the first bedroom. The house was neat. Nikki wouldn't have it any other way. It was also filled with practical, inexpensive furnishings she had picked up at the most reasonable stores around town. Jamal often called their house an old lady's crib for its lack of anything modern, but Nikki didn't sweat that either. It was home. Their home. She couldn't care less if it wasn't stylish.

"Didn't you hear me call you, boy?" She opened his always closed bedroom door. To her dismay, the room was empty. She sighed, praying to God that the boy hadn't defied her once again. Nikki searched the rest of the house to be sure, but it was true. She had told Jamal to come straight home from school today and stay there. But as usual, he had ignored her orders.

Nikki grabbed her keys and headed back out of the door. She was so angry and frustrated that she knew she had to calm herself before she reached her son, or she'd kill him. She could barely stand up due to fatigue, but had to go looking for his disobedient behind. She snapped the gears of her VW in reverse, pulled onto the road, and flew up Firestone Road in a rage. She had a darn good idea of his whereabouts which helped, but it was the gall of him that drove her mad. It had been this way since he was a child whenever he didn't get his way. He'd kick and scream and throw tantrums so violently that sometimes Nikki thought she'd lose her mind trying to control that boy. She knew he was disadvantaged. She knew she had to be father and mother to him at a time when she was too young and ill-equipped to be either. But sometimes she felt as if Jamal knew it and resented her for it.

Nikki found him where she thought he'd be: on the basketball court in Pottsburg, a dilapidated, poverty-stricken housing project not all that far from their home.

His shirt was off and his jeans were down his butt as he and the Pottsburg gang hung out under the lights. Their rap music was blaring at this time of night as if life was just a party to them.

Nikki had no problem crashing the party. She got out of her car, walked up to the court, and ordered Jamal home. All of the other teenagers started laughing, as if it were the funniest thing in the world for a mother to order her sixteen-year-old around. Nikki wasn't the least concerned about what they thought. She wasn't about to sit back and let a child of hers ruin his life because of her indifference. She didn't care how embarrassed she made him or how funny his friends thought it was. They were all high school dropouts anyway. Kids whose parents acted as if they'd already given up on them. So who were they to judge her?

Jamal, however, felt that they were some pretty impressive judges. They were his friends; the coolest boys he knew. He didn't like it one bit that his mother was always treating him like some ten-year-old around them. Jamal angrily snatched his shirt off of the court and headed for the VW. Not because he wanted to, but because he knew his mother. If he didn't do exactly as she'd ordered, she'd grab a stick or whatever she could get her hands on and run him all the way home. And for Jamal, on the embarrassment scale, that would be a ten.

Nikki had barely backed up and driven out of Pottsburg before Jamal was complaining. "Why you had to come here?" he angrily asked. "I was coming home."

Nikki looked at her son and shook her head. He was tall, already taller than she, with a reed thin body and a face that looked as innocent as a dove's. He was no thug. Anybody who looked into those big, scared brown eyes of his could see that he wasn't. But she couldn't tell him that. He thought hanging out with gangsters made him a gangster when all it made him was a sorry excuse for a wannabe. A lamb among wolves. A target.

"I told you to stay home, Jamal. You don't break my rules and expect me to sit back and let you."

"But you could have told me all this when I got home. You didn't have to come running out here like you the police, ordering me around like I'm some child. They already be picking on me as it is. Now here you come."

Nikki exhaled. She never experienced a whole lot of peer pressure herself, because at thirteen, she was living on the streets, too busy trying to survive to have any peers; but she'd read a lot about it. And according to the experts, it was a big deal, bigger than most parents could ever even imagine.

"What are they picking on you about?" She tried her best not to sound too concerned. She and Jamal were alike when it came to any show of affection. It made him uncomfortable and defensive, ready to fight back rather than show any vulnerability.

"What you think?" he said.

"Watch it, boy."

"They be calling me a bookworm and junk."

"Oh, I see. Those thugs—"

"Don't call them that!"

"Those thugs," Nikki went on, ignoring Jamal, "think there's something wrong with you because you haven't dropped out of school? You're a jive turkey because I refuse to let you become a bum on the corner like them? Yeah, okay; let them pick all they want."

"And they be talking about my clothes too. They live in the ghetto and dress better than me. They wear Jordans and Reeboks while I be wearing these cheap behind, Wal-Mart tennis shoes nobody never heard of."

"Jamal, I can barely pay our bills. How do you think I can afford to buy you some two hundred dollar tennis shoes? I've got to rent out one of our bedrooms as it is, just to help make ends meet, and you're complaining because I'm not taking my hard earned money to make sure that Reebok and Michael Jordan and all of those other millionaires stay rich? Child please."

Jamal hesitated, his once angry face now showing signs of concern. He looked at his mother. To him, she was the most beautiful woman he'd ever seen. Even his friends said so; and he was sorry that he'd been nothing but trouble for her. But he'd never tell her that. "You're renting out a room?" he asked.

Nikki nodded. She wasn't at all crazy about the idea. "Have to."

"You don't have to."

Nikki smiled. "Yes, I do."

"I can get a job."

Nikki shook her head. "No way. Your job is to stay in school, stay out of trouble, and make good grades. When you graduate top of your class from college, then talk to me about a job."

Jamal leaned back against the headrest. *If I go to college.*

The leadership of New Life Progressive was packed into the boardroom, with Reverend Wallace and Deacon Atwater at the head of the table. The questions were coming fast and furious, all concerning their new interim pastor, and if all of the rumors about his ruthlessness were true. Sister Aretha Dardell, the head of the usher board, and Sister Wilma McKernan, the Sunday School superintendent, were especially distressed. They didn't see why the entire church should be trembling in their boots over Cochran or anybody else since it was Pastor Crane, not they, who'd messed up. But Reverend Wallace, certain they had no idea of the seriousness of the church's predicament, quickly brushed aside such talk.

"Make no mistake about it, Dardell," he said to the usher board president, "Bishop Cochran is no joke. That man is here to clean house whether you believe it's dirty or not. That's what y'all have got to understand. That man ain't playing. Ask Roosevelt. He's something else!"

"He all but told me I don't have any business being chairman of the deacon board." A gasp filled the room at Roosevelt's reveal. "Said it right to my face. Cecil's right, folks. We got to be together on this here or I'm afraid we might not have a church by the time Cochran's done."

Dardell moved around in her chair. She was a big woman in her early fifties with a bull dog face and an equally tough disposition. "I tell you I don't like it," she said firmly. "Don't like it one bit. They're treating us like we're criminals, sending the head man down here like we don't know what we're doing. We don't need somebody telling us how to run our church. Besides, since they're so disgusted with us, I say we pull out from the national organization and stand on our own."

"Here here," Sister McKernan said, with others joining in agreement.

Wallace refused to even hear of it. "Y'all don't know what y'all talking about," he said with some frustration. "Pull out from the national organization? Pull out with what? They own the church, they own the name, they own all the property associated with the name; so what, exactly, are we pulling out with?"

"They own the church?" Sister Dardell asked, a look of surprise on her long face.

"Of course they own it, Dardell! This theirs. You think they care if we decide to leave? The way Bishop's talking, they'll probably be glad to see us go."

"I don't care what you say, Cecil," Dardell shot back. "I'm not worried about no Dean Cochran or nobody else. Who is he, anyway? Folks always talking about how he's this great man, how he doesn't tolerate anybody's moral lapses, how he'll get rid of you on the spot if he so much as suspects you're not living above reproach. Well, what about him? I wonder if he's as pious in his own life as he expects us to be in ours."

"What are you talking about, Dardell?" Wallace raised his hands in the air and then dropped them to his side. He felt that they didn't understand the magnitude at all. "What difference does it make how he's living his life?"

"It makes a lot of difference," Dardell said. "He's here because of something that's happened in the past. Well, what about *his* past?"

"Make it your business to find out," Sister McKernan suggested. "That's what I'd do."

Dardell agreed. "And that's exactly what I'm gonna do! Who does he think he is? All have sinned and come short of God's glory, and that don't just include us. So yes, I will make it my personal business to see just how short our bishop has come himself, Sister McKernan, because God put me in my position."

"I heard that," Roosevelt said.

"No man had nothing to do with me being where I am," Dardell continued. "And it'll be a cold day in you-know-where before I let some—"

The door to the boardroom opened, and Dino walked in. Dardell looked at the big man and her words remained on her tongue. Like most everybody else in the room, this was her first sight of Walter Dean Cochran, and she was thrown. She knew he was powerful by virtue of his position as head of an organization as large and prosperous as New Life, but it was the power of the man that surprised her. He was tall, broad-shouldered, and his chest was so muscular that it strained the fabric of his tailored suit. Even his face was unusual in its beauty. This man was the embodiment of perfection: handsome, strong, confident beyond anybody's business. It was no wonder that he expected all of them to be perfect too.

"Good morning," Dino said with a smile that nobody could confuse with friendliness as he walked up to the long table. "I understand you folks wanted to see me."

Wallace quickly rose to his feet. "Yes, sir, we did. We were just having a little get-together before we got together with you." He laughed nervously. Dino simply stared at him. Wallace cleared his throat. "What we wanted, Bishop," he continued, "was to ask you a few questions."

Dino glanced around the room. The faces were grim and harsh; hardly the sort of people who would want change. But that was exactly what they were going to get. "Ask away," he said as he slid his hands into the pants pockets of his expensive, brown silk suit. He stood soldier-still; a pose so intimidating that Wallace felt unable to continue. He looked to the always fearless Sister Dardell for help. Dino looked at her too, which made it doubly impossible for her to shirk.

"We want to know what you want from us," she finally said.

Dino looked at her as if surprised by her bluntness. "And you are?"

"I'm Aretha Dardell, the president of the usher board. And let me just say that I think it's a shame the way the national board is treating us." The others in the room sat up straight. They loved it when Dardell took charge. "We didn't do a thing wrong," she continued. "That was Pastor Crane running around with that woman and acting a fool. We didn't know a thing about that. Then you come down here, the head man, like we're the criminals. Well, I tell you, we don't like it. Pastor Crane resigned. The problem is already gone. So why you got to be here?"

Some in the room almost gasped at Dardell's directness, but Dardell continued as if she didn't care what Dino or anybody else thought. Dino liked that. "I've been a member of New Life for thirty-five-some-odd years, and I have never seen the level of disrespect like I'm seeing now. It's as if y'all don't care nothing about what we think or feel. Just so long as we take up our collections and give y'all a cut."

There was a definite gasp this time. Even Reverend Wallace couldn't believe she'd said that. "Sister Dardell!" he said, appalled. But Dardell didn't back down one step.

"Tell the truth and shame the devil!" she said. "If this church is as bad as they claim, then that must mean it's been bad for years. And if it's been bad for years, where they been all this time? Why all of a sudden they come running down here now?" Her mouth was tight and her emotions just inches away from exploding.

Everybody looked at Dino as he turned to Wallace. "I need to see all of the church's financial records dating back ten years, a job description of every paid employee, and a list of all auxiliary heads and their Christian credentials."

Wallace felt as if he had just been blindsided. "Their credentials?" he asked.

"Yes, Reverend. The statement of their Christian experience. Every auxiliary head is bound by the rules of conduct and therefore, must complete a background check. Didn't you know that?"

Wallace shook his head. "No, sir."

Dino was surprised by Wallace's lack of knowledge. "It's not a secret, Reverend Wallace. It is in every New Life leadership packet."

"I was . . . I mean, Pastor Crane was handling that; at least I thought he was, but I'll be sure that one's done on every leader right away."

Dino shook his head. "I'll take care of it."

"It won't be any trouble—"

"I'll take care of it," Dino repeated.

Wallace exhaled. "Yes, sir."

Dino then turned to Sister Dardell. "And as for your comments, I agree that they are valid concerns. We don't mean to be disrespectful, but allow me to be as blunt as you were. It is outrageous what's been going on in this church. Your pastor has resigned, money's missing, and he's pointing fingers at many of the leaders here today. He insists that he paid off his mistress with the full knowledge and blessing of the leadership. He's claiming that there are leaders in this church who aren't even saved, who're committing more sins than even Satan can keep up with, and we've got to get to the bottom of this.

"Now you can point the finger at the board of bishops, and that's fine if it'll make you feel better. But this is a mess. I want everybody here to understand that. Bishop Thorndike, who was in charge of this diocese, has been replaced for his failure to notify the national board that there was a problem. I can't say that there was more that the national board could have done because every safeguard in place in this church has broken down. The bishop didn't notify us of the problem, the deacons didn't notify the bishop of the problem, and the pastor *was* the problem."

"But I don't understand that," Roosevelt Atwater said. "If Bishop Thorndike wasn't notified, why did you replace him?"

"Because this is his diocese. It's not just what he didn't know, but what he should have known, Deacon Atwater. And based on the reports that I received, it was a well known fact here in Monroe that Pastor Milo Crane had numerous moral lapses that were always hushed and disregarded as if they were as simple as the Spirit being willing but the flesh being weak."

"That's exactly what they were, Bishop," Roosevelt said.

"No," Dino corrected him. "He was pastor of this church. That excuse is not good enough. Not for the head of the church." Dino exhaled. "Now I know this doesn't seem fair, but we're in the business of saving lost souls. We can't be fair. We've got to be right. And if a leader isn't right, then he can't hold any positions of leadership in this church. Period. Now, are there any other questions?"

The room was pin-drop quiet as even Dardell couldn't quarrel with Dino's bottom line. Dino looked at Wallace. "I'll take that tour now."

Wallace, evermore certain that his suspicions were right and that Dean Cochran didn't come all this way just for the fun of it, hurried to escort him out.

THREE

The VW was loaded with trays of food to be taken to the soup kitchen at New Life, and Nikki and Tam were driving to the church to make the delivery. Tam found it amusing that Nikki always had something negative to say about church folks and what hypocrites they were, but she never failed, week in and week out, to bring food to those same hypocritical folks to help feed the hungry.

"I don't see the problem at all," Nikki said as she drove slowly through the streets of Monroe, her eyes tired and drained from another late night of work and worry. "I do believe in God, in case you've forgotten; and God does admonish us to feed the hungry. Since New Life has this soup kitchen thing going, I figure why not contribute? But I still say the church is loaded with hypocrites, and I'm not changing my mind."

Tam rolled her eyes. "You're gonna be one tough nut to crack when God decides to do it, and you best believe, baby, that He will."

Nikki smiled. "Whatever."

Tam looked at her through concerned eyes. "Okay, what is it?"

"What?"

"What's bothering you, Nikki?"

Nikki sighed. "Nothing's bothering me."

"Right."

Nikki glanced at Tam, as if trying to convince her. "Nothing's bothering me."

"Is Jamal all right?"

Worry filled Nikki's eyes. "If he ever was, yes. I'm just—"

"Tired?"

Nikki exhaled. "Yeah."

"Why don't you take some time off, Nikki? You're an attractive thirty-four-year-old woman who acts like she's ninety-four. Work, work, work, that's all you know. Just take a break. You are the boss, after all."

"Yeah, I'm the boss all right. A boss who's way over her head with responsibilities."

Tam looked at her. "Still behind?"

"The understatement of the year. I'm even trying to rent out a room in my house, Tam; that's how critical it's getting. But I don't know. I've been at this stuff for a while. Looks like it would have gotten easier by now."

Tam folded her arms and looked at the road ahead. "God is able, Nikki. You've got to learn to put your trust in Him."

Nikki didn't say anything. She rarely did when the talk shifted to spiritual matters. Instead, she drove a little faster and turned into the parking lot of the New Life church. When she saw the new-looking, shiny Mercedes in the pastor's space, she couldn't help but stare.

"That's the bishop's car," Tam said proudly. "Isn't it something?"

"The brother is getting paid."

"I know that's right. I heard his base salary is something like five hundred thousand a year."

Nikki looked at Tam in amazement. "Half a million dollars? Get out! Are you serious?"

"That's what I heard."

Nikki shook her head as she parked her VW near the church's dining hall. "No wonder people are starving."

"Oh, Nikki, please!" Tam said, knowing her friend too well. "The man is in charge of a national organization with churches in I don't know how many states. Paying him that kind of salary is not that big a deal, considering the budget he's over-seeing. Besides, I also heard, for your information, that he already had his own money before he even took the job."

"It still should be a crime," Nikki said as she and Tam got out of the car. "If you want to serve the Lord, you should do it for free."

Tam looked at Nikki as if she were crazy. "Do you do what you do for free? Do I? Of course we don't, Nikki. And you know why we don't?"

"Because working at the Big Turn isn't exactly serving the Lord."

"Speak for yourself," Tam corrected. "The reason employers don't generally want free labor is because they'll get what they pay for."

"True that," Nikki said with a laugh as she began unloading the trays.

Inside the dining hall, Reverend Wallace was introducing Dino to Missionary Stephens, who ran the soup kitchen, when Nikki and Tam walked in. Dino stood with his back against the wall, his arms folded, and his big eyes completely focused on the young, talkative missionary. He didn't see Nikki across the massive hall, but Tam saw him as soon as they placed their trays on the elongated table.

"Umph, umph, umph." Tam shook her head, smiling.

"What?" Nikki asked, too busy arranging the food and unwrapping foil to look up.

"Our new pastor. I'm telling you that man is something good to look at."

"Yeah, I'll bet." Nikki looked up. "Where is he?"

"Over there." Tam nodded her head in the direction of her gaze. "He's with Reverend Wallace and that mouth-of-the-south, Missionary Stephens. That woman can talk a toad to death."

Nikki looked across the big hall, at the numerous people that were milling about. Then her eyes found the corner where Dino stood. At first she thought she was eyeing a distinguished looking stranger; and she had to agree with Tam that he was very good looking. Especially the way his rich silk suit fit his muscular body with tailored perfection.

But then she saw those eyes that she could never forget, and literally had to grab hold of the table. It was a ghost. It had to be! That man standing not forty feet away from her was the bishop of a church? The head of an entire religious organization? How in the world could that man be? That was *Dino*! Her mind was telling her that it couldn't be, it just couldn't be, but her heart knew better.

"Didn't I tell you he was good looking." Tam was still gawking at Dino. "Didn't I tell you he was the finest looking bishop you were ever gonna see in your lifetime?"

Dino laughed at something Missionary Stephens had just relayed to him and Nikki's heart dropped. It was him. She knew it now beyond a shadow of a doubt. His dreads were gone, and Lord knows he wasn't that same tough guy gangster in his early thirties anymore, but that bright white, hypnotic, half-cocked smile hadn't changed one bit. It was Dino Cochran. It was her baby's daddy.

"And guess what girl?" Tam said.

Nikki didn't want to guess or say anything. She just wanted to leave. "What?" Her voice trembled.

"He's single." Nikki looked at her and Tam reiterated. "That's right, Nick. The man is without a wife. Can you believe it? I nearly had a heart attack when they told me that. I'll bet every female in New Life is gonna be knocking over pews to get their claws on him. Won't they, girl?"

"What? I mean, yeah, whatever. Let's just hurry up." Nikki forced herself to look away from Dino.

Tam, however, kept her eyes on Nikki. "What's wrong now?"

"Nothing, Tam. We need to get back to the diner."

Tam rolled her eyes. "You and that diner," she said as she continued unwrapping foil. "I tell you,

Nikki Lucas! I've known you for fifteen years now, consider you my best friend in this whole wide world; but I declare I don't know you at all."

"Good," Nikki said. She tried to smile, but her trembling bottom lip made it difficult to do so effectively.

Missionary Stephens excused herself from Dino's group to take a phone call, and Dino was left to listen to Cecil Wallace sing the praises of New Life's numerous projects to aid the poor. He was only half listening to Wallace. Not because he wasn't pleased with the projects, but because he had to see the proof before he could believe the praise. New Life had been cooking their books far too long. They'd been reporting too many outrageous rosy scenarios, even as the national board's own internal audit was showing just the opposite. Wallace could praise this church until he was breathless, but Dino had to see it to believe it.

Dino listened as Wallace kept talking, but he also began looking around at the newly renovated church. He admired the beauty of the architecture; the elegance of it. But then, when he looked down from the hanging glass chandeliers that swung low above the tables, chandeliers that he thought were a bit much for a church dining hall, he saw her. *It can't be.* But then she looked up at the woman standing next to her and he saw those stunning green eyes of hers. His heart sank.

"Is something wrong?" Wallace asked, following Dino's gaze across the hall to see if he could see it too. Dino began breathing heavily, as if he was going to hyperventilate, but it was his own steel will that kept him from falling apart.

"Bishop, are you all right?"

"Who is that?" Dino managed to say in a voice just above a whisper.

"Who's who?"

"The woman in that white jersey over at the tables. The small one."

Wallace recognized Dino's target and smiled. "Ah, yes. That's Nikki Lucas."

When Dino heard her name, he could barely contain his shock. He never thought he'd lay eyes on her again.

"Pretty little thing, isn't she?" Wallace added with a small laugh.

"Is she a member here?" Dino composed himself enough to ask.

"Not hardly. She owns the Big Turn diner downtown. One of our more colorful residents, I must say." Without warning, Wallace called Nikki over.

Nikki's heart rammed against her chest when Reverend Wallace called her name. She was just trying to get away, just trying to ease away before the ghost of her past could track her down, and now the reverend was calling for her to come there. To come to her ghost. To come to *Dino*. She couldn't move.

"Reverend Wallace calling you, Nikki," Tam said to her, totally oblivious to the trauma her friend was experiencing. Nikki nodded, as if she was realizing it for the first time, and then slowly began to walk across the room.

Dino unbuttoned his suit coat and placed his hands in his pants pockets as he watched her approach. His heart ached as he watched her. She wasn't as thin as she used to be, but she was still too small. Her face looked tired, and her hair looked bedraggled in that thrown together ponytail she was wearing. And her clothes, her beloved jeans and jersey, made her look as if she were still the teenager he remembered sixteen years ago. He should have forgotten Nikki. She was, after all, just one of many indiscretions from his sordid past. But he never forgot her. Not her warm smile and feistiness, and not her amazing dark green eyes that haunted him still. Not that wonderful, terrible night they spent together when she became the prey to the then selfish, ruthless man that he was.

"Hello, Reverend," Nikki said, trying with all she had to hide the trembling and nervousness that was attempting to overtake her.

"How are you, young lady?" Wallace replied. "I haven't seen you in a month of Sundays."

"Just dropping off some food."

Wallace smiled. "Always there to help out. Good for you."

Nikki kept her eyes transfixed on Reverend Wallace, terrified that if she so much as glanced Dino's way, she'd literally dissolve.

"I want you to meet Bishop Cochran, our interim pastor." Wallace nodded toward Dino, as if insisting that Nikki take her eyes off of him and at least acknowledge the presence of the esteemed bishop.

Nikki knew Dino was watching her like a hawk. He always did. She lifted her head and slowly looked his way. She was determined to keep it together in front of him. "Bishop," she said, amazed that the word didn't come out garbled.

Dino's heart dropped even further when their eyes met.

"This is Nikki," Wallace said to Dino. "Businesswoman extraordinaire."

Dino removed one of his hands from his pocket and extended it. "Hello, Nikki."

It was that same concerned, deep voice she once loved so desperately. She did not want to touch his hand; she just knew it would sear her. When Nikki reached out and placed her small hand into his large one, she thought she was going to die. A simple touch from him still made her tremble. She couldn't believe it. She was supposed to hate him. After all, he'd used her like garbage and tossed her out. But her heart wouldn't let her hate. Her heart felt as if the years had stood still and remained in that night when Dino made love to her. Before he broke her heart.

Dino stared into Nikki's large eyes and his suspicions were realized. The pain he used to always see in those eyes was still there, but the years had intensified it, as if life after Detroit had not been kind either. It was there, in Detroit, when he last saw her. He was going into his nightclub with his hand on Sophia's lower back as if he wanted the world to know that she was his. And Nikki was left standing on the sidewalk, lost and abandoned, all because of him and his selfishness. Because of him and his inability to control feelings he had no business having.

Now, he was the master of control. Now, nothing riled him, no impulse got the best of him. But those devastating memories were still there, as alive as the hand he now held in his grasp. A hand he was now smothering and didn't want to release, but knew it was not his to have anymore. He let her go.

Wallace had thought he'd found something he could exploit in the bishop when he called Nikki over. The reverend believed Cochran liked Nikki on sight. That was why he singled her out and asked about her the way he did. But if Wallace was expecting Dino to show his hand, he now realized how foolish that expectation had been. The man simply spoke to her, shook her hand, and didn't say another word.

Cochran wanted Nikki. Wallace was certain that he did. Why else would he stand there staring at her, looking her up and down as if she were a piece of choice meat? But Cochran was a smooth operator, one of the coolest cats Wallace had ever seen, and he knew how to bide his time. But Wallace knew how to bide his too. And when that rock hard shell of Bishop's did crack, as it inevitably would, he'd be right there to bust it wide open and prove to Mister Intolerant that perfection didn't exist; that people couldn't live above reproach the way he wanted them to; that even he, the big man himself, was no better than the rest of them.

What Wallace didn't know, however, was that Dino already knew he was the least among them. He should have died with Sophia in that car crash sixteen years ago. It should have been him, instead of Max, who died at that strip mall ambush. But God spared his life. Not for him to keep going along to get along, but to do better and to expect better. And if Wallace or anybody else had a problem with that, Dino's response was automatic: *"Take it up with God."* It was what he always told his detractors.

Now he stood, unable to take his eyes off of Nikki, still wondering if she found any happiness after Detroit, or more of the same pain that had always cloaked her like a strait jacket. That was why he couldn't say another word. What could he say to the woman whose innocence he'd robbed, whose life he'd undoubtedly ruined?

Having no clue about their history, Wallace tried to reinvigorate the non-existent conversation by asking Nikki about different food dishes the diner was famous for. But Nikki couldn't bear it. She used that same diner as a reliable crutch, telling them she'd better get back to it, and left without daring to look into Dino's eyes again. She didn't stop back at the table either; not even to tell Tam that she'd be back later to pick her up. She didn't wait to help serve the food the way she had always done. Instead, Nikki walked out of the dining hall slowly, unremarkably, but with an urgency that no one noticed. Except Dino.

He didn't realize just how disturbed he really was until he saw Nikki walk out of the hall. Dino thought he was holding up well considering that he'd just received one of the biggest shocks of his life. But now he knew better. The picture was too grim. Here he was, in town to straighten out a church riddled with all kinds of moral turpitude, when the victim of his own moral lapse had just been standing right in front of him. Nikki in the flesh . . . again. The young woman he ruined was right here to remind him grandly of just what kind of man he really was.

Dino asked Reverend Wallace if he'd excuse him, and then abruptly left the dining hall.

Nikki jumped from her Volkswagen, ran into her house, and threw up in her bathroom's toilet. Then she slumped to the tiled floor, crying. All of the memories flooded back, from her hero worship of Dino, to her blind faith in him that led to her pregnancy. Just seeing him again was horrifying enough. But feeling those feelings that she was certain no longer existed, was unbearable.

Even worse than that was the fact that she had committed what she now believed to be an unpardonable sin. She had told her son that his father was dead. Back then, she was hurt and bitter and so certain she'd never see Dino again, or that he'd ever want to see her again, that in her heart, he *was* dead. But now he was here, in Monroe of all places, alive and well. Her son's father had risen from his grave! She sat on the floor of her bathroom, terrified by what it all could mean when Jamal found out the truth; and if that truth would make him resent her even more than he already did.

Dino didn't know he had a son. Jamal didn't know he had a father. And just like sixteen years ago, when Nikki was throwing up in a toilet in another place and time, she was throwing up again. Saddled with trouble all over again.

FOUR

Tam, like everybody else in the congregation, was amazed that a man who presented himself as the epitome of cool could preach a sermon that fiery. Even Sebastian, who'd been a critic of performances all his life, couldn't criticize this. He was too impressed, too blown away, not only by the sheer beauty and power of the man, but by the grace with which he moved. Broadway actors half his size would have given an arm and a leg to move like that.

It was Sunday morning. New Life Progressive Baptist Church was packed to the rafters, and Dino Cochran was in the pulpit preaching. He wasn't preaching the kind of dignified, scholarly, ultimately boring sermon Sebastian would have expected from a man of his stature, but a sweat-pouring, hand-clapping, amen-shouting fire of a sermon that had even the most conservative members enthralled. Dino had shed his suit coat and tossed it over the chair as if it didn't cost the five grand Sebastian was willing to bet it had. And with the microphone in his hand, he was moving like a panther, from one side of that large pulpit to the other, praising God and not caring a twit if somebody didn't like it.

"You don't have to praise Him with me!" Dino shouted from the top of his lungs, to thunderous shouts of "Amen" from the congregation. "You can sit there and act like you don't know what praising God means. You can sit there and act like you're too pretty to praise Him, too sophisticated to praise Him, too educated to praise His holy name. But I'm gonna praise Him anyhow! I'm gonna worship Him anyhow! I'm gonna let the world know that Jesus Christ is the answer and no substitute will do! You can keep your sophisticated gods. You can keep your educated gods. You can sit in church and act like you're ashamed of your little god. But my God Almighty is the awesome God! My God Almighty is the everlasting God! My God Almighty will see you through when there's no way out. He won't leave you, He won't forsake you, He will never let you down! That's the kind of God I serve! He brought me out, saints. He brought me out. I should have been dead. I should have been sleeping in my grave. But the Lord . . . good God Almighty! He had mercy and He brought me out!"

By now, worshippers, that had rarely shouted responses behind any sermon preached to them by their former pastor, were on their feet in the kind of praise and worship that would rival a football stadium's delirium after the winning touchdown. Even the members of the deacon board, who were usually dour and impassive, were on their feet in praise. They didn't think Cochran had it in him. Not Mister Intolerant. Not Mister Cool. But he did.

Deacon Atwater was awed as he watched the man (with the power to replace him), walk back behind the podium in the pulpit and finally tone down his fiery sermon.

"That's why we praise Him," Dino said when the delirium had ebbed and people were finally taking their seats. His voice was raspy now, and sweat poured from his body like rain. He picked up a handkerchief from the podium and began wiping his face. "That's why we worship Him. You don't have to hold that pain deep inside and think that no one cares. God cares. And He will bring you out. Don't you ever let anybody tell you, or even suggest to you that our God isn't real. He's real to the bone. You ever tasted a piece of meat—any kind of meat—that was good to the bone?"

A few chuckles rose from the congregation. "Well, that's how our God is. He's good to the bone. And don't you ever forget that." Dino stood as if he was still coming down from the high of his sermon. He began folding the handkerchief in a fold so neat that it made Sebastian, a neat freak, beam. "The doors of the church are open," Dino finally said, prompting the members to stand. "If you want to know the Lord in the pardon of your sins, if you want to have that joy that the world can't give to you and the world can't take away from you, why don't you come to the altar today? He will bring you out. No matter how low you've gone, the Lord will bring you back from the brink. If you know you need a Savior, if you know you need to give your life to Christ, why don't you come? The doors of the church are open. The choir will give us a ministry in music. Come."

The choir began singing, "I Surrender All," and to the amazement of every man on the deacon's board, many people who had been members for years were coming to the altar for the prayer of salvation. Stunned, Roosevelt looked at Wallace and Wallace looked across the room at Sister Dardell. This confirmed for Dino the problem with this church, and they knew it. The last recorded time that anyone walked down to that altar to give his life to Christ was nearly ten years ago, just before their old pastor passed away and Milo Crane, their now disgraced ex-pastor, became the newly elected head of New Life Progressive of Monroe, Florida.

Nikki leaned back at the head of the table and watched the people she cared about the most eat, laugh and talk during their usual Sunday afternoon good time. This was a custom now, this dinner at Nikki's house every Sunday. And they all showed up as if she were all they had too.

Fern and Mookie always sat together and always had their own little side conversation going, usually with Fern doing all of the talking and Mookie gawking at her. Fern's plate was virtually untouched. She had a figure to maintain. Mookie's plate looked the same as he couldn't seem to take his eyes off of Fern long enough to eat.

Henry sat in his wheelchair, his normally quiet, placid face lit up with gaiety as if he were thrilled beyond words to be a part of this loosely constructed family of theirs. Even Jamal seemed to love it, sitting at the other end of the table and enjoying the natural happiness of a group of good friends.

And of course, Tam and Sebastian were there. They were the two people closest to Nikki in this world. They'd declare on a stack of Bibles that they couldn't stand each other, but were rarely seen apart. Tam tried to be discrete about it, but as they sat beside one another at the table, Nikki could sometimes see her catch peeps at Seb. Sebastian was a very handsome man with age and experience to his credit. Admittedly, his theater background and exaggerated mannerisms made him appear more of a drama king than masculine, but everybody loved Sebastian for his honesty and intellect. Tam was his greatest admirer; Nikki was sure of it. Sebastian was dominating the conversation as he usually did, talking about his theater days and how he almost played Othello at some community theater "not all that far off-Broadway."

"Did I hear *almost played*?" Tam asked, putting a hand behind her ear.

"Yes, I said almost," Sebastian replied.

"That's what I thought I heard. *Almost played* is not the same as playing, okay? Heck, I can say I almost played Ofello too, and I don't even know who he is!"

Jamal and Henry laughed, but Sebastian failed to see the humor. "It's *Othello*," he enunciated. "And a female cannot play the role, all right? But what I was going to say, Henry and Jamal, if you care to hear it before I get rudely interrupted again, is that the actor who did get the role came out on that stage opening night and said—and I kid you not—*'Now is the winter of our discontent made glorious summer by this son of York!'* I tell you, I nearly had a conniption."

Henry and Jamal smiled, although Nikki could tell they had no idea what Sebastian was talking about. Tam had no clue either.

"So?" she said assuredly. "The man came on stage and said those stupid little lines they always get on stage and say. What's wrong with that?"

"Absolutely nothing," Sebastian replied calmly, "if he were playing Richard in *Richard the Third*. But since he wasn't quite playing that particular role, then I would say everything was wrong with it."

A horn blew loudly and repetitively just as Tam was about to zing Sebastian back. Jamal quickly jumped up from his seat.

"Where do you think you're going?" Nikki asked.

"Out," Jamal said, grabbing his jacket from the chair and hurrying through the small living room, toward the front door.

"Out where, Jamal?" Nikki tossed her napkin on the table and rose too. She hurried behind him, not about to let him get away that easily.

"Don't follow me out the door, Ma. Goodness!" Jamal turned before he opened the door.

"Where are you going?"

"Just up the way with some friends of mine, that's all."

"Those hoodlums from Pottsburg?"

"They're not hoodlums. They're just people, a'ight? Everybody ain't prim and proper like you."

"*Prim and proper*?" Nikki said in a high-pitched tone. She couldn't believe he'd sum up a life as hard as hers with such a dismissive phrase. "Boy, move out of my way!" She angrily stepped around her son and stormed out of the door.

"Ma, don't go out there!" Jamal yelled, amazed at the gall of her. Then he looked toward the dining room. "Seb, man, why don't y'all do something? I'm tired of her embarrassing me like this!"

Sebastian hunched his shoulders. "She's your mother, Jamal. She's not trying to embarrass you. She's just concerned."

Jamal rolled his large brown eyes and then hurried behind his mother.

Nikki walked up to the early model bubba Chevy with its thousand dollar shiny rims and booming stereo. The young men inside the car laughed when they saw Nikki coming, but they turned down the music.

Nikki stood there, her arms folded, her pretty face unable to hide her obvious disgust. "Who are you?" she asked the driver.

"Who are *you*?" he replied just as Jamal hurried up to the car.

"His name is Shake, Ma; now will you please excuse us?"

Nikki refused to budge. "Where are you going, Shake?"

Jamal interrupted. "Up the block, I told you."

Nikki looked at Jamal. "I'm not talking to you." Then she looked at Shake. "Where are you taking my son?"

"Here . . . there . . . you know," Shake said. His boys in the backseat covered their mouths and chuckled.

Nikki stared angrily at Shake. She'd known his type all her life. The leader of a pack of losers. The good time boys. She looked at her son. Why he couldn't be into books the way he was into running the streets, she'd never know. "I want you back in this house by ten."

Jamal looked astonished. "Ten?"

"Ten, Jamal. You have school tomorrow. And if you're late, see if you go anywhere else with Shake!"

The boys laughed hard at that one, but Nikki didn't stick around to hear it. She headed back toward her porch, disgusted. Sometimes she wanted to just throw up her hands and forget it the way so many other parents in the area had done; but she never could. Her parents gave up on her, leaving her to fend for herself, and she'd never give up on a child of hers that way. She knew that she was sometimes overbearing, overprotective and tried too hard; expending all kinds of energy she really didn't have to waste, but Jamal was her child. She loved him and she wasn't about to sit back and let him toss his life to the dogs. No matter how badly he wanted to.

Nikki went back into her home, had dinner with her friends, and slowly all thoughts of Jamal and his choice in playmates drifted from her consciousness. She even laughed at Sebastian's jokes and tried her best to relax. Eventually, Henry, Fern and Mookie left, but Tam and Sebastian stayed behind, sitting out on the porch with Nikki and relaxing.

"Had any luck finding a boarder?" Tam asked as she slouched down in her chair. It was a narrow porch with a line of chairs against the wooden frame, and with a magnificent view of a retention pond and thick tree forest across the streets.

"I had a few inquiries, mostly kids from the college, but nothing's panned out. I guess I might be asking too much."

"Don't you dare lower your price," Sebastian advised. "Keep it right where it is. That'll keep the riffraff away."

Tam looked at him as he sat beside her. "What riffraff?"

"Riffraff. People who want something for nothing. People like you, for instance."

Nikki's immediate smile turned into a laugh.

"Forget you," Tam said lightheartedly and then proceeded to try and do just that.

They sat and stared across the street until Sebastian started talking about church service today and how so many people gave their lives to Christ. "I'd never seen anything like it," he said. "Reverend Ike ain't got nothing on Bishop."

"Reverend Ike?" Tam was amazed at the choice of comparison. "Anyway," she continued, looking from Sebastian to Nikki, "he asked about you today."

Nikki frowned. "Who asked about me?"

"Bishop Cochran," Sebastian said.

Nikki couldn't help but feel a tinge of pain at the sound of that name. Dino . . . a *bishop*! She still couldn't get over that one.

"I thought it odd myself," Sebastian added.

"So did I," Tam agreed. "Especially since he'd only seen you that one time. But he surely asked about you."

Nikki hesitated. "What did he say?"

"He wanted to know why you weren't in church today, that's all. And he actually seemed upset when I told him you're never in church, and that because of the way your aunt treated you, you believe all church folks are hypocrites."

Nikki corrected her. "Not *all* church folks."

"But I don't know," Tam continued. "He asked if you were in church, but it seemed like that wasn't really the question."

"Oh goodness; here she goes," Sebastian said. "Madam Tammy, at your service."

"Why do you say that, Tam?" Nikki said, surprising herself with her dying curiosity. "What do you think the real question was?"

Tam thought about it for a moment. "I think he was trying to find out if you were okay," she said.

The luxurious Embassy-Carlton hotel in Jacksonville, some twenty-five miles outside of Monroe, was Dino's temporary home away from home during his stay in Florida. He had hoped that it wouldn't take over a month to complete his work and find a replacement pastor, and paid for a room at the hotel with that length of time in mind. But now, after just a week at New Life, he was certain that his projection was far too wishful.

He sat out on the balcony of his eighth floor room and looked out over the Saint John's River, where the streaming busy bridges provided just the right backdrop for the well-lit business towers. He had showered and ordered room service, and was now in a robe and slippers, his legs crossed as he sipped hot tea to nurse his still hoarse voice. His Bible was open at his side.

Dino thought the record-keeping problems at New Life would be his main concern, especially in light of all of the misinformation Crane and his people had been reporting for years; but that was only a fraction of the problem. Dino realized today that the real dilemma was the total lack of moral authority in that church. Saving souls wasn't even on those people's agenda. Everybody, from Crane down, had been doing whatever suited their fancy, be it in or out of step with God's Word; and the bishop in charge had allowed it right under his nose.

Dino leaned back against the high-back chair and let out a sharp exhale. Sixteen years ago, after his wife and unborn son had been killed in that car crash because of his negligence, all he wanted to do was die. His best friend, Max, had also died, during that strip mall shooting, and Dino knew that that was his fault too. The gangster life had caught up with him in spades and snatched away everything he held dear. He was so devastated and so angry with life during those days that all he could think about was retribution. Somebody had to pay.

But his doorbell rang one night, the night he had a gun in his hand, ready to go out and settle a few scores; and it caused him to shudder. Nobody came to his home. Nobody dared. But somebody was ringing his bell. Dino remembered clearly how he kept the gun at his side as he answered it; too curious to see what fool had the courage to bother him like that.

And there he was. Billy Graham. That street corner preacher who was always urging him to give his life to Christ, the only one of the preachers who actually believed there was still hope for Dino after all, was standing on his stoop. Dino was too amazed by the man's gumption not to let him in. And for the first time, he actually listened to what Billy had to say. Dino accepted Christ that very night, and less than a year later, he was called into the ministry and given a chance to redeem his sorry life.

The New Life Progressive Church in Detroit grew massively under Dino's leadership, from a membership of less than two hundred to nearly twenty-eight thousand; an incredible turnaround, according to many Christian magazines and local newspapers. It made the national board take notice. Soon, Dino was also running the national board, serving as the powerful CEO and final arbiter of any and all things associated with the large family of churches.

Before his ascension, he was content just to be saved and alive, but he soon came to realize that God had other plans for him. Now Dino was at the top of his profession, as high as he could go. But instead of being a fulfilled man, instead of counting his blessings and letting them grow, he still couldn't shake his past. He still couldn't understand why he, of all people, made it out alive. Most times it didn't bother him; most times he was too grateful to God and too thankful to have gotten the chance to please Him to question it. But other times, like now, as Dino looked out at the beautiful Jacksonville skyline, he was as lonely as that dreadful night sixteen years ago, when his wife died at his side.

He sipped more tea and found himself thinking about Nikki. Young Nikki. She was still so pretty and pure, still so wide-eyed and curious. But that spark in her eyes was gone. Dino noticed it as soon as he saw her. She looked at the world with disdain and bitterness that reflected through her eyes like a deformity. Since seeing her in that dining hall, Dino hadn't been able to forget her, thinking about her constantly. He couldn't understand why seeing her again, why seeing that particular ghost from his past, had affected him so. But it had. Like an affliction to his core. That was why he closed his eyes and asked the Lord, for what had to be the hundredth time, to forgive him.

FIVE

A week later, Nikki, Tam, and Sebastian were sitting in the front booth, finally catching a break. The last of the diner's hectic lunch crowd had gone and they were grateful for the peace. Sebastian complained that he'd walked so much that his feet felt like steel. Tam complained that she rang up so many orders that her fingers tingled. Nikki was just too tired to complain about anything. Even when Fern and Mookie decided to take their breaks at the drugstore across the street, or when Henry decided to take his at the same time, she didn't have the energy to tell them to hurry back the way she usually did. A nod of the head was all she could manage. And when they were all out of sight, she laid that same head on the tabletop.

"I feel like crap," she said in a muffled voice, not particularly concerned if anyone heard her or not.

"You look like crap," Tam replied. "Especially that hair, girl. That is the wildest looking ponytail I have ever seen in my life."

"I know better than this," said Sebastian, who was seated next to Tam. "I know you didn't just call somebody's hair wild. At least it's *her* hair."

"And? This mine too. I paid for it. So I don't get your point. Nikki's hair is wild, that's just a fact. It's thick, wavy, rich and beautiful. But it's wild. Now if I had all that hair—"

"It would be wild too," Sebastian said. "From the shock of being on your bald head."

"Forget you, Sebastian! You ain't exactly dropping curls either with those lil' bb's on top of that peanut head of yours."

"Chill, guys," Nikki said without bothering to lift her head. "You two carry on worse than an old married couple."

"Married?" Sebastian sounded as if the thought horrified him. "Bite your tongue, Nikki Lucas!"

"Behave," Tam said, looking out of the large front window beside their booth.

"Behave my foot," Sebastian retorted. "Did you hear what Nikki said?"

"Behave, Seb," Tam repeated. "Bishop Cochran's here."

Nikki's head lifted from the table in a kind of anguished excitement as all three friends looked out of the window at the shiny black Mercedes that had just stopped in front of the diner. Dino stepped out wearing a white dress shirt and Nikki's breath got caught in her throat at the sight of him. Even when he grabbed the suit coat from inside his car and put it on, there was still no denying the beauty of his muscular physique. It was almost cruel how kind the years had been to him. From his sparkling black shoes and that beautiful ocean-blue elegant suit, to the soft tint of his hair; everything about Dino Cochran screamed power and success.

Tam shook her head. "He might be a preacher, and he ain't the youngest brother on the block, but I'm sorry. That is a good-looking man."

"He works out," Sebastian observed, "but I don't see where he's no better looking than, say, me."

"*You*?" Tam laughed so hard that she started coughing.

"It's not that funny," Sebastian said, finding her response insulting at best.

Nikki began smoothing down her hair, which only mildly helped; but Tam noticed it.

The clang of the door as it opened brought their attention back to Dino. He entered cautiously, as if he'd never seen a small town diner before in his life, until he looked to his right and realized that three pairs of eyes were glued on him. When he saw that one pair belonged to Nikki, his chest tightened. "Good afternoon." He was greeting everyone collectively, but Tam beamed like his words were directed toward only her.

"Good afternoon, Bishop Cochran," she said cheerfully. "Welcome to the Big Turn!"

"Thank you, Sister Ellis." Dino moved slowly toward the booth. "For a moment, I wondered if anybody was here."

"On break," Tam explained. "We had an exceptionally busy lunch crowd. Don't tell me that's why you're here too."

Dino stared at Tam for a brief moment. Unlike Nikki, she was a tall woman, around five-eight. Tam had a long, narrow face and overly eager bedroom eyes. Dino could tell that she was a natural flirt, teasing men and smiling that experienced smile of hers to help lure them in; a trait he prayed hadn't rubbed off on Nikki. "I don't quite follow you," he said.

"Are you here because you heard about our world famous double-decker, stacked to the max bacon cheddar cheeseburgers too?"

Dino laughed, revealing a smile so magnetic that Nikki found herself staring into the man's mouth. "Not exactly," he said. After a second thought, he added, "World famous, you said?"

"Surely, surely she jests, Bishop," Sebastian chimed in. "Or, to be more precise, she's lying. At best, she's exaggerating. Reminds me of this time when I played Cyrano de Bergerac off-Broadway, but actually quite close to the Great White Way, and this female—"

"Surely, surely we don't want to hear it," Tam said, effectively cutting him off. Then she looked at Dino. "But for real, Bishop. If not for the cheeseburgers, why are you here?"

All eyes were on Dino again and he suddenly felt oddly uncomfortable. The truth was simple. He couldn't bear to go another second without seeing Nikki again. But he wasn't about to blurt that out. "I came to speak with the owner," he said. "With Miss Lucas."

At first, Tam felt a little jealous that Nikki, who never showed any interest in any man at any time, was once again being chosen over her by men who could have virtually any woman they wanted. Now, even Bishop Cochran, a man everybody knew didn't play anybody's games, was taken by her. Tam didn't know what the sister had, as she looked at her in her wild pony-tail, jersey, and jeans; but whatever it was, men wanted it. "We'll just get out of your way then," she said, elbowing Sebastian to slide out of the booth so that she could get out too.

When they left, bickering nonstop as they made their way over to the counter, Dino looked down at Nikki and sighed. She was a royal mess. Ponytail and all. But even with that, she was a beautiful sight to behold.

"Hello, Nikki," he finally said.

It was that voice, that strong, deep voice that caused her to get out of the booth, certain that she couldn't deal with what his presence back in her life truly meant. Nikki tried to make a bee-line for the counter, but Dino grabbed her by the arm and pulled her back beside him. Her entire body clenched when he touched her, when she smelled the freshness of his masculine scent; but she looked up at him with an angry fierceness that shook him. She hated him. He could see it in her eyes.

"Take your hands off of me." Her voice was controlled and tense.

"We need to talk, Nikki."

"There's nothing to talk about."

"There's plenty to talk about. What time do you close?"

She frowned. "What?"

"What time are you planning to close up this shop and head home?"

"I don't see where that's any of your business."

Tam and Sebastian, pretending not to listen, but hearing every word, looked at each other, shocked that Nikki would speak so harshly to a bishop. Even Dino seemed taken aback by her brashness. His grip tightened on her arm with a kind of unconscious anger of his own, until he realized the truth of the matter. Nikki knew him back in the day when he was everything a man of God was not. He couldn't expect her to instantly respect him as this church leader. But yet and still, Dino wasn't about to sit back and let her get away with it.

"Watch who you're talking to, Nikki," he warned her. "Now I'm going to ask you again. What time do you close?"

Nikki knew that look in Dino's eyes. He was angry, but was trying to control it. Gripping her arm too tightly was the only way he could display it without the world knowing that he wasn't as together as he was pretending to be. She should have told him about his behind right then and there. She should have told him to get out of her diner and leave her alone once and for all. But she couldn't. They did have a lot to talk about; not least of which was the son that thought he was dead. The son that he didn't even know existed.

"Eight," she finally said.

"Okay." Dino loosed her. "I'll be here at eight."

Nikki didn't waste a second getting away from him. He threw his hand up at Tam and Sebastian, who both waved and wished him well. Dino left feeling less worried, but a little embarrassed that two of his members had witnessed his display.

"What was that about?" Tam asked.

Nikki began heading for her office, unable to face anybody right now. "Nothing at all," she said, attempting to appear unaffected.

Tam looked at Sebastian and he urged her, with a nod of his head, to follow Nikki.

"I've got paperwork to do, Tam," Nikki said as Tam walked into the small back office behind her and closed the door.

"This won't take long."

"I'm sure it won't, but I still have paperwork to do." Nikki stood behind her desk and looked at her friend. Tam stared at her. "What?" Nikki asked.

Tam folded her arms. "You tell me," she said. "What's up with you and Bishop Cochran, and don't tell me nothing because I heard that entire little conversation, *Nikki*. That's what he calls you, isn't it? He calls all the rest of us names with religious titles, but you're just *Nikki*. I don't know about you but that sounds a little familiar to me, for a man who'd supposedly only laid eyes on you once before."

Nikki exhaled. Getting anything past Tam was impossible and she should have known not to even try it. She sat down behind her desk and Tam, more than curious now, sat in front of it. Nikki leaned back. "I know him."

"Since when?"

"A long time ago. Before I came to Florida. He wasn't a bishop then, you can bet that. He owned this nightclub called the Bluebird, and I used to boost tapes on the corner right near his club." She paused. "We had a night together."

"A night together?"

"Yes, Tam. You know what I'm talking about. I actually thought I was in love with that player." Nikki hesitated. Then she gave a quick, terse smile. "No thought in it. I *was* in love with that player. Only to find out he was married and about to be a daddy."

Tam couldn't believe it. "Bishop Cochran slept around on his wife? And she was *pregnant*? I don't believe it."

"Hold on there now. He wasn't a bishop then, I told you. Dino was a gangster; one of the most feared gangsters in Detroit for a while. He wasn't thinking about no church."

"And you slept with him?"

Nikki hesitated as the pain seared her. "Yes."

Tam shook her head. "No wonder he was asking about you at church and now wants to talk to you. He probably wants to tell you to keep it all undercover."

Nikki became angry. "He ain't got to tell me that," she said defensively. "Of course it's gonna stay undercover. You think I want this whole town to know what a fool I was? Please. And you'd better not tell a living soul either."

Tam gave Nikki one of her harshest looks. "What do you take me for, Nikki Lucas?"

"The biggest gossip this side of living. But this is off limits, Tam. For real."

Tam nodded. In truth, she had intended to tell Sebastian all about it. Now she knew she couldn't. She stood up. "Are you gonna be all right while he's around?"

"I have no choice. Thank God his stay is only temporary."

"Yeah." Then, as if a lightbulb had just flashed in her head, Tam quickly turned back toward Nikki. "Is it possible?"

"Is what possible?"

Tam swallowed hard. "Could Bishop Cochran be Jamal's father?"

Nikki's heart pounded. "Don't be ridiculous. Why would you say something that crazy? You know Jamal's father is dead."

"I know that's what you told everybody," Tam said. "I was just wondering."

"Stop wondering. The answer is no." Nikki's voice was firm.

"Okay. Good gracious! It was just a thought. Let me get out of your hair before you try to get into mine."

"If Seb was here, he'd say you don't have any to get into."

Tam smiled. "You wrong for that, Nikki." She left the office, closing the door behind her.

Nikki, suddenly stricken, leaned forward as every muscle in her body tensed, and covered her face with her hands.

Night descended peacefully on Monroe as the once bustling town square was now a quiet, empty street. Dino sat in his Mercedes outside of the Big Turn for nearly fifteen minutes after closing. All of the employees had gone, and Tam and Sebastian paused their heated argument over the usefulness of rap music long enough to stop by the car and speak to their pastor. But the silence ensued again as Tam's car cranked up, backed out, and disappeared around the corner.

Dino didn't like it. He didn't like the fact that Nikki was the last to leave, coming out of the diner well after all other forms of life around her establishment had packed up and moved out.

He watched her as she carefully locked the door. Her tight jeans and ponytail made her appear far too young for this kind of responsibility. He wondered why she didn't insist that one of her employees at least wait until she locked up the place.

But he knew Nikki. He knew how stubborn she'd always been, and how she probably wouldn't dream of somebody lending her a hand. When she was just a kid outside his nightclub, boosting tapes as if she was some tough dude, he used to worry about her. He didn't know why, but he did. And he was still worrying, still disturbed that she continued to be so alone in the world that even when the night came, there was nobody there to see her safely home.

After locking up the diner she walked slowly toward Dino's car, as if she didn't really want to. Dino remained seated behind the wheel, staring at her every movement, looking her up and down and remembering her. And when she finally opened the passenger door of his car and sat down to face him before the inside light dimmed, he told her exactly what he thought of her bravado.

"They would have been glad to wait until I left," Nikki responded.

"If you would have asked them?"

"Right."

"And of course, you would never even consider it."

"Look, Dino, this isn't Detroit, okay? There're no drive-by shootings and strong-arm robberies here in little Monroe. Nobody's gonna bother me."

Her lack of concern upset him. "That's when they get you, Nikki. When you think it's not possible."

Nikki rolled her eyes and folded her arms. "Is this what you wanted to talk about?"

Dino stared at her longer, unable to decide whether he liked or despised this toughness about her, a toughness that had undoubtedly kept her alive all these years. He cranked up his car.

"I thought we were going to talk," Nikki said.

"We are," Dino replied, backing out of the slanted parking slot. "Over dinner."

Nikki looked at Dino as he sat back in the fancy leather seat of his fancy black Mercedes, oozing with that air of arrogance that had always cloaked him, and she wished she could protest. She wished she could tell him to take his talk and dinner and anything else he had in mind and shove it. But she couldn't. She was too curious. Despite the rage that bubbled just below the surface of her exterior, despite the fact that he once broke her heart, there was still a part of her that wanted to take the measure of this man. There was still a part of her that wanted to find out what had been up with him all of these years, and if his road to Monroe had been as bumpy as hers.

He took her to Diamond's, a restaurant in Jacksonville whose clientele ranged from the very elite to the barely presentable. Nikki, in her jeans and jersey, viewed herself as the latter. Tam had urged her to take a moment to brush her hair and put on a little lipstick. And Nikki, just to prove that Dino would never again have the ability to alter her life, did one, but refused to do the other. Her lips would have to wait for another day to be decorated.

They ordered drinks, a Coke for Nikki, unsweetened tea for Dino, as they sat at a table near the back of the crowded restaurant and stole occasional glimpses at each other. They exchanged small talk about the weather and Monroe's annual watermelon festival until their drinks arrived. Then Dino, without consulting Nikki, ordered steak dinners for them both.

"No," Nikki quickly said. "I don't want anything."

"Two steak dinners," Dino repeated to the waiter.

"Yes, sir." The waiter glanced at Nikki as he grabbed the menus and walked back toward the kitchen.

"You can order it all you want," Nikki said, "but I'm not gonna eat it."

"You need to."

Nikki frowned. "How would you know what I need?" She didn't think her voice would sound so bitter. She and Dino exchanged glances, both understanding fully where that little outburst came from.

Dino leaned back and looked down at his glass of tea. "I see you're still tough as nails."

"I just try to keep it real, that's all. If that means tough, oh well."

Dino smiled. "You were the toughest kid I'd ever seen when you first started hanging outside of my club. Sometimes I'd walk out of the Bluebird and see you standing there in your baggy jeans and that backward turned baseball cap and just shake my head. Then you'd bug me like a big dog to let you into that strip joint, like I was going to allow that."

"You allowed all those other girls to go up in there."

"Yeah, well, you were different. I wasn't allowing you to go up in there."

Nikki could feel her cheeks grow warm and she looked away from Dino. She wanted desperately to ask him why he used to think that she was different than all the others, but she couldn't bring herself to do it. It wasn't as if it mattered anyway. She wasn't born yesterday. She knew this entire so-called dinner date wasn't about her. It was Dino's attempt to ease his own little messy guilt. She knew that just the idea of the big shot Bishop Cochran having a one-night fling with one of the local girls wasn't exactly great for his image, and he had to make sure, like Tam said, that she kept it undercover.

Dino laughed. "Remember when that dude stole your tapes and you actually thought you were going to run him down and take them back?"

"And I would have too if you hadn't stopped me. I couldn't believe you stopped me. You and Max both were just standing up there letting that joker get away with it."

Dino's smile hardened around the edges of his mouth. "He didn't get away with anything."

Nikki smiled. "Wonk and Sugarman found him?"

"Yeah; they ran up on him."

"I hope they beat him down."

Dino looked at Nikki. She wasn't just tough, she was ruthless. "They definitely took care of him."

"Good!"

"And I definitely wouldn't recommend anybody handling situations in that manner anymore."

"Yeah, yeah, I know. You're Mister Bishop now, and you've got to play that game for all it's worth."

"It's not a game, Nikki."

"Whatever."

Dino looked at her with such intensity that she felt as if she'd been slapped. "It's not a game, Nikki," he said again, as if he were determined that she understood that.

Nikki sipped from her glass and tried to ignore him, but his stare wouldn't relent. "Where is that food?" she asked before she realized it.

Dino smiled. "I thought you weren't hungry."

"I wasn't. But I am now."

Dino studied her. She was fighting against herself, remembering how she used to idolize him so unflinchingly and hating herself for it. He didn't deserve the hero worship then, that was a fact, but he certainly missed it now. "Did you come straight to Monroe after you left Detroit, or were there stops along the way?"

Nikki hesitated. "No. I came straight here."

"You didn't tell anybody you were leaving."

"Like who was I gonna tell, Dino? Amanda the hooker? Or maybe Joe-Joe the drug dealer?"

"You could have told me."

"You?" Nikki asked with a deceptive smile. "And when was I supposed to tell you that? The night when you introduced me to your wife— your *pregnant* wife, by the way—and told her I was Max's girlfriend? Would that have been a good time, Dino?"

"That was a long time ago."

"I know that."

"You have to move on."

"Yeah, well, sometimes life won't let you."

Dino paused. Would that past of his ever leave him alone? "Seems to me you did all right for yourself," he complimented. "Own your own business. Got your health. Still beautiful."

Nikki looked away from Dino when he mentioned her beauty. She wondered just what kind of holy man was he to even comment on something like that. Was he still a player? Was he still the real Dino putting on a show for those folks at New Life? She looked back at him. "How's your wife?" She spit out that question specifically to quickly deflate any more talk of her so-called beauty.

Dino swallowed hard, his droopy eyes staring at Nikki. "I'm not married."

"Yeah, that's right. Tam did say you was single. What, she caught you with another woman and divorced you? Did you claim one time too many that one of your females belonged to Max?"

A strange, sad look came over Dino's eyes. "She died, Nikki."

Nikki stared at Dino. Stunned. "She died? What you mean she died?"

"She died. A couple weeks after you disappeared. I was driving her home from one of her childbirth classes. I was talking on the cell phone and paying no attention, as usual. I ran a stop sign."

Nikki's heart dropped. "You mean you—"

Dino nodded. "I was driving the car. Yes, that's what I mean. Me and my negligence caused her death. They had even toyed with the idea of charging me with vehicular homicide, with her murder; that's how guilty I was. I can still hear the sound of that crashing metal to this day. It sounded like an explosion in my ears. I'll never forget that sound for as long as I live."

Nikki's stomach plunged. She couldn't even imagine what he had gone through. His wife, that beautiful woman, was not only dead, but dead because of his carelessness. And she was pregnant too! Nikki looked at him. "What about . . . the baby?"

Dino swallowed hard. "She died too."

"Oh Dino; I'm so sorry." Nikki words sounded so heartfelt that they caused Dino's chest to tighten.

"Yeah, it was horrible, I'm not gonna even lie. It was hell on earth. Max had died the week before."

Nikki was floored. "Max? *Max*? What happened to Max?"

"He took a bullet that was meant for me outside this strip mall I was thinking about buying. He slipped into a coma before they could airlift him to the hospital, and he never regained consciousness. All because of me and my shady past. All because of me and my . . . I should have been dead, Nikki. No lie. I should have been the one to pay for my sins, not my wife, my child, and my best friend. I became a walking dead man and I was ready to take it out on the world."

Nikki suddenly looked alarmed. "With a gun?

"Yes. Absolutely. What man can live with all of that guilt over his head? You better believe I had a gun. And I wasn't playing either. I was ready to bring it on, to settle every score I even thought needed settling. But I didn't, thank God."

"Why didn't you?"

Dino smiled. "Billy Graham rang my door-bell."

Nikki gave Dino an *are you serious* look. "Come again?"

"You remember that dude who used to always hang around the Bluebird preaching the gospel, and everybody used to call him Billy Graham? The one with the wild afro?"

Nikki smiled. "Oh yeah; I remember ol' Billy." Then she frowned. "He was a pain in the butt."

"Yeah, well, that pain came to my house at the absolute best time possible, and preached the gospel to me. He'd heard about the accident and heard about Max, so he came on over. I didn't exactly have appointments, except the one that could definitely wait, so I let him in and listened to him. I accepted Jesus Christ as my Lord and Savior right then and there."

"A saved man, then a preacher man; now you're running the whole shebang."

"That's how God does it, Nikki. He doesn't bless you halfway. You're going to know when it's Him."

"I heard that," Nikki said. She also wanted to say, *Thank God for Billy Graham*, but she felt it would sound too silly coming from her, so she didn't. She also didn't tell Dino anything about their son. He'd been through enough, and so had she. Sometimes it was better to keep the unspeakable unspoken.

Instead, she took another sip of her soda and looked beyond Dino, at the animated crowd in the oddly relaxing restaurant.

It was pin-drop quiet throughout the entire town square by the time Dino drove his Mercedes into the slanted parking space in front of the Big Turn. He got out quickly to open the door for Nikki, but she was already out by the time he walked around to the passenger side. She lingered, however. He noticed her hesitation before she began walking over to her VW. He followed her, smiling as she fumbled in her purse for her keys.

"Whatever did you see in that bug of a car?" he asked her.

Nikki looked up at him. His breath caught at the sight of those big, green eyes of hers. "Small monthly payments," she replied.

Dino, not expecting that answer, laughed. "There's that," he said.

Nikki felt oddly regretful when she finally laid hands on her keys. "Well, guess I'd better get going."

"Nikki," Dino moved closer to her as she unlocked her car door.

Nikki looked up at him and immediately felt flushed when she realized how close they now stood. "Yes?"

"About what happened that night," he said, not knowing how else to say it.

Nikki sighed. She should have known. "Don't worry, Dino. I don't plan to go around broadcasting it to everybody."

Dino frowned. "Will you stop jumping to conclusions for once in your life?"

"What am I jumping to?" Nikki was perturbed. "I was just letting you know that I wasn't gonna tell."

"I didn't expect you to, Nikki. All right? I just wanted to tell you that I was sorry about what happened. What I did to you was wrong and it was cruel, and I want to apologize for my thoughtless behavior."

Nikki shook her head. "I wasn't exactly an unwilling participant."

"You were a virgin." The pain of that fact still pierced him. "You were young and naïve. Don't you ever try to convince yourself that you were my equal that night. I knew what I wanted, knew I had no business wanting it, and I took it anyway."

"You didn't take anything. I knew what I was doing too."

"Don't fool yourself, Nikki. You were clueless." He reached out and placed his hand on the side of her face, a hand that felt so warm, Nikki found herself leaning into it, a reaction that only hurt him more. Why she would even give him the time of day was a mystery to him. "I'm sorry," he said.

Time heals all wounds, Nikki wanted to smile and say in return, but she couldn't. Because it wasn't true. Dino hadn't just hurt her and left her. In time, she believed she would have easily gotten over that. But he left her with a child, with a constant reminder of how odd her life was. She had loved Dino desperately, believing that he cared for her, and that in him, she'd finally found somebody who might actually love her. It was the most awesome thought in the world to her; the idea that somebody could love her. Everybody else had failed her, including her own parents, but she just knew that somehow, Dino was different. He wouldn't hurt her. She would have bet her entire tape collection on it.

But he did hurt her. That was why, when she saw him with his pregnant wife, a part of her died right where she stood. Because she was pregnant too. With his son. And she knew at that very moment that she was on her own for real, that all of her dreams of being loved by

Dino Cochran were as hopeless as her life itself. And there was never any getting over that kind of pain, that kind of constant, painful reminder every time she looked into the disappointed eyes of her teenage son.

She looked up at Dino. He stood big over her, big and imposing, and suddenly Nikki felt overwhelmed by his presence. She looked further down, at his broad chest and beautiful blue suit, at the soft silk of his crisp white shirt. She almost began to cry, almost allowed him to see her at her most vulnerable when she never allowed anybody to see her that way. But he saved her the shame by pulling her into his arms.

Nikki's breath caught when she felt his arms encircle her. She found herself first alarmed, and then pleased by his nearness. She laid her head on his shoulder, and closed her eyes. He didn't smell the way he used to smell. His scent was more masculine back in the day, where any hint of cologne barely registered. Now he carried a strong cologne scent, a kind of fresh fragrance that seemed to go beyond just his clothes, and ooze deep under his smooth, brown skin. Nikki felt intoxicated by the smell of him, and she didn't want to hug him back. But she did. She collapsed in his arms. She couldn't find the courage or the will to pull away.

It seemed like a sweet eternity to Dino as she allowed him to hold her; as she allowed him to pull her closer to him in a steel grip that even tingled the thick muscles beneath his coat sleeves. He didn't know where this could lead. He didn't know why he would want it to lead anywhere. Not with all of the responsibilities he now carried in his present life, and the horrific burdens he'd never be able to shake from his past. But he kept pulling her closer against him, as if he wasn't going to let her go, as if in Nikki and Nikki alone, he could find some semblance of hope in this life. It was selfish and foolish, and about as cowardly as anything he could think of. But it was there. A sudden, desperate need to keep Nikki in his life, to keep her under his thumb; to keep her against him now as they stood helplessly in the long-deserted, poorly lit parking lot in front of the Big Turn.

Nikki, too, felt some desperation as she held on to Dino. She could have stayed there all night, marveling at how strange it was that no man, to this day, could make her feel the way Dino could. So many men had tried to get the inside track to her heart, but she wouldn't let them. So many men had tried to whisper sweet nothings in her ear, and get her in their beds, but she wouldn't hear of it. She'd been with one man in

her life, and he was holding her right now. No
matter how much she tried to hate him through
those years, no matter how much she convinced
herself that he was the worst thing that had ever
happened to her, it still had always been Dino
and Dino alone. No other man would do.

That was why, when he placed his hand on Nikki's chin and lifted her face to his, she didn't pull
away. She allowed him to look deep into her eyes,
and stare at her lips, and then place his mouth
on hers and kiss her with a kiss that lingered. He
pulled her closer against him, wrapping his arms
tightly around her, and she allowed that too. And
when it was all over, and she opened her eyes, the
tenderness she saw in Dino's stunned her. How
was she ever going to get over this man . . . this
big, awesome man who had so much power over
her that even her own ironclad will couldn't fight
it? She almost shook her head in wonderment.
What was it about Dino?

But there was absolutely something about
him; she knew it sixteen years ago, and she knew
it now. She could have stayed in his embrace forever as he continued to hold her even after their
kiss. But those memories that had sustained her
all these years, but had somehow disappeared,
came flooding back tonight. He'd hurt her. Bitterly. He'd caused her to become an ill-equipped
single parent, to become a statistic she swore

she'd never become; and the needed pleasure of that moment was replaced with that old familiar, unyielding pain. Dino moved to keep her in his arms, but she frowned in anguish and pushed him away.

"Don't, Nikki," he said, refusing to let her go, fighting back easily her attempt to get away from him.

"Please."

The anguish in her voice devastated him when she uttered the single word, and he released her.

Nikki moved away quickly and got into her car, looking exactly like the wounded woman he knew she had to be. He wanted to go after her, to get her to understand that he wasn't that same man who'd hurt her those years ago, but he didn't dare. He didn't deserve her understanding. He didn't even deserve her forgiveness. Dino let her go, knowing that he should have never held her in the first place.

Tears stained Nikki's lids as she hurriedly backed out and drove away, her heart pounding with the painful and the disappointing truth that happiness in this world wasn't ever going to happen for her, not unless and until she could get that man out of her heart. But how could she when she couldn't even stop herself from watching him through her rearview mirror? How could she?

SIX

"*A strip club*?" Reverend Wallace asked in astonishment as Sister Dardell walked into his office the next day with a written report in her hands. Wallace, Roosevelt Atwater, and Sister McKernan sat in amazement, as the news was even more graphic than the rumors had suggested.

"That's what I said," Sister Dardell replied. "With real live strippers. And that ain't all, either. There was a shooting where his best friend was murdered with a bullet that was meant for him!"

"A bullet that was meant for him? Have mercy," Sister McKernan said.

"Told y'all he was a thug," Roosevelt interjected.

"Hold on now," Wallace protested. "We already knew he came from a rough background."

"*Rough*?" Dardell couldn't believe Wallace would try to minimize her information. "I'd call it more than rough, Reverend; especially when you include the fact that his pregnant wife and unborn child were killed in an automobile that he was driving!"

"Dardell!" Sister McKernan said incredulously.

"It's the truth!"

"Was he drunk?" Roosevelt was thrilled by the news that Mister Perfect was nowhere near perfection after all.

"They arrested him," Dardell replied. "Was gonna charge him with murder, but dropped the charges. What you think?"

"That hypocrite!" Roosevelt said. "Calling us to give account, and look at him. Acting like he's some saint around all us sinners. He's no saint!"

"Course he ain't," Dardell added. "These aren't tales on this here paper. I'm telling y'all that man is something else. And here he comes down here like he's Mister Righteous that's gonna show us the way."

Roosevelt shook his head. "I knew it was something about him I didn't like. Always staring at me like I'm a piece of trash. Yeah, he wears all his Armanis and Versaces and got the big cash flow going, but that don't mean he have to be player-hatin' on me because of my style, because of my suits; as if I'm dressing like some kind of clown!"

"You do dress like a clown," Dardell said. "He ain't lying about that."

"I've got style, woman. What you talking about?"

"I'm talking about clowns. Circus. A grown man walking around in those orange, yellow and purple zoot suits ought to be on Ringling Brothers' payroll."

"I designed those clothes myself!"

"And I rest my case," Dardell said.

The door to Reverend Wallace's office burst open and Deacon Frye, a young man with a look of bewilderment on his face, hurried in. "I don't mean to disturb your meeting, Reverend, but I thought you'd wanna know."

Wallace looked at the concerned deacon. "What is it, Roy?"

"It's Bishop Cochran, sir," the deacon replied. "I just got word he's shutting down New Life Academy."

"*What*?" Wallace and Dardell said in unison.

"He just told Principal Whittam that this will be the last term for the Academy and he needed to start notifying parents immediately."

Dardell and Wallace exchanged glances. Before Deacon Frye could utter another word they were heading for the exit. They marched to Cochran's office on the top floor of the church as if they were leading a troop of foot soldiers, going to battle. Deacon Atwater and Sister McKernan were right on their heels. Deacon Frye nervously brought up the rear. Although they felt they had a right to barge in, they were becoming too familiar with Bishop Cochran's sometimes brash style to take the chance. Therefore, they allowed his secretary to announce them first, and then escort them into the large, posh office that for years belonged to Pastor Crane.

"How dare you shut down our school?" Sister Dardell said angrily as soon as they approached Dino's desk. "New Life Academy has been a staple of this church for nearly a decade. How dare you even suggest that it be shut down?"

Dino, who had been seated behind his desk all morning, mulling through a ton of paperwork, half expected this kind of fierce resistance. He removed his reading glasses and leaned back in his chair. His exhaustion showed through the heaviness of his drooping lids. "A thorough review of the Academy—"

"We don't care nothing about what no review says!" Dardell interrupted.

Dino, showing a flash of anger himself, cut her a look so intense that even Dardell felt its warning. Wallace gave a slight tug on Dardell's dress sleeve, just in case she didn't.

"A thorough review of New Life Academy," Dino repeated, this time even calmer and looking directly at Dardell, "made the decision to close an easy one."

"But why, Bishop?" Wallace wanted to know. "There's no reason."

"There are plenty of reasons, Reverend; beginning with the low enrollment."

"We know enrollment is down," Wallace said, "but we expect a great up-tick again any day now. It's just a matter of time."

Dino shook his head. "You haven't had a substantial up-tick in ten years, Reverend. That so-called school would have been shut down long ago if we would have known the true state of affairs rather than the lies your annual reports were telling us. That school is nothing but a drain on church resources. Resources that are needed to help the various ministries win souls to Christ. I simply can't continue to allow that to happen."

"Is that all y'all care about?" Dardell asked. "Money? Resources? What about those poor students who've been attending the Academy for years?"

Dino nodded. "I feel sorry for them; I really do."

"Then don't close down their school!" Dardell exclaimed.

"I feel sorry for them *because* they attend this school, Sister Dardell. I checked out that curriculum. It's simplistic; below grade level at each and every level. It's a sure recipe for failure."

Dardell planted her hands on her hips. "But their grades—"

"Are excellent," Dino finished. "I realize that. Everybody's an A-B student at New Life Academy. Even those students that can hardly read! And to bear that fact out, their test scores on the F-CAT and other statewide exams are dismal. They're far behind in every subject, and I mean *every* subject, because of these low expectations the Academy has allowed to fester. The best thing we can do for those students is to get them away from us and into schools that will not accept excuses for low achievement."

Dardell was beyond angry. She looked at Cochran with such disgust that it took all she had not to tell him about his natural self. And if he weren't the Bishop, if he weren't the man who could also shut down their entire church, she would have told him a thing or two. Roosevelt, however, had no such qualms.

"You're not perfect either," he said bitterly to Dino. McKernan couldn't hold back a gasp. "You owned a strip club. You were in shoot-outs and Lord knows what else. You were even arrested for murdering your own wife. Since you don't believe in second chances, since we're all just sinners and hell-bound folk and our fine school is retarding our youth let you tell it, why don't all of your sins disqualify you? Why don't somebody shut *you* down?"

All eyes turned to Dino, certain that Roosevelt Atwater had gone too far. Dino remained leaned back in his chair, staring in his uncomfortably intense way, at Deacon Atwater. After what seemed to them to be an interminably long pause, Dino finally spoke. "Have a good day," he said to all in an unmistakable tone of dismissal.

Wallace and Dardell wanted to argue further, but that look in Dino's eyes discouraged them. Roosevelt had crossed the line, even Dardell knew that, and they'd be foolish to compound the error. Therefore, they kept their considerable opinions to themselves and began leaving the office.

"And Deacon Atwater," Dino said without looking up.

"Yes?" Roosevelt responded.

"Effective immediately, you are no longer the chairman of the deacon board. In fact, effective immediately, you are no longer a deacon." Then Dino looked up. "Have a nice day." There was no hint of humor in his voice as he placed his glasses back on his face and returned to his paperwork, not even bothering to see the sudden stricken look on Roosevelt's face.

Roosevelt was so upset that he wanted to argue with the bishop, to tell the bishop to step outside to settle this thing, but Wallace hurried him out of Cochran's office before his long-arm of anger, and *demotions*, didn't end with just their colorful deacon.

When they were gone and his door was closed, Dino removed his glasses and leaned back in his chair again. He ran his hand over his face and exhaled. This job was exhausting, frustrating, and emotionally draining. He hated this aspect of his work. He hated getting into it with people, calling them to give account, and making life-altering decisions when they refused to tow the line, as if he were some worthy arbiter of moral behavior.

He'd like nothing better than to be as he was back in the early days of his Christian walk, when he was the overseer of one church—New Life Progressive of Detroit, Michigan—not one hundred churches. Life was simpler then. His mission was clear. Instead of mixing it up with pompous deacons, he was winning souls to Christ, preaching God's gospel, laying hands on the sick, giving hope to those who were as hopeless as he once was.

Now it was all about audits, resources, and unpopular tough decisions. Instead of thinking about his sermon all week as in years past, he now had to think constantly about paperwork and budget authorities and whether one man should retain his position of leadership while another lost his. And as if that wasn't enough, he also couldn't stop thinking about Nikki.

He closed his eyes when she crossed his mind, and a smile tugged at his lips. Nikki Lucas. Samson had his Delilah; he had his Nikki. Not that Nikki was deceptive like Delilah. It was he, not she, who mastered in deception back in the day. But just as Delilah had a hold on Samson, Nikki surely had a hold on Dino. He thought about last night and how desperately he'd kissed her, how he had such a hunger for her that it still made him shudder. Was he out of his mind to consider getting involved with her right now? Was he out of his mind to even think it could be possible? He was thankful she'd pulled away from him; thankful she'd gotten in her car last night and driven out of his sight. If she were smart, and he knew she was, she'd never look back.

But Dino still couldn't stop thinking about Nikki, and wanting her, and having this constant need to see her again. And when he looked at his Rolex and realized it was just after one on a day he hadn't had a bite to eat, he stood without another thought, grabbed his suit coat, and headed for the exit. He had to eat; and if going over to the Big Turn meant that he could eyeball Nikki again in the bargain, then that would just have to be his fate.

Dino knew he shouldn't do it. He knew he shouldn't lead her into believing for a second that they could ever have a future together, especially since they both knew that would be a disaster. But he headed to Big Turn anyway. He was a strong man. Many people marveled at his strength. But Nikki had a way about her, an almost unconscious, innocent way about her, that could cut him down to size.

Nikki leaned forward in the chair behind her desk and stared Jimmy Milton in the eyes. He was a loan officer from the finance company that held the note on the diner. He wasn't coming clean with her, and she didn't like it. "Let's cut the crap, Jimmy, all right?" she said. "What's the deal?"

Jimmy shuffled the numerous papers he had on Nikki's desk, looking, in his usual unorganized way, for a particular paper. "I'm just trying to get you to understand the back story, Nikki."

"I don't need to understand the back story. I know the back story. I know all about the history of my payments. Just give me the bottom line."

Jimmy stopped shuffling papers and looked at her. "Okay." He removed his glasses, his blue eyes clear as crystal. "You will face forfeiture on the note if you aren't completely current within two months."

"Two months?" Nikki was flabbergasted.

"That's the bottom line, Nikki. Two months. That's the longest we can give you. And that's pushing it."

Nikki leaned back, suddenly stricken. "I thought you said y'all were gonna work with me and come up with something, Jimmy?"

"We tried, Nikki. Trust me, we tried. But there's nothing more we can come up with. Your payment history has been awful."

"If y'all wasn't charging me an arm and a leg with those high interest rates, then my payment history would have been fantastic."

"I understand that. But it hasn't been fantastic. It's been awful. When you applied for our loan, we gave you the best rate you could get. You know that. But unfortunately, given your payment history to date, that rate has got to go up. I'm sorry, Nikki. You have two months to get this thing caught up or we will demand payment in full. Given your payment history, we believe we're being more than generous."

Jimmy watched as Nikki thrust her head back and covered her face with her hands. Tension seemed to run through her body. He stared at that body, and at her gorgeous thin neck. "Nikki, you're a beautiful, single woman who could have any man she wanted. You need to take advantage of that. Don't you have a friend, a male friend, who could help you out? Maybe one of your customers?"

Nikki removed her hands from her face and gave Jimmy an oddly suspicious look. "What are you trying to say, Jimmy? Are you suggesting that I prostitute myself for the sake of this diner?"

Jimmy smiled, knowing he had stepped into it. "That's not what I meant, Nikki. I mean you're a beautiful woman. Why don't you use that to your advantage sometimes? Be nice to some of these businessmen around here. By and large, Monroe is a very prosperous town with more than a few prosperous citizens; some of whom would be more than happy to help you out."

Nikki stood up quickly, her temper one word away from exploding. "I'll be caught up in two months, Jimmy. You'll get your money. And I assure you it won't be because I played nice to some man."

"I didn't mean it like that, Nikki," he said again, although he knew she wasn't hearing him.

Up front, Dino, with the *Monroe Gazette* in hand, walked into the Big Turn just as Sebastian was ringing up a customer and as Tam was wiping down the counter top. Tam smiled when she saw Dino, waving at him and elbowing Sebastian.

"What?" Sebastian asked while accepting money from his customer.

"Look who's in the house."

Sebastian looked, saw Dino, and frowned. "So? You're going a bit overboard with your schoolgirl infatuation, don't you think?"

Tam was too busy staring at the object of that infatuation to hear him. Dino walked over to a banquette and took a seat. The lunch crowd was already thinning out and he was disappointed when he looked around at the various faces and didn't see Nikki's among them. Her car was parked outside and he assumed she was around somewhere. He decided to just relax and wait. Dino placed on his reading glasses, unfolded his newspaper, and attempted to read a below-the-fold article about Mayor Luke Granger's controversial bond initiative to help pay for a proposed new stadium at the high school. The only reason the article caught Dino's eye was because Mayor Granger, like most of the elite around town, was a member of New Life.

"Can I take your order?"

The voice came from just above Dino's head. He looked over his reading glasses at a young woman with spiky short hair and a decidedly bored look on her pretty face. She held a pen and pad in her hand and seemed overly anxious to get on with it. Dino smiled. "Afternoon."

Fern shifted her weight and repeated, "Can I take your order?"

"I'll take a Coke, I know that," Dino said. "As for food, I'm not quite sure. What do you recommend?"

Fern frowned. "I don't eat none of this stuff, so I can't tell you."

"Well then, could you get me a menu?"

"A menu?" Fern looked as if she'd never heard of such a thing.

"Yes. It offers a listing of the items served in an establishment."

Fern sucked her teeth, grabbed a plastic menu from a nearby table, and then slapped it on top of Dino's newspaper. She then folded her arms and shook one leg as if she weren't going anywhere until he made up his mind.

Dino shook his head. "Give me a cheeseburger with that Coke." He removed the menu off of his paper. He was about as ready to be rid of her as she was to be rid of him.

"Stacked, double-stacked, or triple-stacked?" she asked.

"Excuse me?"

Fern rolled her eyes. "Do you want your cheese-burger stacked, double-stacked, or—"

"No," Dino said before she could continue her diatribe. "The regular will do."

"Sure about that? The boys 'round here usually get theirs stacked, but most men like 'em double-stacked."

Dino gave her a hard look. "Regular will do."

Fern looked at him as if he were trying to be smart with her, but that icy look in his eyes stopped her from saying what she truly wanted to say to him. Instead, she slipped her pad and pen back in the pocket of her uniform, snatched up the menu she had placed on Dino's table, and walked away from his booth. He shook his head again, surprised that Nikki would allow her waitress to be so lacking in social skills.

Within seconds of Fern's departure, Tam made her way to Dino's table. "Hello there, Bishop," she said cheerfully. "Just the man I need to see."

Dino, who had returned his attention to his newspaper, looked over his glasses at Tam's slender body standing before him. "Good afternoon, Sister Ellis." His tone was far less cheerful than hers.

"May I?" Tam motioned toward the seat across from him in his booth.

"Certainly." Dino stood halfway as Tam sat down. He lowered himself back into his seat and took a quick glance at her unnecessarily low-cut yellow blouse. "What can I do for you?"

"What can I do for *you*?" she replied, smiling. "Would you like something to drink? Some coffee, tea, or . . . *me*?"

Although she said it with a laugh, Dino smiled only mildly. "Thank you, Sister Ellis, but I already ordered." He looked around the diner. "Nikki around?"

Tam was a bit disappointed, especially since Nikki acted as if he were the last man on earth she wanted to be with. Besides, Nikki had already been with the man in the barest sense of the word, which automatically gave her the inside track. "She's in a meeting," she answered. "But it shouldn't take long."

"All right," Dino said. "Now what was it that you needed to see me about?"

Tam smiled and leaned her body forward, doing all she could to entice him. "I heard some crazy rumor that you were closing down the school. Tell me that's not true, Bishop."

Dino folded his newspaper. "I can't tell you that."

"It's true?"

"It's true."

Tam became concerned. "But why, Bishop? What about those poor kids?"

"We weren't helping those poor kids, Sister Ellis; I assure you of that. The entire Academy was nothing but a drain on church resources with no sufficient return. Even the staff wasn't adequately equipped to meet the challenges of this new society. Many of them couldn't pass the tests they were attempting to prepare the children to pass. It's something that had to be done. When and if that school reopens, it will be able to compete with any school in this state. Otherwise, it stays closed."

Tam smiled and shook her head. "They weren't lying when they said you don't play."

"Not a question of playing. It's a question of doing the right thing."

"Mister Righteous, at it again," she said, still smiling. "You know that's what they call you behind your back?"

Dino nodded. He knew that was the image he presented; that of an intolerable, insufferable man. But he also knew that the truth was never that simplistic. "You're a friend of Nikki's, aren't you?" He decided to change the subject.

"I'm proud to say I am."

"Known her long?"

"Fifteen years. We started working at this place the same week. I came on board, then Nikki a few days later. Of course, she was more of a workaholic than I ever was and rose up the ranks ahead of me, eventually becoming the manager. After she bought the place, she made me manager. But that's Nikki. She never forgets her friends."

Mookie arrived with Dino's glass of Coke and smiled at them both.

"Where's Fern?" Tam asked. "I thought this was her table."

"It is," Mookie said, "but I don't think she's feeling well. She's taking a break out back."

"Yeah, I'll bet she is. Tell her if she don't get her skinny behind back to her duties, then she'll be taking a permanent break."

Mookie looked upset by Tam's order, but he nodded and went to do her bidding anyway.

Tam shook her head. "That Fern is a trip," she said to Dino, "but Nikki won't fire her."

"Why not?"

"A million reasons; none of which has anything to do with working on a job. But Fern had a rough childhood. Mookie likes her and Nikki adores Mookie. And I don't know, but I think Nikki thinks of us as her family, as a vital part of her."

"Family's important to Nikki?" Dino asked, as if he didn't know.

"It's everything to her. But she'll never tell you that. That woman can't stand for another human being to even touch her. I ain't joking. You touch her and she just kind of slides away from you."

Dino thought about last night, when he more than touched her, and she didn't exactly slide away from him. At least, not at first.

"Seb . . . Brother Dobbs jokes that Nikki acts like she was raised by wolves, and human affection is a mystery to her. But Nikki doesn't think it's funny."

Dino didn't think it was funny either.

Jimmy Milton came from the back of the diner and began heading for the exit, his paper-stuffed briefcase in tow.

"I see you're still in one piece," Tam said to him.

He displayed a smile that transformed his already handsome face. "Just barely. That boss of yours will sober up a drunk!" Tam laughed, but Dino found himself studying the young man and wondering if he'd tried his hands at getting next to that boss of Tam's. "See you later," Jimmy added as he began heading for the exit.

"Who is he?"" Dino asked her. "Nikki's friend?"

"As in boyfriend, you mean? Please. Nikki doesn't play that. I, however, on the other hand . . ." With a seductive smile, Tam leaned forward again. In turn, Dino leaned back.

Nikki came up front and saw Dino before he saw her. He was too busy staring at Tam, too busy sizing her up the way Nikki was accustomed to him doing her. Dino wore a more conservative black suit this time, with a white shirt and a black and white tie. But even a dress-down day (by his standards), didn't distract one iota from his distinguished look.

Nikki actually felt thrilled to see him again, especially after the way she abruptly left him last night, as if she'd been wrong to act so hastily. She could still remember the warmth she felt when his arms were around her, and when he kissed her, and how so very tenderly he looked at her in the moonlight. But then she saw Tam's hand brush his and saw how he allowed it, and her sudden thrill was gone.

She snapped out of it. Same old Dino, she thought as she moved behind the counter.

As Nikki began helping Sebastian ring up customers, Fern came out of the kitchen with Dino's plate. When Fern arrived at the table, Tam left Dino alone to eat his lunch. Nikki did everything in her power to avoid looking Dino's way.

"I might have a chance, Nikki," Tam said as she lifted the hatch and walked behind the counter.

"A chance for what?" Nikki leaned against the counter as her customer left.

"Love, girl. Love!"

Sebastian looked at her. "Love?"

Tam grinned. "I do believe that if I play my cards right, I just might be able to snag Walter Dean Cochran himself. The catch of the century!"

Sebastian burst into laughter. It was an exaggerated, actor-trained laughter he had to force himself to display; especially since the truth of the matter was that the very thought of Tam being interested in another man disturbed him. Why it disturbed him, disturbed him even more.

Nikki didn't look too thrilled either, which made Tam wonder. "Unless you've got dibs on him yourself?"

"*Me*?" Nikki said as if such a thought was insulting. "Pah-lease!"

Tam smiled. "Alrighty then." She looked in Dino's direction. "Let the games begin!"

Nikki smiled, but felt hurt inside as she excused herself and went back into her office. She stayed there and tried to work, but all she ended up doing was obsessing; first about the diner and how she was going to be able to hold on to it, and then about Dino. She wouldn't trust that man as far as she could throw him. She knew she wasn't going to have a moment's rest until he left town, until that ghost from Detroit went back where he came from.

But knowing Dino, knowing his m.o., she knew he wasn't going away that easily. He was the kind of man who didn't let up until he had a person under his thumb. And then, when he rendered his prey helpless and had her all in love with his butt, that was when he suddenly didn't know her anymore. The more Nikki thought about it, the more it upset her. Last night he had tried it again, holding her and kissing on her and making her feel that there could be happy endings, after all. And maybe there was some kind of crazy chance for them. Now, the very next day, he was here in her establishment, not asking about her or anything, but sitting at a table flirting with Tam. And Tam wanted him too. Well, she could have him as far as Nikki was concerned. She could have every inch of him.

When she finally gave up on pretending to get work done, Nikki left her office, certain that Dino would be long gone and she could at least help out up front. But she was wrong. Not only was he still present, but he had left his booth and was sitting on a stool at the front counter flirting, once again, with Tam.

When Dino saw Nikki, his chest squeezed. "Hello, Nikki."

Nikki looked at him, the anger she had worked up in her mind now boiling over through her mouth. "May I help you?" Her tone was purposefully nasty as she walked behind the counter.

Dino smiled and threw up his hands. "I simply said hello."

"And I simply asked if I could help you."

"Watch it, Nikki," Tam warned.

Nikki frowned. "What I got to watch? I'm doing nothing wrong. I just wanna know what he's doing here."

"What did Jimmy want?" Sebastian asked the question in hopes of ridding the room of some of the uninvited tension.

"What?" Nikki responded with a puzzled look on her face.

"Jimmy Milton. What did he want?"

"What he always wants, Seb. Why?"

"Just asking a question, Nikki; my goodness. Didn't mean to insinuate I was giving you permission to tear my head off. All I wanted to know is what that slime ball, Jimmy Milton, was doing here. That's all I wanted to know.

"Who is this Jimmy?" Dino asked.

Nikki looked at him as if she couldn't believe he'd ask such a thing. "None of your business, that's who he is." Her tone was so harsh and disrespectful that both Sebastian and Tammy snapped their faces in her direction.

Dino was looking too, only his look wasn't incredulous like theirs. His was cold as ice. He stood and walked to the small archway that led into the hall, his tall, muscular body tight with sudden anxiousness. "Come here, Nikki," he said calmly.

Nikki knew she'd crossed the line already, but was unable to draw back from her feistiness. She looked at him as if he'd just insulted her. "Come where?"

Dino inhaled a heavy breath, as if his patience was one false move from exploding. "Come here, Nikki," he said again, this time with that look of controlled fury she used to admire about him, a look that now only heightened her own anxiety. She knew she should have taken that look for a sign and obeyed, for peace sake if nothing more. But after the news Jimmy had just laid on her, after being told point blank the truly critical state her business was really in, she couldn't care less about peace.

"Come where?" As soon as the sarcasm escaped her lips and Nikki saw the, *I've had it up to here* look that crossed Dino's face, she knew she was in trouble.

He moved up to her with a swiftness that belied his forty-eight years as he lifted the hatch and grabbed her by the hand before she could even think of a word to say. Tammy quickly backed out of his way as he jerked Nikki from behind the counter, pulled her down the hall, and then yanked her into the office, slamming the door behind them.

Tam looked at Sebastian and Sebastian shook his head. "I think your catch of the century has already been caught," he said.

Once the office door slammed shut, Dino pulled Nikki in front of him. "Let's get one thing straight right now, young lady." His hands slinging open his suit coat and resting on his waist, his thick chest heaving up and down.

But Nikki didn't care how upset he was. She was upset too. "We aren't getting anything straight," she said angrily as she moved swiftly to leave the office.

Just as quickly, Dino grabbed her by the arm and pulled her back in front of him, refusing to release her this time. "Let's get one thing straight," he said again, this time between clenched teeth. "You may not have a very high opinion of me—"

"*May*?" Nikki asked incredulously, attempting unsuccessfully to snatch away from his grip.

Dino's heart tightened with anguish at the look of hatred he could see all over Nikki's face.

"You may not have a high opinion of me, but you will respect the position I hold even if you don't respect me as a person. Those are members of my church out there, Nikki. And while I'm here, you will not talk to me as if I'm some child; as if I'm one of those punks you used to hustle. Do you understand me?"

"I heard you."

"I said do you understand me?"

"Whatever, Dino, all right? Just leave me alone!"

Dino stared at Nikki, at the hatred he thought she had managed to overcome last night, and frustration swept through his body like a shooting pain. He'd hurt her once, he'd be the first to admit it, but instead of accepting his apology, instead of talking to him about it, she'd apparently decided to hold on to the hurt. To the hate. Well, so be it. He released her angrily, all but shoving her away from him, and hurried out of the door.

Nikki was emotionally exhausted by the time she arrived at her house. And as if she didn't have enough to worry about, Jamal wasn't at home. His bedroom door was closed and it was empty inside. Any other night and she would have raced out of the house, jumped into her VW, and headed for the streets in search of him. But not this night. It wasn't an especially busy day at the diner, only the usuals, *plus one,* showed up. But emotionally, it had been a drain. She went to her refrigerator, grabbed a bottle of water, and plopped down on her sofa.

Nikki's house was eerily quiet and somber, as if her downcast spirit had already overtaken it. She looked at her pastel colored living room furniture, at her Berber carpet, at her matching drapes that swept into a sash on either side of her window, all very modest, but the best she'd ever had. Nikki couldn't stop wondering if she could lose this too, when all was said and done. Jimmy said she had two months, two short months to turn her financial situation around, and she assured him she would do just that.

Yeah, right, she thought, and then she smiled. If she told Dino he has a son, and then hauled him in for all of that back child support, which she knew would be big money considering the kind of money he had, she wondered if they could process her claim in two months time. Then she frowned, her own joke not even funny to her. Even if they could process her claim in time, she wouldn't accept one red cent from Dino. Not one red cent. Not from that snake.

But why couldn't she stop thinking about that snake? Nikki felt horrible after he angrily left her office, as if a part of her was about to be lost forever again. For the rest of the day she could hardly function. Even Sebastian told her that she was wrong, that regardless of her feelings about Dino, that didn't change the fact that he was a bishop worthy of respect. Then he wanted to know why she had such strong feelings against his new pastor. But Tam, as only Tam could, turned his attention away from Nikki and back on her. Not that her rescue was necessary. Nikki wasn't exactly in the mood for giving out details anyway. She was in too much pain, pain she couldn't even explain anymore, pain that she knew was eating her alive.

Instead of dwelling any further on it, however, she decided to sleep on it. A little nap, an hour tops, was all she needed. She'd rest and not think about Dino, or his touch, or his kiss, or the way he made her feel just at the sight of him. But Nikki's plan didn't work. She spent an hour lying on her sofa and doing exactly what she declared she wouldn't do: think about Dino. And his touch, and his kiss, and even his *smell*. She couldn't believe it. And as for Jamal, as for that other headache in her life; if he didn't return soon, she'd have no choice but to get into her car, find him, and drag his disobedient, trifling behind back home where he belonged. That was her final thought as she finally began to drift off.

Nikki woke up nearly eight hours later, just before six in the morning, to the sound of knocks at her front door. At first she opened her eyes and stared at the room around her, as if she didn't quite know where she was. Then she quickly got her bearings and hurried for the door.

It was Ollie Curtis, one of the deputy sheriffs in the county; a young man in his late twenties with big, blue eyes and a friendly smile. Nikki was quick to realize that he wasn't smiling this time.

"What is it, Ollie?" she asked, opening the screen door wider. "Did somebody break into the diner?"

"No, Nikki. Nothing like that."

"What is it then?"

Ollie hesitated. "It's Jamal."

Nikki's stomach plunged. "Jamal?" She nervously raked her hand through her hair and tried to remember if her son had already come home.

"I'm sorry, Nick."

"What are you sorry about? What's happened, Ollie?" Nikki was getting frantic and Ollie immediately realized his error.

"He's okay. He's not hurt."

"He's not?"

"No. But . . . he's in trouble."

"Ollie," Nikki said, trying with all she had to remain composed, "tell me what's happened."

Ollie exhaled. "There was a killing tonight, Nikki—"

"A killing?" she interrupted.

"William Coleman. Dollar Bill Coleman, you know, from the football team?"

"Of course I know him, Ollie. What's happened? Tell me what's happened!"

"Somebody gunned down Dollar Bill over in Pottsburg. Shot him dead on the spot, and Sheriff Peete seems to think . . . the sheriff seems to think that Jamal was the shooter."

At first, Nikki stared at him. Then she shook her head.

She knew she had to have heard him wrong. "You can't mean that, Ollie. You don't mean that."

A grave look came over Ollie's round, cherubim face. "He's been arrested for the murder of William Coleman."

Nikki continued to shake her head. She couldn't even begin to understand such crazy news. William Coleman was dead? The greatest athlete in Monroe's history was dead? And they were saying that Jamal, *her* Jamal, was responsible?

It felt as if the breath had been knocked out of her. And she fell to her knees.

SEVEN

Dino leaned back in the executive chair in his office and let out a booming laugh. Wallace, who was seated on the edge of his desk, laughed too. Dino had been in town for only a couple weeks, but already he was beginning to feel as if he was getting somewhere.

"I'm telling you the truth, Bishop," Wallace said. "Every time Pastor Crane would stand up to give his sermon, ninety percent of the church would go to sleep. And I'm not talking about no lil' ol' catnaps either. I'm talking loud, bear-sounding snoring all over the church, from little old ladies to big burly men. It wasn't sermon time, it was bedtime. I expected members to start bringing pillows and blankets to church on Sunday mornings." Dino laughed again. "I ain't joking. It was that bad."

Dino then let out an exhausted exhale. "It sounds pitiful. How could that man call himself a preacher and not be concerned about lost souls?

And how could Bishop Thorndike not report such behavior? I agree with you, Reverend, it was bad. Still is, really; because we still don't know the full extent of the problem."

Wallace shook his head. "I thought y'all knew, Bishop; I declare I did."

"And thought we didn't care?"

Wallace hesitated, then nodded. "Right."

Dino understood. "I'll take the blame for that. I rarely got in the field. I didn't have time, really. That's got to change."

Loud knocks were heard on his office door and Dino glanced at his watch. He'd only been in his office thirty minutes, but break time, he supposed, was over. "Yes?"

The door opened and Brother Curry, looking flustered, hurried in.

"Where's Sister Maxwell?" Dino asked, referring to his secretary.

"She wasn't at her desk, sir; but this couldn't wait. I've got some horrible news. Just horrible."

"What's the matter, Brother Curry?" Wallace asked.

"Dollar Bill Coleman is dead, sir."

Wallace quickly jumped to his feet. "*What*?"

"William Coleman is dead."

"Dead? But how?"

"He was shot late last night. Out in Pottsburg. They say he died right there at the scene."

"Good Lord." Wallace ran his hand across his bald head. "Have mercy, have mercy! We've got to do something." He looked at Dino "We've got to get over there, Bishop; to the Colemans' house. I saw that boy just yesterday, talked to him and everything just yesterday. The picture of health."

"Who is he?" Dino stood. "Was he a member here?"

"Yes, sir," Brother Curry said. "His whole family is."

Wallace shook his head. "I saw him just yesterday."

Dino grabbed his suit coat from behind his chair and began heading for the exit. "Tell me about him."

"One of the nicest young men you'd ever wanna meet," Wallace said. "The closest thing we've ever come to a local hero. He's a senior . . . he *was* a senior in the high school here, and the best football player this county has ever seen. And when I say the best, I mean the best. Played running back the way Jim Brown played it. That's the kind of comparisons he's been getting. Every major college in the country wanted him, and I'm talking the big boys: USC, Ohio State, Florida. Now he's . . . now he's *dead*?" Wallace shook his head again. "It's unbelievable."

As Dino, with Wallace behind him, approached the door, Sister Dardell hurried into the office, looking frantic too. "William Coleman's been murdered, y'all!" She couldn't get the words out fast enough.

"We're on our way over there now," Wallace told her. "Brother Curry, notify Deacon Frye and tell him to meet us at the Colemans' place. This family is gonna need all the support they can get. They were expecting their son to be a multimillionaire NFL star in a few years. Now he's dead? And murdered?" Wallace's head-shaking continued.

They all headed out of the door and began walking through the secretary's suite, with Dardell leading the way. Dino was right behind her, and Wallace behind him. It felt like a funeral march; a tragedy of the young. Almost too awful to mention, though Dardell had no problem talking about it.

"He got shot down like a dog, right over there in Pottsburg," she said. "Like an old mangy dog. But thank God they caught his killer. Arrested that good-for-nothing Jamal Lucas."

"Jamal Lucas done it?" Wallace asked. "What a tragedy."

"Who's this Jamal Lucas?" Dino asked, putting on his suit coat as he walked.

"Kid from around here," Wallace said as if he wasn't surprised at all. But when he added, "He's Nikki Lucas's son," Dino, in the middle of flapping down his suit collar, stopped in his tracks, causing Wallace to bump into him.

Nikki's son? Did he say *Nikki's son*? Dino didn't even know she had a son. He whirled around to face Wallace, to make sure this wasn't another one of his ill-timed jokes, but there was no humor on Reverend Wallace's distraught face. A young man had been murdered, seemingly the town's hope and glory, and this mystery son of Nikki's, this child she so conveniently failed to mention she had, stood accused as the murderer. There was no humor in that kind of news and even good-humored Wallace wasn't trying to find any. It was enough to slap the smiles off of everybody's face, especially Dino's. He knew the hurt and shame that the mother of the accused had to be going through right now. Nikki was no tough lady of steel as she so artfully pretended to be. This would devastate her. This could throw her into a state of panic that her stubborn disposition might not be able to get her out of.

But he couldn't allow it to devastate him, or to throw him. At least not now, not when there was a family that needed to be consoled and he was duty-bound to console them. That was why he turned back around and kept on walking. His face was markedly pained and anguished, not as a bishop displaying grief over the tragic loss of one of his members, but as a man with a past; a man who had a strong suspicion that he was about to come face-to-face with nothing short of the torment of the damned.

The Monroe County Police Department had never seen the likes of this. Every available deputy was on duty, taking phone calls from angry citizens who wanted to know if it was really true, if Dollar Bill Coleman was really dead.

Then they wanted to know just when the hanging of that murderer, Jamal Lucas, was to convene so they could be sure to attend. They were judge and jury and didn't care. And Sheriff Jeremiah Peete did nothing to try to dissuade them.

Sheriff Peete sat down behind his desk, his burly six-three frame almost too large for the large chair, and sipped from his piping-hot coffee. His hair, once blond, was now white as snow, and his light green eyes were bloodshot from his being jostled from bed far sooner than his normal five A.M. wake-up time. He'd kept the lid on this thing all night, not even notifying the Colemans until early this morning. He wanted to make sure that when he did make notifications, when the news did hit the fan, that he had his men on the job and his own act together. Now the maelstrom was here. The phones were ringing nonstop and the statewide press was making no secret of their intentions to besiege the once-peaceful town for every angle of the story they could get their grubby little hands on. Even the mayor had called, offering more assistance as if he were trying to make sure that Peete was up to the job. Peete wasn't sure himself, but he told the mayor that he was.

He also told Ollie, who stood at the foot of his desk as nervous as he was excited, to send Nikki Lucas on in.

Nikki quickly rose from the chair just outside of Peete's office, a chair she had been occupying for nearly three hours, and hurried inside. Ollie had been kind, even sitting down and talking with her when she first arrived, but he was the only member of the force who had been. All of the cops ate at the Big Turn, every one of them, and they all knew Nikki well. But now they were looking at her as if they didn't know her at all. They acted as if she plotted and planned this awful tragedy; as if she wouldn't move heaven and earth to see William Coleman walking around happy and alive again, and her son safely back home where he belonged.

She walked up to Peete's desk, with Ollie right behind her, and was about to launch into her defense of her son, but Peete held up a hand.

"Save it, Nikki." There was hate in his eyes. It surprised her at first, although she should have known it would come to this. The fact that he had made her wait three hours to see him should have told her something. But even if it didn't, the look on his face now said it all. Jeremiah Peete, who was her friend yesterday, was no friend of hers today.

"I want to see my son," Nikki said firmly.

"I'm sure you do," Peete replied, staring at her. Exhaustion could be seen in her big, stricken eyes, and it was all just getting started. "But you can't see him, Nikki; my deputies already told you that. You need to just go on home and—"

"Home?" Nikki was astounded that he would even suggest such a thing. "I've got to see my son, Peete. I've got to see for myself that he's all right. I want . . . I *need* to see my son. Don't you understand that?"

Peete exhaled. "Look, Nikki, I know what you want and need. We all want and need. The Colemans *really* want and need. But right now it's not going to happen. That boy of yours is still being processed and won't be seeing anybody today. Now, don't you understand *that*?"

Peete had always been one of her best customers, always complimenting her on the excellent food and service. Those days, Nikki was coming to realize, were gone. "He didn't do it." Her voice was unwavering.

Peete nodded. He'd heard that too many times before. "Sure he didn't."

"He didn't!" Nikki was fighting the urge to lose control. "He couldn't have."

"Well, I say he could have and he did. He was a ticking time bomb waiting to explode and you know it. You even told me yourself that he was a problem; that he was always hanging around with those thugs in Pottsburg, which, incidentally, is where this crime occurred. So don't stand up here now and act like Jamal is some angel, because you, me, and every living soul in this county knows that that boy of yours is a long way from angelic."

"Now you wait a minute, Peete—"

"No, you wait a minute!" Peete's brewing anger brought him to a standing position. "You didn't see the look on Bessie and Jimmy Lee's faces when I had to tell them that they won't be seeing their child again. Bessie nearly died where she stood. She'll never be the same again. So excuse me if the cause of that grief isn't somebody I particularly want to help right now."

"But Jamal didn't do it! You know he wouldn't kill anybody. Think about what you're saying, Peete! You're saying Jamal killed somebody!" Nikki had to calm down before she could continue. "You're right. I can't begin to know how the Colemans must feel. I can't begin to even imagine their sorrow. But I know my boy. And I know he's not capable of causing that kind of pain."

Peete quickly disagreed. "I say he's more than capable. And around here, what I say is what counts. So you need to get on home now, Nikki, and let us do our job. There's nothing you can do here today."

"Why can't I just see him for one minute, Peete? He's gonna wonder why I haven't come to see about him." Nikki was near tears, a state Peete certainly had never seen her in, and he was sorry about it. But it wasn't his fault.

"He should have thought about that before he did what he did, Nikki. Now excuse me."

It was a dismissal, no mistaking that. Ollie even touched her on the arm to help escort her out. Nikki snatched away from him. "I'll get a lawyer," she threatened, although she already knew what good that would do.

"Get a lawyer," Peete said without missing a beat. "Heck, get ten lawyers! But not one of them will be seeing Jamal today. Not today. Out of respect for Dollar Bill Coleman, not today!"

The anger in Peete's voice was undeniable and so unflinching that Ollie took Nikki's arm again. "Come on, Nikki," he said.

Nikki snatched away from him again, her eyes unable to leave the sheriff's. "Jamal has his issues, Peete," she said. "Lord knows he has issues. But he would never have killed anybody. Never. I don't care what you say!" Anger, pain and fear assaulted her unlike she'd ever experienced in her life. Nikki looked at the sheriff a moment longer before she walked out of his office.

She drove in a near daze to the diner Tam had graciously opened in her stead. Tam had been nearly hysterical when Nikki called her this morning with the news. Like Nikki, Tam immediately knew that Jamal didn't do it, and she wanted desperately to go with Nikki to the police station to let Peete know it too. But Nikki refused the offer, figuring she could handle Peete herself, and asked Tam to open up the Big Turn instead; to at least try and carry on as if there could possibly be some semblance of normalcy left in their lives.

She parked in front of the diner and sat in her car for a few minutes longer, feeling everything but normal. Her mind was still unable to believe that this nightmare was really taking place. They were telling her that her son was a murderer, that the boy she birthed could kill another human being, and she couldn't even see his face to let him know that she knew better than that. Her son wasn't some animal and they weren't going to convince her that he was.

But she was powerless to do anything about that right now. Powerless to even afford a proper defense for her son. This was Monroe, and in this town, Jeremiah Peete was the law. And as far as the law was concerned, Jamal's conviction was as certain as poor William Coleman's death.

Nikki got out of her car and walked into a noisy diner that was suddenly blanketed by near complete silence as her customers realized who was now amongst them. Some spoke to her, as they always did, particularly those out-of-state truckers who wouldn't know Dollar Bill Coleman from a dollar bill. But many others whispered and pointed and behaved as if she couldn't see, hear, or even feel their disgust. Nikki ignored them, the way she knew she was going to have to do if she stood any chance of keeping her sanity, and kept on walking to her office.

It wasn't entirely surprising to her when Tam and Sebastian, the only two people in this world she knew she could always count on, were in her office in a flash. She was just sitting behind her desk.

"Who's minding the store?" she asked them.

"We're minding it," Tam said. "Are you all right?"

Nikki wanted to cry. She wanted to tell her friends that all right was the last thing she was, but she couldn't do it. This mess was her mess and she'd deal with it her way. "I'm okay."

"You look awful," Sebastian said.

Tam quickly hit him in the rib with her elbow. "Don't mind him, Nikki. Did you see Jamal? How's he holding up?"

"We don't believe for a second he killed that boy," Sebastian added.

Nikki shook her head, her thick ponytail barely clasped in the loose-fitting barrette. "Peete wouldn't let me see him."

"He wouldn't let you see him?" Tam said. "Why not?"

"He said Jamal is still being processed. They've had him all night, but he's still being processed."

"That sounds like Peete," Sebastian said. "He can be something else when he wants to be. I remember when I first came back to town from New York, satisfied that my career would wait until I tended to Mother. He treated me as if I was the scum of the earth. He said, 'What career? You bombed in New York, that's why you came back, so don't you dare try to act like you're some big Broadway star leaving it all behind for dear old Mama. Mama my behind! Broadway star my behind!' And those weren't the exact words he used either. He can be just horrid when he wants to be."

"What are you gonna do, Nick?" Tam had a worried look on her face.

Nikki exhaled. "I'm going to sit down and balance these receipts."

"Nikki!"

"What can I do, Tam? Peete is the law. He's got my boy, and he won't let me see him. He even told me that getting an attorney won't help. So please tell me what am I supposed to do because I don't know."

Tam and Sebastian looked at each other. They didn't know either. All they knew was that this was a mess, a fine mess Jamal had somehow managed to get himself and, by default, his own mother, into.

"He has a right to an attorney, I know that," Sebastian said. "That's the law."

"Peete is the law around here, Seb," Tam replied, "and you know that too. I say Nikki should go to the newspapers, get some publicity behind her cause."

"And what cause is that?" Nikki asked. "The cause of freeing the man every newspaper from here to Miami is probably already declaring murdered a football star?"

"But there's got to be something you can do."

"There's nothing, Tam, all right? Nothing. Now if y'all will excuse me, I really need to get this work done." Nikki looked at them, daring them to question her any further.

Tam wanted to continue, certain that if they thought about it long enough that they could come up with something, but Sebastian urged her out of Nikki's way. Nikki was a basket case. It showed all over her strained face, and reminding her of the hopelessness of her situation wasn't going to help. When they left, Nikki leaned back in her chair and slung her head back. Once again, her son was paying the price for her sins; for having the unfortunate bad luck of being born to a powerless, insufficient, incredible loser of a mother like her.

It was a long morning and Nikki could barely function for worrying about Jamal. Even when she was able to put it in the back of her mind and concentrate on other matters, some customer would whisper something or boldly say something loud enough for her to hear, and the dread would overtake her again. By noon, she'd had enough and told Sebastian she was going home.

Only she didn't go home. She couldn't. Instead, she went back to the police station and tried again to get Peete to change his mind. This time, however, Peete wouldn't even see her, telling her through Ollie that she was wasting her time. Pigs will fly, he told Ollie to tell her, before she sees Jamal today.

Nikki got into her VW and leaned her head against the backrest, fighting tears with all she had as she sat outside of the Monroe Police Department. Jamal was in the kind of trouble she'd never even dreamed he'd get into. Her greatest fear, all those times when she came home from work only to find him not there, was that he'd get shot, that one of those thugs he loved to hang out with would do him harm. It never even occurred to her that he would be the one to harm somebody. Not Jamal. He was always taking in stray cats and feeding them, and helping the little kids with their wrecked bikes. He was a good-hearted boy, a kind young man who once told her that he didn't like to fight; but now he was in the fight of his life.

She prayed. For the first time in her adult life, she actually closed her eyes and began to pray to God Almighty for help. Jamal needed help. He didn't need her pity, her pain, or her anguish over his horrifying situation. He needed help.

Nikki kept saying, "Jesus, help me; Jesus, help me," over and over until it almost sounded like gibberish to her. She didn't even know how to pray! But only God could help them now and she kept on praying anyhow. She leaned her head on her steering wheel, and prayed and prayed.

Until it happened.

It wasn't a bolt of lightning, but it was sudden enough, as if the answer to her prayer was there all the time. *Dino*. He popped into her mind like a sudden flash across her brain, and her eyes flew open. Dino. Why hadn't she thought of Dino before? By far, he was the most powerful man she knew. He could at least use some of that considerable authority to help Jamal, and to help her get in to see him. Instead of fighting the fact of the matter, instead of obsessing on the heart of the matter, Nikki thanked God Almighty for bringing Dino to her remembrance and cranked up her VW, knowing that her wounded pride had to take a backseat this time.

As much as she hated to admit it, Dino was the answer to her prayer. Jamal needed him regardless of how she felt about it. Nikki decided then and there to forgot all of that old mess that was still tearing her apart, and concentrate on this new mess that had consequences far beyond any heartbreak ever could. She steered her car along the square and headed straight for New Life.

EIGHT

The small block house on Amsterdam Road seemed lively from the outside. Numerous family, friends, and members of New Life hovered around the porch, lawn, and sidewalk, talking and remembering all they could recount about William Coleman. Reporters with their cameras and notepads were also outside and the people didn't hesitate to tell how they felt, how a dark day had descended on Monroe, and how Jamal Lucas, the cause of the darkness, had to pay.

Inside, the house was like a tomb. Silence engulfed every room. Bessie and Jimmy Lee Coleman, both in their early fifties, both stricken with grief at the loss of their son, were seated together on the small sofa. Other family members sat passively around the living room and at the table in the adjacent dining room. Dino was at the head of the table, his reading glasses on as he reviewed a photo album someone had placed in front of him. It was an album filled with clippings of William's brilliant high school football career. Reverend Wallace sat beside Dino, his bald head constantly shaking every time he thought about the magnitude of the loss. No words were being spoken. They had already said enough. Dino felt that condolences could only help just so much. At the end of the words, somebody's child was still gone.

Dino felt unsettled as he reviewed those clippings, as if he was intruding into the life of a young man he'd never even met before. He was a smart, handsome young man with broad shoulders and an infectious smile; a talented young man who should have had his entire life ahead of him. Who was he to take a peep at that? Who was he to think that photographs alone could go beyond the surface and tell him anything substantive about that boy's life? And the silence didn't help. The silence only magnified the intrusion.

That same silence didn't break until the front door opened and Luke Granger, the short, dark-skinned mayor of Monroe, stepped inside. Everybody, including the Colemans, seemed to sit at attention when he walked in, forcing Dino, who'd only met the mayor once since he'd been in town, to pay attention too.

"Bessie, Jimmy Lee," the mayor said as he hurried over to the grieving parents. He clasped their hands with his and sat on the coffee table in front of them. "I am so sorry."

Bessie and Jimmy Lee nodded their appreciation and listened. They listened with anguished looks on their faces as the mayor waxed nostalgic for a young man whose life was cut too short. Others started talking too, all about their precious moments with William, with many of them calling him 'Dollar Bill' so often that it caused Dino to lean toward Reverend Wallace and quietly ask him why.

Fond memories prompted Wallace to smile. "It was his gridiron nickname. One of the local sports writers got it started. One day after William had scored four touchdowns in a game against one of our staunch rivals, the journalist just started calling him Dollar Bill Coleman. He wrote that when William got the ball, it was like money in the bank. The name stuck because it fit. Because it was the truth."

Dino nodded and looked at the mayor. "He acts as if he's pretty close to the family."

"Granger? I don't know about close, but his daughter, Sharon, was dating William."

"Dating him? Oh. I see."

"Yeah. I'll bet she's devastated. Her and her crowd. They were all raised right there in New Life too."

Dino wanted to ask about Jamal Lucas, and if he was in church anywhere, but from the snippets he'd been hearing so far about how unruly a child he was, he doubted it and decided to keep his interest to himself.

The mayor spoke again. "I tell you, I've gone over this here thing a thousand times and I still can't believe it."

"It feels so strange," Bessie said as Jimmy Lee grabbed her small hand. "We just don't understand it. How can anybody want to murder our son?"

"It wasn't some anybody," Jimmy Lee said, a bitter twang in his voice. "It was that Jamal Lucas. That boy always been trouble, always driving around town with those gangsters from Pottsburg, getting into all kinds of trouble. I used to tell William to stay away from his kind. I told him that a boy like that don't mean no good. And William listened to me and he told me okay, that he wouldn't have nothing to do with Jamal Lucas. That's what kind of boy he was, Mayor Granger. He listened to his daddy."

Mayor Granger nodded. "He was a good boy, Jimmy Lee."

"Yes he was!" Jimmy fired off in a grief-stricken tone. "A fine boy. Unlike that Jamal Lucas. Nikki didn't half raise that juvenile delinquent right, and now look what's happened."

Dino's heart sank at the mention of Nikki's name, at the indictment of that name.

"Stop blaming Nikki, Jimmy Lee," Bessie said with her own touch of bitterness. "This ain't her fault. She was a child when she had that boy. She was just a young, single mother who did the best she could."

"Well her best wasn't good enough!" Jimmy Lee was unwilling to let go of his anger. "If it was, we'd still have our boy here with us. She shouldn't have had no babies if she couldn't raise 'em right. She knew that boy of hers was trouble. Sheriff Peete said she even told him so herself. But what did she do about it? Nothing, that's what! Now look what's happened!"

Mayor Granger was shaking his head. "You're only telling the truth, Jimmy Lee. We got to tell it like it is. I'm sorry, Bessie, but there's no excuse for this."

"Amen!" a few other family members chimed in, all equally disgusted with the Lucas boy.

"But I'll promise you this," the mayor continued, knowing that he had a captive audience, "I plan to do everything in my power, and I mean everything, to make sure that Jamal Lucas goes from jail to prison and never again sees the light of day."

The proclamation brought applause from many of his listeners. Dino, however, could only look back down at the photo album. At the life of a boy that stopped mid-cheer. And all he could think about was Nikki. All he could think about was how in the world was a fragile creature like her, somebody who'd die before she would let on that she was even in trouble, going to handle a tragedy like this?

They didn't want her there, Nikki could see it in their grim faces, but that was their problem. Jamal needed help and she wasn't about to let some sour faces and bad dispositions stop her from getting him that help. Dino wasn't in, which made it worse. And his secretary, Sheila Maxwell, a woman who had always treated Nikki cordially, was now acting so nasty with her that she decided to wait.

Sheila didn't like it. She told Nikki over and over that Bishop Cochran wasn't expected back any time soon, but Nikki still sat right there in her office, daring her to do something about it. She'd wait all night if she had to. She had to see Jamal, and Dino was the only person she knew who could at least come close to making it happen.

It wasn't all night, but it was nearly two hours later when Dino came through the door of his secretary's office, heading for his own. He couldn't see Nikki at first entrance, because she sat in a chair against the backside wall. But she saw him. He walked slowly, not bothering to say a word to Sheila Maxwell. And Sheila, although she put herself out as this powerful secretary to this powerful man, seemed afraid to say a word to him. Nikki almost wanted to smile at the sight of her glancing at her boss, as if she wanted desperately to make nice with him and prove to Nikki just how in-crowd she was. But seeing his face changed her mind. Dino sometimes came across as very unapproachable. Nikki could see how this was one of those times.

But it was more than that. He didn't look like himself despite being dressed to the hilt in a dark green suit that fit him so well; so well that it looked as though it had been stitched on to his muscular body. But his eyes were drooping more than usual, and his face seemed drained of its customary intensity. He was grieving William Coleman's death, Nikki surmised. He might just hate her too.

She almost froze where she sat, content to stay out of his way given his mood, but she couldn't. Jamal needed him. "Bishop Cochran," she said as she stood, unable to keep her voice from quivering.

Dino turned at the sound of that voice and gave her a look that was, at first, frightening in its harshness. Then, as if seeing the hopelessness that filled her eyes, his eyes became almost soothing. He exhaled sharply, as if she were a sad sight to see, then he gestured for her to come to him.

Dino placed his hand on the small of Nikki's back as he ushered her into his office. He could see Sister Maxwell staring as he turned to close the door, her eyes quickly averting his when he looked at her. After closing the door, he turned and scanned Nikki. She looked so distraught and devastated that his already tormented heart dropped. He had not bargained for this when he came to Florida. He thought it was all about confronting a church and their demons; not his own.

"I need your help, Dino," Nikki said before he could say a word. Then she frowned. "My son . . . I have a son . . . and my son needs your help." There was a pause as Nikki tried hard to suppress the tears that were trying to stain her lids. "They've arrested . . . they've arrested . . . he's been arrested for William Coleman's death, for his murder, and they won't let me see him. I know he didn't do it, Dino. I know him, and he couldn't have done it. Please help him."

A sense of shame washed over Dino as he watched Nikki beg for his help. Why was life so harsh to her? Why!

"Nikki." His voice was so flustered that she shook her head.

"I should have looked for him," she said.

Dino stared at her. "It's not your fault, Nikki."

"I've always looked for him. I've always gotten right back in my car and looked for him, no matter what.

That's how he stayed safe, because I looked for him. I told him to stay home, but he never . . . he didn't listen to me. But I would always go out and find him. That's how he stayed safe. But I was so tired last night. I was so . . . I'm just so tired." She looked at Dino. Tears began to fill her devastated eyes.

Dino's chest tightened in anguish, and he pulled her forcibly into his arms. The look on his face was now one of iron determination, as if his will alone was going to make everything all right. "It's all right, sweetheart," he said, pain searing him. "It's going to be all right." He held her as she clung to him, and his eyes were tightly shut in silent prayer. She was his responsibility. Somehow, from the moment he first laid eyes on her sixteen years ago, he knew she was. He prayed to God Almighty for the courage to do right by Nikki, to not fumble that responsibility this time.

They walked into the Monroe County Sheriff Department and right away, Nikki could see the difference. There were no harsh looks at Dino by the deputies, no nasty remarks under their breaths. And when Dino told the desk clerk that he wanted to see Sheriff Peete, and told him who he was, there was no delay in Peete hurrying out of his office and greeting them. Nikki stood beside Dino, her small frame dwarfed by his large one, and she still wanted to feel his big arms around her. She still wanted to feel that connection to him. It was odd for Nikki to feel this way; she'd always been this woman who made it her business never to depend on anyone, but she couldn't seem to help herself right now. She just couldn't shake that sense of neediness that had overtaken her when she cried in his arms.

"It's an honor to meet you, Bishop," Sheriff Peete said, extending his hand long before he even reached Dino.

He was no fool. He was an elected official. He knew that New Life was the largest church in town and with many of the town's most influential citizens, almost all of whom voted. "I've heard so many positive things about you, sir."

"Hello, Sheriff." Dino shook his hand. "How are you?"

"I've seen better days, I'll tell you that. This is quite a mess we've got going on in our county right now."

"You've arrested Jamal Lucas." Dino stated it as a fact, not a question.

Peete glared at Nikki, then fudged a grand smile at Dino and said, "He's here. He's been booked for murder." The last sentence came with some emphasis and he shot another glare at Nikki when he said it.

"We're here to see him."

"I'm afraid that's not possible, Reverend."

"I'm afraid it is."

Some of the deputies in the reception area glared at Dino when he made such a bold statement. Then they looked at the sheriff, certain he wasn't going to stand for that. But Peete, again, was no fool. He smiled.

"I don't guess it'll do any harm in letting him talk a few minutes with a man of God. Probably just what he needs, considering. Yeah, I don't see any problem with letting you see him, Reverend."

Dino placed his hand on the small of Nikki's back and pulled her slightly in front of him. Nikki suddenly felt warm and protected by his touch, a touch she now needed.

But Sheriff Peete felt cheated, and was about to object stringently. *You, but not her*, he was going to say. Until he saw that look in Dino's eyes. The man didn't look like any preacher he'd ever known. He didn't have that humbled, downcast look many of them had. With Dino, Peete didn't see the humility. There was something dangerous about the man, something volcanic about that fiery look in his eyes that reminded Peete of that same look he'd often seen in the eyes of hardened criminals.

He glanced around at his men, many of whom were waiting to see if their boss would stand up to the likes of Nikki Lucas (bump that preacher), and his anger swelled. Because he couldn't just *bump* that preacher. Because he'd heard that Cochran wasn't just some acting pastor, but was the head of the entire organization, head of the multi million dollar nationwide family of New Life churches. How could he bump that kind of power with the campaign season just months away? His men wouldn't understand, but he did.

Instead of giving in verbally to Dino's silent demand that Nikki be included too, he acquiesced without words, turning to show them the way.

Dino stood with his back against the dingy wall, his arms folded, head leaned back, eyes nearly hid from view, while Nikki couldn't keep still. She paced the floor in her tight blue jeans and white jersey, looking so young to Dino that he couldn't even imagine that she could be the mother of a teenage son. But time hadn't stood still for Nikki, just as it hadn't for him. She wasn't that kid on the corner anymore. Neither of them were the same.

The door creaked open and Jamal Lucas walked in slowly, looking around, his big, brown eyes first on the stranger standing against the wall, and then on his mother. When Dino saw Jamal, when he saw this gangly kid who looked so familiar that it stunned him, he unfolded his arms. And when their eyes met, when Dino was able to take in the full measure of the young man, his heart fell. He was grateful when the kid looked away.

When Jamal looked at his mother, sadness seemed to overtake him. He hadn't planned on crying, Dino could tell by the way his lips trembled as if he was fighting it still. He hadn't planned on showing any kind of emotion. But as soon as he saw Nikki, as soon as he saw the anguish in her eyes, he lost it. He broke down right where he stood and Nikki, her heart in her shoe, knocked over a chair getting to her son. She grabbed him and pulled him into her arms, grabbed this boy who was taller than she was, and Dino's stomach plunged. He had expected to see some foul-mouthed thug, a hard nose, hard to handle and completely out of control hothead. Instead, this kid shows up. This tall, lanky kid with a look of terror, rather than toughness, all over his handsome, devastated face.

Nikki was crying as she held on to her son, and they eventually stopped hugging each other and began wiping the other's tears. "Are they treating you right, Jamal?" she asked, touching his arms and his face and looking him all over, as if she just knew they'd been unkind.

Jamal nodded that he was all right. Even if he wasn't, he would have nodded that he was anyway. Then, as if he'd revealed more than he'd ever intended, the boy's look changed. "What took you so long?" There was a sudden flash of anger on his face, causing Dino to observe him even closer. "Why you didn't come see about me?"

"They wouldn't let me, Jamal," Nikki said, an uncharacteristic plea in her voice.

"They would have let you if you would have tried hard enough."

"I tried all I could."

"I bet you didn't even take a minute off from work. I bet you was at that precious diner the whole time I was rotting in here."

"That's not true!"

"It is true! They probably would have let me out if you would have been here. Now they haven't even set my bail yet and I gotta rot another night in this jive-behind place."

"I did all I could, Jamal. Peete wouldn't let—"

"Ah, I don't even wanna hear that wang. I would have been out of here—they even said so—if you would have showed up. Now I'm stuck here. All because of you!"

Dino quickly pushed away from the wall and moved with a controlled anger toward Jamal and his mother. Jamal looked at him, at this big man with the muscular physique; at this live wire coming toward him in his thousand dollar suit as if he had it going on like that. And that nervousness Jamal felt when they first locked him up began to overtake him again. At first he thought Dino was his lawyer. But looking at him, at that intensity in his eyes, made Jamal doubt that now. He was too much like those brothers behind the bars. Too intimidating to be anybody's mouthpiece.

His concern didn't ease when Dino grabbed him by the collar and slung him against the door. Nikki shouted Dino's name because of the sheer ferocity of his quick movement, but Dino's eyes stared unflinchingly at Jamal. "Who do you think you're talking to?" he demanded. "That's your mother, boy; not one of your schoolyard friends. I don't care if she never came to see you, if she left you rotting in this place for all eternity, you will continue to respect her as your mother. She didn't put you in this predicament. Your disobedience put you in this predicament. She did everything she could to try and get these few minutes with you, including coming to me, which, I assure you, was not what she would have chosen to do if she'd had a choice. She's been so worried sick about your little butt, worried out of her mind, and you're talking as if she couldn't care less?" In an attempt to regain his composure, Dino let out a sharp exhale before continuing. "You're going to cut the pity party, sit at that table, and listen to your mother. Not whine like some punk, but listen. Do I make myself clear, young brother?"

Jamal's heart was pounding ferociously as he stared at Dino, as he looked up at this big man who held him by the catch of his collar as if he were as light as paper; at this strange, tough-acting man who so quickly came to the defense of his mother. No man had ever done that before. Not one time in Jamal's entire life. But this man, who looked like one of those stone cold gangsters Jamal had always admired, was different. He wasn't the kind of brother who could be gamed. Jamal could see it in his eyes.

"Do I make myself clear?" Dino asked again, this time jerking on Jamal's shirt.

"It's clear." The words came quick, and Jamal swallowed hard after speaking them.

Dino stared at the young man a moment longer, at the sadness behind those bright brown eyes of his, and then he released him. He felt odd, exposed for some reason, as he gestured for the boy to take a seat.

Jamal sat down at the small table and Dino pulled back a chair so that Nikki could sit across from him. Instead of sitting himself, however,

Dino unbuttoned his suit coat and began a slow, deliberate pacing in the back part of the room. Jamal looked beyond his mother and stared at Dino. He walked like Morgan Freeman did when he got out of the joint in *Shawshank Redemption* and was walking the streets trying to figure out a way to get back in. He had that same thoughtful look on his face, as if some internal war was going on, as if this meant more to him than just helping a sister out. And Dino looked like it bothered him that it meant more. He plodded along, seemingly lost in deep concentration.

Excitement swelled within Jamal at the thought that this man could be his mother's new boyfriend; that she could have finally found herself a real man. And that maybe she'd finally get off of his back.

"Are you sure they've been treating you okay?" Nikki asked. "You look so tired."

"They been all right, Ma. They just all mad about Dollar Bill and think I did it. They all think that."

"What happened last night, Jamal? Why didn't you stay home like I told you to?"

"I was tired of staying up in that house!" His tone caused Dino to glance at him. Their eyes met again and Jamal shuffled in his seat. "I mean, I just went out, that's all."

"What happened?"

"I was hanging out in Pottsburg like I always do, shooting hoops with some of the guys. Dollar Bill was out there too. Him and Shake was kind of tight."

"Were you tight with Dollar Bill too?"

"Not really. I mean, I took a lot of classes with his girl, Sharon, and he knew me from that, or from when I was with Shake, but never just me and him hanging; nothing like that."

Nikki gave her son a sidelong look. "What? He thought he was too good to hang out with you?"

"I'm sixteen, Ma. He was a senior. He considered me a kid. No seniors be hanging out with no sixteen-yearolds."

"Sharon is sixteen and he hung out with her," Nikki pointed out. "But she was female and beautiful and the mayor's daughter. I guess that made the difference."

"Whatever. I ain't none of that."

"What about the shooting?"

"What about it?"

"How did it happen, Jamal?"

"It didn't happen. Not while I was there. Dollar Bill and Shake were kind of off talking about something, and me and the other guys kept shooting hoops. The guys were thinking about driving over to some club in J-ville, but I knew you was already gonna pitch a fit about my being in Pottsburg. I knew Jacksonville was out of the question, so I started walking on home."

"Before any shooting went down?"

"Before anything went down. I heard some gunshots while I was walking home, and I was curious about it, but I wasn't about to go back and see what was happening. Besides, they didn't even sound like they came from the basketball court. Then I heard sirens heading for Pottsburg and I figured something had happened. But I kept on walking. Then when I was just a block from home, when I was almost there, I heard those sirens coming my way. Coming for me. They slung me in the car and said I killed Dollar Bill. They said I was gonna go down hard for killing Dollar Bill. Ma, I didn't kill nobody. I swear I didn't!"

Nikki grabbed Jamal's hands. "I know. Honey, I know it. And don't you worry, I'm gonna get you out of this."

"But how? They haven't even set bail for me yet, and when they do, it's gonna be so high there's no way you gonna be able to afford it. They gonna see to that. They want me to rot in here, Ma."

"Don't say that," Nikki said.

Dino knew the boy was right. He heard it straight from the mayor's mouth himself. He walked over and stood at the head of the table.

He looked at Jamal. "Have you told this story to the authorities yet?"

Jamal looked from Dino to his mother, expecting an introduction. Nikki was caught short by what she should have expected all along, and had to settle her sudden nervousness before she spoke. "Jamal, this is Bishop Cochran."

Jamal's heart dropped. "*Bishop* Cochran? You mean he's a preacher?"

"Yes. He's the acting pastor of New Life. We knew each other back in Detroit, before I came to Florida and met your father." Nikki and Dino exchanged a glance.

Jamal looked at Dino too. "What does a bishop want with me?"

"Don't you talk to him like that," Nikki said defensively, although Dino certainly didn't need her defense. "If it wasn't for him, they wouldn't have let me see you at all today. And that would have killed me, Jamal."

Jamal looked at his mother and the agony all over her pretty face. He nodded Dino's way. "Thanks, man."

"What have you told the authorities?" Dino's demeanor was one of all-business all the time, although Jamal had only to look into his eyes to tell that wasn't true.

"What do you mean?"

"When they booked you and interrogated you, did you tell them that story you just told your mother?"

"So they could twist around my words and act like I confessed? No way. I didn't tell those jokers nothing. They tried to pry it out of me, threatening to give me the death penalty if I didn't talk and all that crap, but I wasn't about to get into no game with them."

Dino liked the kid's tenacity and smiled a smile so brief Jamal didn't catch it. "Okay," Dino said with a nod of his head. Then he began his thoughtful, concentrated Morgan Freeman pacing again.

It was late evening by the time they left Jamal. They stepped out into the fresh evening air and Dino exhaled. Nikki, however, was still wound tight. Dino looked at her, at the way she seemed a million miles away, going through the motions of life rather than even thinking about living.

Instead of heading for his car, which was parked in front of the sheriff's department, he placed his hand on her lower back again, and steered her along the sidewalk. "Let's walk, Nikki."

The streets were quiet, as many of the town's shops closed early on weekdays. Other than the occasional car driving past, all they could hear was the heavy step-down on the concrete of Dino's leather-soled shoes. Nikki looked at those shoes, at how big his feet were, and then she looked up at Dino. She wanted to thank him for getting her in to see her son, but the words wouldn't come. She hated that she couldn't do it herself. She hated that Dino had to throw his weight around just to help her and her son. She hated that the secrets and lies she'd been bearing alone for all of these years were about to blow up in her face. The truth would come out, she knew; every bit of it. But not yet. Because she wasn't about to risk Dino's alienation until her son was out of harm's way.

They ended up in Remington Park. At this time of evening, ducks and birds were more common than people. Nikki and Dino sat on one of the park benches that overlooked an elongated, peaceful lake. Nikki sat on the bench seat, while Dino sat up on the back top of the bench itself, his expensive black shoes plopped down on the seat.

"He's a good looking kid, Nikki," Dino said.

Nikki nodded. "He certainly thinks so."

Dino chuckled at that. "He's got quite a few girlfriends, I take it."

"Not really. Nothing serious anyway. He'd go out with one occasionally, but Jamal's always been more fascinated with Shake and that thug life out in Pottsburg. In that crowd, females are just somebody to have fun with, not to hang out with."

"Who is this Shake?"

"The leader of the pack. Some chump. I only met him once and didn't like him one bit."

"What didn't you like about him?"

"He's a thug, Dino. A straight-up thug. A bad news brother up and down. I told Jamal what time it was with him, but he didn't wanna hear that. He seems to think that I don't know what I'm talking about; that I've lived some kind of sheltered life and—"

"*You*?" Dino said with a broad smile.

"The boy is gone, I told you. Yes, me. He thinks I don't know anything about street life when it's actually the other way around. He's the one who doesn't know a thing."

Dino nodded. Then he exhaled. "Nikki?"

She hesitated. His tone had changed. "Yes?"

"What about his father?"

Nikki's heart slammed against her chest, but she did manage to speak calmly. "What about him?"

Dino didn't respond to that. He just stared at Nikki's profile, where her high cheekbones, small nose and almost eternally puckered lips, gave her the look of an angel. She knew what he meant. He could tell it by the way her jaw tightened.

Nikki knew she couldn't tell Dino the truth. Not yet. What if he denied it and insisted that she was trying to flimflam him out of his money? What if he refused to help Jamal anymore? The truth could open a can of worms that could not only devastate Dino, but could hurt Jamal even more. And for Nikki, doing that was not an option. "He's not yours," she said almost harshly, and then looked back and up at Dino. His look was so intense, so scrutinizing, that she couldn't hold his gaze. She turned back around. "His father's dead. He died when Jamal was a baby."

Because of where they sat, neither could see the other's facial expression. But both looked stricken with unimaginable concern. Instead of saying another word about it, they quietly, reflectively, looked across the park at the beautiful lake beyond them.

NINE

The diner was only half-full, which was unusual at lunchtime, but everybody knew the reason why. Nikki worked feverishly, almost maniacally, determined to personally handle each and every one of the customers. It was as if the fact that they had showed up to eat at the Big Turn at all meant that they hadn't condemned her son. Tam and Mookie did all they could to help Nikki's drive for excellence that day. Even Fern tried to do her fair share. Sebastian worked the register.

"She's in denial," Sebastian told Henry, who had just rolled his wheelchair from the kitchen and was staring at Nikki's mania. "Those customers are all she has right now, and she's doing all she can to hold on to them."

"Light crowd today," Henry said.

"And probably everyday until after the trial. Monroe can be cruel, and its residents are some of the most unforgiving, judgmental people I've ever met. You should have seen the way they treated me when I came back from New York. I was weird to them, and I guess that made me somebody to be avoided, simply because I had the flair of an actor."

"Yeah. When I got in this wheelchair they didn't wanna have nothing to do with me either; like I had it coming or something. But thank God for Nikki."

"Oh yes. She gave me a job when no one would give me the time of day. But that's Nikki. Always taking in strays." Sebastian smiled and looked back at Henry, but he didn't seem to care to be portrayed that way. He rolled back into the kitchen without responding. Sebastian shrugged his shoulders and watched as Tam, looking exhausted, lifted the hatch and came behind the counter.

"She's gonna work herself to death," she said.

Sebastian nodded. "That's the idea. Not death, of course, but something that feels like it."

"She saw Jamal last night."

This surprised and pleased Sebastian. "Really? I thought she said they wouldn't let her. You mean to tell me Sheriff Peete actually did something as human as changing his mind?"

"Nothing that dramatic. He had no choice. Bishop Cochran went with her, and you know he wasn't turning down Bishop."

Sebastian raised one of his thick eyebrows. "This sudden altruism of our pastor . . . I do not understand it."

"What's to understand?" Tam asked in a lame attempt to make sure that the secret of Nikki and Dino's past remained secret. "He's just a man of conscience, helping a sister out."

"Even if that sister is not a member of his church? Even if that sister is the mother of the young man who allegedly killed a member of his church? *Hello*? I wasn't born two days ago."

"I suspect you wasn't born at all," Tam replied. "My guess is that something dropped you down on us. Something green and ugly, and with *beam me up* powers. The brother from another planet; that's you."

"Then what are you? The sister who can't even be from another planet because they didn't want her either?"

"That's lame, Seb."

"That's me, Tam."

"Knock it off; both of you," Nikki said harshly as she came behind the counter. "Let's not run away the few customers we do have."

Tam looked at Nikki. "Things will pick up. Don't worry, honey." Nikki nodded, although it was obvious to both Tam and Sebastian that she didn't believe that for a second.

The door to the diner chimed as Dino and a very tall, very striking woman walked in.

"America the beautiful has arrived," Tam said snidely, a little disturbed by this development.

Nikki couldn't help but stare. Dino had on another one of his expensive tailored suits, and the woman, all dark, leggy and smiley-faced, had on a gorgeous business suit of her own. The skirt of it was so short it was almost indecent. She appeared younger than Nikki, maybe in her late twenties. And she had that high energy walk about her that made her seem something that Nikki never was: carefree. Yet, what caused jealousy to prick Nikki wasn't the lady's beauty or vitality, but that Dino had his hand on the small of the woman's back, the same way he had touched Nikki the day before. Just seeing it felt so uncomfortably painful that Nikki grabbed a cloth and began wiping the counter top, busying herself again.

"Hello, Bishop," Tam said with a smile.

"Hello, Sister Ellis. Brother Dobbs."

Sebastian grinned. "How're you doing today, Bishop?"

"I'm good." Dino looked at Nikki, who was not even attempting to meet his gaze. "Hello, Nikki."

Nikki looked up, and that pained look in her dark green eyes caused Dino to shift his weight and to remove his hand from his companion.

"Hi." Nikki's smile could only fool someone who didn't know her. But Dino knew her.

"I want you to meet Ida Fox," he said.

Recognizing the name, Tam immediately elbowed Sebastian.

"She's Jamal's attorney," Dino concluded.

That got Nikki's attention and her face transformed, suddenly hopeful. "His attorney?"

"Yes. She flew in from Detroit late last night."

Ida stepped forward. "I saw your son, Miss Lucas. He appears to be a fine young man."

"You saw Jamal already?"

"Oh yes." Ida had a smile that could charm a dead man back to life. "Dean insisted that I see him as soon as he met my plane. That's the reason he had me flown here." She seemed disappointed that that was the only reason.

Nikki ignored her disenchantment. "How is he?" she asked.

"Wonderful. As I said, he's a fine boy."

"Let's go to your office for a few minutes, Nikki," Dino said. "Ida needs to give you some information."

Nikki nodded, glanced at Tam and Sebastian, and then ushered Ida and Dino down the hall that led to her office. Once inside, she closed the door and offered one of the chairs in front of her desk to Ida. Nikki took the other one. "Is there something wrong?" She looked from Ida to Dino.

"Nothing's wrong, Nikki," he assured her as he walked over to the desk and sat in the chair behind it, looking as if he belonged there.

Ida leaned forward. "Miss Lucas—"

"Nikki, please."

"All right, Nikki. Dean is right, there's nothing wrong. In fact, everything's better than could have been expected at this very early stage. I was able to get the bail set."

Nikki sat erect. "You were?"

"Yes. And I have one of the best private investigators in the country ready to descend on Monroe and do a little digging . . . a lot more than the police will ever bother to do."

"A private investigator?" Nikki asked.

Dino could see the concern in her eyes. He knew she was worried about the price tag, and her very next question validated his thoughts.

"How much is this investigator going to cost?" Her question was directed to Ida. "And how much is Jamal's bail?"

The woman opened her briefcase and pulled out some papers. Her hands looked soft, as if she'd never known a hard day's work in her life. In her younger days, Nikki used to despise women like Ida; those that always seemed to be so blessed while people like herself had to scratch and claw for everything they got. But now she knew better. If somebody had offered her a chance to go to college and live the easy life, she would have taken it too.

"The PI's rate," Ida paused to look down at her papers, "is four hundred per day, plus expenses."

"Four hundred a day?" Nikki asked incredulously. "Four hundred *dollars*?"

"Very reasonable, I assure you, considering his normal fee. He normally charges five times that amount. Easily. Trust me; this is virtually pro bono work for him."

Nikki smiled and shook her head. What else could she do? She could barely afford to get her car registration renewed and this woman was telling her to hire an investigator that cost a cut rate fee of four hundred dollars a day!

"And as for Jamal's bail," Ida added. "It's been set at five hundred thousand."

Nikki's jaws dropped. "Five hundred thou—"

Ida smiled. "No no; you misunderstand me. All you'll need to come up with is ten percent of that. Only fifty thousand."

Nikki stared at Ida. Was this woman from America? Where did she think Nikki was going to get fifty thousand dollars from? "Look, Miss—"

"Please call me Ida."

"Look, I don't have fifty dollars right at the moment. There is no way on earth that I can come up with fifty thousand dollars! Couldn't it be lowered?" Nikki looked to Dino for help, but he didn't say a word. He just stared at Nikki, wondering painfully just how hard it had really been for her.

"Surely you can come up with it, Nikki," Ida said, as if everybody had it so easy.

"Really now?" Nikki folded her arms. "And how do you suppose I do that?"

"Nikki," Dino said by way of warning, seeing her temperature rising.

"No. She's telling me what I can come up with. So I want to know just how I'm coming up with it."

"I thought you could get a second mortgage on your home, or this diner here." Ida said with uncertainty. It was her turn to look to Dino for help, but Dino was still staring at Nikki.

"You thought that, did you?" Nikki said. "Well, you thought wrong. I'm about to lose this diner you think is a goldmine, Miss Ida, and my house is already in hock up to its equity from all those years struggling to be able to keep this goldmine open. And you're talking to me like four hundred dollars is four cents, and fifty thousand is fifty cents!" Nikki exhaled to calm herself down. "I'm sorry," she said. "I'm especially sorry for Jamal, because he's the one who's going to suffer thanks to my failures. But I don't have it. I can't even afford to pay *your* fee."

Ida shot a look at Dino. The two of them went back some years, and she cared deeply for him. But working for free was going too far.

Dino stood to his feet, as if upset by the entire conversation. "I'm handling all of the fees," he said as if it should have gone without saying.

"Including Jeff Islick's?" Ida asked.

"Including the PI, yes. All of it."

"So I can give him the okay?"

"I told you that when I phoned you last night, Foxy. Yes. Give him the okay."

Nikki caught it, she caught the almost scandalous little nickname he called the woman, but she was too steeped in her own troubles to borrow more. "How am I gonna pay you back, Dino? I've never had that kind of money in my life."

Dino frowned and began heading for the door, and Ida, as if she were his lapdog, gathered up her briefcase and began hurrying too.

"What?" Nikki stood up and asked, confused by Dino's sudden need to leave.

"Did I ask you to pay me back, Nikki?" He looked at her over his shoulder.

"You didn't have to ask me. When people loan me money, I know it's got to be paid back."

"Did I once say anything about a loan?"

Nikki hesitated. "No. But I don't take charity."

"Fine. Don't take it. I'm not giving it to you. It's for the boy." There was harshness in his voice and he didn't wait for her to reply. Dino stormed out, leaving Ida to scramble behind him.

Nikki sat back down, flustered and confused. If she didn't know any better, she would have thought Dino was offended that she never once thought that he would be responsible for what was clearly her responsibility. If it were true, it was wonderful. But how could it be true?

What was true, however, was Dino's word. She got the call less than two hours after he left the diner. It was Jamal, telling her that he was in the bondsman's office and she could come and pick him up. Nikki was so ecstatic that she left the diner in a blur, forgetting her car keys the first time, then forgetting her car as she hurried out of the diner the second time. She began running along the sidewalk, not caring that people were staring, not even clear where she was running to. It wasn't until Nikki had run nearly a block that she realized what she was doing, that she had keys, but no car. She ran back to her car, jumped in, and drove nervously, anxious to pick up her son.

When she arrived at the office, she wanted to hug Jamal as soon as she saw him. But she knew he didn't play that in public, not with the bondsman and his secretary standing right there. But once in the car, she grabbed his hand. "You okay, Jamal?" It was her third time asking.

He rolled his eyes. "I'm fine, Ma; goodness. I'm just glad to be out of there."

"Me too. I'm glad too, son."

She cranked up her VW and headed home. She would call Tam or Sebastian later and tell them that she wasn't coming back. Not today anyway. She kept glancing at her child who was in a pair of jeans and a regular white T-shirt. He looked as if he wanted to say something. "What is it?"

"What?"

"Come on, Jamal. What's the matter?"

"You mean other than this murder rap over my head?"

Nikki smiled regrettably. "Other than that."

"I was just wondering," he said without looking at his mother.

Nikki turned the corner and drove slower, deciding for once to obey the 25 mile per hour speed limit near the courthouse. "What were you wondering?"

"They said my bail was set at five hundred thousand dollars."

"It was."

"And that you had to get up fifty g's to get me out."

Nikki nodded. "That's true too."

"They didn't expect me to get out."

Nikki smiled. "That was their plan, I'm sure."

Jamal looked at his mother. "Where you get that kind of money, Ma?"

Nikki exhaled, thinking about Dino. "Didn't the bondsman tell you?"

"No. I didn't ask him either. That's not something I need to be talking to him about."

That sounded just like Jamal. He only wanted to know what he wanted to know. Even when he was two years old and asked about his father, and Nikki told him that his father was dead, she fully expected him to want all kinds of details. But he didn't ask her another thing about it. Not his name. Not how he died. Not what death meant. Nothing. All he knew was that his father was dead, and that was all he wanted to know. She looked at him. He was still that little boy.

"Bishop Cochran bailed you out, Jamal."

Jamal looked at Nikki. "Why?"

"I told you we knew each other back in the day. He was just helping us out, that's all."

"Ma, I'm not stupid, okay? What brother gonna give up fifty grand just to help a sister out? I don't care what kind of bishop he's claiming to be. What's his game?"

Nikki rolled her eyes. "What are you talking about, boy?"

"He likes you or something?"

Nikki shook her head. She thought about Dino with Ida Fox, another dark-skinned, leggy female just like his wife had been, neither attribute of which Nikki had. She also thought about how he called her *Foxy*. "Please," she said to her son.

"Please what?"

"Yeah, he likes me, Jamal. Me and my sexy ponytail. Or maybe it's my faded blue jeans. Him and his Italian silk suits. Me and my faded blue jeans. Yeah, he likes me all right."

Jamal looked back out of the passenger side window. "You don't have to be sarcastic."

"Stop looking a gift horse in the mouth, all right? Don't read something into this because there's nothing to it. It is what it is. He got you up out of there. Thank God for that and let's just get on home. Okay?"

TEN

Later that evening, Nikki was in the kitchen washing the dinner dishes, and Jamal was in the living room trying to watch *CSI*, when a car drove onto their driveway. Jamal got off of the sofa and walked over to the double-pane window. A black Mercedes was parked, but there was no immediate movement to get out. "Ma," he shouted, "somebody's here!"

Nikki came out of the kitchen and wiped her hands on a dishcloth she had tucked into the front of her jeans. Jamal opened the front door and he and Nikki stepped out onto the porch for a better view, both praying that it wasn't more bad news. When Jamal saw that it was Bishop Cochran sitting behind the wheel, his panic left and an odd sense of calm overtook him.

Dino was on his car phone, and Jamal smiled at how cool it was to have a man like him in his mother's life. He didn't care what Nikki said about her not being pretty enough or sophisticated enough for somebody like Cochran. Jamal knew better. He knew that no brother on this green earth would give up the kind of money that man had given up on his behalf just for old times' sake. Forget that. The brother wanted more.

Nikki looked beyond Jamal and her heart dropped at the sight of that black Mercedes. She knew that she would have to see Dino again, and thank him for what he'd done for Jamal; but somehow, she never dreamed it would be this soon.

Dino ended his phone conversation and got out of the car. It had been a long day. From dealing with New Life's tangled web to having dinner with Ida Fox and going over the facts of Jamal's case. All he wanted to do right now was go to his hotel room and get some sleep. But he needed to see Nikki and make sure she was all right. He walked up the steps onto the porch. "Good evening." He tried to smile through his weariness. "How's it going, Jamal?"

"All right." Jamal was glad to see Dino, but afraid to show it. "Thanks for getting me out of there."

Dino looked at the boy, at his narrow eager face that made him look younger than sixteen, and nodded. "You're welcome. Just stay out of trouble and do exactly what your mother says."

Jamal smiled. "Yes, sir."

Nikki looked at him. He'd never shown her that level of instant respect, and it bothered her that Dino would so easily be awarded the honor. She looked at Dino. "I appreciate it too, but I want to work out a repayment plan."

Jamal rolled his eyes. "For fifty thousand dollars, Ma?

Dino smiled. "We'll work something out, Nikki." He moved his gaze from her body to her eyes. Nikki found herself looking directly into those eyes, something she could never do without considerable unsteadiness. But Dino wasn't all that steady either, and he, like she, quickly looked away.

"Wanna come in, Mr. Cochran?" Jamal asked. When he saw a hesitation in Dino, he added, "Or we could sit out here."

That sounded more acceptable to Dino since he had no intentions of lingering around Nikki any longer than was necessary. He took a seat in one of the chairs on the porch. Jamal sat down next to Dino, but Nikki took a seat on the top step, turning sideways with her back against the banister post. A part of her wished that Jamal had kept his trap shut and allowed Dino to go on his way. But another part of her was pleased that Jamal had spoken up and that Dino had stayed.

"Glad to be a free man?" Dino asked Jamal.

Jamal smiled. "For real. I didn't think I would ever get out of there. It was weird."

"Was it your first time in jail?"

Jamal hesitated. "Yeah. Kind of." When he saw both adults looking at him, he added, "I mean, I've been down there before a few times, but I never had to stay all night or nothing like that."

Nikki scoffed. "You would have stayed all night if I wouldn't have gone and got your butt."

"But I didn't stay all night, did I?" As soon as Jamal said those words, he screwed up his face in disappointment with himself. Nikki was all he had, and he knew it; but sometimes he treated her as if everything wrong in his life was all her fault. He looked at Dino, half expecting him to jack him up the way he did in the jail, or tell him about himself, but Dino, somewhat to Jamal's dismay, didn't even bother. Instead, Dino leaned back and crossed his leg. Jamal looked at his shoe. "What's that? Stacy Adams?"

Dino smiled. "Ferragamos."

"What?"

"Ferra . . . Italian," Dino said.

"Oh, okay. They cost a little more than Stacy Adams then, huh?"

Nikki rolled her eyes.

"I would imagine so," Dino answered.

Jamal nodded his approval. "They're cool. My mother, as you can tell, don't believe in spending money on name brand shoes. She thinks it's stupid."

"You like name brand shoes?" Dino asked.

Jamal smiled. "Yes, sir. Every kid around here does."

"My suggestion, then, is that you get a job and buy yourself a pair."

Jamal's smile dissolved, but Nikki grinned widely. "School is his job right now," she eventually said. "If he can just get through school without any more interruptions, I'll be grateful."

Dino shook his head. "I'm afraid there're going to be more interruptions before this trial is over."

Nikki looked at him. "How bad is it?"

"It's bad, Nikki. Jamal is facing a murder charge, and the victim isn't some nameless, faceless thug on the corner, but the town's hero. And this town is angry about it."

"I know. They've known Jamal all his life, but they're acting like it was only natural that he would kill somebody. Like I raised him to be this monster that could do something like that."

Jamal looked down. "It's not your fault, Ma."

"That's not the way the folks round here see it. In their view, I created the monster, which makes me just as bad. I've lost half of my customers at the diner already." When she said that, Dino looked at her. "But I'm not even trying to worry about them. If they're like that, I don't want their business anyway." Nikki exhaled. "I just want this over with."

"Ida told me tonight that it's a winnable case," Dino stated.

"You saw her tonight?" Nikki asked before she realized it.

Dino considered her, seeing the uneasiness too. "We had dinner."

Jamal looked at his mother, knowing that that bit of news wasn't exactly welcoming. He'd seen Ida Fox when she visited him earlier that morning. His mother didn't stand a chance if a woman that beautiful was in the running.

Although it couldn't be seen on her face, Nikki was seething with jealousy at just the thought of Dino with that woman. Her envy disturbed her. Why should she even care? But she did care. She was beginning to realize just how much. "Miss Fox thinks it's winnable?" she managed to ask.

"She believes it's possible. We'll fully investigate Jamal's story, minute by ever-loving minute, to make sure every possible lead is exhausted. That's where Jeff Islick, the PI we hired, will come in."

"You hired a PI?" Jamal asked.

"Yes."

"But why? I told y'all I didn't do it."

"And the jury may believe you, Jamal. But they also may not. We've got to make certain the jury believes you."

Jamal leaned forward, feeling that sense of dread again. "One of those deputies said I could get the death penalty."

Nikki looked nervously at Dino. "They can't give no child the death penalty. Can they, Dino?"

"He won't get the death penalty. But if they decide to try him as an adult, he could very well get life."

"Lord have mercy," Nikki said so painfully that it made Dino's skin crawl. "Life in prison?" She looked at Jamal. "How can they even consider—"

"It's all right, Ma," Jamal said, braver than Nikki could ever hope to be right now. "Mr. Cochran ain't gonna let that happen and you know it. Are you, Mr. Cochran?"

Nikki and Jamal looked at Dino as if they would burst unless he spoke. He felt as if he was on trial himself, and they were his jury. "You have a great lawyer and a great team of investigators," he said casually. "They'll do all they can."

It wasn't quite what Jamal had hoped to hear. He wanted to hear that *Dino* would do all he could. Irrational, he knew, but his entire demeanor around Dino, the only human being to ever intimidate him, wasn't exactly normal either.

An SUV drove up, an older model Ford Explorer, and stopped behind Dino's Mercedes. The man who got out of the vehicle was tall and handsome. He appeared to be in his late thirties, and had an easy smile and a confident gait. He was wearing jeans and a Denver Broncos T-shirt. "Good evening, folks. It's a beautiful day in this neighborhood."

Right away, Jamal didn't like him and he gave the man a look that could only be classified as a sneer. Nikki, however, was reserving her judgment.

"Can I help you?" she asked.

"You can if you're Nikki Lucas."

"Who wants to know?"

The stranger smiled. "I'm not the police, okay? You look as if you think I'm bearing bad news or something."

"What are you bearing?"

"Enough money to rent that room you have available."

Dino frowned. "What room?"

"Ma's renting out one of our bedrooms," Jamal said distastefully. "Like that makes sense."

Nikki looked at her son. "That's none of your business, Jamal."

"It is my business. I have to live with these strangers too."

"Shut up, I said."

Jamal angrily looked away from his mother. Nikki knew the deal. She knew she needed every dime she could get her hands on; especially now. But somehow, she could never get Jamal to understand the true state of their financial affairs. She looked at the stranger. "You want to rent the room?"

"I most certainly do. I'm new in town. I'm working on that new homes construction site on the edge of town, and will need a place for a few months. I can pay in advance."

Dino's heart dropped at the mere thought of that good-looking brother living under the same roof with Nikki and Jamal. It felt disturbing to Dino, as if some other man would be taking care of his responsibility; some other man would be all involved in their lives and he would be the outsider; some other man would have full access to Nikki any time he wanted. Dino was about to speak, in fact, to object, but Jamal beat him to it.

"You heard about me, right?" the boy asked the stranger.

Nikki glared at her son.

"What about you?" the man asked, still smiling.

"They claim I'm a killer, that I murdered somebody. I'm just out on bail."

Dino looked at the man. Surely, it wouldn't be his first time around a murder suspect.

"Yeah, I heard about it," he said. "Those folks at the Big Turn seem to think it's a bunch of crock. Won't bother me none."

Nikki smiled and was about to stand up to show the man the room, but Dino spoke, turning everyone's eyes toward him. "It's no longer available."

"It's not?" The stranger's smile faded.

"No, it's not." Dino looked at Nikki this time.

The man looked toward Nikki too. "I was under the impression that it hadn't been rented yet."

"You was under the wrong impression then, weren't you?" Jamal said with a laugh in his voice.

"I'm sorry." Nikki didn't know what else to say.

The man nodded and tried to recover his smile. "No problem." He gave Dino one last look, walked back to his Explorer and quickly drove away.

Jamal laughed.

Nikki frowned. "What's this about, Dino?"

"I'm renting the room."

"You?"

"Yes, me. What? Are there some qualifications I don't know about?"

"You know what I mean. You didn't even know I had a room for rent."

"I know now."

"And you want it?"

"How much are you renting it for?"

Nikki shook her head. "This is crazy."

"How much, Nikki?"

"Seventy-five dollars a week. Three hundred a month. But what difference does it make, Dino? The idea of you living in somebody's lil' tiny room is crazy. Come on."

"You think you know me like that, Nikki?" Dino said this as if it were a putdown.

She refused to back down, folding her arms and bobbing her head in demonstration. "As a matter of fact, I do. You're staying in a hotel in Jacksonville now, aren't you? Which one is it? No, let me guess. It's the Embassy-Carlton. You're telling me you're willing to give up all of that luxury to rent a room from *me*? Please."

"I'll double your asking price." Dino spoke as if Nikki had not said a word.

Nikki shook her head. "What does that have to do with it?"

"Ma!" Jamal jumped in. "What's your problem? He's gonna pay you double and you're acting like you don't want it."

"I don't want his money. And you stay out of this anyway!"

"But he wants to rent the room."

"Jamal!"

"He can pay easier than that joker that was just here."

"Didn't I tell you to stay out of this? Just go on inside. This is my business, not yours."

Jamal knew when to back off. It was all in the sharp edge of his mother's voice. He stood up and prepared to head back inside, but not before trying to get in the last word. "I still don't see—"

"Goodnight, Jamal!" Nikki said, amazed by his sudden great need to have Dino around—a man he'd only just met today.

"See you around, Mr. Cochran," Jamal said. "She's bugging."

Dino wanted to smile but suppressed it. "Do as your mother said, Jamal."

Jamal went on inside the house, but no farther than the front door. When he closed it behind him, he pressed his ear against the wood and listened.

"What's your problem, Dino?" Nikki asked.

Dino looked at her. "You have a room you want to rent. I'm willing to double your asking price. What's *your* problem?"

"My problem is that you're paying for Jamal's attorney. My problem is that you're paying for some big shot investigator that cost another fortune. My problem is that you put up all that bail money that's gonna take me a lifetime *plus* twenty years to pay back. That's my problem, Dino! Now you want to rent this little room in my little house and pay me double what I'm asking, and I'm supposed to smile and act like that's so big of you? Please."

"You're either the biggest chump this side of living, which I seriously doubt, or that guilt is kicking your behind so bad that you're willing to do anything to get it up off of you!"

Jamal's heart sank, certain that his mother's sharp tongue was going to send Dino flying out of their lives. He didn't know what she meant about the guilt, and she had to know that Dino was nobody's chump, but Jamal knew that Dino had a look about him that could chill the sun. He wouldn't put up with anybody's nonsense for long. Jamal leaned closer to the door, praying that his mother hadn't gone too far.

Dino stared icily at Nikki for longer than she would have liked, but her defiance forced her to meet his gaze and hold it. He was angry. She could tell it by the way his whole body seemed to have tensed to where his muscular arms seemed prime to break through the seam of his suit coat, and where the intensity in his eyes felt almost predatory. Yet, when he spoke, he spoke so calmly that it shook Nikki to her core.

"Your room for rent is no longer available," he said. "You wanted it rented and now it is. By me. Which effectively closes the matter. All right?"

"No, it's not all right," she said with concern on her face. "Why you doing this, Dino?"

He considered her before answering her. "I have my reasons."

"I'm sure you do," Nikki responded, resigned to the fact that with Dino, she could never win. "Okay; the room is yours."

Jamal quietly jumped up and down with joy. But he knew his mother. He immediately listened for more.

"But you can rent the room only if the money you've agreed to pay will go toward the money I already owe you," she added.

Dino tossed her that offended look he displayed when he came to the diner with Ida Fox. "No."

"But—"

"I said no, Nikki. One hasn't anything to do with the other." He stood up. "My checkbook is in the car." He began to move past Nikki to head down the steps.

"You haven't even seen it yet," Nikki said.

Dino looked at her, at her slender body first, and then at her flustered face. There was no way he was going to be able to live under the same roof with her. He was sure that she was just as aware of that as he was. "I won't be staying here, Nikki. Just renting the room."

"See." Nikki knew what he meant, but she was duty bound by her own sense of pride to deny it. "I knew this was nothing but charity."

"Call it whatever you like," he told her as he continued walking down the steps.

Nikki leaned her head against the post. She hated that she needed so much help, that she was nowhere near the self-sufficient sister she pretended to be. And knowing that Dino knew it was the worst part. The last person on the face of this earth that she wanted to know anything about her shortcomings was Dino Cochran.

Jamal was thrilled to his soul, thankful that Dino was man enough to stand up to his tough-as-nails, stubborn beyond belief mother. Any other brother would have hit the road, glad to be away from an *out there* female like her; but Dino didn't even lose his cool. Jamal liked that. He reminded him of Shake whenever they encountered trouble. Only Shake couldn't touch Dino. There was something great about Dino, something outstanding, not just because he was a bishop in a church, but because he seemed like somebody a person could depend on.

Jamal and his mother had been on their own for so long, struggling and having to depend only on each other when neither one of them was comfortable with that. It felt good to have somebody else in their corner, somebody else willing to ride the tide with them. Because no matter how crazy it seemed and how unexplainable his feelings were, Jamal couldn't shake the feeling that he, and especially his overburdened mother, needed Dino Cochran.

ELEVEN

"I don't know what you're talking about." Sebastian sighed. "I'm simply saying that a medium rare burger in this day and time is not a good idea, with the bacteria problem and the like."

The young man looked across the table at his buddy, and then looked up at Sebastian. "Bacteria? What you talking about, dude?"

"I'm just pointing out a fact of which I thought all human beings were well aware."

"What you getting at? You trying to tell me that I can't have a burger the way I like it?"

"No, I'm not suggesting that at all. I'm merely—"

"Then bye-bye, birdie." The young men laughed.

"Fine," Sebastian said as he quickly grabbed the menus from the table. "One death burger coming right up." He walked hurriedly behind the counter, yelling the table's order to Henry as he arrived.

Tam looked at him and laughed. "I'm surprised we have any customers left with you around."

"Am I wrong to warn the idiots?" Sebastian asked. "Am I wrong to point out what is obvious to anyone with half a brain?"

"People do what they wanna do, Seb. Besides, they can want it rare all they want. Henry knows the rules. That burger won't be burnt, but it'll be close."

Sebastian smiled. "True. I don't know why I even bother. I guess I just need some intellectual stimulation. Nikki used to be good for it. But lately, forget about it."

"She's worried sick about Jamal."

Sebastian nodded. "Don't I know it. It's like walking on egg shells when she's around. You don't know if you're going to say the wrong thing that'll set her off at any given moment. Where is she anyway?"

Tam sighed. "In the office giving Fern and Mookie a piece of her mind."

"What did Fern make the boy do now?"

"Child, let me tell you. Nikki told her to go into the kitchen and wash the dishes, right? Well, little Miss Thang tells Nikki no problem, then she goes right up to Mookie, in Nikki's face, mind you, and tells him that as soon as he finishes bussing the tables, she wants him to wash the dishes."

Sebastian laughed. "No, she didn't."

"Yes, she did. Nikki couldn't believe it. She yanked that little heifer by the collar and took her straight to the office. I said, 'You go, girl,' because if it was me, I would have kicked Fern and her block-long nails out on her behind a long time ago."

Sebastian nodded his head in agreement. "I don't know why Nikki puts up with her."

"Because Fern reminds Nikki of Nikki when she was that age. All feisty and tough. But I don't buy that. Nikki was never stupid with her swagger. She had plenty sense. You can look at her and tell that. She was savvy enough to own her own business at thirty. But Fern? That girl is young and as dumb as a cockroach trying to teach a trigonometry class."

"Two burgers, two fries up!" Henry yelled from the kitchen as he slung the two plates of food onto the pickup slot.

"Which one is medium rare?" Sebastian asked as he turned to reach for the orders.

"Pick one," Henry said and rolled his wheelchair away from the window. Sebastian laughed and headed for the table with his orders.

Nikki, Fern, and Mookie came out of Nikki's office soon after. Tammy could see attitude all over Fern's face as she broke off and headed for the kitchen. Mookie, looking not too grand himself, headed for the tables.

Tam looked at Nikki. "Tell me somebody got fired."

"Okay," Nikki said. "You got fired."

"I'm serious, Nikki. That girl don't wanna do anything, and Mookie's doing too much."

Nikki grabbed the coffee pot and poured herself a cup of coffee. "Mookie is helping his girlfriend; that's the way he sees it. Fern, on the other hand, I don't know what to say about that girl."

Tam shook her head. "She's a mess."

"A major mess," Nikki stated. "She doesn't even see where she did anything wrong. It's perfectly natural to her for Mookie to do her work."

"I like her, Nikki. Beneath all that attitude, she's a good kid. But this is about business. You can barely afford those of us who are working. You can't keep carrying around that dead weight."

Nikki sipped from her coffee and ignored Tam. She knew Fern was an unnecessary expense, as far as productivity went. But she knew too many girls like Fern. She could see that hunger in their eyes. If it weren't for this job, Fern would be out there big time, with Lord only knows how many kids, maybe even on drugs. Big Turn was all she had. Just like Big Turn was all Nikki had once upon a time, when she was a foolish single parent still trying to nurse a broken heart. There was no way she was firing Fern. Besides, it could all be moot anyway, if she didn't do something to increase her revenues and catch up those payments.

"Mookie?" Nikki called.

"Ma'am?" He hurried over to Nikki.

"Take down that card I placed on the bulletin board, the one where I was advertising a renter."

"Yes, ma'am!" Mookie said, going without question to do just that.

"What's this?" Tam asked. "You got you a boarder?"

"Something like that."

"It's that hunky construction worker, isn't it? He came by here yesterday to grab a burger. Told me he was looking for a place, but wasn't crazy about motel living. I told him about the room you had for rent. Is he the one?"

"He came by, yeah. But Dino, I mean Bishop Cochran, said no."

"Bishop Cochran?" Tam was surprised. "What did he have to do with it?"

"My sentiments exactly."

Tam smiled. "So he's Dino, is he?"

Nikki gave Tam a sidelong look. "I won't even dignify that."

Sebastian lifted the hatch and returned behind the counter. "Is he satisfied?" Tam asked, tossing a look at the boys sitting at the table.

"He was in such a deep conversation with his friend over there that he didn't even give that burger a second look. He just bit into it and kept on talking."

"He better thank God for cooks like Henry."

"I know that's right."

"What's this?" Nikki asked; but Tam nor Sebastian felt it worthy of an explanation.

Tam leaned against the counter. "Let's get back to Dino."

"Who's Dino?" Sebastian asked.

"Our pastor."

Sebastian frowned. "I thought his name was Walter Cochran?"

"It's Walter Dean Cochran," Nikki corrected.

Sebastian glanced at Tam, then back at Nikki. "But he's Dino to you, I take it?"

"We knew each other a long time ago, Seb, okay? Curiosity satisfied?"

"Not quite. What exactly was the extent of this knowledge?"

Tam laughed.

Nikki rolled her eyes. "We were friends, okay?"

Sebastian shook a finger at Nikki. "No. Not okay. You know why? Because I am Sebastian Dobbs, once considered a young James Earl Jones. So spare me, please. I do not believe for a second that you and *Dino* were friends at all because, number one, that man is considerably older than you, Nikki. And number two, and pardon me if this sounds crass, but you don't exactly look like somebody a man like that would shoot the breeze with. If you dig my drift. Now, he might do other things with you—"

"Seb!" Tammy said.

"I'm just saying. He just doesn't strike me as the type of man who'll put up with a type like Nikki."

Nikki smiled, although sadness crept in. "I'm a type now?"

"A type?" Sebastian said. "Honey, you're a piece of work. A veritable jigsaw puzzle! And excuse me, but I just don't see Pastor Cochran putting together the pieces."

"We have really strayed far off into left field here," Nikki said, hoping that Seb was wrong. "I said Dino and I were friends back in the day, and you're calling me a puzzle and assigning him the task of making me whole. It's ludicrous."

"Ludicrous? Isn't he a rapper?"

"Seb!" Tam said. "Can you be serious for two minutes?" Then she looked at Nikki. "So Bishop Cochran said you couldn't rent to the construction hunk?"

Nikki nodded. "Right."

Tam folded her arms. "And why not?"

Nikki jumped defensive. "How would I know?"

"But the guy had the money, Nikki, and he seemed good peeps to me."

"I felt the same way. That wasn't the issue."

"Wait a minute." Tam looked confused. "You wanted to rent a room. You wanted somebody who was decent and could afford to pay for it. You found both qualities in Mr. Hunk, but Bishop said no?"

"Right."

"But why?" Tam asked, her hands clasped as if begging for a more plausible explanation.

"He was a hunk, honey," Sebastian said. "You said it yourself. *Dino* is nobody's fool."

"I see," Tam said with a smile. She would not have minded giving Cochran a try herself, but she was nobody's fool, either. She knew his interests were definitely elsewhere, specifically in Nikki's direction.

"No, you don't see," Nikki said, hoping to quickly squash that notion. "That's not it at all, trust me. I just think he didn't feel I should be renting a room out to some stranger, that's all."

"But you said you rented the room," Tam said. Then she caught herself. "Wait a minute. *He* rented the room?"

"Now that's breaking news," Sebastian said and turned toward Nikki.

"He rented it, yes," Nikki admitted, "but it's not like what y'all mean."

"What are you talking about?" Sebastian asked. "What do we mean?"

"He's renting the room, paying me double the asking price, in fact; but he said he's not going to be staying there."

Tam and Sebastian looked at each other, and then they looked at Nikki.

"Come again?" Tam said.

"He's going to pay for the room, but he's not going to live in it."

"That's stupid," Tam said.

Sebastian disagreed. "I understand it."

"You do?" Nikki asked. "Then enlighten me, please."

"It's quite simple, really. He's a bishop, the head of a religious organization. He wants to avoid even the appearance of evil."

"Oh, come on. The man would have been renting a room from me, nothing more. Who in this whole wide world could see evil in that?" Then she looked at Mookie. "You found it yet, baby?" she asked him.

"Not yet, ma'am," Mookie said, staring hard at the bulletin board. "But almost."

"Well?" Nikki turned back to Sebastian and Tammy. "Who could misinterpret a man renting a room from a woman?"

"Narrow-minded people who think all us Christian folk are hypocrites," Tammy said.

"In other words," Sebastian said, looking Nikki dead in the eyes, "people like you."

Tam laughed. Nikki couldn't help but laugh, too. "Forget y'all," she said just before heading back to her office.

The Ford Bronco runs a stop sign. And then there's the crash, like ramming into a brick wall. But the Bronco tries to keep going, tries to plow through that wall. Dino is driving, and a woman is on the passenger side.

She looks at him, amazed that he could be so careless, that he could keep trying to break down a brick wall. "*Help me, Dino*," she pleads, over and over. "*Why are you hurting me?*"

It's the same voice, the same dream Dino had dreamed for sixteen long years. Only this time, the anguished face was no longer Sophia's, no longer his wife's, but it was Nikki's face now. As soon as Nikki turned to look at Dino, as soon as she mimicked, *help me, Dino* with her beautiful, puckered lips, the sound of knocking was heard. Odd, out of place knocking.

Dino woke up with a start, lifting up his head in terror. When he realized that it was only a dream and that he was not transplanted back into that night sixteen years ago, but was in his hotel suite, he laid his head back down. Dino pinched his temple with his fingers and tried to re-regulate his breathing, praying to God that the dream would end. And that was when he realized that the knocking he'd heard was real.

Getting out of bed, he put on his green silk robe. When he walked through the sitting area, opened the door, and saw that it was Ida, he began to finally relax. "Hey."

"I took a chance that you were still awake," she said. "Looks like I chanced out."

"No, it's okay." He opened the door wider. "Come in."

"If you insist." Ida smiled as she moved past Dino and walked into his room. She was dressed in white pants, a sleeveless red silk blouse, and a pair of three-inch stilettos, making her almost as tall as Dino. "You were asleep, weren't you?"

"Hardly," Dino replied. "Have a seat. What would you like to drink?"

"Wine?"

"You know me better than that. Non-alcoholic beverages are all I cater."

Ida laughed. "Nothing for me, love." She sat down on the sofa. "But you look like you could use a fat shot of caffeine. You look like you've been asleep for about a year."

Dino smiled warily and sat down beside her. "Caffeine is about the last thing I need." He looked at her. "What about you? You okay?"

"Think so. Just trying to handle the remains of the day. This neck of the woods isn't exactly my neck of the woods; know what I'm saying?"

Dino nodded. "I know. Did I thank you for coming?"

"You thanked me." Ida gave him a sly look. "Of course, I would have come anyway."

"Oh, yeah?"

"Oh, yeah. You see, I'm a sucker for this guy . . ."

Dino hesitated, then leaned back and crossed his legs. "Any word on when Jeff plans to hit town?"

Ida didn't like the way he so easily changed the subject, but she played along. "He's here. He came in earlier today. He and his men are already on the case."

Dino patted her lightly on her knee before he could stop himself. He quickly removed his hand. "Good work."

"Not as big a coup as it might appear. He owes me one."

Dino laughed. "Who doesn't?" Then he paused before speaking again. "How bad is it?"

"I told you it was a winnable case."

"That doesn't tell me anything. How bad is it?"

Ida exhaled. "I've got to bring my A game; let's put it that way." They glanced at each other, and then looked away.

Ida hesitated before speaking again. "She's more than a friend, isn't she?"

"Who?"

"The mother. Nikki."

"She's a friend."

"A friend with benefits?"

Dino could not believe she'd said that. "Of course not!"

"I don't mean it that way," Ida quickly interjected. "I mean, as concerning the heart of the matter."

Dino didn't respond.

"That's why I came by tonight," Ida continued.

"You came by because of Nikki?"

"Because of the way you look at her. Because of the way my position in your life, which I was hoping would be a little more secure by now, may be slipping even further in the ratings."

"Foxy—"

"I know, Dean, I know. You have enough to do running all of those churches. I've heard it a thousand times. I know."

"You say you know, but every other week, it seems, I'm having this conversation with you. My life right now is serving the Lord. That's what I do. That's my purpose and that's my calling. That's why I believe I'm alive. How many ways do I have to tell you that, honey? This isn't some job for me. This is my life. I get home at night and I'm so exhausted I can barely get to bed. I take you out occasionally, we spend time together. But I told you the deal."

"I know you did. And I don't mind being number two behind your work. But after seeing you and this Nikki Lucas together, after seeing the way you looked at her, I feel I need to make sure that I'm still number two."

Dino leaned his head back. "You aren't listening to me."

"Yes, I am."

"No, you're not. There is no number two. This isn't a game, Foxy."

"I didn't say it was. But how do you think I feel? You're putting all of this money up for this woman's son. You're sending for me and Jeff Islick and all the best for this woman. I'm no fool, Dean. You don't play that. You let people fight their own battles; that's always been your style. But you have no problem whatsoever fighting hers? That tells me that something more than an old friendship is going on here." She paused, mainly to get control of her emotions. "I've known you for nearly six years now. And I've been waiting for six years."

Dino closed his eyes. "I didn't tell you to wait."

"I know you didn't. You didn't have to. It's all on me, all right? But that doesn't lessen the pain."

Dino opened his eyes and looked at Ida. She was a good friend, a good woman, who'd been there for him for years. He leaned over and placed his hand across her shoulder, leaning her to him. "You've been a friend, Ida, a very good friend to me," he said, then lifted her chin so that she could look him in the eye. "But I told you then, and I'm telling you now, that is all it will ever be."

Ida held back an urge to cry. Then she leaned up and away from Dino. "She's a friend and I'm a friend?" she said, looking back at him.

Dino nodded. "Yes."

"Okay," Ida said and began to rise to her feet.

Dino rose too, his eyes never leaving hers, certain that she had more to say than that. When she opened her mouth to continue, which he knew she would, he braced himself.

"Can I ask you one question? Then I'll go peacefully back to my hotel room where I belong, and continue to prepare for the case."

He hesitated. "What is it?"

"If you do decide to take it to that next level, and I understand that you won't, but if, by chance, you decide to do so, will you go to that next level with me? Or with her?"

Dino studied Ida. She was one of many females he considered a friend. And she was also one of many females who wanted more than a friendship from him. But none of them stood a chance; none of them came even a long-distance second to his service to the Lord. None of them. Except the one he shouldn't have even remembered. "Her." His answer was blunt.

Ida felt as if she'd just been sucker-punched. She wanted to lash out, to tell him that no way was she going to sit back and let some hillbilly like Nikki Lucas take him away from her. But she only nodded her understanding. There was a time and a place for everything. And this was neither. But in time, she would stake her claim. And Nikki Lucas and any other female with designs on Walter Dean Cochran, wouldn't know what hit them.

TWELVE

One week later, almost a month after he first arrived in Monroe, Dino parked his Mercedes on the driveway behind Nikki's VW and stepped out. It was a cool Saturday morning, with a stiff noreaster that forced him to button his suit coat as he walked across the driveway to the steps of the porch. He had a key to the house, Nikki had insisted he take one, but he didn't use it.

When he rang the doorbell and waited, Nikki and Jamal answered together as if they were a tag team. "Good morning." He was a lot cheerier than they. Both mother and son appeared groggy and were still in their bed wear. Dino looked at Nikki, in her oversized yellow pajamas, and Jamal hovering over her as if he was the man of her house. He was still in his pajamas too. "Did I wake you?"

"No,"Jamal answered.

"Yes," Nikki said. "Why didn't you use your key?"

"Didn't want to disturb you."

"How could you disturb us, Dino? You live here, too." Then she screwed up her face and added, "Sort of."

Dino smiled and leaned against the doorpost. "Sort of," he echoed.

Nikki found herself staring at him, amazed that he could be so charming this early in the morning. "Come on in." She and Jamal stepped aside.

Dino shook his head. "I'm okay. Thought I'd take you two to breakfast."

Nikki gave Dino a *you've got to be kidding* look. "Breakfast? This time of morning?"

"Yes, Nikki. This time of morning. It's the meal usually eaten in the mornings."

"It's not that early, Ma," Jamal said. Nikki looked over her shoulder at him. "It's not," he insisted. "It's almost eight."

"Which is early for a Saturday morning. Boy, you know what I mean. Besides," she said, looking back at Dino, "I've got to get to the diner."

"I've already been there. Sister Ellis and Brother Dobbs said they can hold down the fort just fine without you."

Jamal smiled and nodded his head. "I'll get ready." He hurried away from the door before his mother could object. Nikki exhaled.

Nikki looked at this man who stood at her door, a man who, just a month before, had been so suppressed deep down in her memory that he was all but dead in her mind. She'd even told Jamal that he was dead. Now he was back in her life and determined to be there. He was running to, rather than away from, the wreckage that was her and Jamal's life. He was almost acting like the Dino she used to know years ago, the one who would always check up on her, the one who always removed her baseball cap and in amusement, watched her unruly hair. The one she never dreamed would let her down.

"I don't eat breakfast," she said to him.

Dino began perusing her body. "Why not?"

"I just don't. And stop looking at me like that."

Dino lifted his eyes to her face. "Like what?"

"Jamal's willing to go," she said, ignoring his question, "and that's his choice. But count me out. I've got too much to do at the diner, regardless of what my traitorous employees said."

Dino nodded as if he understood and then looked away from her. For a split second she got the odd impression that he was hurt by her decision. "Does Jamal have a suit?" he asked, turning back to her.

"A suit?"

"Yes; a suit."

"You mean does he have a fancy set of threads to rival yours?" Nikki asked almost too defensively.

"I meant what I said. Does he own a suit?"

Nikki paused. Why was she always so combative around Dino? "No."

"Mind if I buy him one?"

Nikki looked at Dino. She wanted to scream her objection in his face. He was doing way too much already. But she couldn't bring herself to deny him the right. "If it's okay with him," she said, knowing that Jamal would be thrilled beyond words. "Although I don't know why he would need one."

"Church," Dino said. "He's going with me tomorrow."

"Oh, is he now?" Nikki folded her arms. "And when did you decide this?"

"It'll do him good, Nikki."

"What good? To be stared at and talked about and treated like he's some murderer for real? I'm not having my child subjected to that."

"He can handle it."

"Oh, and like you know him now? You've been around him for what? Two weeks? And now you're supposed to know my son and be able to give me all of these insights about him? Please, Dino." Nikki knew her tone was harsh, but she couldn't seem to help herself. She looked at Dino, who didn't return her fire; who now, in all of his religious glory, knew all about being Mister Cool. Sometimes she resented it, and she didn't know why.

"What are you telling me, Nikki?" Dino asked. "Are you saying that Jamal can't go to church with me?"

"I'm saying I don't think it's a good idea. I'm saying I don't want him hurt."

"He can't get hurt. He'll be with me."

It made no sense, and it made all the sense in the world. Nikki could only nod.

"I was hoping you'd join us, too," Dino added.

Nikki quickly shook her head. "No way."

"Why not?"

"Because I don't want to, that's why not. I believe in God. I don't need some so-called Christians telling me that I need to do this and I need to do that while they aren't even doing it themselves. No, thank you. I can do bad without their help."

Dino considered her and her bitterness. "All Christians aren't like that aunt of yours." He remembered what Tam had told him about Nikki's aunt refusing to take her in when she first came to Monroe.

Nikki jerked a hard look at him. Then she exhaled. Dino always won. "Sure you don't want to come in while Jamal gets dressed?

"I'm all right."

"Suit yourself," she said, then closed the door in his face.

It was the end of the sermon and Dino was exhausted. He stood behind the pulpit and wiped the sweat from his face as the congregation in the packed church slowly began to take their seats. Jamal sat down, amazed that a high and mighty brother like Dino Cochran could preach in such a down-to-earth, mesmerizing way. He had moved around in that pulpit like a rapper, running from one side of the podium to the other side as if he was too jazzed to stay still. The audience hooped and hollered, apparently jazzed too.

Jamal sat in the last pew in the back of the church, praying that nobody would notice him. Unfortunately, many did, as they began elbowing other people and whispering back and forth. A few bold ones on the same pew with him even stood up and moved. At first, Jamal was stung by their reaction, but he wasn't surprised. They believed he was a murderer. They believed he killed their hero. But when Dino began preaching, his fiery style demanded everybody's attention. They soon forgot about Jamal.

The title of Dino's sermon was "Actions Speak Louder than Words," and it was taken from Acts 16:16-18. After Jamal had read those verses from the nice black Bible Dino had given to him, he was expecting a calm, quiet sermon that would bore him to tears. And it started out calm enough, as Dino talked about Paul and Silas and how they spread the gospel. For all of five minutes, it was very calm. But then Dino removed that microphone from its stand and started moving around in that pulpit, and all the calmness flew from his voice like feathers from a plucked chicken. Everybody in the church seemed enthralled with that sermon. Even Jamal forgot about his own predicament when Dino started preaching.

But then Dino slowed down and that calmness returned, as he neared the end of his sermon. He replaced the microphone back into its holder and was speaking through labored breathing. That sermon took a lot out of him, and for the first time, Jamal began to see Dino, not as his mother's friend, but as a man of God. Not that he was behaving as anything less before. But there was just something different about Dino, something bad-boyish, that made Jamal wonder how a man like him could be anything but a high-class gangster.

"You've tried everything you know to try," Dino said to the congregation in a raspy, winded voice. "You've tried Doctor Ruth, Doctor Phil, Doctor Mike, Doctor Bill, and you still have that emptiness deep inside you. You're still in the same boat you were in before you tried anything. That's why you need to try Jesus."

Dino began slowly folding the handkerchief he held in his hand. "Jesus is the answer. No psychic is going to save your life. When your back is against the wall and your very life is in the balance, what in the world do you think the psychic hotline is going to do for you? You say you believe in God Almighty just as that woman said in Acts sixteen. She said all the right words. 'Paul and Silas are servants of the Most High God,' she told the people. 'Paul and Silas are here to show us the way to salvation,' she proclaimed. Oh, my friends, she talked a good talk. But Paul didn't turn to her and pat her on the head and pronounce that truly she must be a child of God. He turned to that woman and rebuked that evil spirit that was within her. Her actions, you see, spoke far louder than her words. She was a fortune teller, a Satanic-inspired profession if ever there was one. She was dabbling on the dark side, folks. And every one of us who fool with all of these psychics and root workers and voodoo doctors are dabbling on the dark side as well."

Dino hesitated, and then continued. "God cannot dwell in an unclean place. He's not about to sit back and let us commit fornication and adultery, do anything we're big enough to do, never have time for Him, and act like it's okay. You don't have time for Him? What if He doesn't have time for you? What if He doesn't come in that midnight hour when it's your time to leave this place? Is it worth the risk to you? Is it worth the chance? Will your psychic friends forestall that coming night? Try Jesus, my brothers and my sisters. Try Jesus. He's the only answer."

Dino exhaled sharply, staring at his massive audience, wondering if he'd gotten through to anyone at all. "The doors of the church are open," he said solemnly as the congregation began to rise.

"Hello, Jamal," a female's voice said.

Jamal, who was standing beside Dino's Mercedes in the church parking lot, turned to the sound. It was Sharon Granger, the mayor's daughter and Dollar Bill Coleman's sixteen-year-old girlfriend.

"Hey, Share," Jamal said awkwardly, trying to smile but unsure if he should. She was dressed in a lavender pantsuit, looking no worse for wear, considering the circumstances. "I didn't see you in there."

"You were in the back," she confessed. "Daddy thought it would be a good idea if I circulated amongst the people today."

"I'm sure Mayor Granger has your best interest at heart."

"Yeah, well, I did it. I see you did it too."

Jamal nodded. "Pastor Cochran was kind of thinking like your daddy was thinking. Only I don't think these people want me around them."

Sharon nodded. "I know. I heard you was tight with Pastor Cochran."

"Yeah."

"This is his car too, isn't it?"

"Sure is. I'm waiting for him now."

Sharon nodded her approval as she checked out the car. "Cool."

"How can they think I killed Dollar Bill, Share?" Jamal asked and Sharon looked at him. "I ain't down like that, and they should know it."

"That's just how people are."

"What about you? You think I did it?"

Sharon looked away from Jamal. "When my brother, Fred, told me that they arrested you for William's murder, I didn't know what to think. I was just so angry and so upset. And Fred said you were at the scene and everything—"

"But that's not true. William was still chillin' with Shake and the boys in Pottsburg when I left.

When the cops picked me up, I wasn't packing, I wasn't trying to run away from them, I was just trying to get home." Sadness ripped through Jamal when he said this. He knew he should have listened to his mother. He knew a lot of things now. "Didn't make it though," he added, then looked Sharon squarely in the eye. "I didn't do it, Share. I would never do something like that. Me and Dollar Bill wasn't tight or anything, but we was cool. Why would I hurt him?"

He could tell that Sharon still didn't know what to believe. Although she nodded as if she understood, her eyes looked bewildered, as if whoever killed Dollar Bill was far less important to her than the fact that he had been killed at all. She looked away and started to say something, but she saw her brothers walking across the graveled path toward them.

Jamal's eyes followed her gaze and then he braced himself. Although he and Dawson Granger, Sharon's twenty-year-old brother, were cool, it was Fred Granger, her older brother and the family hotshot following in his father's footsteps who would hurl the accusations. He hated Jamal and everybody who wasn't a member of the town's elite. That was just how Fred was.

"Listen, Jamal," she said, suddenly anxious to get her words out before her brothers came within earshot, "about what we talked about before all this happened . . ."

"I remember," Jamal said. "I promised you then I wouldn't tell, and I still won't."

She nodded and uttered a heartfelt, "Thanks," just as her brothers descended on their twosome.

"Is he bothering you, Share?" Fred Granger nearly ran up to his sister. "Is this piece of trash giving you a hard time?"

"No, Freddy," Sharon said, placing her hand on her brother's thick chest. "So knock it off. We were just talking."

"About what? How he killed Dollar Bill?"

"Stop it, Freddy." Then she frowned. "Let's just go." She began grabbing Fred by his shirt and moving him away from Jamal. Meanwhile, Dawson and Jamal exchanged a look and a friendly nod of the head.

"Sup?" Dawson asked. He didn't wait for a response, but followed his siblings back across the graveled parking lot.

Jamal exhaled.

They had an after-church meal at the Arlington Red Lobster in Jacksonville with two other pastors Dino knew, and then drove leisurely across the Matthews Bridge, along State Street in downtown Jacksonville, and then onto Interstate 10, heading back to Monroe. Jamal leaned back against the headrest while Dino, buried in thought, drove.

He looked over at Jamal. "Tired?"

Jamal shook his head. "Not really. Just didn't know what y'all was talking about back there. They ran big churches, you ran a big group of churches, but all y'all talked about was politics."

Dino smiled. "What did you expect us to talk about, champ?"

"I don't know. Church stuff. Going to hell, fire and brimstone stuff."

Dino laughed. "I think we already know about that." Then he hesitated. "What about you?" Jamal looked at him. "Are you saved, son?"

"Yeah, sure."

"You said that awfully fast."

"I mean, I believe in God and all that. If that's what you mean."

"Have you accepted Christ as your personal Savior? Have you asked for forgiveness for your sins? That's what I mean, Jamal. Remember the title of my sermon earlier today? About actions speaking louder than words? Just saying you believe in God is very general. Confessing your sins and asking Christ to save you from those sins so that you may have eternal life is very specific, a very conscious action."

"I know. I did that too."

Dino looked in his direction. "Really? When?"

"When they put me in that jail and told me I wasn't never gonna be free again; that's when. I mean, that woke me up real quick. I was so scared." Jamal quickly glanced at Dino, amazed that he'd just made that kind of confession. He screwed up his face. "I mean, I wasn't scared scared, I was just kind of nervous and junk. I know I didn't do nothing, but people be on death row all the time and it's later found out that they didn't do nothing either. So I was . . . I needed help. So I asked God to forgive me for all the bad things I've done, for the way I treat my mama and stuff, you know?" He hesitated, astonished at how easily he could talk to Dino. "I just told Him to save me and help me out of this mess and I believed that He did. Salvation isn't a feeling anyway, it's believing that God can do it and trusting that He will do it, right?"

Dino nodded. "Right."

"So that's what I did. I trusted and believed. And I know what you're gonna say. It's just a jailhouse conversion and it don't mean nothing. But that's not even how it is. It means a lot to me. That's why I didn't argue when you asked me to go to church. I'm serious."

Dino nodded. "Good, Jamal. You're on the right track now."

Jamal looked at him. "What about you?"

Dino smiled. "Am I on the right track, you mean?"

"No, silly. You always been saved?"

Dino laughed. "Hardly."

"What made you decide to come clean with God then?"

Dino hesitated. The pain was still there. "Many things."

"That you don't wanna talk about?"

Dino glanced at Jamal and then turned his attention back to the road. "Right."

"You're an unusual dude."

"Why's that?"

"I don't know. You just are. You ever been married?"

Dino paused. "Yes. But she passed away."

Jamal was shocked. "She died? That's wild. I'm sorry."

Dino nodded. "Yeah, me too."

Jamal paused before speaking again. "Y'all had kids?"

Dino exhaled. "She was pregnant when she died, Jamal. The baby died also."

"Man. That's tough. Was it a boy or a girl?"

"Girl."

"Had y'all named her yet?"

"No. We were under the impression it was bad luck to name a child before its birth. That's how much we wanted that child. Now I wish we would have named her."

"Yeah."

There was another pause.

"You never remarried though, huh?"

"No."

"So you don't have any kids?"

Dino hesitated. "No. Why do you ask?"

"Just curious. You don't meet too many brothers without a pack of kids somewhere."

Dino smiled. "Not this brother."

"So you're all into this Jesus stuff, huh?"

"I try to be."

"Is it your whole life?"

Dino nodded. "It is."

"But . . ."

Dino waited. When there was no continuing, he glanced at Jamal. "But what?"

"How could a dude like you, all into the church and junk, be friends with somebody like my mama, who don't even go to church?"

Dino hesitated. "Your mother and I go back a long way, Jamal."

"When she lived in Michigan, right?"

"Correct. Before I showed any interest in Jesus myself."

"You was a gangster, wasn't you?"

Dino sighed, knowing that he'd probably never totally shake his past. "A gangster? Why would you think that?"

"You got the look. You got the style, even as a preacher. You don't be bo janglin'; know what I'm saying? You know what you're doing."

"Yeah, well, I actually didn't know what I was doing back in those days."

"Neither did Ma?"

Dino smiled. "She was a kid back then, J. Not much older than you are now."

"But you liked her?"

"I was much older than she was. We were friends."

"I see," Jamal said, somehow disappointed by that revelation. He looked out of the side window as Dino's Mercedes flew past a 70 speed limit sign on Interstate 10, just as they were leaving Jacksonville.

Dino glanced at Jamal, at the young man's profile that was so much like his mother's, and he exhaled. "I suppose Nikki's had numerous men seeking to be more than friends with her," he said as if it were a fact, attempting to sound conversational.

"Not really," Jamal replied without looking at Dino.

"Now that's surprising."

"I mean, what they gonna do? They be interested, but she doesn't."

Dino found that hard to believe. "She's never been interested in anybody?"

"Never. And I mean there was some pretty good prospects once or twice, I thought. But Ma be buggin' big time, man. She don't be tryin' to let no man lay no rap on her. I don't know, but I think that maybe it's because of what my father did."

Dino's heart dropped. He looked at Jamal. "What did your father do?"

"He died on her. I think maybe she really loved him or something, and he died on her and left her all alone to take care of me. Some females don't be gettin' over that. They be all bitter and junk. Like Ma."

Dino thought about Nikki, about all of the pain she'd endured. About his part in most of it. Then he looked at her son. "You ever met your father, Jamal?"

Jamal quickly shook his head. Too quickly, it seemed, to Dino. "Nah. I mean, I met him, but I don't remember it. I was a baby when he died."

"Sorry to hear that."

A worried look crossed Jamal's face. "Yeah; me too." He continued to stare out of the window

at the long and winding road, while Dino continued to glance at him.

Later that night, when even the crickets were
attempting a truce, the sound of crashing glass
shattered the silence around the Lucas home
and caused Nikki and Jamal to jump from their
beds and race into the living room. A brick the
size of a football lay on the floor surrounded by
the broken glass of their shattered living room
window. The word MURDERER was sprawled
in red ink on the brick. Jamal, now more angry
than scared, ran to the front door and slung it
open, praying to see the cowards who'd done it.
But all he saw was the darkness of the night and
the silence of still trees in the field across the
street. He dropped his head, tired of the alba-
tross around his neck, and closed the door.

Jamal looked at his mother, who seemed
somehow lost in the moment, as if she were tired
too. She looked up at her son. She looked like
she had no clue how they were going to deal with
this, or even what they were going to do next.
Jamal had never seen her this way. And although
he didn't know how they were going to deal with
it either, he stood erect and took charge. "Call
the police," he said to her with an edge of authority in his voice. "I'll call Mr. Cochran."

THIRTEEN

Nikki swept up the last of the broken glass and shoved it into the dustpan. She looked at the piece of wood that they had to use to cover the broken windowpane and sighed. These people really hated them now, and it wasn't born out of any proof they had of Jamal's guilt. That was a fact that no longer seemed to matter. Somebody killed William Coleman, somebody ended the life of their hero, and Jamal seemed as good a perp as any. One woman at the diner even said as much, adding that Nikki didn't raise him right and that was all the proof she needed of his guilt. Nikki was about to set the sister straight and tell her that she'd better get out of her face with that nonsense, but she didn't have to say a word. By the time Tam and Sebastian had finished with the woman, nothing more needed to be said.

"What are you staring at?" she asked Jamal as she walked up to the window and stood beside him. When she followed his gaze, she saw Dino getting out of his Mercedes and hurrying across the grass toward the front porch, looking terrified. "He's here already? He must have flown."

Jamal looked at Dino, in his dress slacks and pull-over shirt, his long sleeves rolled up as if he was coming over to get down to business, and he nodded his head. "He cares about us." He said it as if he knew that for a fact, then moved away from his mother to open the front door.

Dino's heart was still pounding as he hoisted himself onto the porch. It wasn't so much because of the brick incident, which was bad enough, but because of the way Jamal had described his mother. He'd said she didn't look right, and that she was just standing there as if she didn't know what to do. That sounded so unlike Nikki that it shook Dino. The last thing he needed, the last thing Jamal needed, was for her to start giving up.

Dino studied Jamal with a doctor's precision when the door opened, as if he came to see for himself that he was really all right. When he didn't notice anything visibly wrong with the young man, he exhaled.

"Hey, Mr. Cochran." Jamal opened the door wider to let him in. "Thanks for coming."

"You okay?" Dino's eyes were still trained on him.

Jamal nodded, unable to conceal his frustration. "I'm okay."

When Dino walked into the living room and saw Nikki standing there in her housecoat and slippers, looking just as flustered as she had the day she told him about Jamal's arrest, he had to fight back a sudden surge of protectiveness. But he couldn't stop himself from moving closer to her. "Hello there," he said as he walked, looking at her, his gaze trailing over her entire body.

Nikki, uncomfortable with his stare, folded her arms and tried her best to appear upbeat. "Hello yourself." She almost sounded lighthearted, even accompanied her words with a smile, but Dino knew her better than that.

His stare lingered, piercing through that forced façade, and then he spared her by looking away and at the window. "What a mess."

Nikki nodded her head. "Yep."

"Already boarded it up?"

"Had to," Jamal said, walking up. "Ma's scared of lizards, among other creepy, crawly things, and she didn't want any of them even thinking about coming up in here."

Dino smiled and looked at Nikki, certain she would tell Jamal about himself for so much as mentioning any weakness she might have. Nikki, however, didn't say a word, as if she didn't even realize that Jamal had just exposed her. Dino's smile disappeared. "Where's the brick?" A frown had appeared on his already concerned face. She seemed unable to respond to even that simple question.

Jamal pointed to the far side of the room where the brick had landed. "Over there. We haven't touched it."

Dino walked over to the rock and crouched down beside it. Neither Nikki nor Jamal could get over how well-dressed he appeared, even in his casual wear. But it would seem unlike Dino if he would have shown up looking any less dapper.

"I wish those creeps would have still been out there when I opened that door," Jamal said with more than a little bitterness. "They hanging me already and don't know squat about the case. Ignorant jokers!"

"What did Sheriff Peete say?" Dino continued to observe the brick; specifically the writing on it.

"What you think?" Jamal's tone caused Dino to look at him. "What I mean is, he don't care. He told Ma he'll see if he can spare somebody to come by tomorrow and take a look. All the good that's gonna do."

Dino stood up. "You mean to tell me he didn't send anybody out here tonight?"

Nikki just looked at him, but Jamal nodded his head.

"That's what I'm saying. He was probably glad it happened. He thinks I'm guilty, too."

Dino looked disturbed as he placed his hands in his pants pockets. Then he looked at Nikki. "Do you want me to give the Sheriff a call?" Instead of answering, she stood looking bewildered, as if she didn't understand the question. "Nikki?" he called again. Now she was really beginning to worry him.

"What?" She blinked rapidly as if being broken from a trance. "I mean, what did you say?"

"Do you want me to call the sheriff?"

Nikki shook her head. "It won't do any good. He may come running out here because you called him, but that doesn't mean he'll try and find out who did this." She exhaled with some exasperation and smoothed a strand of stray hair out of her face.

"Why don't you sit down," Dino said. "You look about ready to fall."

"I'm all right."

"Sit down anyway."

Nikki looked at him, at how demanding he always was, and she knew she should have battled him back. But she couldn't. She hadn't realized just how emotionally drained she really was until she heard that horrible sound of crashing glass and then ran into the living room and saw her window. Just like this so-called life of hers, it was shattered too. It wasn't the worst thing that had ever happened to her by a long shot, but it felt like it. It was the final insult, the last straw, or whatever cliché she could think up. Her life had been harsh enough and she'd tried all she could to spare her son of its callousness. But she'd failed once again. She walked over to the sofa on Dino's order, not because she wanted to sit down, but because in truth, she didn't know what else to do. She felt oddly overwhelmed. Lost.

Dino watched her with a hawk's gaze as she sat down on the sofa and leaned her head back. He'd never seen her so defeated. Even that night when she discovered he was a married man, she didn't appear this confused. It could not have been the simple fact that a rock had been hurled through her window that was causing it. Too many rocks had been hurled, too many stones in the name of life's disappointments, hurled too many times, was more likely the reason.

"Finish getting up this glass, Jamal," Dino ordered with Jamal quickly getting to it, grabbing the broom and the dustpan filled with glass, and taking them into the kitchen. Dino looked at Nikki, at her thin, elegant neck, at her small, almost unbearably tense body, and he walked over and sat beside her. She noticeably stiffened when he sat down, as she could not help but be aware of every inch of him, from the smell of his fresh scent, to the sound of his breathing, to his overwhelming physical presence itself. And a surge of emotion overtook her. All she wanted to do was cry and be held by Dino, to feel as if she wasn't in this thing alone, but she knew it would be a mistake. Being weak wouldn't help her at all in the end and would only give Dino that same life-altering power over her he once had. So, she stiffened, but didn't break.

Nikki felt his large hand when it covered the hand she had resting in her lap. At first he simply touched it, but then he reached around and clasped it into his. "It's going to be all right, Nikki," he reassured. She looked at him. The look in her large, green eyes was so distressing that Dino's jaws tightened.

"How can they be so certain that Jamal did it?" Nikki asked it as if she was expecting Dino to know. "He never harmed anybody before in his life. He got in trouble a lot, yeah. He hasn't been an angel, but that was all stupid stuff. Never nothing like this."

"Don't sweat it, Nikki, all right? It's just how people are. You know he's innocent and I know he's innocent. That's all that matters." Dino squeezed her hand.

Nikki stared at him, at the droop in his already tired eyes, at how close his face was to hers, and her look changed. "Why haven't you condemned him, Dino? You know him even less than the people in this town do."

"But you know him. And you believe in him. That's good enough for me. And now that I've gotten to know the young man myself," Dino shook his head, "there's no way, Nikki."

Nikki's heart soared. Maybe Jamal was right. Maybe Dino did care about them. Although, she also had to admit, it seemed unlikely. What man with all of his responsibilities would want to saddle himself to their drama? The same man who would shell out all of that money for Jamal's defense. The same man who would rent a room from her at double her asking price and not even step a foot into it. Anything was possible when she was dealing with Dino, good and bad. It had always been that way.

Then she began to wonder if he knew; if somehow he didn't buy her tale about Jamal's father being dead and he'd figured out that Jamal was his son. Was that why he rushed out and got him an attorney and shelled out all of that money? Because he knew? Then Nikki looked away from him and shook her head. He couldn't know. He might suspect that it was possible, but he couldn't know for sure. Besides, if Dino knew, then that would mean Jamal would soon have to find out too; and just the thought of Jamal finding out caused her to shutter. Jamal would hate her, would never want to have anything more to do with her if he ever found out about this incredible secret she'd kept from him all of these years.

Jamal came out of the kitchen and plopped down in the chair across from Dino and his mother. An enormous surge of joy suddenly overcame him when he saw that they were holding hands.

Dino quickly released Nikki's hand and leaned his large body forward, away from her. "Have any idea who would have done this, Jamal?"

He nodded his head aggressively. "You can bet I do. Got me a few hunches."

"Who?"

"Some of these jokers around here, that's who."

"But you aren't sure?"

"I didn't catch them in the act, if that's what you mean. But I got me some ideas."

"Can 'em," Dino said sternly.

"What you mean?"

"Put a lid on these bright ideas of yours. Whomever you suspect did this to your home, I don't want you anywhere near them. Do you understand me?"

Just the thought of letting those clowns get away with this angered Jamal, and his anger made him suddenly defiant. "Oh, so we're just supposed to sit back and let them do anything they wanna do to us? Is that what you're telling me? Me and Ma supposed to just be sitting ducks for them to take their best shots at? What if the next time it's a gun? What if the next time it's a bomb?"

"Jamal," Nikki said.

"Jamal nothing, Ma. He's not the one they're calling a murderer." Tears stained the lids of Jamal's big eyes, causing Dino and Nikki both to stare at him. "He's not the one they're pointing at and whispering about every time he step outside the door. He's not the one that's got to spend the rest of his life in some prison somewhere!"

Nikki ran to her son before he finished his last words and fell on her knees hugging him. He fell into his mother's arms, closing his eyes tightly.

Dino lifted his head in the air and then looked down, the guilt beating the life out of him. Suddenly, it became too much. He stood up. "Listen." When they looked up at him with eyes so stricken, it broke Dino's heart. He became hesitant. "I'd better get going."

Nikki stood to her feet, folding her arms and displaying, not her customary defiant pose, but an almost painfully difficult vulnerability. "I thought that maybe . . . I thought that if you wanted, or if you wouldn't mind, that you could stay here tonight."

Dino stared at her. He knew what it cost her to say those words. She was just tired of being alone, tired of having to carry this burden of raising a troubled son alone with all of the ramifications it now entailed, and she was asking for help. Although there was a distinct hesitation in his response, he did respond. "Why not?" His smile was too weak to register. "I'm supposed to be living here, anyway."

Both Nikki and Jamal laughed the laugh of the truly terrified as they attempted, at least momentarily, to turn their tears into joy. And Dino joined in. It was a sad commentary that a line so lame could create this much forced elation. But it was the only hope left in a room already void of hope; a room already too crowded with the anguish, the despair and the fear of three very troubled, very lonely people.

It was the last room along the narrow hall and smelled of fresh paint. Like the house itself, it was a small room, with a queen-sized poster bed, a dresser and chest, and one armless chair. Dino surveyed the room, feeling big and awkward in such a small space, but when he saw that there was an adjacent bathroom, he looked at Nikki.

"I know it's not exactly what you're used to," she said regrettably as she surveyed the room, reading him wrong, "but it's clean and it's quiet and nobody will bother you here."

"This is your room, Nikki," Dino said almost as if he were angry.

Nikki, taken aback by his tone, tried not to rise to it. "This used to be my room, yes."

Dino couldn't believe it. "Why would you rent out the room you were sleeping in?"

"Because, Dino. A boarder needs a private bath. He may not want to share."

"And that would be fine. But once you found out that I was the boarder why didn't you move back in here?"

"Because I rented this room to you; not any other room, but *this* room. Whether you be here or not, this is the room you're paying for."

"That doesn't make sense, Nikki."

"Yes, it does. You get what you pay for from me."

Dino stared at her. As least she was coming out of that lethargic defeatism that had cloaked her earlier, although he still disagreed with her logic. But he smiled anyway. He'd take a feisty Nikki over a lethargic one any day. "You're a very stubborn woman, you know that?"

Nikki smiled too, but didn't say anything in response. The room went silent. Dino looked around the room again, and then he stared at

Nikki. She was still in bad shape despite her feistiness; he could tell it by the way her eyes still had that faraway look about them. Her will to fight still seemed tempered, as if it were one bad word away from breaking again. He sighed. What in the world was he going to do with her? "Come here, Nikki."

At first, Nikki didn't bulge from where she stood. Then she slowly pushed away from her position and walked across the room to where Dino stood. As soon as she was in front of him and looked into his eyes, the emotions of the day overtook her once again, and she could feel the tears fighting for release.

Dino pulled her into his arms and held her against him, his entire being shaken by just the sight of her in all of this distress. He told her it was going to be all right again, and rubbed her hair. She placed her arms around his waist and looked up at him. Before she could stop it, before she could even pretend that she was getting it back together, her bottom lip began to tremble and the tears that she'd been battling burst through into a torrent of sobs. Dino laid her head on his chest and held her closer to him. Somehow, he felt responsible for all that she and Jamal had to go through. It was irrational and didn't make sense on any level, but it was how he felt.

When Nikki's sobbing had ceased to where she was merely sniffling and wiping her eyes with his handkerchief, he lifted her face by the chin and looked at her. His look was serious as he studied her. He still had one arm around her waist, and he still held her tight against him, but she never realized just how close they truly were until she saw that their lips were a mere inch apart. She looked at his lips, and then into his eyes, and she knew he wanted to kiss her. But he didn't. He encircled her again and pulled her tighter into his arms.

"You'd better go on to your room, Nikki," Dino whispered into her hair.

"Why?" Nikki asked, certain that she didn't want to go anywhere. She could have stayed in his arms all night.

Dino closed his eyes. "You know why, honey," he said, and then inhaled.

He didn't release her immediately, but held on to her as long as he could without crossing the line, then he let her go.

Nikki moved out of his embrace, looking down, unsure if she could face him right now. But she did, looking at him squarely. Her heart seemed to skip a beat when she saw the look in his heavy-lidded, beautiful eyes, and she knew then and there that she was in trouble. She was in love with

Dino. She couldn't deny it another second. She was completely, incredibly in love with this tall, muscular man that stood before her.

But what was even worse than that, she felt, as she began to move away from his overwhelming presence, still staring at him as if he would dissolve before her very eyes, was her belief that he already knew it. Somehow, he already knew. But in case he didn't, in case he wasn't as in tune with her as she sometimes felt he was, her eyes stayed on his until she was clean out of his sight. She needed him to know it. As badly as a bird needed wings. She needed Dino.

By morning, Dino sat at the island counter in Nikki's kitchen and sipped the coffee he had brewed for himself. He had on the same dark slacks and shirt he wore the previous night, and knew he would have to drive over to his hotel room in Jacksonville to change before heading over to the church. But he was still pleased that he stayed. Nikki and Jamal were in bad shape last night as both seemed unwilling to wing it alone any longer. It wasn't exactly what Dino had bargained for when he came to little Monroe, not this problematic twosome, but it was exactly what God had laid in his lap. Two people with more baggage than Samsonite. Not to mention the enormous baggage he was carrying around himself.

Back in Michigan his life was simple, filled with the day to day rigors of running an organization as large as many big companies. He didn't know if he wanted to disturb that reality by getting heavily involved with the only two people on the face of this planet who could turn his life upside down. Especially every time he looked at Jamal and thought about that night he spent with Nikki.

Nikki said that the boy's father was dead, and the boy himself confirmed it. But Dino still had his doubts. He looked into his cup of coffee and stared at the milky brown contents. The thought that Jamal could be his child was too painful for him to even entertain. The thought that he had a child in this world, somebody who had needed him, and he had been nowhere to be found, was too reprehensible for him to even try and comprehend. Nikki wouldn't do that to him. Nikki didn't have a malicious bone in her body. But it was a bad time back then. She thought she was in love with him. Everybody on the block knew all about that incredible crush she had on him, and he'd hurt her mightily. Given those circumstances, given the fact that just after she discovered that he was a married man with a beautiful, very pregnant wife, she left Detroit for good, it wouldn't be a question of maliciousness. It would have been a question of survival, of keeping her own sanity, of refusing to let some trifling man completely destroy her own sense of self worth.

Dino sipped from his cup and then stared at its contents again. He could demand a DNA test or even get one of those PI's on his payroll to do a little investigating, but what would be the point? He didn't want to hurt Nikki, or alienate her from her son, especially if she'd told her son something that wasn't quite true. And if it were so, and Jamal was indeed his son, what would he do with him? Take him back to Michigan where he wouldn't be able to spare an hour of any given day to spend with the boy? Would that be worse than him not knowing? And Nikki would be alone. Again. Just as she was that night when she saw Dino with his wife, and realized she'd been had.

Dino decided that he would have to wait on Nikki. She would have to be the one to tell him, if there was indeed something to tell. And if she didn't come clean, if after Jamal's trial was over she still wasn't willing to at least discuss the possibility with him, then he would have to take matters into his own hands. That would be the messy way, the way where everybody got hurt. Dino closed his eyes in silent prayer that it didn't have to come to that.

His prayer was interrupted when he heard Jamal yell, in a voice harsh with disrespect, "Leave me alone!"

He sat his cup on the counter top and got off of his stool. He'd been hearing Nikki's attempts to get the boy up for school over the past few minutes, as she'd occasionally go into his room and tell him to get up. He had tolerated Jamal's insolence, chalking it up to the early morning hour. But enough was enough.

Dino stalked into the hall and into Jamal's bedroom as Nikki was now yelling back at her son, refusing to take a nickle of his ungrateful attitude. But with all of her insisting, he still laid in bed. Without saying a word, Dino moved past Nikki, grabbed Jamal by his pajama top's lapel, and slung him out of bed with such force that it caused Nikki to gasp.

At first, Jamal was ready to fight back, grabbing the thick arms of the man that had grabbed him. Then he realized it was Dino. Instead of becoming defiant, instead of readying himself to give it all he had, he suddenly became scared.

Nikki, too, was shocked by Dino's sudden display of temper, and on some level had a fear for her son's wellbeing. But she also knew that it was about time that somebody finally handled that boy. It wasn't as if Jamal didn't deserve it.

Dino pulled Jamal against him with a violence Nikki had always heard he'd had, and he looked him dead in the eyes. "Go take a shower right this minute and get your behind to school!" he ordered, and then released Jamal from his grasp.

As Jamal looked back at Dino, he stumbled forward, but did not fall. He still had that *leave me alone,* perturbed look on his face, still had all of that attitude, but he didn't mix words with Dino. He stomped out of the room, to the bathroom, where he purposely slammed the door.

Nikki stood in amazement that Jamal would do exactly what an adult told him to do, and she looked at Dino. Dino had taken out a handkerchief and was wiping his hands, the stress all over his face. He could be menacing when he was provoked. Nikki knew a long time ago that that was true; but she also knew that he didn't like to be provoked.

"You okay?" he asked.

Nikki nodded that she was. She knew why he had come into the room. It was because of Jamal's harsh tone with her, and she appreciated his back-up. But as she followed him back to the kitchen, she also felt a tinge of jealousy. She couldn't help but wonder how Dino could do in a few seconds what she'd been unable to do in years: get Jamal to obey.

Dino stood at the countertop in the kitchen and took another sip from his coffee. Already it was too cold and his disappointment with the taste showed in his expression.

"I'll heat more," Nikki offered as she moved from the opposite side of the island to the drainboard and began to brew more coffee.

Dino stood there watching her. She had on a pair of blue dress slacks and a blue and white cotton blouse tucked neatly inside. She was showing off her impressive figure for a change, although her hair remained in its customary ponytail. As the coffee brewed, she turned toward Dino and leaned against the drainboard. And to his surprise, she gave him a look over.

"You look spiffy this morning." She gave Dino a smile that he could have taken for flirtatiousness if he didn't know better.

"I only look spiffy if slept-in wear is your thing," he replied with a smile of his own. He wasn't sure if he liked this kinder, gentler Nikki.

"But that's just you, Dino, isn't it? Always perfectly groomed even after a night like last night. Do you ever have a bad hair day?"

Dino smiled weakly. "Many."

"Yeah, right," Nikki said. The silence, but for the brewing of coffee, ensued. She had been hoping that he'd comment on her appearance, since she had gone out of her way to pull it together, but she was probably hoping for too much.

Once the coffee was ready, she emptied Dino's cup and poured a fresh cup. Then she poured one for herself before sitting down on one of the island stools. Dino remained standing. "You're heading to the church?" she asked.

"Soon as I can change."

"Change? You've got to drive back to J-ville to change clothes? Ah, man, Dino; I'm sorry."

"Nothing to be sorry about. It'll be a breeze." He flashed a smile like the ones that used to mesmerize her.

Nikki had some confessing to do to him, and then they to Jamal, but the time had to be exactly right. She had to be certain that he'd be there for her son, and not just hear the news and go on back to where he came from. "You can't just keep on what you have on?" she asked.

"Nope."

"Why not? If those old biddies at that church don't like it, then that's just tough."

Dino shook his head. "It has nothing to do with any old biddies. It's my preference."

Nikki threw her hands up. "Okay. Don't snap my head off." Then she smiled. "I'm not Jamal, you know."

Dino sipped from his coffee, his eyes trained on Nikki. "He doesn't seem to appreciate you much."

"Appreciate me? What's there to appreciate? I haven't exactly given him the kind of life to be appreciative of."

Dino set his cup down. "You did the best you could."

Nikki quickly shook her head. "Not good enough."

"It is good enough. Nikki, look at me." Nikki obeyed. "I said it is good enough. You were a young woman who had to take on the role of father and mother to Jamal, a role that by its very nature is unnatural. And you did the best you could."

Nikki looked down into her coffee cup. She wanted so desperately to talk about it, to finally admit to someone that she had failed, but she couldn't bring herself to do it. She still wasn't convinced that Dino meant to do right by her this time, or even if he wanted to try. She still wasn't convinced that as soon as she opened herself up to him, he wouldn't crush her again. "Let's talk about something else," she suggested.

"Such as?"

"Such as why a great looking guy like you hasn't remarried." Nikki wanted to cringe at her new brazenness, but last night changed a lot for her. She realized last night that despite the past, despite the hardships she still had to endure because of that fateful night all those years ago, she still loved Dino. And she had to find out if it were possible for him to ever love her, too.

Dino looked at her, at her body first and then into her eyes. "Too busy," was all he'd say.

"Too busy? What kind of reason is that?"

"My reason."

"Oh." Nikki felt slightly embarrassed. It certainly wasn't the kind of response she had been hoping for.

"Want me to get somebody to replace that windowpane for you?" he asked, eager to change the subject. Nikki as seductress disturbed him for some reason.

"No, but thanks," she replied, trying her best to regain her composure. "I'm going to take care of it. I know a guy that comes into the diner everyday who does that kind of work."

"Good," Dino said, although he was suddenly curious to know just how well she knew the guy in question. "How's business, anyway?"

Nikki shrugged. "It's okay."

"Problems?"

Nikki paused before responding. "None I can't handle."

Dino picked up on her hesitation. "Sure about that, Nikki?"

She nodded.

He stared at her.

"What?" Nikki asked in a defensive tone.

Dino wanted to pursue it, to go into more detail about her financial situation, but he decided against it. Like him, she cherished her privacy, and she didn't tolerate snooping around anymore than he did. He sipped more coffee, set the cup on the counter top, and then slid down the sleeves of his shirt. "I'd better go. Tell Jamal I'll see him later." He looked at Nikki. "And you take care of yourself."

Nikki nodded without looking up at him. He couldn't wait to get away from her, which made her feel even worse about that weak and lame, trying-to-catch-a-man act she'd just displayed. Only twice in her life had she been so blatantly flirtatious with a man, and both times it was with the same man!

She could hear the back door close as Dino left, and a whiff of an early morning breeze arrived.

FOURTEEN

Nikki's entire staff found themselves sitting at the table once occupied by Nikki alone. She had been working on the books and drinking coffee, trying desperately not to think of the crisis that the lack of a breakfast crowd exemplified. It was mid-morning and normally, the diner would be packed to the rafters with loud, hungry customers, and Nikki and her staff would be up to their eyeballs in orders. Today, however, there had been only a trickle of people in and out, mostly truckers and out-oftowners, with no one showing up at all over the past several minutes.

"We keep this up," Sebastian said, "and we'll all have a hard time justifying our employment."

"It's only temporary," Tam said. "Isn't it, Nikki? Once those investigators Bishop Cochran hired can turn up evidence that'll clear Jamal, the crowds will come back."

"That's the sickening part," Nikki said. "I don't know if I'd want judgmental folks like that anywhere near my diner."

"Put yourself in their shoes," Henry said, bringing all eyes to him. "I been there. When I got shot and ended up in this wheelchair, people didn't wanna have nothing to do with me either. It was like I was bad luck or something. I didn't like it. I was bitter about it for a long time because that shooting wasn't my fault. But I started thinking about it, and I could see what they meant. I *was* bad news. And people had enough of their own and didn't wanna chance any of mine rubbing off on them."

"That doesn't justify it, Henry," Nikki said.

"Sure don't," Fern said. "Jamal's all right. He wouldn't kill nobody."

"That's not what I'm saying, Fern," Henry replied.

"I like Jamal," Mookie said. "He always be nice to me."

"I think he's a little brat myself," Sebastian said. "But a sweet brat. Certainly not a murderous brat, like this young man I had the displeasure of working with when I played Agamemnon—"

"Seb?" Tam interjected as she sat beside Sabastian.

Sebastian sighed, knowing what was coming. "Yes, Tammy?"

"Do we look like we wanna hear a story that concerns you playing Aga-whoever? Especially since we never heard of Aga-whoever?"

"The point of the story wasn't the fact that I played Agamemnon, but that I worked with this young brat of a boy who—"

"Whatever, Seb," Tam said. "We don't care, all right?"

"They threw a brick through my window last night," Nikki said. Now, all eyes were on her.

"A brick?" Tam was shocked.

"Me and Jamal were asleep and the next thing we knew . . . *bam*! It was the fright of my life. I thought something had exploded. And when I saw the size of that brick and saw that they had written the word *murderer* on it, I just kind of freaked. It's like I froze up; you know?"

"You're tired, Nikki," Tam said. "You're sick and tired of all this foolishness you and Jamal have to put up with."

"What did Sheriff Peete say?" Sebastian asked. "Does he know who did it?"

Nikki shook her head in disgust. "Sheriff Peete basically told me to take two pills and call him in the morning."

"That figures," Henry said.

Tam couldn't believe it. "You mean to tell me he didn't even go out there?"

"Wouldn't even send a deputy out. Dino wanted to call him, but I told him never mind."

"Dino?" Fern asked.

"Bishop Cochran, child," Tam said. Then she looked at Nikki. "Why wouldn't you let Bishop call that lazy sheriff of ours and give him a piece of his mind? He might not have been able to figure out who did it, but I'll betcha he would have had his behind out there."

"I know. I guess I just didn't wanna be bothered with it; I don't know. I told you I froze."

"You were probably terrified," Fern said.

"I guess I was. I even asked Dino to stay the night; that's how bad off I was."

"Ooh," Mookie said with a grin. "You let a man stay with you."

"Nothing like that, Mookie," Nikki quickly pointed out. "He rents a room in my house."

"Oh. He's like your boarder."

"Exactly."

"So, did this boarder stay the night?" Tam smirk was not unlike Mookie's.

"Don't even go there, Tam," Nikki said as the phone began ringing. Fern got up to answer it, with Mookie watching her as she went. "I just didn't want those fools to try anything else. I figure if they saw another car in my driveway—"

"A spanking-beautiful, brand new, black-like-the-night Mercedes," Sebastian interjected.

"I figured they'd stay away if they saw it," Nikki concluded. "And since the rest of the night went by peacefully, I have to assume that it worked." Nikki wasn't about to tell Tam or anybody else about that pit-in-the-stomach fear she had last night, borne more out of neediness and loneliness than any brick crashing through her window. She also wasn't about to mention the way she felt when Dino held her in his arms. She'd been fighting her feelings for Dino since he hit town, but now she couldn't shake those feelings even if she tried.

"Telephone, Nikki," Fern said as she came back over to the table. "It's the school."

Nikki glanced at Sebastian and Tam, then rose quickly and hurried to the phone. "This is Nikki; may I help you?" Her nerves were already on edge.

"Good morning, Miss Lucas," the voice on the other end said. "This is Dr. Stewart."

"What's the matter?"

"And how are you this morning?"

"I'm fine. What's the matter?"

"You're rather cynical this morning."

"I'm not cynical, I'm just realistic. Why else would a principal be calling me if something wasn't wrong?"

By now, Tam and Sebastian had come over to the counter too, worried that this probably concerned Jamal.

"It is about your son," Dr. Stewart said, confirming their worries.

Nikki placed both hands on the phone. "What about him?" She looked at Tam and Sebastian while she spoke.

"I'll just come out and say it, Miss Lucas. We've tried to acommodate Jamal since he returned to school, but his presence has become far too disruptive. Children are refusing to sit by him or stand near him. Some are even refusing to be in the same classroom with him."

"How does that make *him* disruptive?" Nikki wanted to know. "He's not refusing to be around anybody."

"We will allow Jamal to stay in school for the remainder of today, but until his court case is settled, we—myself and the school board—have decided that he cannot come back."

"Can't come back?" Nikki asked, astounded. "Are you out of your mind? Just how do you and that school board expect me to educate my son if he can't attend school?" Tam and Sebastian glanced at each other.

"That's not our problem, Miss Lucas," Dr. Stewart replied.

Nikki couldn't believe the gall of the woman. "Not your problem? Not your problem?"

"Look, I know you're upset—"

"Upset? Lady, I'm furious. How can y'all do this to Jamal? And you, especially—"

"We aren't doing anything to Jamal. Jamal did this to himself."

"So he's expelling himself?"

"He should have thought about the consequences before he murdered William Coleman."

"Before he murdered . . ." Nikki's temper caught fire. "Why, you judgmental old hag! How dare you—"

Tam realized that the fire was lit. She reached over the counter, grabbed the phone from Nikki, and hung it up. Nikki started walking back and forth and couldn't seem to stop shaking her head, her mind buried in murderous thoughts of her own.

"Nikki, calm down," Tam said to her.

"She's already convicted him," Nikki said to no one in particular. "They've already convicted him. No evidence, no confession, but he's guilty as sin in their eyes." Then she stood still, her head still shaking. "What am I going to do?" she asked with a frustrated plea in her voice.

Tam walked around and placed her hands on Nikki's shoulders. "What did she say?"

"He can't come back. Until his court case is settled, he's not welcome at his own school any more."

"What is wrong with these people? What do they expect from you?"

"That's what I asked her. But of course that's not her problem. Me and Jamal, we singlehand-edly put ourselves in this mess, let her tell it." Nikki shook her head again. Then she exhaled. "What am I gonna do?"

"Go to the school board and file a protest," Sebastian suggested. "See what legal recourse you have."

Tam couldn't disagree more. "This is Monroe, Seb, all right? These closed-minded idiots don't give a flip nickel about her legal recourse."

Nikki stood there longer, unable to even for-mulate any kind of course of action, and then she thought of Dino. She needed him once again. It was becoming a bad habit, but she couldn't get around it. Without an education, Jamal wouldn't stand a chance in this world, especially since his prospects weren't all that promising to begin with. No way could she just sit back and let that happen to her son without a fight. Without her at least attempting to do something about it. Dino had always been a wise man. Even during his gangster days he never acted on his emotions first, but thought everything out before he made a move. He might have answers she hadn't even considered. He might even have enough pull to get Jamal reinstated. She went into her office, grabbed her car keys, and returned in a swift pace toward the exit.

"I'll be back," she informed her employees.

"Where are you going, Nikki?" Tam asked worriedly.

"New Life," Nikki replied, without further explanation, without looking back.

Sheila Maxwell was sitting behind her desk laughing with another young woman who was propped on the desk's edge. When Nikki walked into the secretary's suite, both females looked at her as if a piece of trash had just blown in. Nikki caught the nasty looks, but ignored them.

"I need to see Bishop Cochran," she said to Sheila.

At first, Sheila continued talking with her friend, as if Nikki wasn't even there. Then she turned again to Nikki. "May I help you?"

Nikki's temper wanted to flare, but she thought about where she was and repressed it. "I need to see Bishop Cochran."

"Can't."

"Why not, Sheila?"

The sting of Sheila's rudeness seemed to deflate when Nikki called her by her Christian name. She may have forgotten that before Jamal's arrest they were once friends, but Nikki hadn't. "He's in a meeting, Nikki," she said more civilly. "He'll be a while."

"Could you at least tell him I'm here to see him?"

Nikki looked so distressed that Sheila suddenly felt compelled to help her. "I'll tell him," she said, "but he doesn't like to be disturbed like this."

"Then why you disturbing him?" Sheila's friend asked, having no problem keeping her distaste for Nikki going strong.

Sheila ignored her and pressed the intercom button. "Bishop Cochran?"

There was a pause, then the sound of an exhale. "What is it, Sheila?" Dino's tone was decidedly agitated.

Sheila swallowed. "I'm sorry to interrupt, sir, but Nikki Lucas is here and she says she needs to see you."

There was a hesitation, a little too long for Nikki's liking, then the sound of another exhale. "Send her in."

Not exactly the exuberant greeting Nikki was hoping for, but she had never expected Dino not to be Dino, either. "Thanks, Sheila," she said before walking into his office.

Two men were seated in front of Dino's desk while Dino sat in the master chair. All three men stood, with the two visitors grabbing their briefcases.

"It'll require a push," the taller of the two visitors said, "but we could have the full audit completed by late next week, or midweek if push comes to shove."

"Midweek sounds good,"Dino said.

The man smiled. "I knew you were going to say that." He and his partner shook Dino's hand, greeted Nikki, and left.

Dino looked at Nikki. He already knew, just by virtue of the fact that she had come to his office, that something was wrong. "Hello, Nikki."

"Hey," she said in a voice so distressed that Dino suddenly felt burdened. He remembered how she looked at him last night, and how seductive she had tried to behave this morning. Somehow she'd made him her hero again. Somehow she'd forgotten what that kind of worship had cost her before. "I see you've changed," she added.

Dino looked down at his charcoal gray Italian silk suit, and then he looked at Nikki. "Yeah. What's up?" He wanted to get to the point, to discourage her sudden admiration.

Nikki shook her head. "It's that stupid school."

"What stupid school?"

"Jamal's school. Monroe High. The principal just called and told me she was expelling him."

Dino frowned. "Expelling him? Why?"

Nikki rolled her eyes and folded her arms. "Oh, let me see. Maybe it has something to do with the fact that they think he murdered somebody."

"Don't get cute with me, Nikki," Dino said in a harsh tone.

Nikki unfolded her arms. "Sorry. I'm just . . . How is he going to get a fair trial, Dino? These people have already convicted him. He won't stand a chance."

"Yes, he will."

"No, he won't! You should have heard that principal. She's a doctor, a supposedly intelligent woman, and she's convicted him too."

"God has it all in control, Nikki. I need you to understand that."

"But what about these people around here? These potential jurors?"

"We'll get a change of venue if we have to. Don't worry about that."

"I'm trying not to. Especially since you're here, but then I get a phone call like that and the worries return."

"God's got it in control," Dino said again. "I'm not some super hero, and neither is Ida Fox. Only God can get us out of this mess."

The fact that he had said *us* wasn't lost on Nikki, but neither was the fact that he had included Ida Fox in his hero category. She suddenly felt foolish for even coming to his office. "They can't expel Jamal like that, can they? Just because he's been accused of a crime?"

"I wouldn't think so," Dino said, grabbing his suit coat from off of the back of his chair. "But let's find out."

Dino and Nikki sat in the main office at Monroe High School and waited for the principal to conclude the telephone call she was having in her adjacent, private office. The school secretary, a burly middle-aged woman in an oversized blue skirt suit, was seated behind the long reception desk, answering the phone and attending to the occasional student.

Dino was calm as he sat in a chair against the wall, his legs crossed, his hands intertwined and resting on his stomach. On the contrary, Nikki was jumpy, leaning forward, and then back, and then standing up and walking around the small area as if her constant movement could will the principal to end her phone conversation sooner. Dino watched her pace. She was a nervous wreck and he wondered if she'd ever had a sense of ease in her entire life. From hustling on street corners, to running that diner and dealing with Jamal, it seemed to him that Nikki was always in a state of unrest.

When the principal finally came out of her office, looking as if she was dreading this encounter, Dino stood to his feet. Nikki stood beside him, as if just his nearness gave her all the strength she needed. She couldn't stop staring disparagingly at the woman who had spoken as if she hated Jamal.

"Hello, Miss Lucas," the principal said, not even bothering to extend her hand.

"You're not expelling Jamal," Nikki blurted.

"May we go into my office?"

"No, we may not," Nikki replied. "What *you* may do is leave my son alone and allow him to get an education like everybody else. He hasn't been convicted of any crime, and there's no law written anywhere that gives you the right to treat him as if he has."

"It's not a question of a conviction, Miss Lucas." The principal glanced around the reception area to make sure no one was within earshot. Her secretary was, but she apparently had to be tolerated. "It's a question of disruption. And his presence here is disruptive to the rest of our student body."

"And that's his fault? People think he killed somebody and that's supposed to be my son's fault?"

"Will you lower your voice, Miss Lucas?"

"Lower my voice? Would you lower your voice if it was your son?"

Dino could hear the well of emotion creeping into Nikki's voice and he placed his hand on the small of her back, hoping to calm her back down. He had purposely stayed out of it, Nikki much more preferred to fight her own battles, despite the fact that she'd come to him for help. But he wasn't going to hesitate to intervene if she didn't keep it together and not allow her emotions to overrule what was best for Jamal.

"Well, would you, Dr. Stewart?" Nikki pressed.

"This isn't about me."

Nikki shook her head. "You people are something else. No, it's not about you. It's never about you. You just sit back in your fancy office and make decisions that could ruin somebody's life, but it has nothing to do with you, does it? And to think Jamal actually respected you." That, above everything else, was what hurt Nikki the most. Jamal had once told her that Dr. Stewart treated all of the kids with respect, and that was why he liked her. But now he was about to be let down again by somebody he thought was in his corner.

The justice system had failed him by branding him with these charges to begin with; Nikki had failed him just by virtue of being who she was; and now, his own school was trying to kick him while he was down. How much more could a sixteen-year-old take?

Dino, sensing Nikki's growing frustration, removed his hand from her back and extended it to the principal. "I'm Dean Cochran, the interim pastor at New Life Progressive."

"Oh, yes, of course," the principal replied, relieved to be shaking Dino's hand. "I'm Dr. Stewart, the principal here at Monroe High. It's an honor to finally meet you. I've heard many positive things about you, sir."

"About my son," Nikki said impatiently. "Where is he now?"

"He's in the guidance office, Miss Lucas, taking his instruction in there for the remainder of the day. As I told you over the phone, students are refusing to have anything to do with him. I will not disrupt my entire school to accommodate one student."

"Don't you mean one murderer? That's what you called him over the telephone. Why you trying to clean up your act now? Is it because Bishop Cochran's here? Is it because you know people like him don't take this kind of crap?"

Dr. Steward sighed. "I have work to do, Miss Lucas."

"I got work to do too. What's that supposed to mean? My work is nothing and yours holds some great meaning?"

"Nikki," Dino said in a voice laced with warning.

"Don't Nikki me, Dino. I want to know where she gets off treating me and Jamal like we're some second-class citizens. I'm supposed to stand here and let her do that? I can't stand people like her!"

"I can't stand people like you!" the principal lashed back. "Have these babies out of wedlock, too ignorant and uneducated to take care of them properly, and then dump them on us and expect us to be miracle workers and clean up the mess you made!"

Nikki's temper flared as she moved into the principal's face, purposely invading her comfort zone. Dino shook his head and decided to stay out of it. In his opinion, the Dr. Stewart had brought it on herself.

"I don't expect you to do anything for my son but give him an education that I am, as a taxpayer, paying you to give to him!" Nikki said angrily. "Do you understand that, Dr. Stewart? Or am I too ignorant and uneducated to make myself clear? How dare you!" Nikki yelled vehemently into the principal's face. "How dare you act like I'm depending on your sorry behind to raise my child as if I can't do it myself! I'll depend on a bum on the street, a crackhead in a crack house, before I depend on your raggedy—"

Dino grabbed Nikki by the arm and pulled her back beside him. He held on to that arm as he looked her in the eye. "That's enough," he said in a calm, but firm voice.

Nikki knew that look of Dino's well enough to back off, but not before giving her own version of that same look to Dr. Stewart.

Dino also looked at Dr. Stewart. "Is there any way possible for Jamal to remain here in school?"

Dr. Stewart quickly shook her head. "I'm afraid not. As I told Miss Lucas—"

"What about home study?" Dino wasn't at all interested in some heated exchange she'd had earlier with Nikki.

"What about it?"

"Jamal would certainly qualify for it if his presence is as disruptive as you state."

"I don't believe that for a minute," Nikki said. "She just don't want him here."

"Nikki," Dino said, again in warning.

"I don't believe her, Dino."

Dino tightened his grip on her arm. "Did I ask you what you believed?" He stared deep into her eyes.

Nikki rolled hers, making clear her displeasure, but she didn't voice any more opinions.

Dino returned his attention to the principal. "If Jamal is allowed to participate in home study, Miss Lucas or myself can pick up his assignments weekly from his teachers and turn them back in the same way. At least until there's some resolution on this Coleman matter."

Nikki looked at Dr. Stewart as she seemed to consider Dino's offer. It was a solution although Nikki still burned with the anger of knowing that there had to be a problem at all. But she had to admit it. They had a problem. Her son not only had to now deal with the pressure of just being a Black man in America, but he also had to deal with the pressure of being a branded Black man in America. A branded murderer. He didn't do anything. She knew in her soul that her son never hurt anybody, but America didn't believe it. America? What was she talking about? His own hometown didn't believe it!

"I'll see what I can do," the principal finally said, making a point of looking at Dino only.

Dino removed his hand from Nikki's arm and extended it to Dr. Stewart. "Thank you." Then looking at Nikki, he added, "Let's go."

Nikki wanted to drag Jamal out of that school right then and there, but decided against it. Jamal wouldn't want it. He hated when she treated him like some kid, and she wasn't about to give Dr. Stewart the satisfaction of seeing her anger flare again. So, she allowed Dino to lead her out of the main office and the school altogether.

It wasn't until they were standing beside Dino's car in the school's parking lot, and Dino was opening the passenger door for her, did she realize how much control she'd just given over to him and how much she hated that she had. "You had no right, Dino," she said.

Dino let out a frustrated exhale. "What are you talking about?"

"You had no right negotiating on behalf of my son's future without consulting me first. That's what I'm talking about! Jamal used to admire that lady. He believed in her. Now she hates him too. If I don't stand up for Jamal, nobody will. That's my son, Dino."

"I didn't say he wasn't your son, Nikki."

"That's my child!" Nikki said with anger. She was about to lose it.

Dino took her by the arm. "Get in the car, Nikki."

Nikki snatched her arm from Dino's grasp. "Nobody helped me to raise him. Nobody helped me to understand what being a mother truly meant. Nobody told me how to handle his temper tantrums and rebelliousness. I thought it would go away. I thought he would grow out of it. I thought I knew what I was doing." She stared at Dino like he already knew she was clueless even before she confirmed it.

"You did the best you could, Nikki," he said.

"Now you come along with your expensive clothes and fancy cars and you've got my child believing again. Believing in you. Believing that you're gonna be a permanent part of his life when you and I both know you can't wait to get away from us. I saw it in there. I saw it in the way you were so quick to compromise with that witch in there. Jamal is like a burden to you now, one you didn't ask for and can't wait to get rid of. And when you're gone, and you know you will be gone soon, I'll be left to pick up the pieces again. So don't you ever make decisions about my child without my permission. Am I making *myself* clear, Dino?"

Dino stared at Nikki. This was some woman. Despite her vulnerability, despite her understandable distrust of this world that had never been kind to her, she still stood up for what she believed was right. She still fought for her son. "Yes. It's clear," he said. "Now get in the car."

Nikki stared at Dino. She used to wonder if God sent him to her just in the nick of time, or if the devil sent him to add to her sorrows. She and her son needed Dino, it was a fact. But that didn't mean she had to like that fact.

"I'll walk," she said and began to move away.

"Nikki!"

Nikki didn't even bother to look at Dino as she walked away. He stared at her, at the gracefulness in her movements despite her problems, and he wanted to call her name again. But he couldn't. The last thing a firebrand like her needed was to feel completely helpless. She had to retake control, and he wasn't going to stand in the way of her doing so. He'd intervene when that control slipped. He'd intervene when that control of hers became a noose around her own neck, or, even worse, Jamal's. He'd step in then.

FIFTEEN

It was no use. Nikki threw down the pen and leaned back in the chair at her kitchen table. She looked at the papers again, at what amounted to her financial crisis, and she knew she couldn't finesse it any longer. She couldn't borrow from Peter to pay Paul, because Peter was just as broke. She squeezed the bridge of her thin nose and closed her eyes, feeling as if she'd been over her head her entire life. From the time she was thirteen and hustling on the streets of Detroit, to trying to raise a difficult child alone, to trying to run a business now. And she'd failed miserably at everything she'd tried. Now the business was in trouble. And to make matters worse, she not only owed nameless, faceless creditors all around town, but she also owed Dino more money that she knew she'd ever have in her lifetime.

Dino, she thought. What would she and Jamal have done without him these past weeks? Not just the money, but the emotional support.

Nikki used to dread depending on people, and in truth, she still did. But with Dino it was different. She didn't know why, or why she would even think so after how he treated her in the past, but she couldn't seem to help herself when it came to Dino. It was as if he had a pull on her, some invisible string that drew her to him. Even that crazy night when she left Detroit, that night when she found out that he was a married man, she couldn't even hate him.

She was angry with him. Extremely disappointed in him. But she never hated him. Not even when she arrived in Florida and was homeless and on the streets, not even when she looked her young son in his big, brown eyes and told him that his father was dead. By then, Dino was a painful memory that she knew she would have to kill . . . or it would kill her. So she did. He became as dead to her as he was to their son, until God brought him back to life just when they needed him most.

Although Nikki would be the first to admit that she was no holy rolling, Bible-thumping church-going type, she did believe in God and in His almighty power. And she was convinced that God had brought Dino to them. Not to help her specifically, since she was pretty certain that He wouldn't expend that kind of concern on somebody like her, but to help Jamal who was now in as much trouble as a kid his age should ever have to experience.

She had no idea when or how she was going to tell Dino and Jamal the truth about their relationship. Most times she just couldn't even think about that herself. Dino may have already figured it out. That certainly would explain why he was so generous to them. Jamal didn't suspect a thing, however. She was convinced of that. In his young mind, he actually thought that Dino was shelling out thousands of dollars, not because of him, but on *her* behalf. Somehow, in his wishful little mind, he thought Dino actually wanted her, a thought so absurd to Nikki that she couldn't help but smile just thinking about it.

"What's funny?" Jamal said as he entered the quiet kitchen and saw his mother sitting across the room at the table near the window. He leaned on the island counter and glanced at the papers he knew were bills in front of her. "I know you aren't laughing at those."

"Beats crying," she said and stood up. Nikki looked at her son, in his neatly pressed polo shirt and jeans, and she frowned. "Where do you think you're going?"

"Thought I'd go shoot a few hoops."

"Where? In Pottsburg?"

"Around there, yeah."

"Are you out of your mind, Jamal? Haven't you learned anything?"

"It ain't like that. I ain't planning to hang with no Shake 'nem. I'm just gonna shoot some hoops by myself, that's all."

Nikki shook her head as she walked toward the stove. "Boy, sometimes I wonder if you have any sense at all. That same place got your behind arrested for murder, and you wanna go right back up in there?"

"Just to shoot hoops. What's wrong with that?"

Nikki grabbed a pot holder and opened the oven door. "The fact that you don't see anything wrong with it is what's wrong."

"Ah, Ma; you always . . ."

Nikki checked her roast and then closed the oven door. She looked at Jamal, waiting for him to complete his sentence. "I'm always what?"

"Looking on the bad side of everything. Acting like no matter what I do I'm gonna get in trouble. Like you don't trust me or something."

"Child please," Nikki said, moving past her son and walking back toward the table. "What does trust have to do with it? I refuse to let you ruin your life, that's what this is about."

"Look like it's too late for that." Jamal's voice was barely audible, like he didn't really want to be heard. But Nikki heard him.

She also heard a car and looked out of the window behind her as a black Mercedes pulled up into her driveway. Her heart actually leapt with joy at the thought of seeing Dino again. They didn't exactly part company amicably earlier today, and she was hoping all afternoon to be able to somehow make amends.

"Have you finished your homework?" Nikki asked her son.

"Yes, Ma; I told you that already."

"Dino just drove up," Nikki said calmly.

"For real?" Jamal sounded amazed. He hurried to the window to see for himself. Then he started shoving her papers into a pile. "Let's straighten up the place, Ma. I'll get the living room, you get these papers."

"What?" Nikki stepped back and did a double-take at her son.

"Let's straighten up."

"Why, Jamal?"

"Just do it," he pleaded as he hurried into the living room.

Nikki continued to stare. He looked desperate, as anxious to please Dino as she used to be. What was it about that man that would have even a second generation Lucas cow-towing to his butt as if they were born to serve him?

"And Ma?" Jamal yelled from the living room.

Nikki suddenly remembered what Jamal had asked her to do and began clearing off the table. "Yes?"

"Be nice to Mr. Cochran."

Nikki could not believe he'd just said that. "What?"

Jamal poked his head into the kitchen. "Be nice to Mr. Cochran."

"Jamal, me and Bishop Cochran are not an item. Okay?"

"Okay," Jamal said. "But be nice to him."

Nikki rolled her eyes.

The doorbell rang and they both seemed startled. Nikki almost wanted to laugh at the absurdity of it, but she was too excited about seeing Dino again to worry about it. She walked to the front door right along with her son who suddenly began rubbing her hair in place. When she realized what he was doing, she batted his hand away and then smiled, shook her head, and opened the door.

It was Dino, all right. But Ida Fox was with him. The almost giddy excitement that had captured mother and son as they opened the door, deflated immediately. Which was crazy to Nikki, since she knew that this woman, this tall, beautiful woman with Dino, was Jamal's lawyer and his best human hope to get out of this madness he'd found himself in. "Hi." Nikki quickly masked her ridiculous disappointment.

"Busy?" Dino asked.

"Not at all. Come on in." Nikki and Jamal stepped aside and allowed their two beautiful visitors to walk on in.

"How you doing, young man?" Dino asked Jamal.

Jamal tried to smile, although he was disappointed. "All right."

"Your mother told you about the school situation?"

"Yes, sir."

"You okay with that?"

"Yes, sir. Those kids were acting all stupid, like I had a disease or something, when they used to be my friends. I don't wanna be there right now anyway."

Dino nodded in a sad, exasperated way. "Okay."

"Nice suit," Jamal said.

Dino looked down at his charcoal gray Armani. "What? This old thing?" he said with a smile of his own. Jamal couldn't help but laugh.

"Y'all have a seat," Nikki said.

Ida didn't have to be asked twice. She looked tired as she moved toward the sofa and sat down, placing her leather briefcase on the floor beside her and said, "Thank you."

Dino glanced at Nikki, not knowing if they were even on speaking terms. He walked to the sofa and sat beside Ida. The fragrance of pot roast, or some other seasoned beef, filled his nostrils.

"Would you like anything to drink?" Nikki asked them, watching Ida's short skirt become even shorter as she crossed her long legs.

"Any non-caff diet soda would be nice," Ida said with that winning smile of hers.

Dino said, "I'm fine," when Nikki looked to him for his answer.

"I'll get it, Ma," Jamal said and headed for the kitchen.

Nikki had a sneaking suspicion that her son didn't want her to leave Ida alone with Dino for even a second, as if they hadn't already been alone for far longer than that before they got there. Nikki sat down in the chair across from the sofa. Unlike her visitors, she was casually dressed in a pair of brown shorts, a yellow sleeveless blouse, and a pair of strapless slip-on shoes.

Dino looked at those shoes, and at the shapely legs coming down into them.

"What a charming little house," Ida said, looking around at the simple home. "It reminds me of a miniature version of my childhood home."

Nikki knew it was a back-handed compliment, so she ignored it. Instead, she asked, "Any new information on Jamal's case?"

Ida leaned back, placing her shoulder-to-shoulder with Dino. "Not new, exactly; but Jeff is investigating."

"Jeff?"

"Jeff Islick," Dino explained. "The private investigator."

Nikki nodded. "What is this Jeff person trying to find out?"

"Plenty," Ida said. "Jamal gave us a list of everybody who was on that basketball court that night, including their ringleader, Shake. Jeff's getting the lowdown on each and every one of them. Including Jamal. He doesn't need to hold anything back."

"I don't get what you mean," Nikki stated. "Why would Jamal hold something back?"

Ida glanced at Dino, who was staring at Nikki. "I'll be blunt with you, Nikki." She leaned forward again. "These people under investigation were once Jamal's running partners. These aren't strangers. And they've been giving some pretty graphic info about Jamal's activities."

"His activities? What do you mean?"

"Taking the spotlight off of them by putting it on him."

"You mean they're claiming Jamal shot William Coleman?" Nikki asked incredulously.

"That's not all they're claiming. They're also claiming that Jamal was the leader of the pack, the bad boy they all followed, the problem kid of the group."

"Yeah, right. Like somebody's gonna believe that."

"Oh, it could be quite believable," Ida responded. "Don't you ever underestimate the power of a lie. Especially one told over and over and by different people."

Nikki's heart dropped. She looked at Dino with such a pathetically helpless look that he suddenly wished she was sitting beside him, rather than across the room where he couldn't hold her.

"Jeff Islick's a good man, Nikki," he reassured her. "A good investigator. He'll sort it out."

"How's he gonna sort out lies?" Nikki looked from Dino to Ida. "What if they get their stories straight and the prosecution parades them, one after the other, on the witness stand and they all say the same thing? What if they all say that Jamal did it? How can some investigator sort that out?"

"If he can't, then you'll just have to depend on my considerable skills, won't you?" Ida sounded so flippant that it upset Nikki. She wanted to lash back at her, but Jamal came into the room.

"Here you are, Miss Fox," he said as he handed Ida a glass filled with ice and diet soda.

"Thank you, young man," Ida said. "Sprite?"

"Seven-Up."

"I can live with that. Diet?"

"Yes, ma'am."

"Cool. Thank you, Jamal."

Nikki spoke again. "I don't mean to sound doubtful, but what if your *considerable skills* fail? What then?"

Ida took a sip of her soda and then leaned back again, far too close to Dino for Nikki's taste. "Then I'm afraid your son will be up that proverbial creek."

Jamal, suddenly nervous by such a blunt comment, sat on the sofa on the other side of Dino. Nikki's breath caught at how needy her son looked, as if all he wanted was that man's approval.

"What other graphic things are they saying about my son?" Nikki asked.

Ida sipped from her glass again and looked at Dino. Nikki looked at him too.

"Jeff's working on it, Nikki," Dino said. "Once he separates the facts from the fiction, he'll give you a report."

"Oh, I see," Nikki said, her arms folding, her head beginning to bob. "So I can't know what they're saying about my own son, but you know? And Ida knows? But me, the mother—"

"Come on, Ma," Jamal said with great frustration.

"That's not what we mean at all, Miss Lucas," Ida said.

"Then what exactly is meant by keeping information from me? I have more of a right to know what's going on with my own son than you do!"

"Will you stop being so ghetto!" Ida blurted in obvious anger.

Nikki looked at her. She wanted to lash back. It was her natural way. But she didn't. She looked at Jamal and it was obvious by the look on his face that he agreed with Ida's assessment. She *was* ghetto. And it embarrassed him. "Sorry," Nikki said begrudgingly, in a voice barely audible.

Dino's heart dropped. She owed nobody in that room an apology.

Ida, feeling triumphant, smiled mildly and sipped from her glass, thrilled by her small victory over the obnoxious Nikki Lucas, that foolish female Dino had the nerve to say he'd choose if it came down to that. Then she turned her attention to Jamal. "Now to you, young man," she said, leaning forward. "I don't want you worrying, okay?"

"I'm not," Jamal said.

Ida smiled. "Not even a little bit?"

Jamal hesitated. "A little bit," he admitted.

"No need to worry," she told him. "I'm really very good. That's why Mr. Cochran loves me so much." She smiled. Jamal glanced at his mother. "But seriously," Ida added, "I won't let you down."

"You think what Shake 'nem say is really gonna matter?"

"Could. Depends on how articulate they are on the witness stand, how believable they come across. But I've never met a thug I didn't want to cross examine. They never hold up under my withering cross; trust me."

"They're lying about me, though," Jamal said, glancing at his mother. "I mean, I'm no choir boy or nothing like that, but I ain't done what they're claiming."

"And how would you know what they're claiming?" Dino looked at him and asked.

Jamal's nervousness returned. "I'm just figuring."

"Figuring?"

"Yeah. Guessing that it's bad, that's all."

"Uh-huh." Dino wasn't convinced. "When Jeff Islick comes to talk to you, I want you to be completely straight with him. You understand me, Jamal?"

"Sure."

"Don't take that admonition lightly, son," Ida added. "If you don't tell us the truth and the whole truth, your case is doomed. Because if it can be found out, rest assured that the prosecution will find it and use it and make you and me both look like fools at trial. I suspect this is their biggest case in years—a local hero's murder—and they want to shine. Just don't let them shine at your expense."

Jamal nodded. "I won't."

As much as Nikki hated to admit it, she could now see why Dino hired this woman to represent Jamal. She was sharp. She covered her bases well. And she also had a way of getting Jamal to open up, something that always stumped Nikki. That gave her some encouragement. She should have known Dino would only buy the best.

"What about the press," Ida asked. "Have there been any attempts to contact you guys?" Ida looked from Jamal to Nikki.

"Early on there was," Nikki revealed, "but I made it clear that we had nothing to say, and I meant nothing. They respected that. Or at least they accepted it."

"Ma made it abundantly clear," Jamal said with a proud smile.

"Good," Ida said. "Perfect. You cannot utter a word to the press or to your buddies or to anybody about this case. You feeling me, Jamal?"

Jamal nodded. "I feel ya'. You don't have to worry about me. I ain't telling those maggots nothing."

Ida looked at Nikki. "Is he your only child?"

"Yes."

"He appears to be a very good young man. Very bright. After he wins this trial I think he's going to grow up to be a fine citizen."

Nikki nodded. "I hope so."

"He will. Trust me." She looked at the teen and smiled.

"What about you, Miss Fox?" Jamal asked. "You have any kids?"

"Me?" Ida laughed. "Hardly. Mr. Cochran can tell you all about my stance on kids."

Jamal glanced at his mother again. She tried not to show her concern, but he could tell it was there.

"But they're fine," Ida added. "Just not for me. Not yet, anyway."

"I plan to have a house full of 'em," Jamal announced. Even Dino had to look at him.

"Really?" Ida said.

"As many as I can get."

"What an unusual desire," Ida oberved. "Whatever is your rationale?"

"I just like kids," Jamal said. "I like the sounds they make in people's houses. It's like you're in a family and not just all by yourself all the time."

It was gut-wrenching for Nikki to hear and Dino could see the pain all over her face. She already believed she'd failed the boy, now his comments seemed to confirm it. At least that was how Dino knew Nikki would take it. She was a woman in need of some serious TLC, a woman he knew he had to keep his distance from before he found himself deciding to satisfy that need.

"It's certainly a unique perspective for such a young man," Ida said. "Don't you think so, Dean?"

"I don't have an opinion either way, Ida," Dino said in a tone that was hardly light, which surprised Nikki. Then he began rising with Ida following his lead. "We'd better get going. I just wanted to see how you fared at school today, Jamal."

Jamal stood up. "It was cool. I mean, those kids were just acting stupid."

"And you're okay with home study?"

"Yes, sir. I didn't like the way they were staring at me anyway."

Dino glanced at Nikki. "Do you need me to pick up his assignments?"

Nikki stood. "No, thank you. I'll take care of it."

"Sure about that?"

"Positive. Don't worry, Dino. I won't trip."

Dino smiled weakly and then stared at her. He felt odd leaving with Ida. But that was what he got for bringing her with him, as if her presence alone could blunt his feelings for Nikki. As if that was all it took. He began heading for the exit.

"Nice seeing you again, Nikki," Ida said, moving toward the door in front of Dino. She looked at Nikki, who was walking up to the door to see them out. "And again, this is a lovely—"

"Little miniature house," Nikki interrupted. "I know. You told me."

Ida smiled. "Right. Take care, Jamal."

"I will. Bye," Jamal replied.

Dino hesitated at the door and looked at Nikki, who was standing beside it. His nearness caused her to suddenly feel flushed. "You okay?"

She nodded. "Yeah."

Dino stared at her longer, at her body and then into her eyes, and then he reached out and touched her sleeveless upper arm. "Call me if you need me."

"Will do."

Dino hesitated, staring at Nikki, and then he gave her a kiss on the lips. Nikki's heart hammered when he kissed her. Then he said his goodbyes to Jamal, gave her one last brief look over, as if he was contemplating all sorts of things, and then walked out of her home, leaving with the woman that seemed so suited to him. Nikki looked as the twosome walked off of her porch and toward Dino's Mercedes, her heart wishing she could be as suited to him too. Then she looked at her son, who was smiling from ear to ear as if he'd just witnessed something remarkable.

"What?" she asked with a frown on her face, concerned that the way Dino had looked at her, and kissed her, was now causing Jamal to leap to all kinds of conclusions.

"Nothing at all," Jamal said, still smiling, still unable to take that smug look off of his face.

Nikki knew she looked flushed, because she felt all warm inside. She shook her head and moved to close the door. "Child please," she said as if she was annoyed. In truth, she was elated too.

SIXTEEN

The red Ford Focus came to a screeching halt in front of Sebastian's small green house, and Tam and Nikki rushed out and hurried across the lawn. Although Nikki knew that Dino would eventually show up, she slowed when she saw that his black Mercedes was already there. Tam, however, was still in a hurry, ringing the doorbell nearly three times before Nikki even stepped up on the porch beside her.

When the door finally opened and they saw how dazed Sebastian looked, Nikki's heart dropped. "Oh, Seb," she said with anguish, pulling him into her arms. Tam also hugged him, which was astonishing to see. And when Sebastian invited them into his home, Nikki noticed that he and Tam were still holding hands.

It was an old home that smelled of mothballs and medicine, with high ceilings, antique furniture, hardwood floors and an old-fashioned pot belly stove as the centerpiece of the room.

When Nikki looked beyond that stove and saw Dino standing at the window, his strong, straight back to them, her heart lurched with that kind of anticipatory giddiness she was becoming accustomed to. He was in a long-sleeved dress shirt, revealing bulging muscles tight with tension. When he turned their way, Nikki's heart rammed against her chest.

"Hello, Bishop Cochran," Tam said as she began moving away from Sebastian and toward the sofa.

"Sister Ellis. Nikki."

"Hi," Nikki said, following Tam. She hadn't heard from Dino in nearly a week, not since the night he and Ida Fox came to her house. Since then, Jamal had asked more than once about him. That was the worst part for Nikki; knowing that her son was already attached to Dino, when Dino was probably counting the days when he could hightail it back to his high life in Michigan.

"Can I get you ladies anything?" Sebastian asked.

"No thanks, Seb," Nikki said. "You come and sit down too."

Nikki waited for Sebastian to sit on the sofa beside Tam, and then she sat down beside him. She noticed Dino's suit coat folded across the back of the sofa as she sat down, assuming that she was now sitting in the space he had occupied. But when he sat down in the flanking chair, she let it slide.

"You didn't have to come all this way," Sebastian said. "Really; I'm all right."

"You're all right?" Tam asked, staring at him as if he couldn't possibly be. "You don't look all right. You look awful."

Nikki waited for the zing to come, for Sebastian to give Tam another one of his famous one-liners. Instead, he gave a weak smile, waved his hand in the air in a kind of exaggerated shrug, and sighed. "I mean, I'm coping. It's just strange, isn't it? Mother no longer here. For forty-one years, for all of my life, she's always been right here, right in this very home. Now, she isn't any more? It's just that I don't know if I can . . . I don't know if I can get used to that."

"Thank God she didn't suffer," Tam said.

Sebastian agreed. "Yes; I thank God she went in her sleep. She usually took her mid-morning nap just after *The Price Is Right* and just before the twelve o'clock news, and never before phoning me. That was our routine, you see. She'd always phone me to let me know she was all right and was about to take her nap. When she didn't phone me this morning, I knew instinctively that something terrible had happened. Just knew it.

She'd fallen . . . she'd hurt herself . . . something. I never dreamed it would be *this*."

"I'm so sorry, Seb." Tam's words were undeniably heartfelt. "I know how much she meant to you. And you to her. You were a very good son."

"Please." Sebastian said it as if just the thought annoyed him. "Surely you jest. Good is not the word to describe what I was. I was a burden to her. An old burdensome disappointment to her."

"Don't say that, Seb," Tam said; but Sebastian shook his head.

"It's true. Finally, it's true. She wanted me to be a loan officer at the bank." Sebastian shared an anguished smile. "Can you imagine me sitting behind a desk going over loan applications all day? Gracious. But that was what she wanted. But no. I wasn't about to give her what she wanted, because it was all about me, remember? I went to New York, instead. To The Big Apple to try my hand at acting." His tone was harsh, as if it left a bitter taste in his mouth.

Nikki glanced at Dino. He was staring at Sebastian.

A scowl was on Sebastian's face as he continued. "I was going to be the next James Earl Jones. No, Sir Lawrence Olivier. No, wait, Sir John Gielgud! *Please*. The next Pee Wee Herman was more like it." He leaned back and crossed his legs, running his hand through his crop of curly hair. "Don't get me wrong, I had a little success. Got a few good reviews off-Broadway. Way off Broadway, actually. But I never got that break. I never got that chance to even show them what I could do. One day I was this young, good-looking, promising actor, ready to take The Big Apple by storm. Then before I knew what hit me, I was this middle-aged, washed up nobody, trying to get bit parts just to pay his rent. So I stopped trying and came back here. Right back where I started from."

He glanced at Nikki. "You knew, didn't you? Everybody knew. It wasn't about Mother or her illness. It was all about me and my failure and the fact that I had nowhere else to go. If it wasn't for you giving me that job, if it wasn't for you giving me a chance when everybody else was too busy laughing me to scorn," he shook his head, "I don't know what I would have done." Sebastian spoke with the kind of heart-wrenching emotion that automatically caused Nikki to lay her hand on his shoulder.

"Even then, I played games with myself," Sebastian continued. "Telling myself that this was just temporary. This was just a pit stop until I could line up that real job that would utilize my real talents that would make my mother finally proud of me." He shook his head. "Yet I knew all along that this was as good as it was going to get for me. I knew it. No Broadway lights. No Tony awards. No stars on the Hollywood Walk of Fame. This was it. And now Mother's dead, and she had to have died disappointed because she knew this was it too."

Nikki tried to convince Sebastian that he was wrong, that he still had many great things ahead of him. Tam tried to convince him too. For a long while, that was all the conversation was about. Until Dino interrupted.

"Why wasn't your mother in church, Brother Dobbs?" The off-topic question gained everyone's attention.

Sebastian exhaled. "She wouldn't go. I tried to get her to go, but she said no. She used to attend. She was an avid churchgoer, but after Pastor Crane took over at New Life, she just lost interest. She wasn't getting anything out of it," she said.

"Had she accepted Christ as her Savior?"

Sebastian hesitated to admit it aloud, but finally said, "Not as far as I know."

Dino sighed in anguish and leaned his head back. Nikki knew right away that that was where all of his tension was coming from. Another lost soul gone, under his watch.

"It's not your fault, Bishop," Sebastian said, noticing Dino's distress.

Dino shook his head. "It's not a question of fault. It's a question of fact. I should have overseen these churches better; that's a fact. Crane would have never been allowed to pastor here or anywhere else if I would have been on my job. He drove people away from the church rather than to it, and I sat back and let it happen."

"Bishop Thorndike was over our district," Tam said. "He was the one who wasn't doing his job."

"I delegated Thorndike to oversee this diocese, Sister Ellis, but that didn't dissolve my accountability."

Nikki stared at Dino. Those sleepy brown eyes of his were now made wide and fierce by distress. It wasn't his fault that Mrs. Dobbs hadn't given her life to Christ. He didn't even know the woman. But it was just like Dino to take on that responsibility. He did the same thing for Nikki, years ago, when he put the word on the street that anybody who touched her had to answer to him. She was under his protection. Everybody in all of those churches he now headed were under his protection. Apparently, that included those who'd left the church. It was a responsibility no one man could bear. But it was just like Dino to try.

"In any event," he said as he turned his attention back to Sebastian, "I want you to call me anytime, Brother Dobbs, anytime at all if you find you need someone to talk to."

"Thank you, Bishop, but I'm fine. You've all been so kind. And please don't blame yourself for what happened here. Mother was a grown woman. She knew the Word. She knew what she was doing. I only pray that at some point, she gave her life to Christ and I just was unaware of it."

Dino voiced amen to Sebastian's prayer and then stood up, prompting Sebastian to rise to his feet as well.

Nikki's heart suddenly dropped. For some reason she couldn't bear Dino leaving her. She stood too. "Could I get a lift?" She was amazed by her own sudden boldness. "I mean, I don't think Tam is leaving any time soon."

"Who's minding the diner?" Sebastian asked.

"Nikki closed it after you called," Tam answered.

Sebastian couldn't believe it. He looked at Nikki. "Why would you do a fool thing like that?"

"There was nothing foolish about it," Nikki said. "It's just out of respect for your mother."

Sebastian stared at Nikki. She was one of a kind. "Thank you," was all he could say.

Nikki smiled back at Sebastian and then she looked at Dino. His distress hadn't lessened. It may have even heightened since she asked him for a ride. He reached past her for his suit coat, his sweet scent and hugeness making her feel as if it might be a good thing if he said no. Every time Nikki saw him lately, she was becoming more and more convinced of just how hard she was falling for him. She was even dreaming about him at night. He might have been avoiding her for physical reasons only, but her feelings for Dino went far deeper than that.

"If you'd rather not, I can call a cab," she offered when it was apparent by Dino's delay that he wasn't at all thrilled about driving her anywhere. "Or Tam can take me and come back once she drops me at the diner."

"No," Dino said as he put on his ocean blue suit coat, "you're going with me."

Nikki tried to contain her elation as they said their goodbyes and was walked by Sebastian, who seemed to be far more accepting of the idea of his mother's death than he had been when they first arrived. That brought Nikki some relief, but she felt even better knowing that Tam would be there with him, should he need somebody.

As Dino pulled out of the driveway and headed toward the diner, Nikki thought about Sebastian and how sad it was to be alone, and how tired of being alone she really was. She leaned her head back and looked at Dino. He was still her measuring stick, still everything she always believed a man should be. He looked so big and attractive as he carefully drove his car that her heart ached with feelings for him.

"Long time no see," she said, smiling the smile of a woman in love.

Dino looked at her, at that seductive smile he knew all too well, but immediately returned his attention back to the road. "How about that," he said.

"Busy week?"

"Since the family had a private funeral for William Coleman a few weeks ago, we had a special public memorial for him yesterday."

Nikki swallowed hard. "I know. I read about it in the papers. Me and Jamal were like zombies yesterday." *And we needed you badly*, she wanted to add. She looked at him. "How was the turnout?"

"Excellent. Standing room only, and that's saying something for a church the size of New Life. A lot of emotional farewells."

"I'm sure that most of the people who came didn't hesitate to assure the family that Jamal would pay for what he did to their wonderful, All-American boy." Dino didn't respond, which made Nikki immediately regret her comment. "I didn't mean it like that."

"They're grieving, Nikki."

"I know. I wasn't trying to put them down or anything. I'm just . . ." She couldn't finish, because in truth, she wasn't sure what she was, exactly. Tired? Angry? In love? "Why don't you come over for dinner, Dino?" she found herself saying. "I'm a pretty good cook, you know, and we can talk." She immediately looked at him for his initial reaction. As usual, it was slow and hardly enthusiastic.

"I made plans already, Nikki," he said, briefly looking at her.

Her entire countenance fell. "I see." She couldn't help but think that his plans were with Ida Fox.

Dino looked at her again. He exhaled. "Want to come with me?"

Nikki shot him a glance. "With you and Ida Fox?" The words spilled before she could stop them. She screwed up her face, upset with herself for being so impulsive.

Dino's Mercedes came to a stop at a red light. He seemed torn during the hesitation that followed. "I want you to come," he said, reaching over and placing his hand on hers. "All right?"

Nikki's heart pounded at his touch. "Okay," she said, knowing such a quick acceptance made her putty in his hands again. She couldn't believe she was allowing herself to become this way, especially when she knew it was all temporary and Dino would soon go back to his big shot life in Michigan and cease to even care if she were still alive. But it had been so long since she'd had these kinds of exciting, giddy feelings. So long since she'd allowed any man to make her feel this way, that it was a chance she was beginning to believe she just had to take.

Dino also knew he was taking a chance as he squeezed her hand and drove under the green light. A chance he had no business taking. A chance he needed like he needed a hole in the head. But that had never stopped him before.

SEVENTEEN

Ida Fox sat quietly in Palazzo, a fine dining restaurant in Jacksonville, and sipped from her glass of wine. She looked at her watch again and was beginning to wonder if Dino was going to stand her up. She even pulled out her cell phone, prepared to give him a call. That's when she saw him, driving up in that sleek black car of his and handing the keys to the valet. She smiled at the sight of him. He was one gorgeous brother in his nice threads, and she'd been trying for years to get his attention. Ida couldn't be convinced that he didn't have a thing for her. She could tell it by the way he sometimes looked at her, but their relationship still was nowhere near what she wanted it to be. She would love to be his wife, to take his name, to have access to that aura of power that cloaked him everywhere he went. But as Ida looked longer, she saw not just Dino getting out of his car, but Nikki Lucas as well, and she knew then that it would never be. He'd already told her. When it came down to it, that ponytail-wearing waitress was his choice.

Although Ida didn't want to admit it, she could see the attraction Dino could have for a woman like Nikki. She was small against his largeness, she was always in some kind of need of rescuing, which Dino was accustomed to obliging, and she lived in that crisis-mode state of constant drama that unfortunately, was familiar to Dino. Ida used to wonder if his lack of interest in her was because he felt that she was too young for him. She was only twenty-eight. But Nikki was young too; some fourteen years Dino's junior. It wasn't age. It was a certain experienced look Nikki had that she couldn't match. As if she had nothing to prove to people, didn't care what they thought, and would be a perfect woman for a man like Dino because he really didn't care either. He placed his hand on the small of Nikki's back as they walked into the restaurant, and jealousy kicked in. Although Ida knew it was a losing battle, especially since the object of her fight already told her what the deal was, she still felt she had to wage it all the same.

Ida was dressed in customary perfection as Dino led the way to her booth near the windows. She had on a cream-colored herringbone jacket with matching slacks and a pink mock turtle-neck, all of which gave her deep black skin a dazzling appearance. She smiled when they arrived at the booth and that bright, white smile on that smooth, black skin made Nikki instantly jealous. She was so much like Dino's late wife, so much like the kind of woman he undoubtedly favored, that Nikki often wondered what in the world he could ever possibly see in her.

Nikki sat down on one side of the booth and Dino sat beside Ida on the other. Immediately Nikki felt outnumbered. When Ida looked at Dino and gave him that winning smile of hers, Nikki felt grossly out-matched too.

"You're late," she said to Dino.

Dino nodded. "Sorry about that. The mother of one of my members passed away and I couldn't get away any sooner. How are you?"

"Now that's a loaded question," she said just as the waiter came to take Dino and Nikki's drink orders. When he left, she added, "Monroe isn't exactly fun for us, is it?"

Dino smiled. "Not exactly."

Ida looked across the table at Nikki. "What about you, Nikki? How do you like living in Monroe?"

"I like it."

"What's there to like?"

Nikki knew she was being baited, so she opened up the menu. "It's just a nice place. I like it."

Ida nodded. "I suppose you would, wouldn't you? I mean, it beats the street corner."

Nikki looked at her, ready to rise to the bait and tell her a thing or two. But instead, she smiled knowingly and returned her attention to the menu.

Ida, realizing defeat, tried a different tact. "About Jamal's trial," she said. Both Nikki and Dino looked at her. "I'm afraid I may have to put you on the stand, Nikki."

"Me? Why?"

"As a character witness for your son. They are sadly lacking in your town. I mean, I could call on your employees, which are his only support- ers around here, but the jurors will figure they're just trying to hold on to their jobs, and will dis- miss their testimony."

"I'll be glad to testify for Jamal."

"Not so fast, now," Ida said, relishing her au- thority by virtue of her knowledge. "It's not go- ing to be as easy as you think. I'll have to ask you some pretty tough questions. Mainly about your background."

Nikki frowned. "What background?"

"Come on, Nikki. Let's not play games with each other. For Jamal's sake, let's not do that."

"But what are you talking about? What back- ground?"

Ida leaned forward. "Number one, you're a high school drop-out."

"I got my GED."

"You also got a baby when you were eighteen years old."

Nikki glanced over at Dino, and then brought her attention back to Ida. "So?"

"So, Nikki. You weren't married, were living in a hooker motel, and were selling stolen goods to earn your living."

'I didn't steal those tapes! I was—"

"Yeah, yeah, whatever. But that's what the prosecution is going to say. They're going to paint you as an unwed, unfit mother who never gave her son a chance." Nikki swallowed hard, her throat suddenly constricted with fear. "You're the villain too, Nikki," Ida continued, "not just Jamal. Many people around Monroe belive that your promiscuity, your less-than-upstanding lifestyle and your immorality are what caused this to happen. You're the town's trash to them. You have nothing going for yourself, nothing that anybody would say is outstanding about you. And Jamal, they believe, was just unfortunate enough to be your son."

Nikki's heart dropped. Hearing those words, words she'd said to herself a million times, devastated her. She immediately began sliding out of the booth. "Will you excuse me?" Without waiting for an answer, she excused herself to the ladies' room.

Ida felt triumphant. Now Dino would wake up and realize how ludicrous it was for him to even consider hooking his prestigious, image-driven wagon to a broken down old saddlebag of a horse like Nikki Lucas.

"She's a mess," Ida said after they both watched Nikki flee.

Dino looked at her. "Enjoyed yourself, Foxy?"

"Pardon me?"

"Got your thrill on with that little exhibition?"

"Whatever are you talking about? Those are the actual accusations the prosecution will not hesitate to level against your little friend there, make no mistake about it."

"Oh, I'm sure they'll allege those and more. I'm sure I cannot begin to know how badly they will try to beat up on Nikki and Jamal. But make no mistake about this: I will not stand by and let you beat up on them too."

"Me? What did I do? All I did was tell the truth."

"With glee, yes you did."

Ida's attempt at levity turned serious, and ice cold. "What do you see in her?" she demanded. "What does she have that I don't have?"

Dino looked into Ida's eyes and shook his head. "That's not the point, Foxy, and you know it."

"But it is the point! You're willing to choose her over me, to defend her like that, and I have a right to know why. What does that . . . *waitress* have on me?"

"Is she prettier than you? Is that what you're asking? No, Foxy, she's not prettier than you. Few women are. All right?"

"Not all right. Not the way you look at her."

Dino leaned back.

"Why her, Dean?"

"It's not her, all right? It's not anybody. I told you that."

"But why are you so . . ." She regathered her thoughts. "Before this Nikki person came along we were tight. I wasn't just your attorney, I was your friend. Your close friend. I even thought that we would eventually . . . But now, you're acting as if I'm supposed to just sit back and let some ponytail-wearing waitress take you away from me."

Dino exhaled. He looked at his friend. "Let's get something straight right now, Ida. Nobody can take me away from you because you never had me. You're a young, beautiful woman who's infatuated with an older man. I told you a long time ago, years ago, that it was going nowhere and you needed to go on and find you a young, beautiful man who would want nothing better than to be your loving husband. I'm not that man. I told you then and I'm telling you now. My duties are to God and that's where I intend for them to stay. But you didn't listen to me then and you're not listening now. Perhaps I encouraged you." He stared deep into Ida's eyes. "Perhaps I wasn't forceful enough. But my goodness, Foxy, what do you want me to do? Spell it out?"

Ida leaned back and picked up her glass of wine. "Well," she said, trying not to behave as the child he obviously took her for, although she felt like sulking now, "you can begin by stop calling me Foxy." She batted her big eyes at him. "That has definitely been an encouragement."

Dino's heart dropped. He'd been doing it to Ida too. Leading her on. Tossing her just enough to keep her coming back. Was it his ego that demanded he always keep some female on his tail? Was that a part of his sinful nature that he still hadn't overcome? And why did he even bring her here? She was a good lawyer, no doubt about that, but he knew others equal to the task. Why did it have to be her? Was he using her to help keep his feelings for Nikki at bay? Was it all about him again, just as it was the night his wife and baby died and his best friend took a bullet for him? *Good Lord. What have I done?*

"You can begin by stop spending time with me," Ida continued, oblivious to his misery, "and stop treating me as if I'm somebody special to you."

Dino nodded in agreement with her, but also in acknowledgment that he had to make a decision, and by default, a choice. His speech was slow and agonizing. "I can also begin by taking you off of this case."

Ida stopped twirling her wine around in the glass and looked at him. "What?"

Dino exhaled. "Go back home, Ida."

Ida's eyes stretched. "Go home?"

"Yes. I thank you for coming, I even apologize for asking you to come, but you're right."

Ida swallowed hard, staring at Dino. "What am I right about?"

"You're right about me. I have led you on, or at least I haven't done all I could to stop it. That's why I've got to stop it now. That's why your being Jamal's attorney isn't going to work."

Ida folded her arms, her anger rising. "So you're firing me, Dean? Is that what you're saying?"

It was a crushing blow. Dino was always cast as the heavy, but in this scene, he knew it was appropriate. "Yes. I'm sorry." He said it as sympathetic as he could, but he knew she didn't want his sympathy either. She wanted him, just as so many other women over these past years, and he roped her into his inner circle, spending time with her, sharing too much of himself with her. Now he was hurting her, the way he always, inevitably, did every woman who dared to love him. He looked at her and saw the tears forming in her eyes. "Ida," he said heartfelt, but she dismissed his concern with a shake of the head.

She wiped away a lone tear trickling down with a quick wipe of her hand and began sliding across the booth seat. "Please move," she said, her progression stifled by his refusal to stand and let her out.

"Ida—"

"No, Dean!" she said harshly, looking at him. "No. You can't tell me to get out of your life and then tell me not to be hurt, or say we can still be friends, or whatever. You say it's over, then it's over." She smiled through her tears. "I never thought this would be it. I never thought in a million years that it would be another woman that took my place. Your duties to the church, yes. God, certainly. But never another woman. I didn't think you handled your business that way. I thought you were . . ." She didn't even bother to finish the sentence.

You thought I was your hero too, Dino wanted to say, as if saying it would prove the foolishness of it, but he didn't say another word. He stood and let her leave. And she left with fire under her feet. Dino sat back down, and leaned his head back. Just as he did, the waiter, who undoubtedly was waiting for the smoke to clear before he came over, arrived with their drinks.

When Nikki returned to the table, looking almost as glum as Ida had looked, as if she'd been crying too, he felt another pang of guilt. "Where's Foxy?" she asked snidely as she sat down across from Dino.

"Gone," he said, trying his best to minimize that monumental word.

"Gone where?" Nikki was too puzzled to be relieved. She didn't see her come near the ladies' room.

"She's not on the case anymore, Nikki."

Nikki frowned. "Not on the case? You mean to tell me that heifer walked out on Jamal?"

"No." Dino turned angry. "It wasn't her fault, you hear me? I fired her. I gave her her walking papers. It wasn't on her, it's on me." He wasn't about to let Nikki or anybody else blame Ida for this fiasco.

Nikki was a little surprised by Dino's defense of her, and why he would give her her walking papers at all, especially after the way they seemed so chummy just before she had headed for the restroom. But if she didn't know anything else, she knew that she'd be dead and sleeping in her grave before she ever understood Dino Cochran. "What about the trial, Dino? She was Jamal's lawyer."

"I'll get him another one."

"Another lawyer? But that's not good, is it? In the middle of a trial, I mean."

"Middle of what trial, Nikki?" he asked, irritated. "The trial hasn't even begun yet. And I told you I'll get another lawyer, so don't worry about that." Dino looked at her. She had every right to worry and he knew she did. But the idea of him causing that worry was the reason for his agitation. "It'll be all right," he said, looking into her eyes, not even pretending to be reassuring.

The ride home was a quiet one. Nikki had wanted Dino to take her to pick up her car from the diner, where she'd left it earlier, but she decided to catch a ride to work with Tam in the morning and get it then. Truth was, she didn't know if she was in the right frame of mind for driving. This was some overwhelming news Dino had just laid on her. As of right now, her son, who was facing a murder charge, didn't have an attorney. She could hardly believe it. Did Dino really know what he was doing? Had he thought through this rash decision of his? Was he thinking about *Jamal*?

She looked over at him. He was driving faster than usual as they drove up San Jose Boulevard, heading for the Buckman Bridge. The Jacksonville traffic was heavy at night, and it was as restless as Dino seemed to be. Nikki knew that Dino wouldn't hurt Jamal. He was aware of the seriousness of what her son was facing. She wasn't used to this, but she knew she had to let him handle this lawyer predicament they were in. It wasn't as if she had a choice, after all. He would be stuck with some public defender that may or may not have skills, if it were left up to her and her sorry means.

Nikki didn't speak a word of her concerns as they drove across the Buckman, along Interstates 295 and 10, and into Monroe. When they drove up into her driveway, she immediately noticed that her entire house appeared dark. After Jamal's release from jail, he'd been very careful about keeping an outside light on for his mother when she came in from work at night. Nikki even told him how much she appreciated his thoughtfulness and he seemed pleased by her gratitude. Now, perhaps, he was just reverting back to form, back to his trouble days. But it didn't feel like that to Nikki. It felt like Jamal was gone.

She just sat there, wondering where in the world he could have gone. Dino got out, walked around, and opened the door for her. It was then, when he opened the door, that she realized if Jamal was gone, if he'd defied her once again, she didn't even have transportation to go and track him down. She looked at Dino and it hurt her to her heart to drag him into her mess again. As if he needed this. "He's not home."

Dino frowned, then looked at the house. "You sure?"

She nodded. "Yes."

"Well, where is he?"

"I don't know."

"What do you mean you don't know?"

"I wasn't here, Dino, all right? How am I supposed to know where he went?"

"You're supposed to know because I told you how this town felt about that boy, how deeply their hatred went. I told you to keep an eye on him!"

"I kept an eye on him! What did you want me to do? Take him to work with me and bring him back home?"

Dino exhaled. This was getting them nowhere. "When did you last speak to him?"

"What do you mean?"

Dino looked irritably at Nikki. His fear for Jamal's safety was translating into anger toward her, which stunned her. "When did you last talk to him, Nikki. You know what I mean."

"This morning."

Dino couldn't believe it. "This morning? You mean to tell me you haven't checked on your son all day, given the climate in this town?"

"I was at work, Dino. Then Seb called with news about his mother and I closed down the diner and just went on over there. I didn't think . . ." She didn't think about her own son. She knew that was what Dino wanted to say. But he didn't.

After another exhale, he asked, "Does he have a cell phone?"

She looked away from him. "No."

"Why not, Nikki? Everybody has one."

She looked at Dino, her anger flaring too. "Well, my son doesn't, okay? And neither do I. A cell phone may be a cheap necessity to you, but it's another bill to me. So excuse me for not being wealthy enough for you."

Dino ran his hand through his soft hair. Times like these made him wish he could get on that plane with Ida. "Go in the house and make sure he's not there. Then we'll drive around and see if we can find him."

Nikki got out of the car. They stood close, although Nikki hardly felt his equal. "If he's not there, all you have to do is take me to my car. I'll go find him."

"Nikki?"

"Yes?" she responded almost defiantly.

"Don't push me; you understand? Go see if he's inside."

Nikki felt as if the last vestige of her once ironclad control was slipping away. Dino was in charge now. He was calling the shots. Once again, he was picking her up and refusing to let her run after that dude that had stolen her tapes all those years ago, because he had decided that it wasn't her battle. They were her tapes and it was her rep and her wounded pride, but it became his fight. Now, the drama that was her life and Jamal's life was his fight. A fight he didn't even want. She could see it in his eyes.

Surprising even herself, she didn't take back the fight. She knew that she eventually would. But not now. Not until she was certain that Jamal wasn't in jeopardy. Nikki went into the house and searched in a futile attempt to see if her child had done something remarkable for once in his life: obeyed her.

He wasn't on the basketball courts in Pottsburg, which was their first stop, but was much farther away, at Monroe High, a place they decided to drive by on a whim. And there he was. Not merely hanging out with the thugs he once idolized, but he was in the middle of the school grounds, shirt off, arms flailing, fighting those very thugs.

"Stay here," Dino said firmly to Nikki as he jumped from his Mercedes. He left his door open in his haste to run toward the action.

Nikki jumped out of the car, forgetting Dino ever said a word, and ran behind him. She wanted with all she had to run up there and help her son defend against those hoodlums, but she also knew Dino was right. She had to stay out of it. She was no match against those strong young men.

There were three of them, and although Jamal was besting one and sometimes two, three were just too many. Dino slung each one of them off of Jamal, lifting them up as if they were weightless. When they saw, not just who he was, but the sheer muscles on those thick arms of his, they didn't try to reenter the fray. It was Shake who was doing the most damage to Jamal, holding Jamal down in a headlock that could have been taking the life out of the boy.

Although it took a little more effort, Dino pulled Shake away from Jamal too. He lifted him up and held Shake by the catch of his shirt as he looked him dead in the eyes. "You wanna fight somebody?" he said "Fight me!"

Shake was still defiant as he stared at the big brother that held him so easily. Then he jerked himself away from Dino. "What kind of preacher are you?" he asked, amazed.

"The kind you don't want to mess with," Dino replied.

Shake didn't like that look in Dino's eyes and quickly looked away. At easier bait. Jamal. "Can't fight your own battles, Jamal?" he taunted as if it were the unforgivable sin. "Punk! he spewed as he and his boys began gathering themselves together and walking back toward their old Buick.

Nikki ran past them, making sure she looked Shake in the eyes, and up to Jamal and Dino. Jamal was still on the ground, touching the small trickle of blood on his lip and then looking at it on his fingertip.

"Are you all right?" Nikki asked, falling down on her knees beside him.

Jamal nodded. It was obvious that he was more angry than hurt. He stood up, refusing Nikki's assistance, and grabbed his shirt from off of the ground. He glanced at Dino, who seemed so upset he could explode at any moment, and it was too much. Tears began to appear in Jamal's eyes. He felt like a chump, crying in front of a macho man like Dino, but he couldn't help himself. He wanted Dino's sympathy. For some crazy reason he *needed* Dino's sympathy. But Dino began walking away.

"Let's get out of here," he said in a voice unmistakably void of any kind of compassion.

When the car returned to Nikki's house, everybody just sat where they were for a moment. It was as if they knew this couldn't be the end of it. Not like this. Not a simple getting out of the car and leaving. Nikki looked at Dino from the passenger seat. Jamal was staring at Dino from the backseat. It was as if they were waiting for him to give them their *walking papers*, to tell them that it was nice knowing them but he couldn't deal with their drama a moment longer. But Dino didn't say a word. He exhaled, unlatched his seatbelt, and got out of the car.

Jamal and Nikki got out too. They began walking toward the front door. To Nikki's surprise, Dino took out his own key and unlocked the door, and then waited while they walked in ahead of him, as if he were the real head of this household. When the lights were turned on, Jamal was about to open his mouth, to try and explain himself, but the look Dino gave him

made him think better of it. Even Nikki could
see the tension all over Dino's face. This episode
with Jamal tonight had affected him in ways she
couldn't even begin to understand, as if it was
the last straw in a long succession of last straws.
Especially tonight. First he blamed himself for
Sebastian's mother's lack of faith, then he had to
fire Ida Fox, effectively leaving Jamal temporarily without counsel, now this. If they had thought
for a minute that this was the end of it and he
was simply going to see them in and say good-
bye, they now knew better than that.

"Excuse us, Nikki," Dino said in a remarkably soft tone, and then began walking toward
Jamal's room.

Jamal glanced at his mother but eagerly followed Dino, certain that he just wanted to take
him in the back and have a man-to-man with
him. Nikki, however, wasn't nearly as sure as her
son. She even jumped when she heard the bedroom door close, as a sudden, nervous curiosity
began to overtake her. She hurriedly walked into
the hallway near Jamal's room, but instead of
standing at the door the way she really wanted
to, she walked across the hall to the dining room,
where she sat at the head of the table and listened.

First there was nothing, not a sound, as Dino undoubtedly was pulling his staring routine on Jamal. It was a style Dino had perfected. That quietness before the storm. But then Nikki suddenly tensed as Dino began to speak.

"Didn't your mother tell you to stay at home, Jamal?"

"I just went up the block to shoot a few hoops."

"Didn't she tell you to stay at home?"

"Yeah, but I was tired of sitting up in here. All I did was go and shoot a couple of hoops. That's all I was gonna do."

"Why did you disobey her?"

"I wasn't bothering them. That's why I didn't go to Pottsburg. That's why I went up to the school. Shake came up on me."

"Okay. Now answer *my* question. Why did you disobey your mother?"

"I told you. I was tired of sitting up in here."

"And that was a good enough reason to disobey a direct order from your mother?"

"Man, it ain't even like that."

"Jamal?"

When Dino said her son's name that way, Nikki's chest tightened. Jamal, as usual, didn't realize the warning.

"Jamal?" Dino said again.

"I heard you. What?"

"I'm not your *man*. You understand?"

"Yeah, whatever."

Nikki closed her eyes. If her son had one knack, it was for showing that disrespectful attitude of his at the exact wrong moment.

"You talk to your mother that way, don't you?" Dino asked.

"What you talking about? I'm trying to tell you what went down and you don't even wanna hear it. You just like her. All you know is that I wasn't here. But I didn't start no fight. That was Shake. He came up on me. I didn't even go to Pottsburg. He came where I was."

"Am I supposed to be impressed by that ability of yours?"

"What? What ability?"

"Am I supposed to forget my point and get caught up in yours?"

"What you talking about?"

"That's how you do your mother, isn't it? Get her caught up in your nonsense until she's too exhausted to remember her own valid argument."

"Man, I ain't even trying to hear all this stupid stuff. I'm getting out of here!"

Nikki opened her eyes in anticipation of what was coming next. Was her son nuts? Did he not see that look in Dino's eyes tonight? Was he *blind*?

And sure enough, before Nikki could even think it, it was happening. First ,there was a crash against the door, as if Dino had deliberately slammed Jamal against it.

"What you doing?" she heard Jamal say in that high-pitched voice he used whenever he was scared.

Then she heard the sound of a belt buckle and then the lashing sounds of a belt hitting flesh. Jamal was trying to fight back. There was a lot of scuffling sounds coming from the room too, so much so that Nikki stood up with the intention of going to see what was going on for herself.

But she sat back down. Dino was only doing to Jamal what she should have done a long time ago. She'd spared the rod and spoiled the mess out of her child. Now it was second nature for him to disobey her. That was why he got into it with Shake tonight. That was why he was arrested for murder that tragic night. Disobedience. Nikki was no Bible scholar, but she did know that somewhere in the Bible even God said it was better to obey than to sacrifice. But she failed to teach that simple lesson to her son. She failed, once again.

Nikki went into the kitchen and put on a pot of coffee. Jamal would be highly upset with her later, she was well aware of that. He would want to know why she would let some stranger beat the mess out of him when even she never lifted a finger to him. But Dino was no stranger. That was what Jamal didn't understand. Dino was his father. His *father*. The burden of that revelation began to overtake her. She leaned against the drainboard and raked her hand through her hair. He had the right to chastise her child. That was why she was leaving him to it. She hadn't done it right. All of these years. Why in the world would she try and stop Dino?

The noise finally stopped and even Jamal's mouth wasn't heard anymore. She wondered for a quick second if she should run in there and make sure Dino hadn't killed her child, but she got off of that position fast enough. Anything could have happened to Jamal tonight out at that school, and she and Dino knew it. Shake, given his leadership status in the gang of thugs, was more than likely the person who killed William Coleman. What if he'd still had that gun with him? What if he would have used it on Jamal? It wasn't as if the citizens of this town of theirs would have shed any tears. They'd already given up on Jamal. If he was murdered, that was fine by them. It would save them the cost of incarceration.

Nikki moved over to the island counter and covered her face. She knew she couldn't think like that. After all, not all of the residents of Monroe had turned on them.

She thought about Sebastian and Tam. They were true friends . . . through thick and thin friends. They hadn't forsaken her son. Then she began to wonder about Sebastian and if he was handling his mother's death any better, and if Tam decided to stay with him all evening, or all night.

Dino came into the kitchen just as the coffee had brewed. He looked so tired, so spent, breathing so heavily, that Nikki almost asked if he was all right. But that would have been a stupid question. Of course he wasn't all right. He was caught up in her craziness. How in the world could that be all right?

"Want some coffee?" she offered.

"No," he said curtly, as if the tension from the bedroom was still weighing heavily on him. He exhaled. "No, thank you." His tone was softer that time. "I need to head on back."

"You still have your room here, you know." It was a bold invitation but Nikki felt a need to extend it.

He looked at her and nodded his head. "I know, but I'm going to need some quiet prayer

time. This hasn't exactly been a spiritually en-
riching night."

"Oh," Nikki said with a slight smile. "I'm real
sorry that I dragged you into this."

"You didn't drag me into anything." Dino's
voice was harsher than he had intended. He exhaled again. "I'll talk with you later in the week,
once I have the new attorney on board," he said,
rubbing his neck. "All right?"

Nikki decoded his words in her mind. *Don't
call me, I'll call you.* "All right," she said.

"And Nikki," he added, "stop babying that boy.
If he disobeys you, you've got to punish him. You
can't tolerate his foolishness any longer. And
if you can't handle it, if you can't do something
about him, then you call me. It's late in the game,
but we've got to start somewhere. Understand?"

He said *we.* Maybe he wasn't giving her the
brush-off after all. "Understood," she complied.

But then he looked at her with what she could
only interpret as a look of disappointment, as if
he knew all about her failings and was tired of
making excuses for them, and that little shred
of hope she'd just grasped, slipped away. "Goodnight," Dino said. He left without waiting for her
response.

Nikki's shoulders slumped. He couldn't wait
to get away. He just couldn't wait.

EIGHTEEN

The heavy rains that had torn through Monroe all morning were nothing more than a noticeable drizzle by the time Sebastian's Honda Civic pulled into the Big Turn parking lot. Fern was the first to see him as he made his way into the diner and wiped his feet on the welcome mat. She elbowed Mookie.

"Hey, Mr. Sebastian," Mookie said with a big smile when he looked across the room and saw his friend. He was wiping tables after a so-so breakfast crowd, and Fern was sitting at the table, apparently keeping him company while he worked. "Good to see you this morning."

"Good to be seen," Sebastian said as he moved toward the counter.

"Sorry about your mama," Mookie added.

Sebastian hesitated. The pain still lingered. He looked at Mookie and nodded. "Thank you."

Tam, who was ringing up a customer, looked at Sebastian as he sat at the counter. "And what are you doing here?"

"I had to do something. Couldn't mope around the house all day."

"All day? It's only ten in the morning."

"Long enough," Sebastian said.

Tam shook her head and handed change to the elderly couple waiting to receive it. "Have a nice day," she said to them.

"You too, Tammy," the woman said. "And tell Henry the omelet was a trifle soft this morning. Not like his usual *at all*."

"I'll sure tell him," Tam said as she watched the couple make their way out of Big Turn. She looked at Sebastian. "When pigs fly, I'll tell him. Can you imagine Henry accepting constructive criticism about his cooking?"

Sebastian smiled. "No."

"What are you doing here, Sebastian?" Nikki's voice could be heard from down the hall. Both Sebastian and Tam turned in her direction. She stood just outside her office looking at them.

"And good morning to you too, Miss Lucas," Sebastian said.

"How are you holding up?"

"I'm all right. I'm blessed."

"Good. Tam, could you come here for a minute? And since you're here, Seb, you come too."

Nikki went back into the office. Tam and Seb looked at each other, wondering what was the matter now, and then went down the short hall and into the small office. They sat down.

Nikki, who was leaning on the edge of her desk, had planned to get right to the point, but found it harder than she thought. "You shouldn't be back so soon, Seb," she said. "You haven't had a chance to grieve."

"I know. I just thought I'd come in for a few hours, that's all. Just to break up the monotony. It just doesn't seem like home since Mother's gone. This seems more like home than home does."

That didn't help Nikki's mood, especially what she had to say.

"What's wrong, Nikki?" Tam asked, sensing her concern. "Is Jamal all right?"

"Other than getting into a fight with those thugs from Pottsburg, he's fine."

"A fight?" Tam asked. "When?"

"Last night, child."

"In Pottsburg?"

Nikki shook her head. "Over at the school."

"Not those same boys who might have had something to do with Dollar Bill Coleman's death," Sebastian said.

"One in the same. I know. I couldn't believe it either."

"What was he doing over at the school?" Tam asked.

"He claimed he walked over there to shoot some hoops. Shake and the boys saw him and jumped him."

Tam shook her head. "That's a long way to walk just to play basketball."

"Don't you know I know that? I don't know who Jamal think he's fooling. But that's his story and he's sticking to it." Then she smiled. "Dino didn't buy it either."

Tam laughed. "Bishop Cochran set him straight, huh?"

"Bishop Cochran beat his behind. You should have heard my son. He must have thought Dino was me and he could tell him all those tall tales and get away with it. He didn't get away with jack."

"It's about time," Sebastian said. Both Nikki and Tam looked at him. "I'm serious. Jamal is a nice young man; you know I'm very fond of him, but he's spoiled rotten. Your idea of discipline, Nikki, is to yell at him and send him to his room. A room, I might add, equipped with a TV, a stereo . . . you know where I'm going with this."

"I know," Nikki said, folding her arms. "Dino told me as much last night. But I just felt Jamal had enough strikes against him. He didn't need

me knocking him down, too. In any event, that's
not why I called y'all in here. Wish it was, but it's
not."

"Diner problems?" Sebastian asked.

Nikki nodded. "Afraid so. I have worked it and
overworked it, and I tell you there's no way."

Tam's heart dropped. "No way for what, Nikki?" she asked, fearing she already knew the
answer.

"There's no way I can keep this diner open. In
six weeks the mortgage will become due unless I
catch up, which is impossible since the revenues
coming in have dried up to half their normal
intake. It's not possible to survive like this. How
we've managed this long is only by the grace of
God because it certainly wasn't any ingenuity on
my part. But now it's over." She hesitated, hating
the fact that she wasn't clever enough to have
figured something out. "Come next month, guys,
the Big Turn will have to close. That's when the
finance company will seize it anyway. I've con-
tacted a realtor, but as you can imagine, she's not
optimistic that she can do much with this situation." Nikki swallowed. "I'm sorry."

It was the final blow. Sebastian didn't know if
he could bear the idea of losing his mother and
his anchoring all at the same time. The Big Turn
wasn't much, but it was the only true family he'd

ever known. He loved coming to work here and earning a living that might have been far below his own expectations, but perfect for his lifestyle. Now all of that was leaving him too. He looked at Tam.

Tam stood up. "Anything else, Nikki?"

Nikki, surprised by Tam's tepid response, nodded her head. "That's all."

"I need a couple of hours off," Tam announced.

"Now?"

"Yes."

Nikki hesitated. "What's up, Tam?"

"Nothing's up. May I have the time I've requested?"

"Sure. You can have it. There's hardly a mob out there. But why do you need it?"

"Thank you," Tam said and left the office.

Sebastian looked at Nikki in confusion, but excused himself and hurried behind Tam. "What is your problem?" he asked as they walked along the short corridor to the counter. "And where do you all of a sudden have to go?"

"I'm going to see Bishop Cochran," she said.

"Bishop Cochran?"

"That's right. He cares enough to discipline her son. You heard her in there. Maybe he cares enough to help her hold on to this place."

"But is this our business?" Sebastian asked reluctantly, already knowing that it was.

"What else we gonna do? Let Nikki close this place? This all we have. This place can't close. If Nikki wasn't so prideful, she'd go for help herself, like she does whenever Jamal's in trouble. We can't sit back and let her pride destroy Big Turn." Tam grabbed her purse and car keys from behind the counter and started heading for the front door. Sebastian hesitated, and then followed.

Later that day, hours after Tam and Sebastian had gone to see Bishop Cochran and returned, certain that he did not understand the urgency at all, Nikki, who was joking around with one of the truckers inside the diner, saw his car drive up. Her heart lurched in anticipation. She honestly didn't think she'd see him today. Not after last night. But there he was, walking like an athlete in that well-tailored dark striped suit. She could also see some tightness across his chest, as if his visit wasn't as accidental as she might have thought.

Tam also saw him coming, and she elbowed Sebastian, who was standing behind the counter with her. They both smiled with hope, but when Nikki glanced their way, they immediately got back to work.

Dino walked into the diner without breaking his stride. It had been a month and a half since he first stepped foot into little Monroe, but he felt as if he'd been there a lifetime. And now this. He looked at Nikki, who couldn't help but gawk at him, and pointed toward the back. "May I see you in your office, please?" He continued his walk through the dining area and down the narrow hall. Nikki looked at Tam and Sebastian, who both shrugged their shoulders as if they had no clue. She then hurried behind Dino.

As soon as Nikki followed Dino into her office and they closed the door, Tam and Sebastian ran up to the door and weren't the least ashamed to press their ears against it.

Inside, Dino was taking off his suit coat and flapping it over the back of the chair behind Nikki's desk. The tenseness she had noticed in his muscular frame when he had first stepped out of his car, was straining the fabric of his silk shirt now, but Nikki would not be distracted, especially since he looked more drained than sexy.

"Where are your books?" he asked her.

"My books?"

He looked at her. "Everything to do with this diner. I want to see them. Now." He seemed angry with her, as if her financial woes were an affront to him.

Nikki shook her head. "Tam went to see you, didn't she?"

Outside the door, Tam placed her fist to her mouth, hoping that Dino wouldn't give her up that easily.

Dino refused to even go down that road. "I don't have all day, Nikki." Weariness leaked from his voice. His manner was calm, his delivery even calmer, but his eyes told another story. Nikki hesitated before providing him with all of the records he needed.

He sat behind her desk, placed on a pair of reading glasses, and methodically reviewed the books she had put in front of him. At first, Nikki tried to point out various situations that the records might show to him, but when he looked at her as if her voice alone was grating on his nerves, she sat back down in front of the desk and let him have his look.

It wouldn't do any good. Dino was a smart businessman. Even he knew it made zero sense to put money into a money pit like Big Turn. What Nikki didn't understand was his attitude. She didn't know if he was angry about her finances, which wouldn't make any sense at all, or just plain angry that he was always getting caught up in her drama, day in and day out. To her credit, this was one drama she had no intentions of ever drawing him into. But, thanks to good ol' Tam, he was already in. Nikki was going to strangle that Tammy Ellis as soon as she got her hands on her.

Dino looked up from the books in front of him and stared at Nikki above his gold-rimmed glasses.

Nikki wrinkled her brow. "What?"

"Twenty-one percent, Nikki?"

She knew it was an incredible truth: a woman supposedly with all this smarts taking out a loan with a twenty-one percent interest rate. But at the time . . . "I would have gotten it lower if I could have, Dino."

"Why would you agree to something this ridiculously high? That's what I don't understand. And for a business loan at that. A crackhead would have shown better judgment."

That hurt. That hurt Nikki to the core. "Now you just wait a minute," she said, but Dino interrupted her.

"No, you wait a minute." He was fired up, too. Nikki didn't understand why, but it was obvious as the day. "Why would you put yourself in this kind of position? This loan was going to be difficult enough for you to pay off at a respectable rate, given the history of this diner even before you purchased it. Yet you sign your name on the dotted line like some doggone fool, and you worry about the consequences tomorrow. Well, the consequences are here, lady, and they're here in living color." Dino lifted the papers and then slammed them back on the desk. "You never stood a chance with these kinds of odds, Nikki!"

Nikki didn't like his tone, as if she had gotten herself in this situation on purpose. "Look, Dino; it's not like you think, all right? You think I wanted to go that route? You think I looked around and said, 'Oh, I guess I'll find the place with the highest interest rate available for my start-up loan?'"

"Don't minimize this."

"I'm not minimizing anything, but you act like there were all these choices out there for me. I didn't have a choice, okay? My life hasn't ever been simple like that, and you know it. The truth is if I didn't go with the twenty-one percent interest rate, then I wouldn't have been able to buy this place. That's the truth."

"Then you should not have bought it," Dino said with less vigor, understanding fully Nikki's dilemma.

Nikki, however, found his comment so insensitive that it hurt. "What do you want from me?" she asked him with more emotion than she had intended. "I was stupid. Is that what you want me to say? Okay, I was stupid. I shouldn't have gotten it. A crackhead's got more sense than me. Satisfied?"

Satisfied? Dino took off his glasses and leaned back. He didn't know the meaning of the word, especially not in his dealings with that darn Nikki. He ran his hand across his face with a bewildered sigh, as if he was beyond annoyed by this situation. Then he looked at Nikki through thoughtful, squinted eyes, and shook his head. "Am I that disgusting to you?" he asked her.

Nikki was dumbstruck. She frowned. "What are you talking about?"

"Am I that horrible a human being to you?"

"Dino, what are you trying to say?"

"You would let things get this out of control, to a point where you would have to give up this place, before you would even think about coming to me for help?"

Nikki almost smiled. So that was why he was so angry. That was why he could hardly contain himself. She didn't go groveling to him for help. She didn't place her business, the way she had to place herself and her son, under his control. She exhaled. "It's not even like that," she said half-heartedly.

Outside the door, Tam disagreed. "It's exactly like that," she whispered.

Sebastian nodded in agreement. They had been joined by Henry, Fern and Mookie, who weren't at all sure yet what was going on, although Fern had some idea. But every time she asked for details, Tam shushed her.

Back inside, Dino nodded his head. "That's exactly what it's like," he said, echoing Tam's sentiment. "That foolish pride of yours prevented you from coming to me. Oh, you'd come if Jamal was threatened, you'd come to me then. But when it concerns you, if it were your neck on the chopping block, you'd let them chop away before you gave me the satisfaction."

"That's not true, and you know it. I'm just tired of failing, Dino, don't you understand that? I'm tired of all of my hard work never being good enough, never quite right, never what I tried so hard for it to be. This was my dream. Yes, this little diner was my dream come true. And I slaved and I slaved to make this work. I gave it my all, Dino. And my all wasn't good enough. It felt like I was thirteen again and my mother were telling me that if I was a different kind of child, then maybe she would take me with her. But I had too much mouth, you see, and I had these weird green eyes, and I would attract too much attention."

She hesitated. "I begged her to take me with her. I begged her, Dino. When I told you about that scene, I made it sound as if it was no big deal at all. My mother walked out on me, left me with some pervert, but that was cool with me. Yeah, right. I told her she could cut out my tongue. I told her I would wear dark shades or she could buy me colorless contact lenses, anything she wanted. Just take me with her. But she wouldn't do it."

"I didn't realize how alone I was until later that night, after I'd gotten away from that old fart she left me with, and I was sitting up against a garbage can in a dark alley. Nobody loved me. That was what I realized. Nobody in this world gave a darn about me. It wasn't my looks, or my mouth, or my eyes. It was me. *I* wasn't good enough. Now it's the same thing. I'm failing again. I'm not good enough again. And you want to know why I didn't go running to you with the big news? I would have preferred to die than have to face this failure. All I want to do now is get it over with, not listen to you tell me what I already know."

Dino stared at Nikki in a lingering, anguished stare. Then he sighed. "What about your employees?"

By now, there wasn't a dry eye to be found among the gang outside the door, but they willed themselves to listen harder. They expected Dino to come back with words of encouragement, but he didn't. The man was all about business.

At first, Nikki was caught off guard by his question. It was a question she'd thought about but had dared not ask herself. "What about them?" She bit her lower lip.

"Nikki, your decision to give up doesn't affect you only."

"So what are you saying? I'm responsible for their lives, too? It's not enough for me to bear my own disappointments, but I've got to shoulder theirs too?" Tears came to Nikki eyes. "I know I'm letting them down, Dino, dang. Don't you think I know that?"

As soon as he saw that tears were in her eyes, as soon as she said his name, he jumped up and moved around the desk, not slowing his progress until he had her in his arms. "Nikki, don't cry," he pleaded.

Her tears could only be matched by the tears that came to the eyes of the gang outside the door. Tam and Seb looked at each other. The idea of Nikki crying, *their* Nikki, was incredible to them. They listened, as only Nikki's sobs could be heard. Then Dino started talking again.

He pulled her closer against him, as she sobbed into his chest, his face lying against her thick hair. "You trust me, don't you, Nikki?" Nikki didn't hesitate to nod. She didn't know exactly what she trusted about Dino, especially in light of their past, but she did. He took her chin in his hand and lifted her face to his. "Then trust this," he said. "You're not going to lose your dream."

The gang outside the door nearly leaped for joy. They could hardly believe their ears. Henry frowned, told them with his hands to be quiet so they wouldn't miss anything, and they all gathered back together and listened.

Nikki stared into Dino's beautiful eyes. She wanted to kiss him, and would have if she had not remembered those few words he had just said to her. "What do you mean?" She sniffed.

"Just what I said. I'm going to pay off the loan on this place, and you'll pay me."

"Dino—"

"At zero interest."

"Dino," Nikki said, pushing away from his embrace. "I can't do that."

Dino could not believe her stubbornness. "You can't?"

"No. No way."

"You don't want this place?"

"Of course, I want it."

"You don't want to keep your people employed?"

Nikki furrowed her brow. "Stop twisting it around, Dino. Of course, I want this diner. Of course, I want to keep everybody employed."

Dino began moving back behind the desk. "Then it's settled."

"Nothing's settled," Nikki said, wiping leftover tears and following him toward the desk. "What are you talking about? I can't let you do this."

"Let me?" Dino glanced at her.

"You know what I mean, Dino!"

"It's settled, Nikki," Dino said firmly as he began putting on his suit coat. "I will buy the diner and you will buy it from me. End of discussion. I think I'll also make an investment in fixing this place up," he added, looking around at the small office. "Give you a little capital to make some needed renovations."

"But I can't let you . . . How can you afford to just buy this place like that, Dino?"

"Don't worry about it."

"Yeah, right. Like I'm gonna sit back and be responsible for you having to file bankruptcy or something because you decided to help me."

"Bankruptcy?" Dino almost laughed. "Nikki, and I'm not bragging, but I can buy this diner and one hundred more like it without a sweat, okay? Don't worry about my bottom line. You just stop letting your pride and unreasonable need for self-determination affect your business decisions. My way, the diner stays open, you keep your dream alive, and your people stay employed. Your way, the diner closes, your people have to scramble to find jobs in a town with too few already, and your dream dies. I don't know about you, but my way sounds like a winner to me. Now do we have a deal, or don't we?"

Nikki folded her arms in frustration. It was no use. How could she turn it down? It wasn't exactly by her own wit and imagination that it all came together, but why did that have to be the criteria? Her friends would still have jobs and she would still have the Big Turn. There was no other answer. "We have a deal," she said somewhat reluctantly.

It startled both of them when a sudden and exuberant burst of cheers rang out on the other side of the door. Nikki frowned and hurried to the door, jerking it open, only to find Tam, Sebastian, Fern, Mookie, and even Henry and his wheelchair, dancing around that narrow hallway like pure fools. Or like, as Nikki's slow-coming smile was beginning to realize, her very happy, very wonderful friends.

NINETEEN

The Lucas dining room looked like a board room. Jamal and his mother sat at the table and listened as Jeff Islick, the tall, razor-thin private investigator Dino had hired, and Bobby Matthews, Jamal's new attorney from Michigan, lay down the law. With them was Darryl Pratt, an attorney from Jacksonville who grew up in Monroe, and yet another attorney, a female who took a lot of notes but never said a word. Jamal now officially had himself what Nikki often heard referred to as a *team of lawyers*, as if Dino was making certain that his hasty decision to fire Ida Fox didn't come back to bite them. He would leave no stone unturned. It had been two months since Jamal had been arrested for the murder of William Coleman, and the stakes were getting higher.

Dino sat at the head of the table, leaned back and stared down at the bottled water he held in his hand. He looked his usual intense self, but appeared far more relaxed than everybody else in the room. He was even dressed in a relaxed manner, wearing a pair of jeans and a black turtleneck. When Nikki first saw him, she knew she was perusing every inch of his athletic body like some idiot, but when all of the other players in this drama started arriving, the reality of why Dino was in her life again in the first place sank in. That laid her gawking to rest.

"Right," Bobby Matthews said as he often did before he got to his point. He was a tall, dark-skinned man around Dino's age, with cowlicks on either side of his narrow face and a skull-low haircut. He also had a British accent that had to be as strong as it was when he first left his homeland and came to America thirteen years ago. He often talked about his homeland, as most foreigners did, although Nikki couldn't help but wonder why he left it in the first place if it were as grand as he claimed.

Bobby Matthews sat in the middle of the three lawyers, and they all sat across the table from Nikki and Jamal. "I'm the lead attorney, but the actual trial presentation will be handled by Darryl here . . . Mr. Pratt. He's the local boy. He knows these people. Me, my accent, and my 'up north,' as they say, credentials, may not bode well for young Jamal. An undue prejudice, I'm afraid. But my skill is always working backstage, away from the spotlight. I think of myself as the Wizard of Oz. The man behind the curtain. And, as in the movie, we want these locals to ignore the man behind the curtain, although in truth, he'll be the one pulling the strings."

Jamal smiled. "But wasn't the Wizard of Oz a fraud?" he asked, and then shot a nervous look at Dino, praying that his little joke wasn't out of bounds. When Dino's thin lips curled into a smile, and everybody else laughed, Jamal inwardly sighed in relief.

Since that night of his fight with Shake, when Dino put the fear of God in him, Jamal had been a little leery of Dino. The punishment was unnerving because it was new, but Jamal wasn't all that sure if he didn't welcome it.

"The Wizard of Oz may have been fraudulent in the end," Bobby said, "but Dorothy didn't know it until the end. Correct?"

Jamal nodded. "I see what you're saying."

"After that trial is over, they can call me anything they like, just as long as you're free to go."

Jamal smiled. "I like that."

"Right." Bobby turned and faced Nikki. "Now, to you, Miss Lucas—"

"Nikki, please."

"Very well, Nikki. Mr. Cochran tells me that you're quite the anxious one." Nikki didn't know if she cared to be described as anxious, but undoubtedly, it was true. Bobby understood her apprehension, and added, "Not that any mother wouldn't be in these rather dreadful circumstances."

"What are his chances?" Nikki asked. "That's what I need to know." All eyes diverted to Darryl Pratt.

"What are the lad's chances, Mr. Pratt?" Bobby asked.

"Here in Monroe?" Pratt asked, and then answered, "Zero."

Even Dino looked up on hearing that one.

"What do you mean zero?" Nikki asked. "You mean to tell me my son doesn't stand a chance to beat this thing?"

"I was born and raised here, Nikki," Pratt said. "A lot of people here know me and, I hope, respect me. I have been from one end of this town to the other end and I will tell you, I could not find one individual who thinks Jamal may not have done it; may not be guilty. I wasn't asking them to declare him innocent, okay, I just wanted them to admit, for the sake of argument even, that there was a chance that he wasn't guilty. I couldn't find one person willing to go that far.

Not one. So if the judge doesn't give us a change of venue, a win for Jamal is improbable. Even if we can get the trial moved to Jacksonville, which I still think is too close, we will have a much better chance."

"I agree," Bobby Mathews said.

"Here, Jamal can't possibly get a fair trial. It'll be an issue for appeal if he's convicted, of course, and we're keeping newspaper articles and statements by local residents to that effect, but we can't allow the conviction."

"This change of venue," Nikki said. "What are the chances that they'll grant it?"

"It's possible," Bobby said, "but not bloody likely. Unfortunately."

Nikki leaned back, feeling as anxious now as she had when Jamal was first arrested. She and her son, as if synchronized to do so, both looked to Dino.

Dino looked at Bobby. "Is it a foregone conclusion that he'll be tried as an adult?"

"Frankly, yes. They have not officially said, of course, but the word Pratt is hearing around the state attorney's office is that they have every intention of filing this lawsuit that way. And they are not at all amiable to even a plea down to second degree."

Dino nodded. He didn't look very disturbed by this revelation, which gave Nikki and Jamal some hope. "What about your end, Jeffrey?" Dino asked Jeff Islick, who sat beside Jamal.

Jeff began by leaning forward, as if he wanted to address his boss directly. "The state's theory is that Jamal and William Coleman were in love with the same girl."

"*What*?" Jamal said, surprised.

"Sharon Granger?" Dino asked, ignoring Jamal.

Jeff nodded. "Sharon Granger. We discovered that less than a week before Coleman's murder, Sharon, the mayor's daughter, mind you, had purchased herself a fake ID and had had an abortion."

"An abortion?" Nikki was astounded. "Are you sure?"

"I'm positive. I'm also positive that your son knew."

Nikki shot a look at Jamal.

"That don't have nothing to do with this," Jamal said.

"You still should have told me, Jamal," Jeff insisted. "I hate being blindsided. When I came to talk to you, and I told you to tell me everything, you should have volunteered this information."

"But what do rumors that she had an abortion got to do with this?" Jamal asked defensively. He glanced at Dino, who was staring at him.

"It has everything to do with this, Jamal," Jeff said as if he couldn't believe the young man's lack of insight. "Especially in light of what we know the state's theory is going to be. Especially since she was William Coleman's girlfriend. Come on, Jamal; I told you to tell me everything, I didn't care how trivial you thought it was." Then he looked at Dino. "But he didn't do that, Mr. Cochran."

"What is the state claiming exactly?" Dino asked, refusing to get into some *I told you so* over Jamal.

"The state believes that Jamal and Sharon Granger were fooling around behind Coleman's back, and there are some witnesses willing to say that they were pretty tight."

"We were just friends," Jamal said. "She was just being nice."

Jeff went on, still directing his responses to Dino. "The state believes that they were more than friends and that Jamal, in fact, was the father of that baby."

"The father?" Nikki shrieked. "That's crazy."

"Is it, Miss Lucas?" Jeff asked.

"Yes, it is."

"Then please tell me why your son accompanied Sharon when she went to have this abortion, and why did he, according to our information, pay for it?" Nikki looked at her son. She could not believe her ears. "Perhaps he went with her as a friend to just be there for her," Jeff added. "But I don't know of too many brothers willing to pay for an abortion when they're not the baby's father."

"It's not even like that," Jamal said.

"Then tell me what it's like," Nikki demanded. "Did you go with her? Did you pay for somebody to get an *abortion*, Jamal?"

"Yeah, I went with her, but I didn't pay for it."

"Who paid for it?" Jeff asked.

"No, first of all," Nikki said, interrupting Jeff, "why did you go with her?"

"She asked me to, Ma, all right? She said I didn't run my mouth with people and she knew I wouldn't tell. And I didn't."

"Who paid for it?" Jeff asked again.

"She did. I was holding the money, but it was her money. She just wanted those abortion clinic people to think that the man was paying for it, that's all."

Jeff nodded. "So you went to a clinic in Jacksonville because she didn't want anybody who knew her in Monroe to see her?"

"That's right. But it wasn't my baby. Dollar Bill was that baby's daddy. She said she didn't tell him she was pregnant because she knew he would want her to keep it. And she didn't want that."

Nikki placed her hands over her face and shook her head.

Bobby Matthews shook his head too. "And you didn't think we needed to know this wealth of information?"

"It wasn't that big a deal."

"Anyway," Jeff continued, "the state alleges that William Coleman, or Dollar Bill as he is also known, found out about this little trip the Granger girl and Jamal took to the clinic and he confronted Jamal. Jamal then pulled a gun and killed Coleman. That's the state's theory in a nutshell."

"That's a lie," Jamal said.

"They have five witnesses, all of whom claim to have been there, willing to back that theory up."

"Lord have mercy," Nikki said in anguish, still shaking her head. This was beyond a nightmare for her. And it was getting scarier by the second. She looked at Dino.

He stood up, walked behind her chair. "Let's go," he said, patting her on the shoulders. Nikki didn't know where he wanted her to go, or why he all of a sudden wanted her to go there, but she stood up without questioning him. Dino looked at Jamal and laid out an order. "You will sit here, young man, and tell Mr. Islick and these attorneys everything, and I mean everything they need to know. You begin at the moment of your conception until this moment in time. You leave nothing out. You tell them every encounter you ever had with William Coleman. You tell them every encounter you ever had with Sharon Granger. You tell them all about Shake and his crew and about that fight you had with them the other night."

"Fight?" Bobby said. "What fight?"

"If you leave anything out, Jamal, anything at all, you'll be answering to me." Dino's expression brooked no debate. "Is that finally clear enough for you? Do you finally get what we mean by *everything*?"

Jamal had a frown on his face, but he nodded his understanding. "Yes, sir." Dino stared at him a little longer, and then said his goodbyes to his team.

To Nikki's surprise, she and Dino didn't go very far; just out of the front door and around the house to the backyard. It was a quiet area surrounded by trees and less grass than Nikki would have liked. And as with everything else around her, the porch itself was slowly falling apart. Dino sat on the top step of that wooden porch while Nikki decided to stand. She was dressed in shorts and a T-shirt, hardly the proper attire for a breezy spring night. But she was too distressed to worry about a little wind.

"It's looking bad for him, Dino," she said, as if she wanted him to contradict her. But he didn't.

"I know," he replied. "But we'll salvage it."

"We will?" Nikki looked at him. He was leaned forward, his elbows resting on his knees, looking more gorgeous than ever in his turtleneck.

"Nikki," Dino said as if he was determined that she understand this time, "you've got to put your faith and trust, not in those lawyers, not in Jeff Islick, and certainly not in me, but you've got to trust in Christ. He is the only one who can get us out of this situation. He's the only one who can."

"I know. And you're right. It's just that, well, it seems almost like stealing."

Dino frowned. "What seems like stealing?"

"I haven't been thinking about the Lord. Now I'm in trouble and I'm calling on His name left and right. It's hypocrisy. It's like I want God to give me something that I don't deserve to have."

"And I deserve to have His love and mercy and everlasting kindness? Of course not, Nikki. Nobody deserves it. If you're waiting until you get yourself totally together to come to Jesus, then you'll never get there. We all have come short. Don't you ever forget that. It's a trick of the devil to have you thinking that you must stop sinning, stop disappointing God, then come to Him for salvation. We'll all be condemned to hell if that's how it's done. God tells us to come to Him just as we are and let Him reason with us, and He'll change our lives. Only He can set us straight. And only He can save Jamal right now. Because you're right, Nikki, it looks bad for him."

Nikki took in a deep breath of anguish, then released it. "He says he's accepted Christ as his Savior, Dino."

Dino nodded. "He told me."

"I pray it's true because that boy, I tell you, sometimes he just makes me so crazy. You heard him in there. He didn't think it was a big deal. Just before Dollar Bill Coleman was murdered, his girlfriend had an abortion, an abortion he took her to get, and he doesn't think that's a big deal. And that's what I don't understand either. How can somebody who claims to be saved be taking a girl to have an abortion? You telling me God is okay with abortions now?"

"Of course He isn't. But Nikki, you aren't listening to me. Christians aren't perfect, okay?

Besides, Jamal hadn't accepted Christ when he helped Sharon Granger. It wasn't until after he was arrested that he accept Christ."

Nikki smiled and shook her head. "Another jailhouse conversion."

"Don't laugh," Dino replied. "Sometimes it sticks. But the point is, even if Jamal had been saved when he helped his friend, that wouldn't mean he was never saved and is condemned to never be. That's what the devil wants us to believe."

"But that's hypocrisy, Dino," she said. "What you're saying is that you can do anything you're big enough to do and still be saved. That's what you're telling me."

"That's not what I'm telling you at all. God knows your heart, Nikki. If somebody's confessing salvation and has no sin consciousness when they do wrong, no regrets or awful feelings about their conduct, as if it's okay, then they're playing. You're right. They are hypocrites. But God knows their hearts. Sin separates us from God's love. When we sin, as Christians, we temporarily lose our fellowship with the Almighty, which is a scary thought. And if we continue to sin, He's faithful and just to forgive our sins and to cleanse us of all unrighteousness. But nobody's pulling any wool over God's eyes. He knows

His children. He knows those who are earnestly seeking Him, who want so much to please Him, from those who are Christians in name only. Be not deceived, God is not mocked. Whatsoever a man sows, that shall he also reap."

Nikki smiled. "You sound like a preacher."

Dino laughed. "I am a preacher, Nikki. First and last." He paused and added, "A very flawed, very human preacher."

"What about this Bobby Matthews, Dino?" Nikki asked with more than a little concern in her voice. "Why him?"

"He's the best. He was my first choice originally, but he couldn't get away unless it was a matter of life or death. After Ida left, I told him that's exactly what it was."

"And this Pratt dude? He seems kind of second rate to me."

"That doesn't matter. Bobby Matthews is running this show. Pratt is just here for color commentary, just in case we don't get that change of venue. But if we do, if the trial moves to Jacksonville, then Bobby's no longer the man behind the curtain. He'll take over completely."

Nikki smiled and shook her head. "You've got it all figured out, don't you?"

"God's got it all figured out."

Nikki smiled. "Why are you so good to us, Dino? Are you atoning for all of your past sins?"

Dino didn't smile, but nodded his head. "Yes," he admitted, to Nikki's surprise. "Every day of my life."

Nikki hesitated. She wanted to ask him more about those past sins, but she didn't dare. "Why did you fire Ida Fox?" she asked instead.

Dino rubbed his hands together and exhaled. "Many reasons."

"Such as?"

"I'm not going into that, Nikki." Dino never discussed his private affairs with anyone, and Nikki wasn't going to be excluded from that. "Suffice it to say that I did what was best for Jamal."

Nikki immediately understood. After all, Jamal's best interest was all she needed to be concerned with. She wrapped her arms around herself and began to move from side to side.

Dino looked at her, at her small body as it rocked in what he viewed as pretty good rhythm. "Cold?" he asked.

She nodded.

"Come here."

Nikki moved over to Dino, no longer hesitant as she had been when he first hit town. He sat her on his thigh. She smiled. "Little inappropriate for a church bishop to be holding some female on his lap, don't you think?"

"Yes," he said and pulled her closer against him.

She laid her head on his chest and to Nikki's surprise, that was all he said about it. They sat in the quiet of the backyard, the sun long since gone down, the trees rustling against each other in the throes of the breeze, and neither felt the need to fill the space, the perfectly peaceful space, with any more words.

TWENTY

Sharon Granger looked out of the bright bay window of her parents' lakeside home and called off the maid, who was preceding her to the front door. The doorbell had chimed only once as she was leaving the kitchen and walking toward the staircase, and instinctively, she knew it was for her. Now, looking out of the window and seeing Jamal's mother standing at the door, she knew that her instinct was right.

Sharon opened the door and stepped outside. It was a warm late afternoon and she'd only been home from school less than an hour, but she had the look of somebody who still wasn't fully awake, who still wasn't going on with her life, as her parents, as everybody who knew her told her that she must. Nikki felt sympathetic when she saw that faraway look in Sharon's eyes, the same look she once held herself when she first arrived in Monroe. It was a feeling of helplessness, of a kind of loss of control, and it wasn't a feeling

Nikki would wish upon anyone. Especially someone like Sharon, who seemed so fragile. Who was so small, so slight in build that she seemed to Nikki to be an odd choice of girlfriend for a big, muscular jock like William Coleman. But then Nikki thought about her and Dino, who was even brawnier than William, and she dismissed the oddity from her mind.

"Hello, Sharon," she said to the young lady before her.

Sharon folded her thin arms. "Hey, Miss Lucas."

"How you doing?"

"I'm okay."

"Sure?"

Sharon smiled weakly. "Yes, ma'am."

"I'm so sorry about William. I know you loved him very much."

Sharon nodded. "Yeah. I'm sorry too. He was one of the good guys, you know? It's still hard to believe he's not around anymore."

Nikki understood. It was too much for a child Sharon's age to have to face. She even felt guilty coming to see her at a time like this, but Jamal was young too. He was facing the battle of his life too. "Sharon, I don't want to add to your burden at all, but I felt I needed to come here."

"About Jamal?"

"Yes. It's about Jamal. I've known you for many years now, and I've always liked you and saw a great kindness in you. That's why I felt I had to come." Nikki hesitated, as guilt began to overtake her confidence. But she knew she had to say it. "Jamal's in trouble, Sharon."

"Miss Lucas—"

"Listen to me. I know you loved William, and I know a lot of people in this town are saying some awful things about my son's part in his death. But it's not true. Jamal is your friend. When you needed somebody, you know he was there for you."

"I never said Jamal wasn't a friend of mine. He is my friend. But they're saying he killed William. What do you expect me to do?"

"You can tell those prosecutors the truth."

"What truth? I don't know anything about what happened."

"Those prosecutors are going to say that Jamal was the father of that baby."

Sharon's heart dropped. Jamal had said he wouldn't tell. "What baby?" she asked nervously.

"That baby you aborted, Sharon," Nikki said.

The stunned look that came over Sharon's face was heartwrenching. "Abortion," she said breathlessly. "What are you talking about? How did they . . . How did you . . . ?"

"Everybody's gonna know. The prosecutors are planning to use your abortion as the motive."

Sharon was stricken. "But they *can't*! My father would kill me! How could Jamal tell them about that?"

"Jamal didn't tell them anything. There were rumors all around the school and they followed those rumors. Haven't they spoken to you?"

"They asked some questions, but not about no abortion. That has nothing to do with what happened to William."

"They think it does. They think William found out that you had an abortion and that Jamal was the father—"

"That's not true."

"I know it's not true, Sharon. But they believe William thought it was true and he confronted my son. And they think that's when my son pulled out a gun and shot William."

Sharon closed her eyes. "This is too much." Then she looked at Nikki. "What do you want me to do?"

"William knew about the abortion, didn't he?"

Sharon nodded. "I told him afterward. He wasn't even mad. He knew we were too young. Plus his career and all."

"And he knew that he was the father, didn't he?"

"Yes, he knew. He knew I wasn't with no other boy."

"Then that's what you've got to tell those prosecutors so they can stop this foolishness. They've got all of these thugs from Pottsburg lined up to testify against Jamal and you can prove to the prosecution that they're all lying, that William knew Jamal had nothing to do with your pregnancy. These so-called witnesses are all they have on Jamal."

Sharon shook her head. What in the world was she going to do? Her father was the mayor of Monroe. The mayor! He couldn't survive this kind of scandal. He was the main one blasting Jamal, telling all of the townspeople that he was going to personally see to it that Jamal rotted in jail. And now his own daughter was caught up in this mess? His own daughter had an abortion? Tears began to sting her eyes. She knew Nikki was in pain, too, but how could she expect her to go public with something like that?

The high-revved engine of a red sports car drove into the Granger driveway beside Nikki's VW. Fred and Dawson Granger, Sharon's brothers, got out of the car in a hurry, with Fred looking as if he was coming for blood.

"What are you doing here?" he asked Nikki as impolitely as he possibly could. "I know you ain't on our property!"

"Fred, that's enough," Sharon said, but Nikki shook her head.

"That's okay. I'm leaving," Nikki told them. "Just think about what I said, Sharon. Please."

"You'd better leave," Fred said, walking up the steps, "and I mean now!"

"And you'd better watch who you're talking to, boy," Nikki said, with equal venom. "You may not have any home training, but I'll teach you some!"

Nikki, who was no stranger to playing it tough herself, could tell that Fred Granger was a big talker and little else, as she slowly walked by him, staring him down on purpose, and headed down the steps. She spoke to Dawson, who was coming up the steps, and then walked across the lawn and toward her car. Fred started his big talk again, after Nikki got inside of her car, but by then, she wasn't thinking about the boy. Sharon was on her mind. And how in the world was she going to convince her to sacrifice her family pride and her father's position, for the sake of Jamal.

Even Sister Dardell couldn't believe the talk as she walked with Mayor Granger across the parking lot to the backside of the church, until she saw it with her own two eyes. There was the bishop, the head of their entire family of churches, sprawled out on his back underneath the church bus, attempting to loosen the screws of the hard-to-access alternator. When one of the young people came and told her what Bishop Cochran was doing, she didn't believe him. She kept on with her work and dismissed such talk as silliness. But it was true. Cochran had gone over the edge. And what a time to display it when the already upset mayor was there to have a word with him.

"Afternoon, Sister Dardell," Luther, the bus driver, said while knelt down in the front of the bus where the pastor was working. Then he nodded toward the mayor. "Mayor Granger."

"Hey," Luke Granger said with little interest in putting on his usual political smile. He was too hot to even attempt civility.

"Will you please tell the pastor we would like a word with him?" Dardell said.

Luther quickly complied, getting down on his knees and relaying her message to the bishop.

Dino, who had been trying mightily to loosen the screws out of the stubborn alternator ever since he drove up and saw Luther having a time with it himself, slid from beneath the bus and then hoisted himself to his feet. He was in a long sleeves shirt and immediately began wiping his hands on an old rag. For a man who had just been under an oily bus, he didn't look too worse for wear.

"Hello, Sister Dardell," Dino said. "Mayor Granger."

Granger could only manage a grunt. Dino knew immediately that something was wrong. "What can I do for you?" he asked him.

"Excuse us, Luther," Dardell said, and Luther, always the faithful servant, hurried away from the power elite of the church. Dardell then turned to Dino. "It's that Lucas woman again," she said.

Dino almost stopped his hand wiping, but refused to give Dardell the satisfaction. "What about Sister Lucas?" he asked, attempting to sound unaffected.

Granger tried his best to maintain his cool. "That woman had the gall to come to my house."

Dino frowned. "She went to your house?"

"Yes! Disturbing my daughter."

Dino forced himself not to shake his head. That Nikki. "And how did she disturb your daughter?"

"How do you think?" the mayor replied. "You're new here, Bishop, and you may not know this, but my daughter and William Coleman had a bond that was unbreakable. They truly loved each other. And that Nikki Lucas was trying to get her to tell all kinds of lies about that relationship, to help that murderous son of hers."

If Nikki had been within reach right about now, Dino would have strangled her. The prosecution was going to have a field day with this nonsense. They could turn that visit of hers against Jamal even more effectively than the mayor was attempting to do. "What lies are you talking about?"

"I'm not repeating that foolishness. I'm just telling you that you'd better keep her away from my family."

"You don't tell me what I'd better do," Dino said without hesitation, reminding the mayor, by his willingness to stand up to him alone, just who he was. It worked. Granger backed down. Dino calmed too. "I think Sister Lucas is who you need to discuss this with."

"The prosecutor told us to stay away from those Lucases and that's what we've been doing. Since you're so close to them, bailing that Jamal out of jail, hiring those big time lawyers for him and all, then I figured you could have some influence with his mother. My daughter is going through too much already and I won't have Nikki Lucas or anybody else upsetting her. Now I'm sorry, Bishop, if I'm coming across as disrespectful, but put yourself in my shoes. What if it was your daughter?" Then he exhaled. "Just tell her to leave my family alone or you'll be hiring a lawyer for her too." With that, he began walking away before Dino, if he so inclined, could get a word in edgewise.

Dino had no such inclination.

It was closing time at the diner and Nikki, Sebastian, and Tam were the last to leave. As Nikki locked up, Sebastian looked at Tam and Tam nodded her head.

"Wanna join us, Nikki?" she asked.

Nikki looked over her shoulder at her friend, confused. "Join you? Join you where?"

"Me and Seb thought we'd take in a late movie over in Jacksonville."

Nikki looked from Tam to Sebastian and then smiled. "Oh really now? Thanks, but no thanks. All I want to do right now is go home and go to bed."

"I heard that," Tam said as she and Sebastian walked toward Sebastian's car.

"I'll give you two lovebirds your space," Nikki snidely threw in.

Tam turned around and looked at her, ready to correct her little comment, but Dino's Mercedes drove up. He didn't pull up into any of the empty parking spaces in front of the diner, but parked on the street. At first Nikki waited, but Dino didn't get out of his car.

"See y'all tomorrow," Nikki said to her friends as she began walking toward Dino's car.

"Okay," Tam said. "We'll let you two love-birds have your space." Both she and Sebastian laughed and got into the car before Nikki could say a word. As they were backing out they waved at Bishop Cochran, and kept on going.

Dino, who had not even turned off his car's engine, lowered his front passenger window. Nikki poked her head in. "Get in." His voice was so void of warmth that she wondered if it would be wise if she did.

"What's up?" she asked.

"Get in the car, Nikki."

Nikki looked inside the car, at those cool leather seats, at an even cooler Dino, and she shook her head. "Thanks, but no thanks. I've got to get going."

Dino looked at her as if he could not believe she was being stubborn again over something as trivial as getting in a car, but then he remembered their last time together. How he held her in his lap. How he had all of the control—again. How she had to hate that. He turned off his ignition, unbuttoned his seatbelt, and got out of the car.

Nikki felt suddenly uncomfortable as he moved toward her. Something wasn't right. He had that same dark expression on his face that he had the day he came into the diner and demanded to see her books. He was upset. She could see it in his eyes.

"What have I done now?" She tried to sound lighthearted, but Dino wasn't just standing before her on that quiet street in front of her quiet diner. He was crowding her, invading all of her personal space, as if he wanted to make certain that she heard him and heard him well.

"I have time for this, don't I, Nikki?" he asked.

Nikki was puzzled. "Time for what?"

"I just sit around waiting for the next opportunity to get caught up in your nonsense, don't I?"

Nikki stared at Dino, unable to figure out what in the world was he talking about. Was he trying to say that he'd had it with her? That he'd had it with *Jamal*?

"You went to see Sharon Granger," he finally said.

Nikki, though still concerned, inwardly sighed with relief. "Yes, I did." She tried her best to look up and meet Dino's gaze, but she found his presence too commanding, just too close. She even stepped back in an attempt to regain at least some of the territory he was taking from her, but he merely stepped forward and effectively took it back.

"You asked her about that abortion."

"Yes, I asked her," Nikki said with bite in her voice. "So what?"

Dino stared at her as if she'd just slapped him. "Do you suffer from some kind of brain malfunction, Nikki?"

"What's that supposed to mean?"

"Are you so impulsive, so emotion-driven that you just act before you even think about thinking about it?"

"Dino, what are you talking about? I went to see Sharon Granger; darn right I did. She knows Jamal isn't the father of that baby she aborted. William Coleman was the father, and William knew it too. She told me so herself!"

"And?" Dino said with a fierceness that slightly rocked Nikki. "What difference does that make? That's no news!"

"But Bobby Matthews said the state is going to claim that William found out about Jamal getting Sharon pregnant and confronted him, and that's why Jamal shot him. But if William already knew that Sharon's baby belonged to him, and that she wasn't having an affair with Jamal, then there would have been no reason for him to confront Jamal." She frowned when Dino looked at her in disgust. "What? Don't you get it? The state's theory is based on a lie, Dino!"

"And, what? You thought it was based on the truth?"

"Of course not."

"Of course not. So what the devil difference does it make if Sharon Granger confirms that it's not true? It's not true. We've already established that."

"But she can get on the witness stand and establish it. She can tell those jurors that what the state is saying about Jamal isn't the truth."

"While five other witnesses get on that same stand and tell them that it is the truth."

"Come on, Dino. She has way more credibility than any of those so-called witnesses combined."

"You think so? This pure little girl who's dating the local hero, the beloved local hero, mind you, but still has time to hang out with the local thug? She's sleeping with the local thug, in fact, if that jury chooses to believe the prosecution, and gets pregnant by that thug. Then she has an abortion, further adding to her purity, and now claims that yeah, the thug was a friend of hers. Yeah, the hero's murderer was the one who went with her to have this abortion, but it's not so, ladies and gentlemen of the jury. The thug wasn't the father, after all. The hero was the father. And you think *she's* credible?"

Nikki looked emotionally exhausted. She had not even considered the possibility. "You're twisting it around."

"I know I am."

"And Jamal is not a thug."

"I know that too. But does the jury know it, Nikki? That's the point. A good prosecutor will rip Sharon's story to shreds! Don't you understand that? And now you've given them even more ammunition to use against Jamal."

"Me?"

"Yes, you! Absolutely you! If they put Sharon Granger on that witness stand, the first thing they'll ask her will be all about your little visit to her house today. They'll make it look as if you were trying to get her to lie for Jamal!"

Nikki was horrified by the prospect. "That's not true."

"Of course, it's not true! The fact that Jamal was arrested at all hasn't anything to do with truth. But he still was arrested, Nikki. Don't you get it? Am I finally getting through that thick skull of yours?" Dino said as he angrily placed a finger to Nikki's forehead and then removed it.

He ran his hand through his cropped-off soft hair and breathed, attempting with all his might to regain some sense of calm. He knew that his anger was largely misplaced. Nikki grated on his nerves worst than any human being alive, that was true. But she warmed him too, whenever he held her, whenever he looked across a room and saw her in it. And his feelings for her were growing, not diminishing with every passing day. It was a serious truth that had him up at night, wondering just what in the world was he going to do about it.

"I don't have Jeff Islick and his people combing the streets of Monroe for nothing, Nikki," he said. "They're here to do a job. A job you have got to let them do or your interference is going to sink this case. I know you're anxious. I know you want Jamal out of harm's way. Well, don't you think I want that too? Or do you figure I'm going through all of this crap for the fun of it?"

Crap? Was that how he saw his involvement with her and Jamal? As crap? She released a puff of air. "I'm sorry you feel this way, Dino." Nikki wanted desperately to tell him that he could leave their *crap* alone and they'd manage just fine. But she held her tongue because she knew it wasn't true.

"You don't know how I feel," Dino said, not letting up. "You don't know the half of it." He paused to calm himself again. "Mayor Granger paid me a visit today."

Nikki looked at him. "You?"

"Yes, me, Nikki. And he was hot."

Nikki frowned. "Like I care how hot he is. My son's life is at stake, excuse me if you please, and I'll do all I can to help him even if it does offend the sensibilities of your upper crust friends!"

Before Dino knew what he was doing, he'd grabbed Nikki by the arm and pulled her even closer to him. "You will do exactly what I tell you to do," he warned her with clenched teeth. "I'll not have the mayor of this town, my church members or anybody else coming to me and telling me that you're doing anything other than what I'm telling you to do. I've got this, Nikki, and whether your little need for independence can deal with it or not, you're going to let me handle this!"

Nikki looked into those fiery eyes of Dino's, those droopy eyes that were a long way from the lazy sexiness they used to remind her of. Now he looked disgusted with her, disappointed again, and she was tired of never being able to please him. To her own amazement, she remained calm, but that didn't stop her from shooting back with venom that matched his.

"You've been handling it, Dino," she said, "but it hasn't exactly been a ringing success, has it? But I guess that's the difference between you and me. I protect my responsibility. I look out for them. You hurt yours, kill yours, and then forget about yours."

Nikki knew it was a low blow. She knew it would hurt Dino to his core. And it did. The fierceness in his eyes left almost immediately, and was replaced with a kind of anguish she'd never seen before in her life. He looked like a dying man staring into the eyes of his attacker, trying to figure out why in the world she would do this to him.

He let go of her arm and just stood there. He looked at Nikki as if he was baffled by her, as if he just couldn't understand how she could have said that to him. She knew how responsible he felt for Sophia's death. And his child's death. And Max's death. And even her and Jamal's life. She knew how he had been determined to destroy his own life before God Himself intervened. How could she believe that he'd forgotten about all of that blood on his hands? Didn't she realize if he could have changed places with *any of them,* he would have?

She didn't understand. He doubted if anybody ever would. And he didn't try to explain it either. He left, walking toward his car in a staggering gait, as if he was dazed. Once inside, he drove away.

Nikki got into her car too, and headed for home. She felt as if she was going to be sick every time she thought about that look in Dino's eyes. He was so stricken, so *hurt*, that he could barely stand. If her goal was to get him, to sucker punch him so that he could understand how two could play that righteous indignation game, she'd succeeded mightily. He was devastated. She'd never seen another human being so distraught. Invoking his dead wife and unborn baby into their little argument had sent him reeling. Dino would not have expected that from his worst enemy. Let alone from the woman he'd been nothing but kind to since the moment he'd laid eyes on her again.

She didn't even think about what her actions could mean when she opened that big mouth of hers, or if her actions would cause Dino to turn against Jamal too. She still hadn't even told him yet, not because she didn't want to (there was little else she wanted more), but because she still wasn't sure about Dino. One moment, like that night he put her on his lap and held her against him for nearly an hour, he was so tender, and so caring to her. The next moment, like this night when he talked so harshly to her, he was the old Dino, the one who slept with her when he knew he was a married man, and then dumped her like a pile of trash. He was saved now, and a church leader and all that, but there were still sparks in him that worried her. It would be better if the truth about him and Jamal never came out. Especially if it came out and only alienated Dino from them even more than he already was.

Of course, Nikki's mouth, tonight, pretty much took care of that singlehandedly. Her only prayer was that he wouldn't abandon Jamal because of her nastiness, that he'd at least see this trial through to its conclusion. Because if he did decide to pull his support, if he did decide to leave her and her son to whatever fate had in store for them, she'd have no choice then. She'd use guilt and anything else as her weapon to make him keep those lawyers and investigators helping Jamal. Then Nikki shook her head in disgust, amazed at how low she would be willing to go for that son of hers. And that was when she felt the first bump.

It was a barely noticeable thump on her bumper, but she could feel it. Her eyes flew to her rearview mirror and saw the pickup truck driving up behind her. It was too dark to make out what kind of truck it was, or who was driving it, but she wasn't about to stop on the dark Mills Road junction to find out. She kept driving, hoping that no damage was done. But the truck bumped her car again. And then again. Nikki picked up speed, understanding now that this was no innocent accident. But her VW was small, and hardly powerful. Her attacker easily matched her speed. Before she could even look into the rearview mirror again, the truck was upon her, and this time pushing her so violently that she ran off of the road.

The sand and rocks caused her out of control tires to spit out the debris as she attempted to steer her wheel and slam on brakes. Then one tire lifted. Then another. Soon, she was airborne and flipping. Nikki could feel the spinning, the careening, and then there was a harsh, throat-throttling ram sound. Silence took over as her VW landed, like an upside-down bathtub, into a shallow, pitch black ditch.

TWENTY-ONE

Dino sat in his car outside of Monroe's Saint Luke's Hospital and gripped his steering wheel. It was one in the morning and he was dead on his feet. When Jamal first called, he almost hung up the phone. He couldn't bear to deal with anything or anybody even remotely associated with Nikki again this night. But he didn't hang up, because he knew what had gone down between him and Nikki had nothing to do with Jamal. He listened to the young man, listened as he frantically told how his mother had been in an accident on Old Mills Road and was now at the hospital. Dino had laid his head back on his pillow and listened in anguish as Jamal all but begged him to come and see about his mother.

Dino got out of his car and walked slowly toward the hospital's entrance. He'd spent nearly an hour praying for Nikki in his quiet hotel room before he even got dressed to go anywhere. Now, he was casually clad in a pair of jeans and a blue polo shirt. His expensive Italian dress shoes were completely out of place on such an outfit, but they were the first pair he could lay his hands on.

Dino had seriously considered packing up and leaving Monroe after he had left Nikki standing in that parking lot. He felt like a chump as he had waited down the road until she was safely in her car and driving away. He had wanted to walk away from it all and just go back to his own stomping ground. This was the high-tech age. He could handle New Life and their problems long distance; especially since all of his hard work thus far hadn't done all that much good anyway. That church needed new leadership, not new rules and regulations as was his charge to establish. The hearts of the people were what most needed changing. But the people's hearts were the one thing that was completely beyond his ability to change.

Therefore, it wasn't New Life that kept him from packing up and taking off. There was the *small* matter of Nikki and Jamal. They were the two people he least expected to encounter when he first decided to leave his comfortable Michigan lifestyle and journey to this backwater town. For nearly sixteen years, Nikki had been nothing more than a small ache deep within his soul that reared up every now and then, whenever he'd see a feisty kid on a street corner, or a beautiful young lady defying the attention of some young man. He thought about her over the years, but no more than he thought about all of those other ghosts of his past.

Dino never knew just how far-reaching and deep-seated his feelings were for Nikki, until he saw her again. And when he heard that she had a son, a sixteen-year-old troubled youth, and that this son had been accused of murdering someone, he thought he was going to die. Leaving was not an option for him. He was in this for the duration, for the long haul, for all that was right and true for once in his life. Nikki accused him of forgetting about the people he'd hurt, but she was wrong. His problem wasn't in the forgetting, but in the remembering. He could never forget all of the hurt he'd caused. *Never*.

The automatic double doors of Saint Luke's opened and he walked inside. Jamal was sitting in one of the round-back chairs that lined the wall near the nurses' station. He looked dead on his feet too, as he sat there with his eyes closed, his gangly body slumped down in the uncomfortable seat.

Dino leaned down and touched the young man's narrow shoulder, causing him to open

eyes so big and brown and beautiful that Dino
wanted to pull him into his arms. So he did. As
soon as Jamal stood up, he embraced the young
man. It wasn't an awkward embrace, as would
seem the case with two men in the middle of a
hospital hall. It was more like a long overdue
gesture.

Dino shut his eyes tight as he held Jamal. The
pain of all of those years that Nikki had to care
for him alone, those years that he didn't know
the boy existed, came down on him like a flood
of shame. If he had not used Nikki, slept with
her and discarded her, then she would never
have run off the way she had, away from what
she knew and could handle, away from *him*. Sister Ellis had said that Nikki had been homeless,
sleeping in the streets, while he lived in a man-
sion for all she knew. She had gotten pregnant
almost immediately by this mysterious man who
died all of a sudden. This man who had given
her a child and then dropped dead, leaving her
to take care of that child alone. How could he
believe a tale like that?

Tears were in Jamal's eyes when they stopped
embracing, and Dino had to suppress an urge to
pull him in his arms again. "You okay?" he asked.

"Yes, sir." Jamal sounded like a frightened
child. Not some sixteen-year-old murder suspect.

"How is she?"

"I don't know." Worry filled Jamal's eyes. "They won't tell me anything."

Dino exhaled at the heartlessness of some people. How could they keep information from the patient's own child? He walked over to the nurses' station with Jamal right on his heels, and asked to see Nikki Lucas.

"Like I told the young man," the stout, jowly nurse who stood behind the desk said with a mile-wide attitude, "I'm not at liberty to give out that information."

"Then let me speak to the person who is at liberty," Dino said.

The woman hesitated. "And you are?" There was growing animosity in her voice.

"I'm Bishop Walter Dean Cochran of New Life Progressive Baptist Church."

The woman knew the name, and definitely knew the church since it was by far the largest and most influential in town. "One moment, please," she said as she picked up the phone. The hostility in her voice had all but disappeared.

Dino turned and leaned his back against the tall desk. He looked at Jamal, who had on a T-shirt and jeans. The shirt had been placed on backward. Dino touched the inseam and smiled. "In a hurry?"

Jamal noticed his error and nodded. "Yes, sir." He removed his shirt, revealing a stomach so thin his ribs appeared to be showing.

Dino frowned. "Do you and your mother ever eat?" He immediately regretted his harsh tone. He softened as Jamal quickly put back on his shirt, correct side out. "You need to take better care of yourself, Jamal."

"I will," he said so accommodating that Dino knew he wouldn't get much out of Jamal until the boy was certain that his mother was all right.

"When the hospital called you, what did they say?" he asked.

"They said that Ma had been in a car accident on Old Mills Road and that I needed to come and see about her. I asked if she was okay and they said yeah, but that was all they would tell me. I tried to call you but you weren't in your hotel room."

Dino was there, and he heard the ringing phone, but he was in prayer and ignored it.

"So I got on my bicycle and came on. When I got here and they still wouldn't tell me nothing or let me see her, I called you again. I didn't mean to disturb you like that, but I didn't have nobody else to call. Nobody who could help Ma, anyway."

Dino nodded and patted Jamal affectionately on the arm. "You made the right call," he assured him.

A fifty-something man in a white lab coat came out of the back rooms of the hospital and extended his hand to Dino. "Bishop Cochran; hello," he said. "I'm Dr. Marshall, chief of emergency services here. I understand you're inquiring about Miss Lucas."

"Yes, Doctor, how is she?"

"She's fine. It was a horrific accident. She and her vehicle ended upside down in a ditch, but she's remarkably unscathed."

"Thank God," Dino said, running his hand through his hair in relief. Jamal also relaxed. Dino looked at the doctor. "This is her son, Jamal," he said.

The doctor shook Jamal's hand. "Hello, Jamal."

"You couldn't come out here and tell him what you've just told me, Doctor?" Dino still couldn't get over them withholding news from the patient's son. "This boy was worried sick about his mother."

The doctor swallowed hard. "This is an emergency room, Bishop," he said, smiling. "I was very busy."

"Then why are you out here now? Because a title is in front of my name? Because I invoked the name of New Life Progressive so that ill-mannered nurse of yours could take me seriously? Do you have to throw your weight around just to be treated civilly around here? Is that the kind of hospital you're running?"

"I'm not running any hospital," the doctor said defensively, "just the ER. And I apologize for any slight Mr. Lucas may have felt."

Dino didn't buy that apology for a second. Dr. Marshall, like everybody else in Monroe, knew who Jamal was and didn't give a twit if he knew of his mother's condition or not. But Dino was far too tired to take on that fight tonight. "Where's Miss Lucas now?"

"She's about to be released as we speak."

"Take us to her," Dino said more as a command than a request. The doctor didn't quarrel with him.

Nikki was fully clothed in a pair of faded jeans and a white, Florida Gators jersey, as she sat on an examining table. Her hair was loose and hung down her back in a spark of wavy thickness. Her shoes swung back and forth, her legs too short for them to touch the floor. Jamal ran past Dino and the doctor toward his mother and she grabbed him in her arms.

The doctor shook Dino's hand, apologized again for any inconvenience, and left as if he'd done his PR duty for the night. Dino walked further into the room as mother and son stopped embracing. Nikki's heart began to pound when she realized he was there. Why did Jamal have to call him? Didn't he know this was the last place Dino wanted to be?

"Hello, Nikki." Dino spoke in his signature commanding voice.

"Dino," she said without looking at him.

"How do you feel?"

"Like I've just been pulled from a ditch. Other than that, I'm fine."

Dino exhaled. The reality of what she'd just been through, and the thought that he could have possibly not seen her alive again, overwhelmed him. He smoothed down her hair with his hand and moved closer to her. She finally looked at him and he stared into her eyes, into eyes so green and stark with pain that he had to look away. He removed his hand from her when a nurse walked into the room.

It felt as if a load had been lifted from Nikki as Dino stopped on the driveway of her small, beloved home. It was Jamal who got out and opened her door for her as Dino made his way around the front of the car. It was Jamal who placed his arm around his mother as he helped a gingerly walking Nikki make it toward the front door. Dino felt a sudden pang of jealousy as Jamal assisted his mother, but he quickly dismissed such triviality. Just a few hours ago, he was thinking about skipping town because of that very woman. Now he was jealous that her own son, instead of him, was helping her? He should be thankful and hit the road now. But he knew he wasn't going anywhere.

It was Dino who unlocked the front door, using the key he had to the house, as he allowed Jamal and Nikki to enter the home ahead of him. Nikki cut a glance at him, as if she was concerned that he was going to leave her again. But he entered the house and locked the door, as if he was planning on staying.

Jamal looked back at Dino, like he was just as worried as his mother, and then he moved to help sit her on the sofa.

"Take her to the bedroom, Jamal," Dino said as he walked toward the kitchen.

"I'm okay," Nikki insisted. Dino glanced back at her, but didn't break his stride. Nikki sat down on the sofa.

"Ma," Jamal said, looking distressed, "do like he said."

"I'm not his child, Jamal."

"Don't run him away. You know how he is."

"No, I don't know, Jamal," Nikki said, folding her arms. "How is he, since you're now the authority on him?"

"You know what I'm saying."

"Enlighten me, Jamal. Give me some of this great wisdom that you have acquired about Dino Cochran."

"We need him," Jamal said bluntly, tired of denying it himself. "You more than me. But every time he's around, you just be buggin' for no reason. Like you enjoy hurting him. Like you want to run him away."

Nikki stared at her son. Maybe he did know the deal better than she did. Jamal had pointed out what any blind man could see: they needed Dino. Not because they couldn't make it without him. But because they were tired of trying. Nikki stood up and allowed her son to help her to the bedroom.

In the kitchen, Dino poured himself a glass of cold water and leaned against the counter top. The kitchen was spotless. The center island and the small kitchen table looked as if no one had ever eaten a bite anywhere near them. It was just like Nikki to run a tight ship where everything was always in place, neat and tidy. Even when she was a kid hustling tapes outside of Dino's nightclub she was a control freak. Always trying to get the last word in even with him, as if she thought she could handle him. Dino smiled and shook his head. She actually thought she had some control over him just because he paid her some attention. Just because he inexplicably felt responsible for her that very first time he laid eyes on her.

Jamal came into the kitchen and opened the refrigerator. "I took her to her bedroom like you said." He said it with such an obvious attempt to win Dino's approval that it made Dino cringe. What had he ever done to deserve this devotion Jamal seemed determined to reap on him? Was it because he shelled out a few bucks on his behalf? Or was it because he beat his behind for disobeying Nikki? Dino doubted the latter. He didn't see where the former made him devotion-worthy either.

Jamal pulled a can of Coke from the fridge and popped it open. He stood beside Dino, nearly shoulder to shoulder, and drank half of it. Dino looked at him. "Little late for caffeine, don't you think?"

"Not really."

"What did you have for dinner?"

"Dinner?"

"Yes, Jamal. That little meal that we tend to eat every night?"

Jamal smiled. "I ate a bowl of cereal."

"A bowl of cereal?"

"I just don't feel like eating much right now. Not with all this over my head."

Dino couldn't help but think that the boy sounded far too advanced for his years. No child his age should ever have to speak of such. "Okay," Dino said and allowed the conversation to lag.

Jamal, however, reinvigorated it. "You're gonna stay here tonight, aren't you?"

Dino looked at his glass of water. "I don't know."

"Ma don't mind."

"It hasn't anything to do with whether your mother minds or not. It's my decision."

Jamal screwed up his face, upset that he had upset Dino.

Dino felt the sting of his own words and felt the need to smooth things over. "Thanks for wanting me, buddy." He placed his glass of water in the sink. "But it's probably not a good idea." Dino looked at Jamal, who looked away from him quickly. Dino, feeling burdened again, walked out of the kitchen, down the hall, and into Nikki's bedroom.

He stared at Nikki momentarily. She was sitting on the edge of the bed taking off her shoes.

She looked gorgeous with her hair down. She seemed almost enchanting sitting there on that bed. He wanted to frame this look Nikki was conveying into his memory bank, that same soft, sweet, innocent look that made him, all those years ago, have to have her.

"Knock knock," he said as he began walking into the bedroom.

Nikki looked up with those big, green eyes that dominated her face and continued removing her shoes. "Hey."

"Glad to be back home?"

"Better believe it. When that doctor first started talking about keeping me all night, I almost cried. But then all my tests came back negative so they didn't see any reason."

Dino sat down on the bed beside her, causing her to suddenly tense. "What happened out there, Nikki?"

Nikki shook her head. "Like I know."

"The doctor said you lost control of the wheel. Was it because of what happened between us back at the diner?"

Nikki shook her head. "That wasn't it at all. I mean, I was thinking about it, sure. I was sorry." She looked at Dino. "I didn't mean to hurt you like that."

Dino nodded. "I know."

"I was thinking about it, but that wasn't why I lost control. A pickup truck came up and bumped me from behind, and then pushed me off the road."

"A truck pushed you off the road? Nikki, are you sure?"

"I'm positive. I was looking at it in my mirror and wondering what was wrong with that nutcase. Then the next thing I know, I was off the road, then airborne, then crashed."

Dino's heart plummeted. He looked at Nikki, suddenly stricken to hear her speak such a thing. His arm slipped around her. Instead of fighting his comfort, instead of shunning it any way she could, Nikki welcomed it. She leaned against him and placed her head on his shoulder. "I'm so sorry you had to go through that, honey," he said. "To go through any of this."

"It was so scary. I actually thought I was gonna die."

"Don't say that." Dino squeezed her tighter. "Thank God you're all right."

"Yeah, that's what Ollie said."

"Ollie?"

"He's a deputy sheriff. A friend of mine. He arrived at the scene."

"So you did get a chance to report this to the police?"

"I told them, sure. But whether they believed me or not is another story."

"Why wouldn't they believe you?"

"The same reason they didn't even bother to investigate why somebody threw a rock through our window. They don't really care if it's true or not. They figure I deserve it. I'm the murderer's mother and that's all I am as far as they're concerned."

"Including this Ollie friend of yours?" Dino asked, amazed at his sudden streak of jealousy.

"Not Ollie. He's cool. But what can he do? He's just a deputy."

Dino pulled Nikki closer against him and became more aware of her presence. Her sweet smell and the softness of her body against him. And when she lifted her head and looked into his eyes, as if she was just as aware of him, his control broke. Dino kissed her. He meant for it to be a peck, just a comforting kiss to remind her that he was there for her, but it became something far different than that. It became passionate as she placed her arms around him and moved even closer to him, the feel of his lips on hers making her dizzy with need. Dino was dizzy too, with the kind of desire he thought he had long ago suppressed, and he kept pulling her closer, and pulling her closer until he was near the point of no return.

Jamal saw it all as he walked from the kitchen up to his mother's bedroom. It was something he never thought he'd live to see. Dino wasn't just kissing on his mother. That would have been remarkable in and of itself. But he had laid her down on the bed and was nearly on top of her. Jamal couldn't believe it. He even started to walk away so he wouldn't interrupt them, as a strange feeling of triumph overtook him. But his mother's eyes opened and she saw him standing there.

Nikki pushed Dino off of her and immediately sat up. In the sixteen years that Jamal had been on this earth she had never allowed him to see her in any compromising positions. Embarrassed by his own lack of control, Dino stood to his feet and walked over to the window, still breathing erratically as if he was some school kid caught in the act, still unable to reconcile how unrestrained he'd just been. He was the pastor of a church, for crying out loud! A bishop, no less. And here he was fooling around in the middle of the night with a woman whose life he'd already managed to ruin. He shook his head and ran his hand through his hair, disgusted with himself.

"What is it, Jamal?" Nikki asked.

Jamal couldn't repress his smile. "Nothing. I was just checking to see if you was all right."

"I'm fine." Nikki attempted to smooth her hair in place.

"What about you, Mr. Cochran?" Jamal looked over at Dino, whose back faced him.

Dino didn't seem to appreciate the lightheartedness that was in Jamal's voice. "Hit the sack, champ," he said without turning around. Truth was, he was too ashamed to turn around. Jamal understood. That was why he kept his jokes to himself, told them both good night, and left.

Nikki looked at Dino. "Sorry about that," she said.

Dino faced her and smiled. "Thank God for that," he corrected. "I'd better get going."

Nikki suddenly felt alone and cold, dying for the comfort of his warmth again. "It's so late, Dino." She rubbed her arms to ward off the sudden chill. "Couldn't you just stay here until daylight?"

Dino walked over to the bed and grabbed his keys. They fallen out of his pocket during their time of passion. He looked at Nikki, who still seemed as if she was on fire, who was more than willing, to give herself completely over to him again. "No," he said. "I can't."

Nikki's heart plunged, but she understood. "Sure," she nodded. "Drive carefully then."

Dino smiled. "I will." He stood there longer, staring at her, wanting desperately to kiss her again but not daring to follow through. "Take care of yourself, Nikki."

"Does this mean," she said too eagerly, as if she'd suddenly remembered to ask it. She settled herself back down. "Does this mean that we're friends again?"

Dino considered her, and then smiled. "Always, Nikki. No matter what."

Nikki returned his smile; then Dino walked out of her room without looking back.

As soon as Dino was back inside of his car, he picked up his car phone and called Jeff Islick, apologizing for waking him, but telling him that first thing in the morning he wanted him to check out the Grangers more closely. Including the mayor. "Nikki was the victim of a hit and run tonight," he said into his phone, "on the same day that she confronted Sharon Granger about her abortion."

"Is she okay?"

"Yes, thank God."

"Coincidence?" Jeff asked.

"I don't believe in coincidences," Dino replied. "You check out that family. I'm beginning to believe that the answer to the riddle that is the Coleman murder, just might rest with the Grangers."

TWENTY-TWO

The choir was singing "Near the Cross" in a slow, old-fashioned cadence, and Dino sat in the pulpit in a meditative state. He was leaned back, his legs apart, his eyes closed, his elbows resting on the arms of the high-back chair. After his behavior with Nikki, he felt especially unworthy this Sunday. He wondered if he could even make it through the sermon he had to preach. He had avoided Nikki for the rest of the week, and Jamal as well, and had instead prayed nearly without ceasing for both of them. God had to be their deliverer, not him, although they seemed determined to put him in that role. He could still see Jamal all but begging him to stay with them, and Nikki with pleading eyes asking for reassurance that they were still friends, as if his presence alone was going to get them out of this nightmare they'd found themselves in.

Once the hymn had ended and the congregation had returned to their seats in a shuffling sound that only belied the fact that the church was packed for yet another Sunday service, Dino stood to deliver his sermon. The scriptural reading had already been given, the sixth chapter of the book of Galatians, and he immediately got to the point.

"Be not deceived," he said, "God is not mocked: for whatsoever a man soweth, that shall he also reap. The text teaches us that having faith in God, and in the promises of God, are all directly related to what we choose to do about it. Again, remember that our actions speak far louder than our words."

As Dino preached, first in a slow build-up to a thunderous sermon, late-arriving members continued to trickle in and ushers continued to walk them down the aisles to their seats. But none caught Dino's attention, and indeed the attention of the entire congregation, until Nikki, along with Tam, Sebastian, and Jamal, walked into the sanctuary.

Dino's heart nearly stopped when he first saw Nikki. For one thing, she wore a dress . . . a very elegant black sleeveless dress in a chevron pattern. It had a drape neckline and a beautifully lettuce-edge hem. Dino had never seen her so adorned and was astounded by the beautiful figure she projected. With her hair down in thick waves, bouncing as she walked, she looked angelic, the absolute picture of grace and beauty. And she wore it well, walking down the aisle with her head held high. The congregation was gawking at her, and whispering their disdain, but she followed the usher without acknowledging any of it and took her seat, for the first time in years, among the faithful.

Jamal was with her, in the suit Dino had purchased for him, and he sat beside his mother. Although Dino was pleased by their appearance, he wasn't thrown by it. He continued to preach his sermon and within minutes, was able to forget that they were even there.

"No more games!" he shouted into the microphone. "You can't fool God. You can fool me, you can fool a million men, but you can't fool God. Don't deceive yourself."

"You can't turn faith on and off. You can't talk about faith as if it was an emotion, a feeling, where you feel good about it one day, and don't feel it at all the next day. Faith is a belief! A belief that God Almighty can and *will* see you through. We know He can. But we've got to believe that He will. Life can knock you down. Life can deal you an awful hand over and over and over again. But it's up to you how you deal with that hand. You can complain about it, and feel that it's so unfair that you have to hold all the wrong cards, or you can have a little talk with Jesus."

The congregation stood to their feet in applause on that line, including Jamal, who just stood there and watched Dino, his eyes riveted on him.

Dino, nevertheless, was riveted on God, his entire countenance as one of a man obsessed with preaching God's Word. "Jesus knows what you're going through," he continued. "Jesus knows that it's not fair, that it's not right, that you're doing all you know how to do and still coming up short time and time again. But that's what faith is all about. It's believing that Jesus Christ can make a way out of no way. It's believing that Jesus Christ can carry you through despite the odds, despite what man says are your chances, despite the overwhelming evidence that tells you to throw in the towel, you can't make it through, girl, you must be crazy to believe that any good can come out of this! I want to tell you, saints, that if God be for you, who can be against you?"

Nikki hadn't planned to stand, but before she knew it, she was on her feet and she kept her eyes and ears completely tuned to Dino.

"I want to tell you, saints, that if God Almighty is working on your behalf, the very gates of hell will not prevail against you! I want to tell you, saints, that if you just believe, if you just give your heart to God and believe that He will handle it with care, that He will take you to heights beyond your wildest dreams, that He will answer your prayer when all you have is a prayer, then you will make it through. Then you will be able to say as Joshua, that prophet of old, said: I don't know about you, and I don't know about you, but as for me and my house, we will serve the Lord. Praise the Lord, everybody. Praise His holy name!"

Dino was well-winded and barely able to catch his breath as the congregation shouted and applauded and cried out to Christ with words of thanksgiving and praise. He walked back behind the podium, set the microphone down, and waited in thoughtful prayer as the congregation continued their spontaneous worship. And then slowly, appreciatively, they all sat back down.

Nikki sat down too, her eyes filled with tears. She'd always believed in God from afar, in only a philosophical way. But she knew now, unlike she'd ever known before, that if it wasn't for the Lord she would not be here today. It wasn't just that accident He delivered her from three days ago. It was when she was thirteen, and sitting in that dark alley all alone in this world. God didn't desert her then. Jesus didn't allow predators to prey on her and dogooders to try and imprison her with what they thought was best for her. He taught her how to survive, how to make it in this cold world when, as Dino had just said, all she had was a prayer. If it weren't for the Lord, where would she be? Dead? On drugs? *Worse*?

That was why, when the altar call was given, when Dino asked if there were any among them who wanted to give their lives to Christ, to try Him out and see if He could give them better results, Nikki decided to be in the number. To Jamal's shock, and even more so, to her own, she stood up. Without looking around, without wondering who was watching her, who was disapproving, who thought she was not sincere, Nikki walked up to the front of the church and stood, along with a handful of others, in front of Dino.

Initially, Dino didn't see her. He was too deep in meditation, too steep in his own sense of the presence of God in the sanctuary. It wasn't until he opened his eyes and looked upon the faithful that had decided to come to the altar, did he realize Nikki was in their midst. His heart leaped with joy as soon as he saw her. Her face was turned upward, and tears were streaming down her cheeks, as she, like all of the others at the altar, poured out her heart to God. Dino looked out at Jamal, who was standing at his seat, his head bowed, too, and tears appeared in Dino's eyes. His prayer had been answered. The two people, who he now realized were the two most important people in his life, were now on God's side; they were now in the household of faith where they could become heirs of God, and joint-heirs with Christ, in the wonderful adventure that is the Christian life. He silently thanked God Almighty for answering his prayers, and then began to pray the prayer of repentance for all of those assembled.

Because Dino had numerous other commitments directly after service, including officiating at a member's Sunday afternoon wedding and preaching at a Sunday evening gospel program for a pastor friend in Jacksonville, he didn't get a chance to spend any time with Nikki until later that night, when he showed up at her door and asked her to go for a drive with him.

Nikki was thrilled to see Dino and she hurried to get her brown leather jacket. She told Jamal she'd see him later, and went out onto the porch with the giddiness of a teenager on her very first date. Earlier that day, when she saw that Dino had tears in his eyes because she'd decided to accept Christ as her Savior, she knew right then and there that he cared. Not just in that guilt sense, not just in that *because I hurt you I owe you one* sense. But he cared in a loving sense, in a deep down, heartfelt sense. She also knew then and there that now was the time to tell him the truth.

He was standing against the porch rail when she came out of the house. He looked a little weary to her, but oddly upbeat at the same time. He smiled, for instance, when she first came out, and placed his hand on the small of her back as they walked to his car. She was beginning to feel as if she was a part of Dino now, although he had yet to stake any claims to her or even suggest that he was interested in doing so. But she also knew that a man like him didn't get emotional for no reason; and witnessing what had happened earlier made her certain that if it wasn't exactly love he was feeling for her, it was close.

He drove her, not aimlessly around Monroe as she had thought he would, but to Remington Park, where they got out of the car and began walking along the lonely path overlooking the lake. It was a dark and quiet night, but the breeze was strong as Nikki placed her hands inside the pockets of her leather jacket and enjoyed the view. When they stopped, and sat side by side on the bench near the shoreline, both leaning forward and staring out across the lake, she exhaled.

"I feel different, Dino," she told him, "but the same too.

Dino nodded. "That's why you don't base your salvation on your feelings. You base it on your belief in God. Your feelings will deceive you like a roller coaster ride, but belief comes from within and isn't subject to whims."

"I just keep believing I'm saved, no matter how I feel?"

Dino nodded. "That's right. You study your Bible to understand what you're believing, and you believe no matter how you feel."

Nikki hesitated. And then she looked at Dino. When he returned her gaze, fear suddenly struck her. What if she had read him wrong? What if she told him the truth and it was too heavy for him, too much on a plate already too full?

"What is it, Nikki?" he asked her.

"Now that I'm getting my act together, or at least trying to, I think I need to tell you something." Anguish overtook her. "But I don't know how."

Dino's heart squeezed. "Just tell me, Nikki."

Nikki looked away from him, at the lake that seemed to keep her calm; then she looked back at Dino. "It's about Jamal."

Dino didn't blink; he didn't move a muscle, as even his heart seemed momentarily inoperable. "What about him?"

Tears began to appear in Nikki's eyes. And she just said it. "He's your son."

At first, Dino did nothing. At first, he stared at her as if he were still waiting to hear what she'd just said. His normally drooping lids wide open now. Then, as if the enormity of the words she had just spoken had finally dawned on him, Dino leaned back in a kind of anguished manner, his legs spread apart, his head tilted back in a distressful pose.

"I'm sorry, Dino," Nikki's tears flowed freely now. "I was gonna tell you as soon as I found out; I promise I was. But that was the night you showed up at the club with your wife and . . . and I was so *hurt*." Dino looked at her, the distress in his eyes almost palpable. "And when you told her that I was Max's girlfriend, and you just left me standing there like the stupid idiot I was, I knew I couldn't tell you then. You didn't want to have anything to do with me. I knew I couldn't even face you again. So I ran away. I packed my bags and went to the only place I had somebody who at least knew my name. My auntie, who lived right here in Monroe. And she wouldn't even let me inside her house. I came all this way, with nowhere else to go, and she, the woman who was always talking about Jesus this and Jesus that, wouldn't let me in her door. I was so terrified,

Dino, I was so alone. I slept in alleys and home-less shelters and tried to find work. But there just wasn't any, at least not for my kind. I was like a fish out of water in the south. It was like another country to me. I hated it here. But it wasn't like it mattered. It wasn't like I had anywhere else to go. It wasn't like I had anybody in this whole wide world who even cared if I was alive."

Dino pulled her into his arms.

She leaned against him and wrapped her arms around him, her head resting on his chest. "So I stayed," she went on, "and I struggled, and I had our son." Dino kissed her hair and rested his chin on her head. She tried to smile. "He looked so much like you when he was a baby. Not by the eyes so much, except that they were brown, but by the mouth and the forehead and the tough-ness. He was a tough baby, let me tell you. Prob-ably would have still been tough, if I would have raised him right."

"Don't you blame yourself," Dino said ten-derly, still holding her, still frowning and still unable to fully comprehend what she was tell-ing him. He'd had his suspicions, he'd had them the moment he found out Nikki had a son, but suspecting that something might be true was one thing. Finding out that it was, in fact, true was something altogether different. Jamal was his son. His *son*. He'd been an absent father, a deadbeat dad, for sixteen long years, and didn't even know it!

He removed himself from Nikki and stood up, the rising breeze whipping his suit coat back and away from his body as he stood with his back to Nikki and his eyes staring across the lake.

Nikki wrapped her arms around herself, immediately missing his warm presence beside her. "I know I should have told you, Dino," she said. "But you've got to understand, I never thought I'd see you again. In my mind, you were dead. You didn't exist anymore. I thought that was the best way for Jamal. Why make him think he had this big, important father somewhere who cared about him, when it wasn't true? So I said his father was dead. I never dreamed you'd come here. To *Monroe*. I thought I was seeing a ghost when I saw you here."

Dino placed his hands in his pants pocket as the wind continued to whip his suit coat around and away from his tense, muscular body. Nikki got off of the bench and stood beside him, her small frame nearly huddled against his large one. Dino removed a hand and began rubbing his four fingers across his forehead. He didn't know what to say.

"You're the only man who's ever touched me, Dino." His entire body stiffened at Nikki's words. "Many have tried, trust me on that. But I couldn't let them do it. It was like I would be betraying you. Can you imagine? That was so crazy to me. But that was how I felt. Year in and year out. It was as if that night we spent together was the beginning and the end for me. Some women can love twenty men in a lifetime, and be truly in love with each and every one. I'm not that kind of woman. I've only loved one man in my entire life. And the awful thing is, he didn't love me back. And the awful thing is, there've been good men that I've treated badly, because that one man didn't love me back."

Dino didn't say anything. He wasn't sure if he could, but he did reach out and place his arm around Nikki. She drew closer to him, needing his warmth like she needed air to breathe, and then she slung her arms around him, clinging to him, burying her face into his chest in hurt and shame. Dino held her too, his eyes closed, his mind unable to pierce through the guilt that racked his soul. She was homeless, with his child, relying on the benevolence of strangers, while he was given a reprieve, a new life, a wonderful, prosperous, new beginning. Nikki was a good woman, and she did the absolute best she could in her attempts to raise their son, but she was no man. She couldn't teach him what it meant to be a man. That was Dino's job. A job he'd neglected, unwittingly, for the boy's entire life.

He placed a hand on Nikki's chin and lifted her face to his. The tears were still streaming down her eyes, her beautiful, sad eyes. He wiped them away with his hands. "It's going to be all right, Nikki," he said, causing her to flush with hopefulness. "You did what you had to do."

Nikki stared at him, certain that he understood. Certain that he wasn't judging her and despising her and ready to forget her and Jamal as quickly as he could get away from her. He was pulling her closer to him, not away from him. He understood. She thanked God that of all the people on the face of this earth, the one person who she needed to understand . . . the one human being who had the power to devastate her completely if he didn't understand, did understand. She held him tighter and kept pushing her small body against him, to get close to him, when there was no way humanly possible for them to get any closer.

TWENTY-THREE

As far as it went, considering that they were only serving about half the customers they normally served before Jamal's arrest, it was a busy morning. Sebastian and Tam stayed busy, and Mookie too. He had to cover for Fern when she called in sick, coughing with that phony cough she used as she told Tam that she thought she had the flu. "Yeah, right," Tam had said when she hung up the phone.

But Tam forgot about Fern and returned to satisfying her customers. They were all busy bees like Nikki now, who was helping Henry in the kitchen, as they worked hard to hold on to the faithful customers they did have. Somehow they all believed that things were going to change, that the Big Turn was going to make it through this low turn in its history, as soon as those cops and prosecutors came to their senses and realized that they had accused the wrong man.

"A penny for them," Sebastian said as he came and stood behind the counter beside Tam.

After Sebastian's mother's funeral, they came to an unspoken truce. No more putdowns. No more snide remarks. No more jokes at the other's expense. It was a difficult transition for both of them early on, but they were thrilled to have it. Sebastian told Tam last night, at dinner, that they needed each other. Tam knew it was the truth, perhaps she knew it the first time Sebastian showed up at the diner going on about his big Broadway days when any fool could see that he was no more a big-time actor than she was a Wall Street wiz.

"That man needs a woman," she remembered whispering to Nikki when he left.

And they both laughed. But it was true. And she needed a man. Not any man who would bore her, or she would bore him, like so many times in her past, but she needed Sebastian Dobbs. The only man who could make her laugh, not by telling her clever jokes or making funny faces, but just by being himself.

"What?" Tam said.

"Your thoughts. A penny for them."

"Oh." She smiled. "I was just thinking about us."

"I want my penny back."

"Too late. I was just thinking how glad I am that we're . . . you know."

Sebastian wanted to smile. He frowned instead. He had already come to the inevitable conclusion about his feelings for Tam. He just needed her to stop denying hers for him. "What do I know?"

"That we're . . . you know, Seb, friends."

"Friends?"

Tam hesitated. She was a flirt, and a big talker to boot, but she was never very good with putting her feelings into words. "Okay, more than friends. All right? Am I sufficiently humbled for you?"

Sebastian smiled. "Sufficiently," he said. Then he looked around. "You and me, Tam, are like these customers right now in this diner."

"How's that?"

"We aren't much, but at least we're faithful."

Tam laughed. "Amen to that." Then she hesitated before saying, "Seb?"

Sebastian turned back toward her. "Yes?"

"What do you make of this thing Bishop Cochran seems to have for Nikki?"

"What do I make of it?"

"Yeah. I mean, you think he's serious?"

"Well, I think he has to be. I mean, the man came up with fifty thousand dollars to bail Jamal out, not to mention all of these lawyers and investigators he's hired. And if it wasn't for him, Nikki wouldn't still have this diner and we wouldn't still be employed. I doubt if any more proof of his seriousness is possible."

"I hear what you're saying, Seb. But beyond the money. He had tears in his eyes Sunday when Nikki went to that altar."

"Yeah, that was something, wasn't it? I was amazed, first of all, that Miss *All Christians Are Hypocrites* would even ask me to pick her up for church, forget everything else. And when she went down to that altar I couldn't believe my eyes. I did a triple take, you hear me?"

"I know. She's been through so much and it was a blessing to see her up there. That's why it's good to see that she might just have somebody in her corner now; a good man. I just hope he hangs in there with her."

"Now you're beginning to worry me. Why wouldn't he hang with her, Tam?"

"You know how stubborn Nikki can be."

"Yeah, I know. But I also know that's not what you meant."

Tam looked at Sebastian, at his large, round, expressive eyes. "If I tell you, do you promise not to tell a living soul?"

"I promise."

"I'm not playing, Sebastian."

"I promise, Tam. What is it?"

Tam leaned closer to him and said, in a near whisper, "Jamal's his son."

Sebastian's big eyes stretched even larger. "*What?*"

Tam nodded. "Nikki told me last night. When I asked her nearly three months ago, when Bishop first came to town, she declared I was being crazy to even think it. But I was right all along. I told y'all I'm psychic."

"But how could he be Jamal's father? I mean, I know how, and I know that they used to know each other, but I would have never thought in a million years.—"

"That a man like Bishop would have anything to do with a hot head like Nikki?"

"That Nikki would have anything to do with him, or any man for that matter! Don't you remember all those men—wonderful men—that she'd turned down? You think it was because of—"

"I sure do. Nikki's been in love with Bishop Cochran all these years, that's what I believe. You know how Nikki is. She gives her all to whatever she does. She gave her all to him one night all those years ago, and she wasn't about to let his absence or some new man give it back."

"But how could Bishop stay away like that? Didn't he know he had a son who needed a father?"

Tam shook his head. "Nope. That's the thing. Nikki left Detroit when she found out she was pregnant and never told him anything. Then when he came to Monroe, she told him Jamal's father was dead, just like she had told the rest of us."

"She's told him the truth now?" Sebastian asked. "Please tell me she's told the man the truth."

"Him, yes. But they haven't told Jamal."

Sebastian frowned. "Why the devil not? He, above them all, has a right to know."

"Nikki says she's waiting for Dino to get over the shock. Then she's hoping they'll be able to tell Jamal together, as a united front. I don't know. You know how Nikki is. On any give day she could win the lottery, fall in love with a Denzel-fine brother and be at peace with the world. But if, on that same day, one little detail is out of order, just one, then suddenly she's having a bad day. She's got to have her ducks in a row first. That's just how she is. And that's why you have got to keep your mouth shut about this."

"Do I look stupid, Miss Ellis?" Sebastian asked. And as Tam began to open her mouth, he shook his head. "Never mind all that. I won't tell," he added.

The diner door opened and Jimmy Milton, from the finance company, came in. Tam rolled her eyes.

"Here comes Double Digit," she said, referring to the nickname she placed on Jimmy when she found out that his company was charging Nikki such a high interest on her loan.

"Thank God for Bishop Cochran," Sebastian said, "or we'd be out on our rears if it was left up to Jimmy."

"I know that's right," Tam agreed.

"Hello, Tammy, Seb," Jimmy said as he walked up to the counter.

"What's up, Jimmy?" Tam asked. "Oh, I forgot. It's your interest rates, right?"

Jimmy smiled. "Cute. Is Nikki around?"

"Nikki!" Tam yelled over her shoulder. "Double Digit's here!"

Jimmy laughed and shook his head as Nikki came out of the kitchen, wearing a full apron and wiping her hands.

"What's the matter now?" she asked.

Jimmy quickly held up his hands. "Whoa." He backed up a step. "I come in peace."

Nikki smiled. "Sorry. What's up?"

"You are, my friend." Jimmy placed his briefcase on the counter, reached in it, and pulled out a folder that he handed to Nikki. "Congrats all around."

Nikki frowned. "What is this?"

"It's the deed to this place. Free and clear."

"Praise God!" Tam said as she and Sebastian hurried over by Nikki, looking at the deed.

Nikki looked at Jimmy. "Why are you giving it to me? Dino, I mean, Bishop Cochran should have this. He's the one who bought this place."

"Not according to our records," Jimmy said.

"What are you talking about?"

"Look at the deed, Nikki," Sebastian instructed her. "It clearly names you and you alone as the owner of this property."

Nikki looked at Sebastian and Tam, who could not contain their elation, and then she looked at Jimmy. "But there's some mistake. Bishop Cochran was going to buy this place and I was going to buy it back from him."

"Well, apparently he cut out the middle man," Jimmy said as he shut his briefcase and smiled. "Again, congratulations. I'm glad it all worked out. Nikki, you deserve that piece of paper. Don't think you don't." He said his good-byes to Tam and Sebastian, and then left.

Nikki shook her head. "The nerve he's got."

"He was just being nice, Nikki, come on," Tam said.

"I'm not talking about Jimmy. I'm talking about Dino. The nerve he's got!" She went into her office, came back out with her shoulder bag, car keys and that deed still danging from her hand as if it were a snake. She headed for the exit.

"Nikki, the apron!" Sebastian called.

Nikki lifted the apron over her head and threw it in Sabastian's hands. "I'll be back."

Sebastian smiled. "She sounds like Arnold Schwarzenegger."

Dino was at the conference table in his office sitting sideways, with one leg folded over his thigh and one hand massaging his temple. Braid and Newton, two auditors, were also sitting at the table, their papers spread out before them.

"Tell it to me again," Dino said without looking at them.

"Plus twenty," Newton said.

"Twenty percent upswing?"

"Yes, sir."

"Already?"

Newton nodded. "Already."

Dino nodded too. "That's rather remarkable, gentlemen."

"We thought you'd be pleased. We were shocked to be quite honest. This church was fast heading toward financial ruin when you first got here. Now it's actually turning a profit, with shrewd investments for a change. The membership has soared—"

"Yes," Dino interrupted in agreement. "But far more importantly than any statistic you have in front of you, many souls have given their lives to Christ. That was the problem with this church, gentlemen; the underlying problem. The money woes were just symptomatic of that problem."

"And the fact that the former pastor was a crook," Braid said with a quick smile that Dino ignored.

"Bishop Cochran," Sheila's voice could be heard over the intercom.

"Yes, Sheila?" There was an annoyed tone to Dino's voice.

"Nikki Lucas is here to see you, sir."

Dino hesitated. He didn't know if he should jump for joy or head for the hills. He did neither. "Send her in," he said to his secretary, and looked at his auditors. "Five minutes, gentlemen."

"Certainly," Newton said as both he and Braid rose and headed for the door, speaking to Nikki as she came in. She closed the door behind them.

"We need to talk, Dino," she said as she walked up to the conference table.

"Good morning," he said, leaning back in his chair, his leg still crossed, his demeanor still one of nervous hopefulness.

"Good morning. Jimmy just left the diner." Nikki began pulling the deed out of her purse.

"Have a seat," Dino said, refusing to rise to her urgency.

Nikki looked at him. Dino looked so calm that she calmed down, too. She sat in the chair closest to him and suddenly felt odd, as if she were a kid in the principal's office.

"Now," he said, "what can I do for you?"

Nikki handed him the deed. He put on his reading glasses that lay on the table and looked over the paper carefully. Then he looked at her. "Congratulations."

"Dino, what are you doing? I haven't bought that diner. I haven't paid you a dime yet."

"Don't worry about that."

"How can I not worry about it? That deed is a lie."

Dino frowned. "A lie? How is it a lie?"

"It's a lie. I don't own that diner."

"You do own it."

"And how, exactly, can I own something I haven't bought?"

"You own it because I went down to that finance company and paid off that ridiculous loan. That's how!" Dino threw down the deed on the table, his patience with her all but gone.

Nikki was unable to suppress the frustration all over her face. "I can't keep taking from you, Dino."

"It's not called taking when you're in a relationship, Nikki."

A relationship? Was he trying to tell her something? Was he finally ready to tell her something? "What relationship?" she tested. "You're Jamal's father, and I'm Jamal's mother, but I don't see how that automatically translates into a relationship."

Dino looked at her, at the way her eyes danced with uncertainty. She was as terrified of their future as he was. "No, I suppose not," he said and stood to his feet. "But whatever you want to call it, it's done." He picked up the deed and handed it to her. He still seemed heated, exacerbated with her.

She hesitated, in some awkward show of defiance, but then she accepted the paperwork and stood.

"I wish I had more time," Dino said, walking her toward the door, "but I'm in the middle of an audit right now."

"I understand," Nikki said. Once at the door, she stopped and looked at Dino. "The rent you're paying me for that room you're not even living in . . . you keep that as monthly payments on this loan until I can do better."

Dino looked at her and all he saw was that same kid on the corner, still battling him to the bitter end, still determined to have her will win in the end. "I didn't give you a loan, Nikki."

"But you said I was to pay you instead of the finance company; that's the deal we made."

"Things have changed since then."

"You mean your guilt has increased since you found out you're Jamal's father? Is that it? Is this supposed to be some kind of guilt offering?"

Dino released a heavy sigh. "No."

Nikki frowned. "Then what's changed?"

If it were as easy as saying words, he would have said them a long time ago. He didn't because it wasn't easy, because how could he tell her that nothing was the same since the day he first arrived in Monroe and saw her standing in that dining hall, even before he knew Jamal existed? *Everything's changed*, he wanted to tell her. *Especially me.* "See you around, Nikki," he told her instead.

TWENTY-FOUR

Dino was leaned against the passenger side of his Mercedes as Nikki locked her diner and began walking toward him. She wore a pair of white boot leg pants and a mauve button-up sleeveless blouse, tucked in to reveal her petite, but curvy figure. Dino folded his arms and crossed one foot over the other one as he watched her, as her upbeat smile and bouncy movements made his heart pound.

Her VW was totaled in the accident, a car that only had liability insurance coverage, which meant she would have to purchase another car on her own. Given her financial situation, that was impossible, Dino knew. And he also knew that she'd have a hissy fit if he so much as hinted at purchasing one for her, something he'd gladly do, if she'd let him. But she wouldn't even let him pick her up from work, making it clear to him that Sebastian had already volunteered for the job. The only reason he was there at all tonight was because tonight was different. This was the night that they had both decided, at Dino's insistence, to tell Jamal the truth.

"Good evening," she nearly sang as she walked up to Dino.

Dino stood erect and opened the passenger door, his eyes never leaving hers. "You seem mighty happy."

Nikki smiled and got into the car. She watched Dino as he closed the door and walked around the front toward the driver's side. He wore another one of those expensive suits of his, this one either a dark blue or black, she couldn't tell which in the night. And when he sat down on the driver's seat, his all-familiar fresh cologne smell caused her to smile again. The suit, she realized, was brown.

"What?" he asked when he looked over and saw that smile, curious about what could possibly be causing it. It certainly couldn't be because of their upcoming conversation with Jamal, especially since Dino was the one who had to persuade her to stop putting it off.

"I was just thinking," she replied.

"About?" He put on his seatbelt.

"How blessed I am. How I need to finally start giving the Lord some credit and stop thinking that my world is going to fall apart at any moment. God's got it all in control, just like you said."

Dino nodded, but his curiosity still wasn't satisfied. "What brought this on?"

"When you called and said tonight is going to be the night that we tell Jamal, I panicked at first. I didn't know if I was ready for that. Then I started thinking, and praying about it. And I was able to deal with it. I realized things I hadn't realized before. I'm blessed. Better than blessed. Like this diner, for instance," she said, looking out the window at the establishment which stood dark against the night. "It's a good feeling."

"What's a good feeling?"

"Owning my own business. I mean, really owning it where no banks or finance companies can come and take it away from you just because you have a bad day or a bad week or even a bad month. It's a blessing." She looked at Dino. "I thank God and I formally thank you for giving me that, Dino."

Dino looked at her, at her eyes now more cheerful than sad for the first time that he could recall. "Anything you want, Nikki," he said, "no matter where I am, I'll get it for you."

Nikki smiled as if she fully appreciated his comment, although she suddenly felt queasy inside. *No matter where I am*. What did he mean by that? Was he leaving them? Was he about to tell Jamal he was his father and then *take off*? She leaned back on her seat as her chest began to tighten with anxiety.

"Put on your seatbelt." Dino touched her lightly. "I thought we'd drive over to Jacksonville so that I can pick up a few clothes."

Nikki's heart dropped. "Pick up clothes?"

"I'd like to spend a few days at your place if that's okay."

Nikki smiled, relieved. Dino spending time with her and Jamal sounded perfect to her. "Sure," she said. "Especially since you're paying for the room anyhow."

"Good," Dino said and began to drive away from the curb.

Nikki turned toward him and folded her arms. "May I ask why you've suddenly decided to grace us with your presence?"

"Wasn't so sudden. Great deliberations, I assure you. But I just thought it would be more practical. In case Jamal doesn't take this news we're about to lay on him very well."

That threw Nikki. "Why wouldn't he take it well? He worships you."

"Sure, when he thought I was some new-on-the-scene black knight ready to make all of his dreams come true. But when that new-on-the-scene knight happens to be his father, a father who he'll believe has no business being new-on-the-scene but should have been here years ago, that worship is certain to become something entirely different."

Nikki was horrified. "Dino, you think so?"

"I think so."

Nikki shuttered at the thought. "You mean he might hate you?"

"Nikki, what do you expect? You and he have been struggling for years while I was living the life of a king far as he's concerned. He's got to resent that."

Nikki looked out of the window. If Dino was right and Jamal did have a problem with his absence, she could only imagine what their son would think about her. She was really the one responsible for that absence. Jamal would hate her bitterly for keeping Dino away from him, and all the advantages he could have given him. Those advantages would have kept him far away from thugs like Shake, because Dino would have been all the role model he needed. A heaviness began to overtake her. That was the main reason she didn't tell Jamal about Dino as soon as he came to town. She didn't want her son to hate her. Now, if Dino was right, it seemed almost inevitable. A guarantee, given how emotional Jamal could get.

Dino sensed her distress. "He'll never know, Nikki," he said.

Nikki looked at him. "What do you mean?"

"He'll never know that you kept this from me. He doesn't have to know all of that."

"But Dino, that's everything. What are you talking about? It's not your fault that you haven't been in his life. I kept you in the dark. I did that. I made that decision to run away without telling you."

"And I was just the innocent bystander in all of this; is that how you think I'm going to approach Jamal? Put it all on you? Forget that."

"But it is all on me, Dino. All I had to do was tell you and I'm sure you would have—"

"I would have what, Nikki? Run and told my wife, 'Guess what, honey? You're pregnant with my child and so is this other woman?' Is that what you're sure I would have done?"

Nikki looked distraught. "No. I don't know."

"I was no saint, Nikki, and I want you to stop trying to remember me as one. I was a lowdown, dirty, cheating dog."

"That's not true."

"Yes, it is true."

"Then why were you always checking up on me, Dino? Why were you always making sure I was all right and telling all those hood boys not to mess with me, if you were so lowdown? And don't tell me it was because you wanted some. The way I gawked at you all the time you knew you could have had that a long time before it happened. But you didn't. You told me to stay off the streets. And you got mad because I was boosting. You cared about me."

Dino looked at Nikki. At her small body on his leather seat. And he smiled. "I'll tell you what," he said. "We'll pray before we talk with Jamal and let the Lord lead us. Deal?"

Nikki smiled and nodded her head. "Deal." She began to relax again, but there was still that part of her that wondered if either one of them were worthy of that kind of redemption.

The Embassy-Carlton was the most luxurious hotel Nikki had ever stepped foot into as she took the glass elevator with Dino up to his room. When he swiped the keycard and she walked into that room, she nodded in approval. It was a spacious suite of marble floors and pastel-colored furnishings, and just the thought that Dino could give this up for her tiny bedroom, even for just a few days, was remarkable to her. She looked at him. "No wonder you decided not to stay at my house."

Dino laughed. "Nothing like that." He gestured toward the wet bar. "Why don't you get yourself something to drink while I throw some clothes together."

"I'm fine," Nikki said as she moved toward the sofa, too jazzed to drink even a glass of milk. "Let me make myself at home while you throw all those Armanis and Versaces in a paper bag and come on over to my place with me."

Dino laughed and escaped into his bedroom. Nikki explored the suite, mainly the massive wall-sized window that gave a panoramic view of the Jacksonville skyline. Then she took a seat on the edge of the sofa. A chessboard that looked like it was made of solid gold was set up in front of her on the low table, and she marveled at the artistry. When Dino, surprisingly swift in his packing, came back into the living room with his leather garment bag, she asked him about it.

"Is this real gold, Dino?"

"Far as I know." He walked to the front door, setting down his luggage in front of it.

"Aren't they afraid y'all might steal this stuff, the way we common folks do when we take the soap and shampoo from the Motel 6?"

"It's already in their contingency plan. That's why they charge us these outrageous rates."

"Oh, I see. They do it to you before you do it to them."

Dino laughed. "Exactly," he said, moving toward the sofa.

"You play chess?" Nikki asked.

"Sure. You?"

"I've always wanted to, but it seemed a little beyond me. Tam said it was just like playing checkers but I didn't think that was right."

Dino smiled and tapped Nikki on her back. "Move over. I'll give you a crash course."

Nikki made room for Dino to sit beside her and in front of the chessboard. She flushed with warmth at being this near to him. "The key," he said, "is knowing what you have and what each piece can do. Pick up that first piece." Nikki did. "That's the pawn."

"The pawn?"

"Yes. It moves straight ahead, one square at a time. Then there's the rook or the castle that moves along the file it's on or in a straight line, but it can't jump. Now the knight, that piece there . . ." Dino pointed.

"That looks like a horse."

"Right. Unlike the rook, the knight can jump over other pieces, which means it's a valuable piece. The bishop—"

Nikki smiled. "Like you, for instance."

"Yeah, like me. The bishop moves along a diagonal line, but on the same color, which makes it really interesting. But it can't jump a white or black piece. And the queen is the prize." Nikki felt his eyes turn to her. "She can move straight ahead, lateral left or right, or on the diagonal."

Nikki looked back at him. "She can do it all."

"Compared to the others, she can, yes."

"Is there a king?"

"Yep."

"What can he do?"

"Generally, he can move only one square at a time."

"While the queen's hopping all over the place?"

Dino laughed. "Right." He pulled Nikki against him in a bear hug. "While the queen's hopping all over the place." Quiet briefly took over, but Dino spoke again. "You're one of a kind, you know that? That's why I love you so much."

Those words came out in a haze of amazement. Nikki didn't know what to do. She didn't know if the comment was genuine or if Dino was just playing around. But she knew Dino wasn't the kind of man who played. She turned and looked at him. "You love me?" she asked him point blank.

Dino stared into her eyes. He didn't mean to say those words. Somehow they were on his tongue and flew out. But he didn't regret them either. "Yes." His one-word answer was heartfelt.

Tears came to Nikki's eyes so quickly that it stunned Dino. She leaned sideways against him and hugged him graciously. "I love you too," she said and began kissing him on the side of his face. Then she looked into his eyes, and he into hers, and he kissed her.

Only Dino's was not the nervous, excited kisses she had given him, but a long, passionate one. So passionate that he couldn't seem to stop it. So passionate that he found himself pulling her closer and closer and then, to even his astonishment, unbuttoning her blouse. And even that didn't stop him. It wasn't until the last button was unbuttoned, and he was about to remove that blouse, that he finally forced himself to stop.

He looked at Nikki, who was still on fire with desire, who sat beside him like a wounded woman ready to take another chance. With the same man who'd hurt her before. And she was hungry for him, and needed him, and was terrified by his power and how easily he could use it to hurt her again. But she was still willing to try. He pulled her into his arms. If she could take a chance on somebody like him, who'd already shown her what he had been about, then surely he could take a chance on her, who'd shown nothing but remarkable courage, given the harsh hand she had been dealt.

When Dino stopped embracing her, still breathing heavily, still trying to shake the feelings that would only consume him if he gave into them, he began rebuttoning her blouse. "A little too far again," he said, smiling, trying his best to lighten the tense mood.

Nikki tried too. "It's becoming a habit."

Dino looked her in the eyes. "We'll have to do something about that, won't we?"

She wasn't at all sure what she was agreeing to, but she agreed anyway. "Guess so."

When they made it to Nikki's house, she could tell immediately that Jamal was not there. The house was dark for one thing, and the porch light he always left on for her was not turned on. She looked at Dino. "I don't think he's home."

Dino exhaled and turned off his ignition. "Let's go inside and make sure first. Then I'll go look for him."

We'll go look, Nikki thought, as she and Dino got out of the car and made their way inside the house. She turned on the living room light and was glad to at least see, on the lamp shade, that Jamal had stuck a note.

Dino's cell phone rang as Nikki grabbed the note. "Hello?" Dino said. "Bobby, what's up?"

When Nikki heard Bobby Mathews's name, her heart began racing. Dino listened intently to the phone call, but he stared at Nikki, causing her to look worriedly at him. What was it now?

Why was Bobby Matthews calling him at this time of night?

"Okay," Dino said. "I'll let them know. Sure, Bob. Tell him not to hesitate. Right. I'll wait to hear from him."

When Dino closed his phone, Nikki pounced. "What is it?" Anxiety filled her voice. "Please tell me it's good news."

Dino smiled. "It's great news."

"Really?"

"Really. Jeff Islick and his people have apparently turned up evidence that not only vindicates Jamal, but points the finger directly at Dawson Granger as the murderer of William Coleman."

Nikki was floored. "*Dawson*? That good boy? You sure he didn't mean Fred Granger?"

"Nope. He said Dawson. The quiet one. And Bobby says Jeff is certain about it. He would have called me himself, but he's pulling it all together even as we speak. Then he'll call me."

"Oh, Dino, could it be true?" So much hopefulness was in Nikki's voice that Dino's heart sank. She'd been through too much. She and Jamal, he decided, would never go through any of this kind of all-out drama ever again.

"Yes," he said. "It's true."

Nikki ran into his arms. He held her, feeling not burdened anymore by his responsibilities, but now welcoming of them. "What did the note say?" he asked, pulling back from her embrace. "Where's Jamal?"

"Oh," Nikki said, looking at the slip of paper. "I haven't even read it. That phone call scared me so." She read it aloud. "*Don't worry, Ma, I'm not off in any trouble or anything. Dawson Granger wanted me to meet him at the school.*"

Dino snatched the note from Nikki's hand as soon as he could register the name she'd just said. *Dawson Granger.* The one Bobby had just said was the real killer. The good one Jamal would have no qualms believing would help him. Dino finished reading the note: "*He says he has some info to help my case. I should be back within the hour. Love, Jamal.*"

Dino looked at Nikki in a kind of delayed response as both seemed immobile with fear. Then, as if something pushed their inaction into action, Dino pulled out his cell phone and began dialing 911. He and Nikki ran out of her front door as if their lives depended on their swiftness.

Sharon Granger stopped her car in front of Monroe High school, beside her brother's truck, and jumped out. The school itself was always locked down for the night, except for the outdoor basketball courts and track field. She ran toward the back in that direction. Her only prayer was that she wasn't too late. Her only prayer was that Dawson would have come to his senses by now and stopped this madness.

She ran on the side of the school building but didn't have to go anywhere near the basketball courts. They were right there, as soon as she ran past the end of the building, with Jamal standing with his back to her. Dawson, looking almost too serene, was standing in front of him. The bright lights from the courts and field were the only lights back there, but they cast a clear brightness over them.

Dawson frowned as soon as he saw his sister. "What you doing here?" he asked, prompting Jamal to turn in her direction. He looked calm, which meant he didn't feel as threatened as he should feel.

"Let him go, Dawson," Sharon said.

Jamal smiled. "Let me go? What are you talking about, Share? Dawson says he knows who killed Dollar Bill. He can help my case." Then Jamal leaned away from the building. "What's the matter?" He felt a need to ask, given the stricken look on Sharon's face. He looked from her to Dawson. "Is it a lie?"

"No," Dawson said with a grin. "It's the absolute truth. In fact, I don't think there's a human being alive who knows more about who killed William Coleman than I do."

"Just leave, Jamal," Sharon said, grabbing him by his shirt. "Just run!"

Dawson quickly pulled a small .22 caliber handgun from his pocket and stifled, not only Jamal, who immediately turned to completely face Dawson, but Sharon as well. "He's not going anywhere," Dawson said.

Sharon began walking toward her brother. "Dawson, please. Don't do this!"

"What's going on?" Jamal asked, his heart in his shoe. "I thought you said—"

"And I wasn't lying. I am going to tell you who killed William Coleman. I am going to tell you who had no choice but to kill Dollar Bill Coleman."

"He killed him, Jamal," Sharon said, sounding defeated, and then dropping to the ground in anguish. Tears appeared in her eyes. "*He* killed him."

"I had to kill him!" Dawson spewed. "You act as if I wanted to do it. I didn't want to hurt anybody. But I had to do it."

"Why did you have to kill him, Dawson?" Jamal asked. He was about to move to aid Sharon, but Dawson pointed the gun directly at him.

"Stay right where you are or I declare, you won't even know why you had to die too!"

Jamal quickly stiffened, staring, not at Dawson's face, but at his hand on that trigger.

"As I was saying," Dawson continued, "I had to kill Dollar Bill. Absolutely had to do it."

"But why, Dawse?" Jamal asked, trying with all he had to keep it familiar.

"What do you mean why? He knew too much, that's why."

"He knew the secret," Sharon said, sitting on the ground. She appeared dazed and far away from both Jamal and her brother.

"What secret?" Jamal asked, more in an attempt to keep Dawson talking than for information's sake. He was amazed by this. Never would he have suspected Dawson Granger. Fred, maybe. Even Mayor Granger. But not Dawson. "What secret?" he repeated.

"I was pregnant, Jamal," Sharon said.

"I know that." Why was she telling him something that she knew he already knew? Jamal looked at her with curious eyes.

"But the father of my baby—"

"Was William, I know," Jamal interrupted.

Sharon shook her head. "It wasn't William."

"No, it wasn't," Dawson jumped in. "My sister, you see, is a slut. She enjoys enticing these men."

"It was Dawson," Sharon said.

At first Jamal just stared at Sharon, certain that he had heard her wrong. Then he looked at Dawson. "What? But Dawson's—"

"My brother," Sharon said with distaste in her tone. "My good and kind brother. The father of my baby." She looked up at Jamal, tears streaming down her face. "William found out."

"You told him!" Dawson yelled. "He didn't *find out* anything!"

"I didn't tell him!" Sharon shouted back, looking at her brother. "He started asking questions. He wasn't stupid. He saw the way you looked at me. The way you handled me when it was just the three of us, away from the public eye. And *he* told *me*. I didn't tell him anything. He was just guessing. It was just a lucky guess that cost him his life." Sharon broke down in deep sobs and buried her face in her hands.

Dawson looked at Jamal. "We can't have that," he explained. "You see, our father is the mayor of this town and he can't survive this kind of scandal. You and your investigators were asking too many questions. Which I didn't mind. People are always asking questions. But your investigators started asking the right questions, just like William. If they would have kept snooping around trying to find out why those five thugs from Pottsburg would be so willing to lie on the witness stand to implicate you, then hey, I would have no problem with that. I paid them; that's why they were willing to lie. I promised them a lot more where that came from. But they didn't ask those kinds of questions. If they had, I just would have taught you a lesson, the way I did your mother when I ran her car off the road; the way some of the other conscientious folks in this town did when they threw that brick through your window.

"Yeah, Sheriff Peete told our daddy all about that little incident." He smiled and added, "'Don't worry, Mayor; I'm not even investigating that nonsense. They got what they deserved.' That's what he told good ol' Dad. Y'all got what y'all deserved. And after I kill you, after I splatter your brains all over this wall, he's gonna say the same thing about you. You got what you deserved. Oh, he'll do his little hick town investigation; you know, where he concludes that the trail is cold and he closes the case unsolved, or he'll find some unlucky stiff around here and blame him. The way I made sure he did you."

Jamal was still unable to understand all of this. "But—"

Then Dawson Granger stiffened his back, as if he was tired of the confusion too. "It doesn't matter. It's your time to die, Jamal." He aimed his gun directly at the boy.

It was then, in that split second between Dawson's aim and fire, that Dino ran around the building without breaking his top-sprinting speed and grabbed Jamal from the back, knocking him to the ground. Jamal fell just as Dawson fired. Dino tried to remove himself from the line of fire too, but he was a fraction too late. He first felt the heat piercing through his body like a blade thrust, and then he saw blackness and heard screams, including the terrified voice of his own son, as he fell to the ground.

Deputy Sheriff Ollie Curtis arrived just behind Dino, pointing his gun deliberately, intensely as soon as he heard the blast. "Drop it now!" he yelled hysterically at Dawson. "Drop your weapon now!"

Ollie, the first deputy to respond to the 911 call, had arrived at the school at the same moment as Dino's car pulled into the schoolyard. He chose not to use his sirens for fear that it would cause a panic and Jamal's certain death. Ollie had been running toward the scene with Dino, but was no match for the older man's speed and determination. In the distance now, the sounds of sirens heading their way were sudden and deafening.

Dawson realized it too. He realized that his plans had gone badly awry and he was now as cornered as a man on death row. He dropped his weapon.

As Ollie ran to secure the weapon and to place Dawson Granger in handcuffs, Jamal tried to aid Dino, but Dino had fallen on top on him, as if his personal shield, and was now unconscious.

"Ollie, help!" Jamal pleaded in a muffled voice, unable to budge the big, muscular-tight body on top of him.

Ollie quickly subdued Dawson, chaining him to the down-spout against the building, and then helped to move Dino off of Jamal.

Nikki, who had been running as fast as she could, but was no match for even Ollie, finally arrived on the scene just as Dino was pulled off of Jamal and turned over on his back. Nikki cried out and covered her mouth as soon as she saw that Dino was injured. She ran to him, falling to her knees beside him. She looked at her son, at his thin body. "Are you all right?"

"Yes," Jamal said as he stayed on his knees by Dino's body, tears staining his lids. "He can't die," he said, staring at Dino.

"He's not gonna die," Nikki said, cuddling Dino's head.

"Dad," Jamal called, ignoring all else. "You can't die on me, Dad. You can't die on me."

Nikki stopped rocking Dino and stared at Jamal. He said *Dad*.

When the paramedics arrived to assist Dino, and while Sheriff Peete and his men continued to question Sharon, Nikki and Jamal moved out of the way. Nikki just wanted to make sure Jamal was really all right. Jamal just wanted to oversee how the medics were handling his father. That was why he didn't even look his mother's way.

"Is he gonna be all right?" Jamal asked. One of the medics nodded and gave him the thumbs up sign. Jamal closed his eyes, thanking God for answering his prayer, and then relaxed, inasmuch as he could.

"They say Dawson killed William Coleman," Nikki said.

"He did. He said so. But I don't wanna talk about that."

Nikki nodded. She understood. Then she looked at her son. "I'm sorry, Jamal. I'm so sorry I didn't tell you about Dino."

"Don't be sorry. Nothing to be sorry about. You were a kid when you had me, right around my age. You didn't know what you were doing no more than I know what I'm doing." He looked at his mother and frowned. "You blame yourself for too much, Ma."

Nikki felt relieved beyond words. Then she thought about it. If Jamal wasn't blaming her, was he going to blame his dad? "Jamal, Dino didn't know he had a son. I didn't tell him until a few days ago. He had no idea."

"I know that."

"You know?"

"Course I know, Ma. He would have helped us if he would have known."

Nikki looked at her son. How could he be so certain? She believed it too, now. But it took her sixteen years to realize it. Jamal knew already. "What makes you so sure?" she had to ask.

"Because he's a good man, Ma. A great Christian man. I saw that right off when you first brought him to my jail cell and he jacked me up." Both Nikki and Jamal smiled and then looked at Dino's large body. "And all the things he did for us. And still does. You even said he bought that diner for you. You tried to act like it was no big deal, but I knew it was the dream you've always wanted to come true. And that man made it happen. You don't have to worry about me blaming him for anything. If he would have known I existed, he would have been here."

The paramedics caught mother and son's attention again as they hoisted Dino up on the gurney. Nikki looked at her son and wanted to know more. "When did you figure it out, Jamal? When did you know that Dino was your father?"

"I was hoping all along," he admitted, "but I wasn't sure until just now, when he took that bullet for me."

Nikki, filled with joy, filled with all kinds of conflicting emotions, released a choked sob, and then pulled her son into her arms.

TWENTY-FIVE

Dino's Mercedes stopped on the driveway of the Lucas home and Jamal, the driver, jumped out and ran into the house. Within minutes, less than two, he was out again, and running again toward the car. He jumped in, cranked up, and backed out cautiously. Then he drove as if he were driving away from a gunfight, up Firestone Road, all along Old Mills Road, through the town square, past the Big Turn, and up to the parking space reserved for the pastor of New Life Progressive Baptist Church.

He got out and ran up to the double doors, stopping long enough to catch his breath and to straighten his purple tux. Then he walked, with dignity, into the church.

The church was packed, not only with Tam, Sebastian, Fern, Henry and Mookie, but with nearly the entire New Life membership. Even Bobby Matthews was there, and Jeff Islick, and other people from Michigan that none of the locals knew. Jamal halfway wondered if Ida Fox was going to show up too, as he walked down the aisle.

Dino, in a purple tux also, was standing at the altar, relying on a crutch to help keep the weight off of his injured leg; and Nikki, in a white gown, was standing beside him. Sebastian Dobbs, who had given the bride away, had walked Nikki down the aisle in his purple tux, and seemed to relish the role as if this was his day, not hers. Tam, who was now seated beside Sebastian, looked over at him and smiled just thinking about how he'd strutted his stuff up that aisle. She had a million zingers she was going to sling at him when they got out of that church, and she could hardly wait to get started. She couldn't help it. She loved him.

Jamal took his place beside his father. The minister, a friend of Dino's Jamal didn't know, asked for the ring. This was where they had left off when Jamal had reached into his pocket and remembered that he had forgotten that all-important piece of jewelry, a necessity that caused him to race home and retrieve it. This time, however, it came out of his pocket as if it had been there all along, and he handed it to his father.

Jamal stared at his parents as they recited their vows, his big, brown eyes glued on their mouths. He wanted nothing, nothing to stop this union from taking place. For him, it was a long time coming. He looked at his mother, who was beautiful in white, who had endured so much and was still standing despite all of her setbacks. He used to hate her stubbornness. He used to despise her refusal to let anybody help her with anything. Now he admired her. Now he understood.

He looked at his father, who had been the most intimidating man he'd ever met, who looked even more powerful and handsome on his wedding day, as if it suited him. Dino had decided to become the permanent pastor of New Life, relocate to Monroe, and give up his position as head of the national organization. All for Nikki and Jamal. Nikki, of course, objected, but Dino wasn't about to be deterred. Nikki had sacrificed for sixteen years to be both mother and father to Jamal, now it was his time to sacrifice. In truth, Dino told them both, it was no sacrifice at all.

Jamal was proud of those two people standing at that altar. He was honored to be of their tough stock. Yet when the minister asked if there be one today who had a problem with this union, ordering that they should speak now or forever hold their peace, Jamal froze where he stood. He wasn't worried about any objections coming from the audience, since both his parents had long since refused to let others define their lives. Rather, it was his parents that he was worried about. Would they back out? Would they finally decide that it had been too long a wait, and too tumultuous a ride for them to believe that they could get it together? Intellectually, he knew it wouldn't come to that, but emotionally, his heart was pounding as if he didn't know a thing.

It wasn't until it was crystal clear that no one was going to rain on this parade—especially since Nikki and Dino were still smiling happily at one another as they eagerly said *I do*—that Jamal Lucas Cochran finally relaxed that death grip he had on hope, and was able to smile.

Reader's Group Guide Questions

1   Is Nikki's view of the world pessimistic or realistic? What circumstances in her life led her to acquire her worldview?

2   During Dino's days as a Detroit nightclub owner, a series of events caused his life to unravel. What were those events, and were they self-inflicted hardships, or circumstances beyond his control?

3   What motivated Dino's interest in Nikki? Was it altruistic, predatory, or both?

4   How did Nikki view herself as a mother and as a businesswoman? Did her view of herself contradict or support her underlying worldview?

5   Nikki often characterized Christians as hypocrites. How did her view of Christians change over the course of the story, and why did it change?

6   Why did the New Life leadership initially resist Dino's presence in their congregation? Was their apprehension justified?

7   Discuss the irony of Dino's mission for coming to Monroe against the reality of his past that confronted him when he arrived. Was the contradiction detrimental to his ability to heal the divisions in the church?

8   Dino arrived in Monroe a mere two weeks before Jamal was accused of murder. Would you describe this fact as a coincidence or as divine intervention?

9   Why was Jamal so excited about Dino's presence in his mother's life? What larger issues did it portend for his future?

10 Tammy and Sebastian spent the better part of the story in conflict with each other. Was there always an attraction or did something happen that changed their perspective?

11 Discuss the moral complexities of Nikki's decision not to tell Dino that Jamal was his son.

12 Why was Nikki so resistant to Dino's financial help? Did her refusal represent stubbornness or independence? Was her decision morally right?

13 Many in the town of Monroe indicted Nikki for the sins of her son. Was this indictment justified? Discuss what Nikki did right or wrong to add credence to your answer.

14 What made Nikki realize that she was still in love with Dino? What kind of future do you foresee for this couple?

AUTHOR BIO

Teresa McClain-Watson is the author of six published novels, including *When He Hollers, Let Him Go*, her first Christian work. She received her bachelor's degree from Florida State University and her master's degree, in History and Education, from Florida A&M. She has also attended law school and numerous graduate programs, from the University of Mississippi at Oxford's CLEO Institute, to the University of North Florida's mental health counseling program.

A born again Christian since 1978, Mrs. McClain-Watson has worked as a protective investigator, a clinical social worker, a senior counselor, and a magazine editor. She currently resides in Florida with her husband, John, and Mr. Kitty, their cat. She loves to hear from her readers. Please visit her website at www.teresamcclain-watson.com and leave a question or comment.

UC HIS GLORY BOOK CLUB!
www.uchisglorybookclub.net

UC His Glory Book Club is the spirit-inspired brainchild of Joylynn Jossel, author and acquisitions editor of Urban Christian, and Kendra Norman-Bellamy, author for Urban Christian. This is an online book club that hosts authors of Urban Christian. We welcome as members all men and women who have a passion for reading Christian-based fiction.

UC HIS GLORY BOOK CLUB pledges our commitment to provide support, positive feedback, encouragement, and a forum whereby members can openly discuss and review the literary works of Urban Christian authors.

There is no membership fee associated with UC His Glory Book Club; however, we do ask that you support the authors through purchasing, encouraging, providing book reviews, and of course, your prayers. We also ask that you respect our beliefs and follow the guidelines of the book club. We hope to receive your valuable input, opinions, and reviews that build up, rather than tear down our authors.

WHAT WE BELIEVE:

- We believe that Jesus is the Christ, Son of the Living God

- We believe the Bible is the true, living Word of God

- We believe all Urban Christian authors should use their God-given writing abilities to honor God and share the message of the written word God has given to each of them uniquely.

- We believe in supporting Urban Christian authors in their literary endeavors by reading, purchasing and sharing their titles with our online community.

- We believe that in everything we do in our literary arena should be done in a manner that will lead to God being glorified and honored.

We look forward to the online fellowship with you. Please visit us often at www.uchisglorybookclub.net.

Many Blessing to You!
Shelia E. Lipsey,
President, UC His Glory Book Club